I0699027

SOUL OF A VILLAIN

BLEED FOR ME

A SAVAGE WORLD NOVEL

APRIL MORAN

SILVER BEE PUBLISHING, LLC

Soul Of A Villain

April Moran

No part of this book may be reproduced in any form or by any electronic or mechanical means, including information storage and retrieval systems, without written permission from the author, except for the use of brief quotations in a book review.

This is a work of fiction. Names, characters, incidents, certain locations and dialogues are products of the author's imagination and are not to be construed as real. Any resemblance to actual events or persons, living or dead, is entirely coincidental, except where otherwise noted.

SOUL OF A VILLAIN Copyright © 2024 by April Moran and Silver Bee Publishing, LLC

All Rights Reserved

Editing by Katie Awdas https://www.spicemeupediting.com

Cover Art by Dragonfly Ink and Design https://www.dragonflyinkpublishing.com

*For the dark romance lovers who love the idea of being chased
through the woods by the villain wearing a skull mask.
And for those of us running slow enough to be caught...*

WARNING

SOUL OF A VILLAIN contains several triggers which may be upsetting to readers. A list is provided here but listing one for every situation that might affect a reader is impossible. Please take care of your mental health and read responsibly. This book is a dark romance work of fiction and meant to be enjoyed as such. I do not condone nor endorse the type of behavior in which these characters engage.

*Dub/Non-Con
*Abduction/Captivity
*Somno
*S/A
*BDSM elements
*Hand Necklaces/Breath play
*Violence
*Blood play
*Knife play
*Forced orgasms
*Orgasm denial
*Non-con tattoo
*Punishments
*Bondage
*Spankings
*No safe words
*Praise kink
*Virgin h
*M/F no sharing of h
*J/P and OTTH

PLAYLIST

https://open.spotify.com/playlist/
3ukdf3SZNlKUAqTQwd9CT1?si=3sOixZmhREik1S5ngRSakg

Villains Aren't Born ◆ PEGGY
Bad Guy ◆ Billie Eilish
Throne ◆ Saint Mesa
Enemies ◆ Shinedown
You Could Be Mine ◆ Guns & Roses
Howl ◆ Beware of Darkness
Lose Control ◆ Teddy Swims
You? ◆ Two Feet
Make Me Wanna Die ◆ Pretty Reckless
Two Against One Dangerous ◆ Dangerous Mouse w/ Jack
White
Sin With A Grin ◆ Shinedown
Come Down ◆ Bush
Follow Me Down ◆ Pretty Reckless
Pain Killer ◆ Dreamers
I Wanna Be Your Slave ◆ Maneskin

Blackflowers ◆ Chris Issak
We Stand A Chance ◆ Tom Petty & The Heartbreakers
Never Gonna Let You Go ◆ Kickstand Jenny
Addicted ◆ Saving Abel
Call Me ◆ Shinedown
Ain't No Sunshine ◆ Black Label Society
Savage ◆ Defecto
Save Today ◆ Seether
Coming Undone ◆ Korn
The Reason ◆ Hoobastank

PROLOGUE

I'm the villain. And this is my fairy tale.

liver Benedict Winter

THE INCESSANT BUZZ in his pocket was annoying as fuck.

Oliver dug out his cell phone, glancing at the screen. The number was one he immediately recognized but hesitated to answer. He wasn't really in the mood to speak with his half-brother. Not that it mattered. Kingston Winter was a persistent asshole. Persistent and stubborn.

He'll just keep calling. Might as well get it over with.

Steeling himself, he clicked the call open. "Yeah?"

"It's me. Where are you?"

Oliver sighed. "In a limo."

Kingston did not say anything for a moment. There was rustling on the other end of the line. A woman's soft voice and Kingston's murmured reply. He waited in silence until his brother's attention swung back to him.

"In a limo? Where are you going?"

Oliver's laugh was exasperated. "On my way to Diamond Lake Ranch, if you must know, big brother. Don't worry; I did all my chores before heading out for some fun."

"I know you finished the job," Kingston huffed. "When I didn't hear from you, I got worried."

"Aww. That's sweet," Oliver said, sipping the scotch he'd poured from the limo's bar.

"It was a hazardous assignment. You can't blame me for making sure you are still alive."

A pang of guilt assailed Oliver. Although he'd spent nearly a year away from New York and their family stronghold, The Den, he and Kingston kept in regular contact. There were jobs to be done and assignments to be completed. These phone calls were unavoidable, and Oliver experienced a strange pleasure in them. It wasn't too long ago that any interaction with his brother was something he dodged whenever possible.

"Sorry, King," he breathed. "Guess I should have touched base."

Kingston cleared his throat. "So, you're going to Diamond Lake?"

Oliver settled back against the leather seat. "Yeah. Got an invite and thought I'd visit while I'm in Colorado."

"Be careful, O," Kingston said. Oliver could almost see his brother's concerned frown through the phone connection. "They've been delving deep into the darker side of auctions. Dangerous shit. And since Ava...well, that's something I have no interest in. I can't condone it anymore." The unspoken insinuation was that Oliver should distance himself from such activities if he wished to remain in Kingston's good graces. "Besides, I can hardly believe you are welcome there after you backtracked on your deal."

A twinge of unease assailed Oliver. Fuck. He didn't need the subtle reminder of when he tried to sell Kingston's fiancée through the same organization.

"Just using their facilities, King. Nothing more than that."

"Understood. But still, be careful, will ya?" Kingston laughed softly. "Anyway, on a more personal note. Are you coming home for the wedding?"

Oliver's stomach clenched. Kingston and Ava's wedding was two months away. And he still hadn't decided whether he could face either one of them.

"Ava and I both want you here, Oliver," Kingston said, intuitively understanding the reason for Oliver's silence. "Don't you think it's time to put the past behind us?"

Letting out an inaudible sigh, Oliver said nothing. It was impossible to explain simply how he'd changed and yet stayed the same over the past year. He was still a bad guy. He still murdered people. Still treated women like objects. Still selfishly took what he wanted and cheated when necessary. Juxtaposing those attributes with scarce moments of contrition was difficult. And confusing. And a fucking waste of time to try and understand.

"I don't know if I can. Or if I should. You know me, Kingston... I'll find a way to ruin things. It's in my nature, and you damn well know that is the truth. Hell, didn't they teach you at your fancy college that my middle name means betrayal?"

"Look. You're my brother. We've spent the past year hashing this shit out. If I can move past it, you can, too." Kingston's voice contained the stubborn tone Oliver knew all too well. "It's time to put your nightmares to rest like I have.

You think it can't be done, but you're wrong. Ava has forgiven you. I've forgiven you. Come home, O. Let us show you how different life can be."

"It's all moonlight and roses for you, Kingston." A thread of resentment laced Oliver's words. "You have Ava. She loves you. I'm just the sadistic asshole who terrorized her every chance I got. The brother who was waiting and hoping for the opportunity to put a bullet between your eyes. You know, you can try turning a wolf into a pet. You can keep it in a nice cage. Love it. Feed it. Even train it to do some tricks. But it's still a wolf. Eventually, it does what centuries of ingrained instinct tell it to. And it ends up ripping you to pieces." Oliver sighed heavily. "That's the truth of it, man. I can't be trusted. Or hell, even liked."

"That's bullshit. You use that excuse as a way of keeping everything buried deep. It shields you from facing the reality that the real monster was our father. It masks the pain of losing your mother in such a horrific way. I get it, Oliver. I carry my own guilt, too, for my actions when we were growing up and what happened with Rebecca. They must be faced head-on. You must trust me on this. Come back for the wedding, O. Let's work things out together. It's not too late to be a real family."

"I'll try, King," Oliver finally acceded with a growl of defeat. Kingston's use of the affectionate nickname he'd given him during childhood was a low blow. A sledge-hammer reminding Oliver of the times his brother protected him. It also brought up shared nightmares of a shitty child-hood with a sadistic father. It was almost more than Oliver could stand. It made something burn deep inside him. A hatred once reserved for his older half-brother but now—more often than not—turned inward. "Really, Kingston. I'll try to make it."

"I hope so. We'll talk again soon and finalize our plans. Until then, be safe, brother."

Oliver ended the call, poured another finger of scotch, and tossed it back with a grimace.

Hate was a funny thing.

After living with it for so long, its absence proved disconcerting.

Oh, he still hated, of course. Burned with it, actually. Loathing for his deceased father. Hatred for his enemies. Disgust for liars. But the overwhelming emotion once harbored toward his half-brother had melted during the months roaming the country.

Love had worked some crazy magic on Kingston. His happiness and that of his bride-to-be were evident in the photos Oliver saw splashed across social media and paparazzi outlets. The two of them fucking glowed with adoration despite the brutal violence coloring the beginning of their love story.

But even as his hate for Kingston had dissipated, Oliver still suffered from jealousy. There were moments when he craved the same peace and contentment his brother had found with Ava. It hit him the hardest during those intermittent phone calls with Kingston. The five-minute conversations existed as reminders that his brother cared for him. Worried about him. There was no mistake that Kingston and Ava wanted him home so the tattered relationship could be mended for good.

Oliver wanted that, too. Sometimes. But the blackness inside him inevitably snuffed out any glimmers of light. The promise of happiness was not meant for a man like himself—a coldhearted monster who once negotiated the sale of the woman his brother desperately loved. It did not matter that Oliver killed his partners in the illicit deal following an unexpected change of heart. It did not matter that he saved Ava's life for Kingston's sake. Even if he no longer hated his brother, darkness still poisoned his soul. Kingston and Ava might have forgiven him, but it didn't fucking matter. How could it when forgiving himself for what he had become over the years was impossible?

The truth was simple. Whatever drops of humanity he managed to squeeze out would not change a damn thing. His heart was twisted and black. It would be that way until the day he took his last breath. And he would pay for his many sins during an eternity in Hell's deepest pit.

There was little hope of salvation for the soul of a villain.

ONE

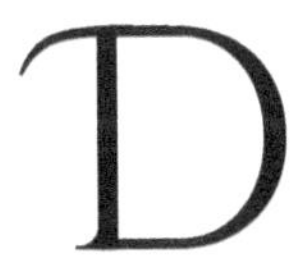

iamond Lake Ranch, Colorado

OLIVER

OLIVER RAKED a hand through dark hair while half-heartedly listening to the Diamond Lake Ranch director.

"Fine set of girls tonight," Erik commented in a thick Russian accent, his thin lips curved into a grin. "Maybe you bid, eh? Get girlfriend for small price."

Oliver almost snorted in disbelief. Small price? No such thing existed here at this exclusive compound nestled deep along one of the more remote ranges of the Colorado mountains. Every service offered at Diamond Lake Ranch came at an exorbitant cost.

"I'm just here for a scene or two," Oliver replied with a

shrug. "Been a while since I've had the chance to visit the ranch." He did not mention that it had been nearly four months since he'd last fucked a woman. It wasn't for lack of female attention. Recently, no woman piqued his interest enough to put forth the required effort.

Erik leaned closer, his voice lowering. "We have special offering tonight after the usual auction, Mister Winter. A man of your tastes will appreciate."

Oliver's eyebrow lifted. "A man of my *tastes*?"

In addition to the normal operation as an exclusive and remotely located kink club, Diamond Lake Ranch also organized a series of expensive auctions. The world's elite were offered a buffet of women willing to serve as companions and sexual partners. Vetted participants entered the auction with the protection of a contract and rules. Everyone walked away happy—especially the women who were paid outrageous sums of money and treated like royalty during the requisite thirty-day time span.

The Russian's eyes narrowed. "*Da*. It is no secret, my friend, the things you like. I took the liberty and preapproved you. You will find the necessary information in your room."

Oliver did not respond as Erik led the way to the suite reserved for his stay. He had no interest in bidding on a woman, much less being responsible for her care and well-being for the next thirty days. He'd only come for the quick, string-free encounters and extensive BDSM activities the ranch was famous for.

His curiosity pissed him off when he found himself gravitating to the security-enforced chambers where the auction would take place. Deep within the subterranean network of tunnels beneath the sprawling compound, Diamond Lake Ranch auctions required prior financial approval, an invitation, and a mask to enter. All thoughtfully provided for Oliver's convenience. He ignored the internal voice echoing Kingston's warning about the ranch's recent forays into the darker aspects of the business. These voluntary auctions were common; he saw no danger in attending one merely as an observer.

There were two selections of masks available for bidders. Picking one up, Oliver considered the sickly gray devil mask accented with curved horns. He tossed it back onto the heavily carved side table and picked up the second one. He slid it on. The half mask covered his features from the mouth upward. A gruesome skull with black, hollow eyes could have served as the prototype for the tattoo inked on his back.

Before moving toward the auction chamber, he accepted a tumbler of scotch from a bartender whose features were concealed by a simple black mask. Other men slowly filed in, choosing their own masks and taking advantage of the elegant bar.

Low, thumping music set the mood as attendees moved through the queue, the space lit only by flickering gaslight lanterns anchored into roughly hewn stone walls. Once his credentials were verified and paddle number registered, Oliver entered the inner chamber and took up a stance against the back wall. He tucked his bid paddle into the inner pocket of his black tuxedo jacket and glanced around the room.

From this vantage point, he could easily see the circular stage bathed in a pool of white. Attendees could view the offerings while remaining hidden in shadowy darkness. It was cold; the stone walls and floors only enhanced the chill in the room. Cavernous and dark, the chamber was illuminated only by the wall lanterns and that singular light blazing over the stage. It reminded Oliver of a surgical room in a horror movie where the attention was focused on the operating table and the patient. There was no seating, but several high-top tables of the same heavy dark wood stood within the antechamber. Men gathered around them, talking in low voices, their low chuckles barely audible over the background music.

"I knew you wouldn't resist the auction, Winter."

Oliver cursed under his breath. Despite his devil mask, he immediately recognized the middle-aged man who sidled up beside him. The burn scar marring the top of his right hand gave his identity away. Lee Barlow was a mean son-of-a-bitch and as dirty as one might expect a career politician to be.

"Mere curiosity. I'm not in the market for a pet."

"Ah," Lee chuckled, running a hand through salt and pepper hair. "Wait until you see the offerings before setting that statement in stone. I hope to find a suitable replacement for the last one, myself. Rumor is this is an exquisite group of girls. Of course, I'm also intrigued by the special surprise the ranch has planned. It's my understanding she's a last-minute addition."

Oliver sipped his scotch. "Like I said. I'm not interested in the auction."

Lee's reply was cut short by the beginning of the auction. The music's tempo slid into a slow, seductive grind that screamed of sex. A beautiful blonde girl wearing a scarlet silk teddy and high heels to match sauntered onto the stage and into the spotlight, a smile curving her lips.

"Gentlemen, welcome Item Number One--our first offering of the evening. Blonde hair. Blue eyes. One hundred and ten pounds... she enjoys shopping, sunbathing, and catering to your every need. Bidding starts at the standard two hundred thousand. Do I have a bid for this lovely creature...?"

The auction continued until the fourteen women listed on the program were placed. Winning participants could claim their new companion immediately or in a more intimate setting. More than half of the men in attendance vacated the chamber, ready to take possession of their prizes. Oliver frowned as Lee Barlow approached him and clinked his glass to his.

"Gorgeous girls, but none truly caught my attention. I hope the final one is worth the wait."

"I wish you luck," Oliver murmured, preparing to duck out of the chamber. His lack of interest in the proceedings surprised him. He'd spent the past hour shifting from one foot to another, hoping one of the girls offered in the voluntary auction might pique his attention. It was disappointing none had. Maybe it was because they were too fucking excited about selling themselves.

Hopefully, someone would whet his appetite in one of the scene rooms. A beautiful, reluctantly willing girl ready for a long, hard fuck after a bit of impact play. His fingers itched for the feel of a sturdy whip. Or the smooth hardness of a paddle's handle.

When the doors to the chamber clanged shut, Oliver cursed under his breath. Any thought of escaping was cut off as the armed security previously loitering in the background now sidled in front of the exit.

"Gentlemen, we apologize for the temporary inconvenience. Diamond Lake Ranch has one final auction tonight," the disembodied voice of the auctioneer rumbled over the sound system. "This sale necessitates extra precautions, and special parameters must be strictly adhered to. Two bidders with the highest offers will be entered into the next stage of the auction, which will consist of a hunt. The initial bid and the hunt must be completed before the sale is considered final. Win the hunt, and you win the item. All bidders understand and agree that the customary thirty-day contract associated with Diamond Lake Ranch auctions will not apply. The item is completely and irrevocably yours upon completing the final stage. The winner is free to do whatever he wishes, for as long as he wishes with the exception of a secondary sale. Secondary sales will be conducted through Diamond Lake Ranch only. The winner of the initial auction has the right to end possession of the item with the extermination of the item if desired. No penalties will be assessed if extermination is selected."

Oliver could not help the tingle that raced inside his veins. *A hunt? This could be interesting.*

An excited murmur rippled through the thirty men occupying the chamber. Oliver recognized many of them despite the masks. Like himself, those pressing closer to the stage boasted extreme wealth and power. A familiar tension swelled inside the room, a stench reeking of violence and depravity. It was one Oliver knew well. It had permeated every fiber of his being for longer than he could remember.

A door opened in the back corner of the chamber, and two large, muscular men clad in black suits with simple black masks entered the room. Anchored between them was a stunningly beautiful girl. She wore a black lace bandeau-type bra, matching thong, and a thick black leather collar encircled her slender throat. Attached to the collar's ring was a glittering length of chain, its length clutched in the fist of the man on her right. She looked no older than twenty.

The girl stumbled as the men dragged her forward, her bare feet digging into the slick floor and finding no purchase. Dark, chestnut-colored hair tumbled to her waist in a riot of messy, loose curls, and her hands were cuffed behind her back. Once she was wrestled onto the stage, Oliver realized that although he could not see the color of her eyes, the flesh below one was shaded black. Her full bottom lip was split, a trickle of blood marring the corner. In the soft stage light, there was no mistaking the multiple, fingerprint-shaped contusions dotting the creamy white skin of her thighs. One high cheekbone bore evidence of a bruise where someone must have struck her.

Every man in the room pressed closer to the stage and the girl, except Oliver. He did not move from where he leaned against the chamber's rough stone wall. The coil deep inside the pit of his stomach wound tight.

"Gentlemen, it would be remiss of this organization if we did not explain the unusual circumstances of this sale. During transport to this auction, Item Number Fifteen killed an employee of the organization. Because of this, the directors removed her from the voluntary auction and placed her for sale in this format. Tonight's hunt winner will assume full responsibility for her care and disposal. There will be no records of the transaction once all financial obligations are fulfilled. There is also no recourse should you encounter difficulties with said item. The Virgin status of Item Number Fifteen has been confirmed and certified. Additionally, a clean bill of health has been established, and birth control is in place for one year. Those of you interested in satisfying a breeding kink will want to sit this auction out."

"Spin around. They want to see you," one of the men holding the girl's arm stated impassively.

Item Number Fifteen appeared frozen with fear, her bottom lip trembling as she scanned the sea of anonymous, mask-wearing men. She was terrified, as any rational girl in her position would be. The scene before her—strange men all wearing devil-inspired and ghoulish skull masks—was something out of a depraved nightmare. But her eyes flashed with foolish defiance; it was like waving a hundred red scarves at a herd of bloodthirsty bulls.

"Go to Hell," she snarled, the words slurring a little. Whatever drug they'd given her as a means of ensuring compliance was not having the desired effect.

One man released her arm and, with frightening calmness, reared back and punched her in the stomach.

Oliver's hands tightened, squeezing the crystal tumbler of scotch with such ferocity it was miraculous that the glass did not shatter.

The girl gasped, her body doubling over as she absorbed the blow. Her shoulders quivered as the one who struck her tried jerking her upright. She resisted until the man gripping the chain attached to the collar gave it a vicious tug. Eyes glistening with helpless tears, pained puffs of air escaped her lungs as she wobbled back into an upright stance between the two brutes holding her aloft, only to have them abruptly force her to her knees. The brute holding the chain yanked it again while grasping a handful of her hair to push her head back. The position mimicked how she would look while giving a blow job.

Oliver's blood surged as an aroused murmur swept through the crowd of men.

He wasn't the only one imagining how delightful it would be to fuck this girl's mouth. To be the one holding the leash and commanding her submission.

Stupid girl. She had no idea what was in store for her after that pitiful display of disobedience. Now, she would become a meal for one lucky man in this pack of wolves.

Oliver's eyes narrowed behind his mask, a sigh of resignation escaping him.

This was going to be a *very* expensive evening—expensive but far more satisfying than anything he would have found within Diamond Lake Ranch's scene rooms.

"Item Number Fifteen possesses a stubborn streak. Which one among you will be the lucky one to break it?" The auctioneer chuckled, then announced, "The bidding begins at three hundred thousand dollars."

CHAPTER

TWO

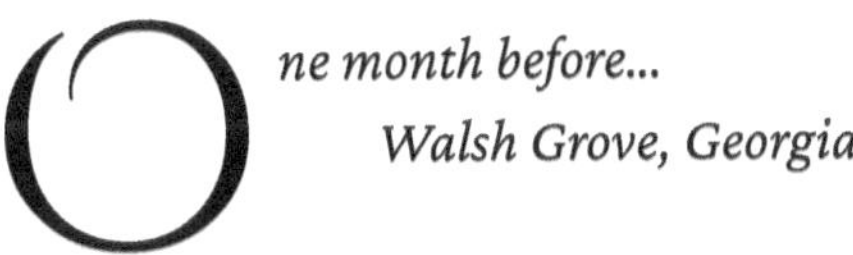

ne month before...
Walsh Grove, Georgia

LONDYN JULIETTE SKYE

"YOU LOOK SO PRETTY TODAY, PARIS," Londyn murmured, pushing her older sister's golden-brown hair away from her forehead. With gentle fingers, she tucked the strands behind Paris's ear and forced a smile to curve her lips. "As pretty as the flowers blooming outside your window."

Paris stared ahead, her gaze vacant and unseeing.

Londyn bent down, peering intently into Paris's eyes. "I'll bring flowers for your room next time, okay? Would you like that?"

There was no response, but Londyn did not expect anything different. Paris's condition had remained unchanged

15

from the day she came out of the coma. Things had not improved when Paris transferred from the hospital to the care facility six weeks before. There was hope, but it faded with every passing day.

Biting her bottom lip, Londyn moved away from the hospital bed and opened the small closet. Grabbing the extra pillow from the shelf, she carefully slid it behind Paris's shoulders until she was more upright.

"There, that's better. Do you think you can eat some of your soup today? It's your favorite... chicken and wild rice with carrots." Londyn pushed the tray closer to Paris and sat on the edge of the bed. "Can you smell it? It looks really good. Like Mom used to make when we were sick. Do you remember that?"

That was a bit of a stretch. Mom had rarely done any cooking. But it was true that she made chicken soup sometimes, even if it was straight out of a can. Keeping up a steady stream of conversation, Londyn spooned little bits into her sister's mouth, glad when the older girl mechanically swallowed the broth. "Before too long, you'll be doing this yourself, you know. You won't need your little sister to help you with things like this. You'll get better and come home where you belong. I'll help you, sis. I'll stay with you for as long as you need."

Paris did not respond. There was not even a flicker in the hazel green of her eyes to indicate she understood Londyn or even recognized her.

Londyn swallowed a muted sob before steeling herself. Despite the devastating stroke Paris had suffered, hope that she would recover completely would not be abandoned.

She must get better if there was any chance of bringing justice to the man responsible.

The door creaked open, and the charge nurse's gray head

appeared in the opening. "Hello, Londyn. How is our patient today?"

Londyn quickly dashed the tears from her cheeks. She smiled at the elderly lady as she entered the room with Paris's chart in her hands. "The same, Mrs. Hill," she said, turning away from Paris so she couldn't hear the sadness in her voice. "I wish I could say differently, but I can't."

Mrs. Hill *tsked* under her breath and approached to pass a gentle hand over Paris's forehead. "I know seeing her in this state is difficult for you, my dear. It is a small blessing, but she is not experiencing pain. You are doing the right thing, coming every day like you do. Talking to her about normal things. I think it helps."

"I believe that, too, Mrs. Hill." Londyn lifted another spoonful of soup and guided it between Paris's slack lips. "I know it's rather sudden, but I'll be out of town for a few days. An unexpected job opportunity has come my way, and it's too good to pass up."

"Oh?" Mrs. Hill said, surprised. "What kind of job, dear?"

Londyn's mouth tightened into a thin line before she forced herself to smile. "It's highly confidential, so I cannot reveal the details. But I can say I will be unavailable for thirty days with no access to a cell phone during that time. My trust in you and the rest of the staff is the only reason I can consider doing so. I know you will take excellent care of Paris while I am gone."

"Thirty days? Lord, what kind of job is this?" Mrs. Hill asked, her brow furrowing with concern. "It sounds dangerous. It-it's not something illegal, is it?"

Londyn's expression was crafted of just the right amount of amused shock. "Oh, no, Mrs. Hill. Of course not! However, the terms are quite clear, and I was required to sign a nondisclosure agreement. Thirty days isn't so long, and the pay is very generous. I'll be able to continue Paris's care here for years if that becomes necessary." She gave Mrs. Hill a reassuring smile. "I'll be perfectly fine and back before you know it. It's truly a once-in-a-lifetime opportunity."

"What about school? Doesn't the new semester start soon? I'm sure your sister would not want you to miss one hour of your education."

"I took the fall semester off under hardship purposes, so I have a bit of breathing room. I've already made arrangements to transfer home if it becomes necessary."

Mrs. Hill still did not look convinced. Londyn's hand shook a little as she dabbed a white napkin at the corner of Paris's mouth. If only the motherly woman knew the truth of the new job, she would probably do whatever was necessary to make sure Londyn did not take it. After all, placing oneself in a secret, underground auction might be the height of stupidity. Even if she stood to gain a small fortune for simply giving up a month of her time.

Not just your time. Don't forget your virginity is part of the deal. Your virginity and *your body.*

It was the only way of ensuring Paris would continue receiving the same level of care once the insurance benefits leveled off. And it was the only path open to ensure Sheriff Adam Franklin paid for his crimes. There *must* be revenge for Paris. Revenge for the beating Adam administered before injecting her with the drugs that caused her stroke. He'd left her for dead that night, confident his actions would keep their illicit affair a secret and his department's rampant corruption hidden. For a year and a half, the sheriff had been cheating on his beauty-queen wife with the young emergency dispatcher while also involving her in situations of extortion and violence. No one knew Londyn was aware of her sister's involvement with Adam and all the horrible things he'd done.

The first time Adam had come to the nursing care center, dripping with false sincerity as he checked on his "dear employee," Londyn had nearly thrown up. She calmly thanked the man for his concern while ensuring he understood the severity of Paris's injuries.

Adam's handsome features expressed smug relief when he realized Paris would never, *ever* be the same again. Londyn wasn't sure how she kept herself from snatching up a pair of scissors and stabbing him straight through his black heart.

It was little consolation, but soon, she would have enough money to see Adam Franklin pay for his crimes. He would either pay with the loss of his job, his wife, and his fine, upstanding social status, or he would pay with his life.

Londyn was terrified to realize she much preferred the latter.

CHAPTER

THREE

DURING THE THICK of the heated bidding war, Item Number Fifteen finally lapsed into some sort of complacent trance after resisting several times. Oliver loved a woman's submission, so it was inexplicable that he enjoyed this girl's moments of resistance.

Each time, she paid dearly, however. He found himself keeping a tally of every blow she'd endured, growing increasingly agitated as evidence of her stubborn nature became more apparent with each passing moment. Maybe they would have given her more drugs if not for the planned hunt. After all, how much of a challenge would it be if their prey could barely walk?

"Congratulations, Mister Winter and Mister Barlow. As the two highest bidders, you now advance to the hunt phase." The auctioneer shook the hands of both men before laying out

20

forms for their signatures. "Diamond Lake Ranch will instruct you on the rules once your funds have cleared. Mister Winter, as the leading bidder, you will be given a two-minute head start before Mister Barlow is permitted to join the hunt. When Item Number Fifteen has been captured within one hour, the item will officially become the winner's property, and ownership will transfer immediately. Please remember that no record of this transaction will be kept other than the auction's internal log and payment transaction. This information is encrypted, and if the files containing that information are ever breached, the record is programmed to self-destruct. This is as much for your safety and peace of mind as for Diamond Lake Ranch."

Oliver nodded in agreement, with Barlow doing the same.

One thing could be said for Diamond Lake Ranch. They certainly knew how to capitalize on an unusual situation. The auction's setup meant two bids were collected, although there could only be a single winner. One man would lose an extraordinary sum of money with nothing to show for his greed-fueled lust. Between Barlow's bid and Oliver's, the total paid for the privilege of hunting and owning this girl was nearly five million dollars.

"Hell of a price to pay for a bit of pussy," Lee drawled as he scribbled his signature on the required form.

Oliver's lips twisted in a parody of a smile. He handed the fountain pen to the auctioneer. The man hurried away, Erik accompanying him. No doubt, the two were heading straight to the ranch's financial office so the transactions could be approved right away. "Wondered when you would give up, Barlow. Seems the answer is somewhere around two million."

Lee pushed his mask until it rested atop his head. Producing a cigar, he bit off its end and chuckled as he lit it. "I should have known you wouldn't back down. Could tell right away you wanted that one even before the bidding started. If you happen to win the hunt, would you consider sharing? All for the sake of good sportsmanship, you understand. Doesn't seem fair that one of us will be left holding our dick in our hand while the ranch collects a fortune."

Revolt quivered throughout Oliver's body. He tamped it down while schooling his expression into one of serene calm. "Having just paid two-point-five for the privilege of hunting that—bit of pussy... I assure you I'll have no interest in sharing the treasure. If I catch her first, that is."

Lee shrugged, but his eyes were shrewd. "Suit yourself, Oliver. Just know the offer stands. Maybe we can work out a deal when it comes time to exterminate her. If there's anything left worth buying, that is."

Oliver considered punching the politician. He would, too, if he could not extricate himself from the conversation before his temper flared any higher. "You heard the rules, Barlow. Whoever catches her must go through the ranch if a secondary sale is considered. But we're getting ahead of ourselves here. Let's get through the hunt before there's any talk of extermination. Or secret deals."

"BETTER MAKE those two minutes count, Winter," Barlow taunted as people gathered on the wide stone terrace steps.

Oliver ignored the man, focusing on Item Number Fifteen instead. She'd been given a pair of gray track pants and a white sports bra, but her feet were still bare. The handcuffs had been removed, although the collar was still latched around her neck. One of the two brutes present during the auction held the end of the attached chain while the other had her arm in a punishing grip.

Caught in the floodlights illuminating the small grove, the girl appeared like a fragile, pale waif. Oliver wondered if it was true that she had killed a man. It looked like she barely had the strength to stand, her gaze roaming over the guests who'd gathered to observe the special event. When she caught sight of the two men waiting on the edge of the clearing wearing their masks from the auction, her chin trembled, fear etched across her features. It was painfully obvious how terrified she was, but it did not distract from her beauty. Dark-brown hair tumbled over her shoulders, and even in something as simple as workout garb, she was fucking stunning.

Oliver's heart clenched, and he frowned, caught off guard by the foreign sensation. *That's fucking weird.*

"Gentlemen, remember the rules for the auction. One hour to capture the target." The man speaking to the assembled guests was Ruril Andrey, the managing director and owner of Diamond Lake Ranch. His brother, Erik, stood beside him. Together, they presented a united front in their bespoke suits and heavy, gold-and-diamond-encrusted rings flashing from thick fingers. Five blonde women, all as gorgeous and svelte as supermodels, crowded close to the two men and subtly shoved each other for the chance to hang off a brother's arm. "She must be presented here, under your control, for the sale to be complete. You have zip ties and flashlights. Use them at your discretion. Your masks will remain on during the hunt. Makes it more interesting."

"This is madness," the girl said, shakily, that somehow shimmered across the grove. It was carried on the wind, shifting through the aspens and thick pines. "You are all evil, evil people... every last one of you..."

The guard holding the chain leash gave it a quick, vicious jerk. Item Number Fifteen landed on her knees, her free hand grasping the collar around her neck. Tears ran down her cheeks and mingled with the blood staining the corner of her mouth.

"Unleash her," Ruril commanded with a wave of his meaty hand. From his perch on the upper terrace, he might have been a king issuing orders to the peasants below. "Girl, this is your chance to run."

"Go on," the man holding her arm instructed in a guttural voice as the chain was unclipped. He hauled her to her feet, then shoved her with such force the girl landed on her hands and knees. "Run so they can chase you." Using the toe of his boot, he kicked her in the buttocks, propelling her forward and sprawling into the dirt.

Item Number Fifteen clenched her fists against the earth, scrambling forward to escape the guard's boot a second time. Oliver thought she might stay down, sobbing in defeat, but in a flash, she was up and hurling handfuls of gravel and dirt into the faces of the men tasked with guarding her.

Howls of laughter erupted among the observers as the girl sprinted to the edge of the clearing. While the guards cursed and brushed away the dirt stinging their eyes behind the simple masks they still wore, she was gone in an instant. The ebony black of the woods enveloped her.

"Fucking bitch," one of the guards muttered as they stepped back from the clearing. "They should have given her to us. We'd make her sorry she ever entered the auction."

"Pretty sure she's already sorry," Oliver dryly commented as the two men took positions beside him and Lee. "Can't imagine she signed up for something as depraved as this. Hunted like an animal and torn to pieces by men wearing masks."

The one who had kicked the girl scowled at Oliver. "She shouldn't have murdered one of us."

"Noted," Oliver said. He really didn't care what the girl had done that landed her in this predicament. His interest lay in catching her and then fucking her hard enough to justify the money he'd ponied up for the privilege of placing the bid. But the fact this particular guard enjoyed hurting her was royally pissing him off.

Five minutes later, Ruril once again waved his hand. "Proceed with the hunt, Mister Winter. Remember you have a two-minute head start before Mister Barlow begins. Good luck."

Oliver nodded, and contrary to what he knew the crowd expected of him, he strolled toward the edge of the trees as if all the time in the world lay at his disposal. After tucking the zip ties into his back pocket, he flicked on the flashlight and melted into the forest.

FOUR

L *ondyn*

LONDYN'S HEART beat like a wild thing.

She took a deep breath and expelled the air in a measured release. The key was to focus on not gulping in another panicked breath. That would only lead to an episode of hyperventilation. And *that* must be avoided if she had any chance of getting as far away from this place as possible. With a determination born of desperation, she went through the calming technique a second time, gratified when her persistence paid off.

Her heartrate leveled out, a sense of calmness seeping through her body. Now that her initial burst of frantic reaction was subsiding, she could think with a bit more clarity. Although her brain still felt addled from the drugs they'd injected her with, she possessed enough of her wits to assess the situation. And, more importantly, figure out a way to escape. Convulsively, she swallowed as she touched the collar still around her neck. It was tight enough that she could not get a finger between it and the skin of her throat. It felt like she was choking, even though she knew she wasn't.

I must get away from here...

But how? They have my driver's license. I have no money, no transportation, no cell phone, and, for God's sake, no shoes.

She glanced down at her feet. They were already scratched and bleeding, but it wasn't as bad as it could have been. Thank God she'd spent her childhood traipsing barefoot around the Georgia countryside. Hopefully, it had toughened her up enough to survive.

She'd taken refuge beneath a small ridge of stone not too far from the clearing where she'd been set loose earlier. If the men chasing her shared anything in common with the parade of Neanderthal boyfriends her mother accumulated while she was alive, they would not expect her to circle back to the source of danger. It was a maneuver she and her sister employed many times in those dark years of escaping hard, grippy hands and cruel fingers. How many times had they both slept in the woods on the outskirts of the trailer park? Waiting in the darkness for the clumsy, unkempt animal chasing them to give up and settle back on her momma's sagging couch with cold beer in his hand.

Outwitting those monsters and staying just beyond their reach as she grew from child to young woman was an accomplishment. A testament to her resiliency and will to live. And Paris, too. Without her older sister, Londyn knew she would not have made it out of her nightmare childhood in one piece and physically unscathed.

I will outsmart them all. I must... There's no other option. I have to get back to Georgia somehow. For Paris's sake...

Her best hope lay in finding a vehicle, which meant doubling back to the ranch house or one of the outlying buildings. At the very least, she could follow the ranch's entrance road until it connected with a highway. Hitchhiking out of the area was not ideal, but it would be the only option available if she could not find a car with the keys left inside.

Taking another deep breath and slowly letting it out, Londyn listened to the silence of the night surrounding her. A pale half-moon provided her with very little light, but it was enough that she could make out the trail just below her hiding spot. If anyone ventured close, she'd see them first.

Her fingers found and closed around a rock small enough to fit within the palm of her hand. She squeezed it until the rough edges bit into her skin while considering her options. What kind of damage could such a meager weapon inflict? Was it enough to knock a man out? Enough to buy a few precious seconds to escape?

A gun would be better... like the one she used to kill her escort during the journey to this damned ranch.

A shudder raced through Londyn. The details of the incident were fuzzy, but she'd never forget the look of surprise on the man's face when his hand clamped over the hole in his side. The blood that dripped from the wound onto her bare stomach began as a hot liquid, only to cool quickly into a sticky mess that left her chilled.

She hadn't meant to murder him; it just... happened. He had attacked her with the finesse of an experienced rapist, and she reacted blindly. Protecting the only thing of value she owned was paramount. If she arrived at the ranch in a condition less than promised, it would have affected the amount of money she was supposed to receive.

She did what was necessary to keep it from being stolen, but the people in charge did not seem to care about any of that.

In fact, this turn of events seemed to suit them just fine. They would double the anticipated amount and not have to pay her the previously agreed-upon price. They would keep it *all*, and she would eventually lose her life.

"Girl."

A man's voice boomed in the night, the single word bouncing off the trees and the boulders. Londyn stifled a gasp and crouched lower, squeezing herself into the crevice under the ledge. She could not see who called out, but he sounded very close.

Peering through the darkness, she focused on the part of the trail she could see from her elevated vantage point. It was still empty, with no sign of movement or sound. Even the wind had died down, leaving everything motionless, silent, and limp.

How she wanted to scream at him. Rage and cry and hurt him as she'd been hurt. *Londyn!* She ached to tell them all. *My name is Londyn.*

It took all her willpower to hold her breath, fighting to keep the terror inside her. Twigs crunched on the forest floor, and the rustle of bushes as someone pushed through them signaled the man was coming closer. The sounds echoed in the vast space, making it difficult to tell which direction he came from.

"Girl… if you can hear me, I want you to listen very closely to what I'm about to say," the man explained.

His voice sounded calm. Smooth. Londyn wondered if he could hear her heart pounding. It was beating so hard that she was becoming dizzy. Was it a side effect of the drugs they'd pumped into her to make her more compliant during the auction? Was it from the injection they'd given her just before the hunt began? The guard chuckled when telling her she would be slower and clumsier.

"Of the two of us, I promise you'll be better off if I am the one to catch you. I'll treat you like a queen," the man crooned. "Cater to your whims. Fuck you until you are certain you will die from the pleasure. My opponent, well—he is another story. Take my word on it. He's a monster who *enjoys* hurting women. Loves making them cry and beg for mercy. I'm the better choice of the two. Come on out, honey. Let me take you back to the main house. We'll get you cleaned up. Feed you. Get you some warm clothes..."

There was still no movement on the trail, but through the thick underbrush, there was a sweep of illumination that could only come from a flashlight. Whoever it was, they were nearer than she liked. Panic galloped through Londyn. She clutched her inadequate protection harder, taking comfort in the unforgiving hardness of the stone in the palm of her hand. She decided she would wait until he moved past before continuing toward the main house. Hopefully, both men out there, hunting her as if she were a prized game animal, would continue trekking deeper into the forest in their effort to find her. She crept out from under the safety of the ledge, her eyes trained on the distant illumination of the flashlight.

God, please don't let them catch me. Please help me get away from this awful place and these awful men. These monsters.

There was silence. Thick. Encompassing. Scary. Then, the world came crashing down on Londyn. At least it felt like it, anyway.

"Caught ya."

LONDYN SCREAMED in terror as the man gripped a handful of her hair, using it to drag her out of her hiding spot. Once she was on level ground, he dropped the flashlight and wrapped his arms around her, squeezing until she could not breathe. His laughter was cruel as she struggled to free herself. When she managed to knock the devil mask slightly askew, he grunted and wrangled her into a position where her arms were tightly pinned against her sides.

"What a hellcat you are!" His chuckle turned into a surprised yelp when Londyn kicked backward, her heel connecting with his knee. "Vicious, too." He released her just long enough to spin her around so he could backhand her across the face. "We'll have to do something about that." His hand, scarred and ugly, gripped her chin. Holding her still, he glared down at her, his features hidden behind the mask's grotesque visage. "Now, let's get these zip ties on, get you back to the ranch, and make this official."

With a strength she didn't realize she possessed, Londyn swung the rock at the man's head. Gripping it like it was her only salvation, it collided with his temple, knocking the mask completely off. Even in the diluted light of the moon, the surprise on his face was apparent. Blood trickled from a cut left behind by the weapon's sharp edge.

"You little bitch," he snarled. "You're gonna pay for that."

He struck Londyn again, knocking her to the ground. The rock fell from her hand, lost in the sooty darkness. Then he was on her, his hands ripping at the sports bra, pulling and tugging the jogging pants she'd been permitted to wear. Guttural, animal-like sounds came from deep in his throat as he tore at her clothes.

Londyn fought back even though she was becoming dizzy and disoriented from his blows.

"Fucking chasing you through these goddamn woods for almost an hour..." the man growled. He tore the jogging pants off her and used his body to pry her legs apart while trying to catch her mouth with his. Locking her hands in a tight grip, he wrenched them high above her head and pinned them in the dirt. When she tried bucking him off her body, he reared back with an ugly laugh. The moonlight caught on the gray streaks in his hair as he quickly unfastened his pants. Feeling the hot length of his cock searing the inside of her thigh, Londyn screamed again.

"That's what I want to hear..." he laughed. "I like it. Do it ag—"

Thud.

The man's eyes widened in shock. Londyn stared up at him, uncomprehending when the attack abruptly stopped.

Thud.

Again, that sound.

The man slumped forward slowly and then toppled sideways, trapping Londyn's legs beneath his weight. She tried scooting out from under him, but he was too heavy. She was trapped. Trapped and choking on hysterical sobs as a shadow loomed, growing larger and more ominous by the second.

No. Not a shadow but the Devil himself, with shoulders broad enough to block out the moonlight and clad in a midnight-black tuxedo. A tousled mess of dark-brown hair fell over the edge of his terrifying skull mask, and a jawline of chiseled perfection was evident when his attention turned to the fallen man. Gripped in one of his large hands was a heavy, tactical-type flashlight identical to the one Londyn's attacker carried. In the faint glow of the moon, she saw tattoos on his fingers but could not make out what they were.

Using his boot, the man kicked the injured man aside. Startled by her sudden freedom, Londyn belatedly tried scrambling away as the man's firm mouth curved in cruel amusement. He watched for a few seconds, apparently entertained by her reaction, before tucking the bloodied flashlight into his back pocket. Stooping, he silently grabbed her by the ankles, his fingers wrapping neatly around the delicate network of narrow bones and using his grip to jerk her closer.

Zip ties appeared in his hand. The hazy part of Londyn's brain registered his actions. With quick, efficient movements, as though he'd done this thousands of times before, the man flipped her onto her stomach and securely tethered her hands behind her back.

"Let's go, little killer." His voice was low and melodic as he hauled her up onto her feet, pressing his body against her back. His cologne teased her nose. Sharp and clean. Like the winter air spiked with pine needles and cardamon. Stronger than iron, his grip was impossible to break.

Londyn screamed in frustration. When the man clamped a hand over her mouth to shut her up, she promptly bit him, her teeth sinking into his skin.

He allowed the assault for a few seconds, then with terrifying calm, yanked his hand free. Drawing her closer, his mouth skimmed her ear; his breath warm, his words chilling. Pressed against his body was like being held to an open flame. He was so hot. Londyn nearly melted into him, her icy skin delighting in the unexpected warmth of his embrace.

"Do that again and I'll have the absolute pleasure of fucking you and killing you on this very spot. Do you understand?"

Londyn stomped her foot on top of his in response, hating that his amused chuckle frightened her more than any uttered threats.

"You're a feisty little thing, aren't you? Guess I need to take you down a notch," he murmured. "You still want to play this pointless game of cat and mouse? All right. I can do that. I'll let you go. Give you a head start and hunt you again. But know this. When I catch you—and I will catch you—I'll fuck you. Hard. Without mercy or kindness. Right here in the dirt." He kicked the body of the fallen man, eliciting a pained groan from him. "With this fucker watching."

"Let me go," Londyn seethed.

"Want to get fucked that badly, do you?" Trailing his hand over her neck and the leather collar, he gripped it suddenly, pressing his thumb against the underside of her chin until her head was forced back. The night sky filled her vision. An endless, vast expanse of darkness punctuated with glittering stars and the watery light of a silver moon.

"I want you to go to Hell," she snarled, throwing caution to the wind while an uncontrollable quiver somewhat ruined the ferocity of her words.

His laughter burned her ear, his lips tracing the curve of her neck as she strained away from him. "We'll go together. It'll be fun."

She did not respond to that. Something in his tone told her this man was well acquainted with Hell.

"Ah, you going quiet on me now?" he chided.

"There's little sense in talking when you have no intention of listening." Londyn clenched her teeth as his hand drifted from her neck to her stomach. He kept her positioned with her back to his front, and although he still wore the skull mask, she stupidly wished she could see his face.

"He ripped your pants."

Londyn frowned at the iciness of her captor's statement. Honestly, she'd forgotten the state of her clothing until he mentioned it. Now, as if her body needed the reminder, she shivered uncontrollably. "Yes."

"He broke the rules," was his gruff response. His large hand splayed across the bare skin of her stomach, his fingers gently stroking her and familiarizing himself with her curves. Inexplicably, he abruptly stripped off his elegant formal jacket and draped it over her shoulders.

She didn't want to, but Londyn huddled into its warmth. "You cheated, too," she mumbled, the adrenaline of the chase and the innate desire for survival quickly wearing off. Suddenly, she was so very tired. Exhausted, cold, hungry, and thirsty.

"There are no rules against my actions, but he would have raped you before being declared the winner." The injured man chose that moment to groan, and her captor's attention shifted to him. His amused laughter tickled her ear. "Can't say I'm terribly sorry about this turn of events, Barlow," he said to the man who was now pushing himself up to a sitting position. "Better luck next time."

"Fuck you, asshole," Barlow muttered, glaring up at them. Noting the jacket slung over Londyn's shoulders, he smirked. "I should have known you were stalking us both."

"Now, now. Don't be such a sore loser. It's poor sportsmanship." The man gripped Londyn's wrists, turning her away from Barlow's stare and pushing her toward the narrow trail. "I hope you won't forget I showed you mercy," he called over his shoulder, his voice chipper as though he'd just won a game of bingo rather than ownership of an unwilling woman. "I just as easily could have bashed your head in, and no one would have blamed me."

 *liver*

"WILL you be staying with us for the remainder of your reservation, Mister Winter? Or have your plans changed?" the front desk concierge inquired.

Oliver rubbed a thumb over his bottom lip. Every fiber of his soul screamed that he should get the hell out of Diamond Lake Ranch sooner rather than later. But the impossibility of finding suitable lodgings at this hour could not be ignored. Besides, he couldn't check into a new hotel with the bruised, naked girl he'd just chased through the forest. No, leaving the ranch would wait at least until morning.

"Staying, Mister Phillips. Although I'll need a change in accommodations due to current developments. One of the outer cabins equipped with a cage will do nicely. I would greatly appreciate your handling the necessary arrangements."

"Of course, sir. It will be taken care of immediately." The concierge snapped his fingers to gain the attention of a porter. He spoke quietly to the man and handed him a master key to Oliver's rooms.

"I do not blame you for being in a hurry, Mister Winter," Erik said with a smile of approval. "Knowing how rough you play; I hope she lasts through the remainder of the night. For the sake of your bank account, anyway."

"Thank you, Erik." A familiar tingle of warning nagged Oliver as he accepted a congratulatory cigar from the Russian. Something felt off about this entire situation, but damn if he could ferret out the precise cause for concern.

Sure, he'd backed out of a lucrative deal of selling them the woman his brother loved, but the organization offered multiple assurances that his standing had not suffered. Besides, in addition to the exorbitant sum he coughed up for acquiring a new prize, he'd been assessed a sizable fine for reneging on that contract. Money had a way of smoothing out problems. The Russians would overlook many things if paid enough. That was a universal truth in many aspects of this life he led.

"Enjoy, my friend. You will let us know if you need anything, yes?" Erik asked, his gaze shrewd.

"As long as Barlow doesn't want payback for those knots on his head, we should be good."

Erik waved a hand in dismissal. "Ruel gave him the choice of girls in the play dungeon. He'll be kept busy and will forget about the hunt."

Oliver nodded before heading to the expansive bar area mere steps away from the ranch's lobby. While waiting for his cabin to be prepared and his new possession cleaned up, he might as well have a drink and contemplate everything he planned on doing with her.

The cabins of Diamond Lake Ranch were hardly cabins in the traditional sense. The buildings along the outskirts of the main lodge were luxury chalets. They came complete with a lower-level room set up for all manners of erotic play and heated plunge pools overlooking the huge lake. They had an isolated feel, surrounded by mature aspen trees with leaves that shimmered and sang in the spring and summer months. They were very popular with guests requiring more privacy and no prying eyes.

Oliver had never stayed in one before this visit. He preferred the convenience of staying in the main building and having the amenities close at hand. Staying in a cabin meant one either undertook a short walk to the main lodge or used the ranch jeep assigned to that cabin.

Having settled in almost an hour ago, Oliver now waited impatiently for the delivery of Item Number Fifteen.

Although he'd been given a dossier file containing all pertinent information related to his new toy, Oliver did not open it. He preferred to unpeel her layer by layer. Piece by ragged piece. He truly was curious to see what she would reveal on her own. Would she share her secrets willingly in exchange for promises of mercy? Or would she stubbornly keep it all hidden while waiting for death at his hands?

Taking a drink of his favorite scotch thoughtfully stocked in the well-appointed bar, Oliver drifted around the luxurious cabin. At one point, he paused in the living room area and admired the beauty of the lake below the wall of windows. The moon illuminated the water while creating dark shadows in the trees still holding onto the late summer leaves.

Oliver continued his exploration while lingering in the doorway of the cabin's sole bedroom. A circular iron cage occupied one corner, standing about seven feet high and six feet wide. The cage door had a number keypad and a padlock to secure whatever real-life treasure was placed within its confines. An elaborate but sturdy birdcage that he intended to make full use of.

Oliver's cock hardened at the images his mind conjured. Item Number Fifteen. His little killer. Naked and shivering. Locked in this beautiful cage. Unable to escape while he made use of her lithe, warm body.

A knock on the front door alerted Oliver, and a quick check of the security camera confirmed it. The girl hung limp between the same two burly guards. Her head was lowered to her chest, and despite the chill in the air, she was scantily clad in the same bandeau bra and thong she'd worn at the auction. She was also sporting handcuffs, although this time, her arms were not pulled behind her back like before. Oliver's annoyance at the lack of care demonstrated for his property revealed itself in a heavy scowl as he flung open the cabin's front door.

"Where do you want her?" The guard speaking was the same who'd kicked the girl at the start of the hunt. A fresh scratch marred his cheek, and frustration radiated off him. In his hand, he carried an overnight bag. Oliver realized it must belong to the girl. It was probably filled with personal items from home. Her own clothes. Toiletries.

"Bedroom." Oliver stepped aside so the men could enter. They practically carried their charge through the foyer, and Oliver's anger simmered when he saw the girl trembling from exposure to the cool air. Whose decision was it to deliver her in such a state? It was unacceptable.

"Not wasting any time, is he?" one guard muttered as they half-marched half-carried the girl down the wide corridor. Oliver watched with narrowed eyes from the doorway as she was unceremoniously tossed onto the bed.

Instead of remaining there, however, she rolled to the side of the mattress, her movements lethargic. New bruises adorned her upper arms, and although she'd been washed clean of the grit and scrapes associated with her desperate foray in the woods, her cheeks were wet with tears. The leather collar was still around her neck, but there was no longer a leash attached to its center ring.

Her gaze frantically searched the room. And Oliver finally saw the color of her eyes when she found him standing silently in the doorway. Deep, dark gray. Fathomless and full of secrets and questions. Wide with terror. It was like gazing into approaching storm clouds while lightning illuminated the universe from the inside out.

A moan escaped her throat as she twisted away from the rough hands keeping her hostage. Was she more frightened of the men restraining her? Or was it the sight of her new owner that induced her panicked response?

"Hold her still," Oliver instructed, his voice calm, although whatever he was experiencing in that moment, deep inside his gut, was far from rational. It went beyond possessiveness. Beyond ownership. It was something so wild, so fucking feral, it scared him. This girl... this girl was his. His from this very moment until she drew her last shuddering breath beneath him. *His.* "I want to see *everything* I paid for."

"She's a goddamn handful, that's for sure," the taller of the two guards grunted as he pressed the girl down into the thick mattress, oblivious to the danger of his rough actions. "You see what she did to Carl? It's why we had to cuff her again."

"Has she been sedated?" Oliver asked, his lips tight. He already knew the answer. He just wanted confirmation.

"Yeah. Same stuff she was given at the auction. Should have tied her feet, too. Maybe even hogtied her. Just about kicked ol' Rodney right in the balls when we got her out of the Jeep." Carl grabbed the girl's ankles, yanking them with such force that she cried out.

The pain woke her from the semi-conscious state. She began fighting, weak as a newborn kitten at first, then with increasing ferocity until she writhed against captivity like a wildcat. Teeth flashing, she snapped at anything that came close to her mouth. During the frenzied attack, she latched onto Carl's forearm.

Letting out a sharp curse, Carl cuffed the girl's temple with a meaty fist. She instantly went limp, her head lolling from the force of the blow.

"Fucking bitch! You gonna pull that shit again?" Carl bellowed at the unconscious girl, spittle flying from his mouth in his anger.

"Goddamn it, Carl," Rodney swore, scowling up at his partner as he rolled the girl onto her back. He pushed the hair out of her face, assessing the damage. "How many times you gotta be told, you stupid asshole? Never hit them in or around the face. *Never.* No matter what. No matter how pissed off they make you."

"Yeah, well, she deserved that and a hell of a lot more for all the trouble she's caused."

Oliver did not think. He let the fury sink in and drown him. He did not question his reaction or consider reining in the red-fueled rage swamping him. When the guard sank into a low chair, he quickly approached the distracted man from behind.

"Fucking bite me," Carl grumbled as he examined the bloody wound, "and think you can get away with..."

In a flash, Oliver captured Carl's head in his hands with a forearm caught beneath the man's chin. One quick twist, a sickening crunch, and Carl slid from the chair to the floor in a motionless heap.

"Holy shit." Rodney jumped off the bed, backing away from the girl's prone body as Oliver advanced toward him. Hands raised in supplication, the look of terror on the guard's face was comical. "Mister Winter... What the fuck? He shouldn't have hit her, but goddamn, sir, you didn't have to kill him."

"On the contrary. It was an absolute necessity. That's not the first time he struck her. While I had no right to object before, I certainly do now." Oliver paused long enough to shove Carl's lifeless body out of the way and fixed a stony glare on Rodney. "Now, I would advise you to get the fuck out of my cabin and take this piece of shit with you. And when you report this incident to the directors, let them know that I'll happily explain why I killed the bastard who mistreated my property in front of me."

"I-I understand, Mister Winter." Rodney swallowed hard. "Can you help me move him?"

"I'm sure you can figure it out," Oliver replied, shaking his head. "I suggest you get busy."

It took Rodney nearly ten minutes to wrestle Carl's body out of the cabin and loaded into the Jeep. Once the man was gone, Oliver pocketed the key to the handcuffs, set the security system, and returned to the bedroom.

The girl lay unmoving on the bed, her long, rich-brown hair streaming across the covers. Her eyes were still closed, her handcuffed hands resting on her bare stomach.

Oliver examined the bruising on her soft skin in the room's soft lighting. Some marks, like the mottled red discoloration along her jaw, resulting from the scuffle with Lee Barlow in the woods. The darker ones, the purplish-yellow ones, must have occurred during the time leading up to the auction. But a few were so fresh, so vivid, they could only have happened during the transport to the cabin and into his custody.

"Fuck. I should have insisted on different guards," Oliver muttered, disappointed in his lack of foresight. Why the abuse this girl had suffered bothered him so acutely was a mystery, but it couldn't be ignored. If it wouldn't have caused unwanted hassle, he probably would have exterminated the second guard for good measure. But that would not be overlooked by Diamond Lake Ranch. Murdering one was justifiable. Two? That was a reckless and foolish move he refused to take.

Showing restraint was surely a sign of his personal growth over the past year—an example of newfound rationality and maturity.

A rueful chuckle escaped Oliver. Mature? Yeah, possibly. But rational?

No fucking way.

CHAPTER
SIX

 *liver*

Climbing onto the bed, Oliver straddled the girl and, with gentle fingers, examined the side of her face where Carl struck her.

The thought that she could have a concussion was mildly concerning, especially if she began exhibiting signs such as vomiting. It wasn't ideal that she was still knocked out. He was no fucking doctor, but after a few moments, Oliver decided her unconscious state had more to do with sedation and extreme exhaustion. Obviously, she'd been through a lot over the last few days.

He smoothed a finger over her dark eyebrows. With impossibly long eyelashes and a perfectly shaped mouth, she possessed classically beautiful features. She was fucking stunning.

Oliver's right hand moved to her throat, encircling the slender column. What he saw sent a dark thrill shooting through his body.

MINE, the letters tattooed on his fingers declared as he gently squeezed. Her pulse thumped rhythmically beneath his fingertips, echoing the pounding in his own veins.

MINE, everything inside him screamed. It didn't make sense to feel so intensely for a girl he knew nothing about, but it didn't matter.

Holding her in his grasp felt right. Claiming her with just a hand wrapped around her throat felt right. Everything about her was *right*, and although he did not understand it, he was ready to be swallowed by what might become a new obsession.

"You're already obsessed," Oliver muttered. He'd paid a fortune for her. Cheated to win her. And killed to protect her.

Sinking his hand into her thick dark hair, he cradled her skull and tilted her head with the force of his thumb to the underside of her chin. Her lips parted on a soft sigh, but her brow remained smooth as he handled her. She remained lost to the world, and Oliver took advantage of it.

He liked his women submissive, silent, and in servitude. It was in his nature to expect complete obedience in all things. His upbringing in a dark and dangerous world where women existed to serve a man's pleasure set that in stone a long time ago. But this girl was proving herself different from his usual appetite. Her feistiness was adorable, but the ferocity he witnessed earlier thoroughly entranced him.

A sprinkling of freckles danced across the bridge of her small nose, and it was impossible to resist brushing his lips over her silken skin. Tasting her. Inhaling her. Learning the sweetness of her breath and how it affected him. He owned this girl. *Really* owned her. Her very breath was his to take or give, and the power that came with that was some heady shit.

Letting go of her head so it fell back against the bed, Oliver let his gaze drift over her body. Removing a switchblade from his back pocket, he quickly cut off the meager lingerie she wore. But he hesitated when it came to the collar that encircled her pale throat. He could not deny he liked the idea, but he'd rather she wore one of his choosing. Making the split-second decision, he sliced through the leather and tossed it aside.

He repositioned her arms so her cuffed wrists were stretched high over her head. Every bruise and every scrape was mentally cataloged as he drank in her beauty.

Deliciously round breasts crowned with nipples of dusky pink had Oliver's mouth watering. The supple mounds of flesh fit perfectly into his hands as he tested their weight. Except for a few scratches from the hunt, her skin was amazingly soft and velvety in texture. He pinched her nipples in turn, loving how they puckered in response. Sucking one tip into his mouth, he rolled the pebbled flesh between his teeth.

"Fuck, you are delicious," he murmured reverently. Delicious and goddamn addictive. He couldn't seem to stop smoothing his hands over her; first, her breasts which he continued to suck and nibble, then her flat stomach and the curved flare of her hips. Maybe he should have her nipples pierced before killing her. Seeing her pretty breasts adorned in jewelry would be something quite memorable. She'd probably object but he could always strap her to a chair for the procedure.

Oliver's lips tilted in a self-indulgent smirk. Everything about this situation was illegal, depraved, and immoral, but he did not care. He was too far removed from normality to feel even a sliver of shame. Whether she was conscious or not, he had every right to examine and play with his new possession.

And he would, regardless of the morality of it. He would do what he wanted, when he wanted, and that's just how it was going to be. He didn't need permission, and he didn't need her consent. Not after he spent nearly three million dollars for the pleasure of fucking her.

With an index finger, he traced a line from her belly button to the top of her pussy. Item Number Fifteen was waxed bare of any hint of hair because the Russians liked it and foolishly believed every man who visited the ranch did, too. Oliver preferred a woman to be neatly groomed with a narrow strip of curls to tease his nose when he licked her pussy.

Oliver frowned, thinking of the procedures she endured to be readied for the auction. Jealousy, sharp and almost painful, stabbed at him. He wanted to scoop out the eyeballs of every person who had seen her naked and vulnerable.

Moving her long legs wider, Oliver settled between them, his mouth lined up with the junction of her thighs. Fucking hell, her cunt was gorgeous. So plump and pink. Sheer perfection. Gently, he spread her flesh, allowing him complete access.

A quick check of her face revealed she was still unconscious. Emboldened by her lack of response, Oliver bent his head, lapping at her clit before raking the sweet bud with the edge of his teeth.

The girl's hips shifted slightly, bucking upward at the sensation. Oliver grinned, flattening his tongue against her clit and pressing harder until her body twitched.

There was no mistaking that involuntary, automatic response. It would be easy to make her come like this. Even in this oblivious state, he could drive her body to a shuddering, helpless orgasm. She was his, even if she would inevitably hate that fact. She could fight until her body was bloody and bruised, but it would not matter.

Oliver savored this first taste, swirled his tongue around her softness, and administered tiny bites here and there. As his cock throbbed painfully, demanding to sink into her, he slid a finger into the warmth of her cunt and fucked her with slow, shallow thrusts while devouring her with his mouth. She was delightfully wet. Wet and warm, and soon, he would take every sweet piece of her.

After a few more minutes feasting on her, he reluctantly gave her pussy one last swipe of his tongue then rolled off the bed. Rubbing his aching cock through his pants, he knew if he did not stop, he'd end up fucking her.

That's not what he wanted right now. Not like this. He wanted her awake. Awake and aware the first time he fucked her. He wanted her tears. Her screams. He wanted to hear her cries, begging him to stop then pleading for more.

Glancing at the cage occupying the corner of the room, Oliver made a decision. The rational thing to do was to lock her up in the contraption. With the possibility she might murder him in his sleep and escape the cabin, he needed to secure his little killer. It was also very likely his willpower would evaporate, and he'd wind up fucking her unconscious body six ways from Sunday. Not to mention, the nightmares he occasionally suffered made it hazardous for a bed partner. For her own safety and his sanity, she'd sleep in that cage this first night.

CHAPTER

SEVEN

L *ondyn*

THE FIRST THING Londyn saw when her eyes fluttered open were vertical bars like those found in a prison cell. And her first thought was a simple one.

The police have me. They found out about the man I murdered.

She sat up, grimacing as pain shot through her body. Every part of her ached and throbbed, including her head, which pounded like the devil was trying to beat his way inside.

The room was dimly lit but as she became more aware, she realized she was indeed inside a cage, only it wasn't a jail cell. The bottom of the round metal cage was cold and hard, but soft, fluffy pillows covered its floor, cushioning it from being too uncomfortable.

A blanket of dark fur rested over her shoulders. Londyn clutched it closer when she abruptly realized she was nude beneath the blanket. And she certainly was not safely incarcerated in police custody.

"You're finally awake."

The low, husky timbre of a man's voice drew her attention. He sat in a low-slung chair just outside the elaborate cage. Londyn scrambled back as far as she could, pressing against the farthest point of the enclosure.

Images flashed through her mind. Memories of everything she'd gone through over the past few days. The plane ride. The attack by the guard. Being starved before the auction and those horrible hours when strange hands held her down and prepared her for sale. She'd been waxed, plucked, bathed, her hair shampooed until every inch of her was clean. And then there was the examination by the house doctor...confirming her innocence. She swallowed the bile that rose in her throat. All of that paled in comparison to that terrifying hunt through the woods and the moment she was claimed by the victor.

Her gaze darted around the room, taking in the massive bed and the elegant rustic furnishings. Her chin wobbled when she remembered being tossed upon that bed and held down by cruel hands. She remembered biting one of them and then... blankness.

Her gaze flew back to the man, waiting patiently for her attention to refocus on him. His mouth curved in a smile.

"Do you know who I am?" His voice was calm and assured, as if he had all the time in the world. Londyn shook her head, not trusting herself to say anything. She was afraid that if she opened her mouth, she would begin screaming and never stop.

He chuckled a little and leaned forward, resting his forearms on his knees as he studied her. "You don't remember last night? That chase through the woods? I paid a fortune for the right to hunt you. To catch you. I'm your new owner."

She pulled the blanket closer, the soft fur tickling her nose.

She wanted to forget those moments in the woods. Wanted to forget how brightly hope flared only to be stomped out under a heavy heel. Another man had assaulted her, then was clubbed for his trouble by the one now watching her so intently.

The guards who delivered her into this man's possession last night called him 'Mister Winter.'

Despite her resolve to stay strong, to continue fighting until she escaped this nightmare, tears tracked down Londyn's cheeks.

The man made a *tsking* sympathetic noise. He had a beautiful smile with straight, white teeth and the sharply cut jawline of a Greek god. "Oh, baby. Do you think your tears make a difference?"

Londyn shivered at the unabashed cruelty in his tone but said nothing. Instead, she calmed herself with a deep breath.

He was frowning when her eyes lifted to meet his. Her unwillingness to play his games annoyed him, but even in a pissed-off state, he was probably, and unfairly, the most gorgeous man she'd ever laid eyes on.

Thick, dark-brown hair tumbled over his forehead, and his eyes, an unearthly shade of ice blue, were fringed with eyelashes so lush they'd make any girl jealous. He wore a fitted black T-shirt and black jeans, the muscles in his forearms on full display. Several tattoos decorated his lightly tanned skin—from letters inked across his fingers to a band of barbed wire that encircled one powerful bicep.

He couldn't be much older than herself, although a hard edge added years to his demeanor.

With a sigh, he reached beside the chair and picked up a bottle of water she'd not noticed before. Then he dug something out of his pocket, leaning closer to the cage and offering the items to her.

"Are you thirsty?" His voice was that same husky softness.

He was trying to soothe her with it. Lull her into thinking she was in no danger. She didn't move from the back panel of the cage, remaining pressed against the bars.

He waved the bottle in her direction. "You should drink something. You're dehydrated." Setting the bottle just inside the bars of the cage, he also placed two pills beside it, his lips quirking upward when he saw her glare full of suspicion. "It's just ibuprofen. It will help with the pain."

He was right about the pain, but why he was concerned was a mystery. Her face was sore, and when Londyn gingerly touched her temple, it ached. Her mouth was so dry it felt like it had been packed with cotton. She wanted that water, but how could she trust a man who had locked her in a cage?

"Are you going to kill me?" Londyn blurted out suddenly.

"Not today," the man replied with another charming laugh. He scooped up a black folder lying on the floor between his feet. "I've not gotten my money's worth out of you yet."

"I-I need to use the bathroom," Londyn said quietly. That was the truth. She really did. She could also look for a way of escaping.

The man's eyes darkened as he stared at her while slowly flipping through the folder. "I'm sure you do, but we'll go over a few details before I give you even an inch of rope. Let's start with the most important detail of this arrangement. When I tell you to do something, I expect obedience. Now, take that medicine and drink the water like I've told you."

Londyn scooted closer to the side of the cage where the bottle sat. Although she despised the necessity of following his commands, she twisted the seal of the bottle's cap and took a long swig. It wasn't fair that plain old water should taste so good. She took another deep swallow, holding the blanket tightly at her chest so her nakedness remained hidden, which was stupid since he was likely the one who undressed her in the first place.

"And the medicine," he prodded, not even bothering to glance her way as he perused the contents of the folder.

Londyn examined the round orange pills. They certainly looked like common ibuprofen. While debating the wisdom of ingesting something unknown, she slowly put them in her mouth and took a sip of water. Swallowing them, she hoped he was telling the truth and had not just given her poison.

"That's a good girl," he murmured, and Londyn's stomach tightened. As a third-year psychology major, she understood the powerful yet fundamental dynamics behind those words of praise. Men used them as a way of enticing and encouraging obedience.

"Will you let me out now? I did what you wanted." Her voice was strained and hoarse from the crying she'd done over the last few days, but the note of challenge it contained, and the derisive curl of her lip had the man's head snapping up. Those scary, glacially hued eyes narrowed.

"I will not tolerate defiance. Or insubordination."

Londyn gulped, her mouth suddenly drier than before she drank half a bottle of water. She nodded in a short, jerky motion and waited silently as he flipped through the folder.

"You have a very pretty name. Unusual spelling, too. Were you born in London?" he asked, his eyes flickering back to her. "Or perhaps your parents enjoyed vacationing there?"

Londyn suspected that the folder he held lightly in his large hands contained every bit of information the ranch had gathered on her. Within those pages was her life story, including how she'd ended up trapped inside this ornate birdcage of a prison.

"No. I was not born in London. And my older sister was not born in Paris. My mom barely had enough money to buy a can of soup when she was pregnant with me, much less take vacations." Londyn could not keep the sad bitterness out of the words. The meager amount of money her mom had made working as a waitress was wasted on alcohol, cigarettes, men, and rent on the dilapidated trailer they called home. "I never knew my dad. He was out of the picture by the time I was six months old."

Londyn bit her tongue, appalled at herself for spilling such personal details. This man, her *owner* as he referred to himself, did not have the right to know these things about her life.

"Hmm," was his noncommittal response to her sharing painful truths. He silently read for a few moments, then gave her a sharply quizzical look. "You entered the auction voluntarily. Why?"

Answering his questions was pointless when all the information was in front of him. This was simply a way of exerting control. Her lips thinned as she realized she must appease him while subtly asserting herself. "Please... may I use the bathroom? I'll answer your questions after."

He considered it for a long moment, his gaze scrutinizing her for any signs of deception. Londyn forced her face into a blank mask and did not blink under his perusal.

"Let me make something clear to you, Londyn. There is no escape from this cabin. There are alarms on *all* the doors and windows and if you try opening one, I will know immediately. And the punishment for that, for trying something so stupid, will be severe. Do you understand?"

"Yes," Londyn breathed. She didn't care if the alarms went off like a breakout at a maximum-security prison; if there were a way of getting a window open, she would be gone before he could get to her. "I just want to use the bathroom. And maybe... maybe clean up a little?"

He unfolded himself from the chair to stand at his full

height. Londyn swallowed nervously. He was so tall, at least six foot three, perfectly proportioned with a lean build and well-defined muscles. Taking a key out of his front pocket, he unlocked the door and punched in a code on the keypad. When the lock clicked twice, the door swung open.

"Come on." His hand extended to her, waiting for her to accept his assistance. Londyn trembled, clutching the blanket around her as she placed her hand in his. He pulled her onto her feet and waited until her cramped limbs acclimated to the change in position. When she swayed a little, his arm snaked around her waist. "Steady, now."

This unexpected benevolence confused Londyn. It was almost... tender.

Such strange behavior from a man who would likely eliminate her soon.

CHAPTER

EIGHT

L*ondyn*

LONDYN HELD the blanket tighter around her as he led her to the bathroom. It was a large space. Sleek and cold, with every amenity of a five-star hotel.

"You can take a shower if you like." After pulling a few towels from the cabinet, he motioned to a hook where a clean, lush bathrobe hung. "Put that on when you get out."

"I'd rather have some real clothes..." she began, but her words faltered when she saw his smirk.

"Sorry, Londyn. I won't allow that at the moment. Be grateful for the robe. After all, I could require that you are nude at all times." He stepped closer, tilting her chin using the knuckle of his index finger. The light in the bathroom was bright and unforgiving, finally revealing the letters inked onto his fingers.

MINE.

Londyn's stomach flip-flopped. It was hitting home just how fucked-up this situation was. This man had purchased her. To use. To rape. To possibly murder. She became light-headed at the reality, her skin tone turning pale.

"Are you okay?" her captor asked. "You're trembling."

Was he that oblivious to the reasons for her current state? Of course, she was shaking like a leaf. She was terrified.

"I'm fine," she gritted out between clenched teeth. From his expression, she knew he did not believe her, but he nodded and took a few steps toward the door.

"Come to the kitchen when you are done. It's down the hall from the bedroom. You have fifteen minutes before I come and collect you."

Londyn dipped her head in agreement, wrapping her arms around her midsection. One thing she must do was humanize herself to him. She needed to be more than just an object if she was going to survive this. They must have some sort of connection. A relationship she could exploit the moment an opportunity to escape presented itself.

"Thank you...um...Mister..."

He grinned, so charming and handsome that crazily enough, Londyn almost smiled back.

"My name is Oliver. Oliver Winter. And I can't wait to hear you scream it."

Londyn's chin lifted. She knew her reaction was foolishly reckless, but she couldn't help herself. "You'll be waiting a long time, then." Her glare should have blistered his flesh, but her fierceness only amused him.

Resting a hand on the door handle before exiting the room, Oliver swept her body with a look of absolute possessiveness. "You will scream for me, Londyn. The reason why is totally up to you."

The minute he closed the door, Londyn ran to it and clicked the lock. Her gaze darted around the room, frantically searching for any type of weapon she could find.

Hopeless.

The vanity mirrors over the sink were large plates of glass attached to the wall. Smashing them to bits would bring her captor back immediately. He'd likely break the door down before she could find a piece suitable for use as a knife. The towel bars were heavy metal pipes. Tugging at one only revealed how securely they were attached to the wall.

No artwork decorated the smooth, white marble walls and a quick search of the vanity drawers revealed nothing but high-end toiletries and a blow dryer. Unless she planned on bashing his head in with a bottle of expensive shampoo, there was nothing that could inflict any kind of real damage.

She couldn't even open a window, as they were a series of rectangle-shaped openings stacked on top of each other in a geometric pattern and placed along the length of one wall at ceiling level. The design allowed a ton of natural light to flood the room, but the windows were far too narrow for a body to pass through.

Defeated, Londyn sank onto the toilet seat, fighting back tears. Taking deep breaths once again staved off a panic attack, but her heart pounded as though she was once again running through the woods in fear for her life. She was trapped. Really trapped.

WHILE SHE QUICKLY SHOWERED, Londyn noticed the strange marks on the inside of her thighs. Their presence was mystifying since they almost appeared to be bite marks. There were also scrapes, as though something rough had rubbed against the tender skin. Multiple scratches and bruises covered her body along with scrapes from rocks and branches, but these were entirely different. Even the marks caused by the rough handling of her guards did not resemble the bruising.

With a towel wrapped tightly around her body, she stood in front of the enormous vanity mirror. Brushing her teeth with a new toothbrush discovered during the search for a weapon, Londyn examined her reflection.

The bruising under one eye was a bit darker, and there was a nasty abrasion on her chin, but the cut on her lip was already healing. Experimentally, she ran her tongue over the wound, wincing when the toothpaste stung.

The most noticeable of her injuries, apart from the unexplained marks on her inner thighs, was the mottled bruises around her neck. They had come from the collar and leash being forcibly jerked as a way of controlling her. Her body stiffened as she recalled that humiliation during the auction. When she'd been forced to her knees while cruel men salivated over her helplessness.

After rinsing her mouth, Londyn probed the sore area around her temple with gentle fingers, wondering how that particular injury might have occurred. Her last memory from the previous night was biting Carl, the guard, and his instant rage while shaking her off.

Everything else was blank until she woke that morning in a cage. Had the man struck her so hard that it knocked her out? Was that the explanation for the black hours that must have surely followed? What had the three men in that bedroom done to her last night?

Maybe they had raped her. Maybe they had held her lifeless body down on that huge bed and took turns violating her.

Londyn shuddered. She would surely be in agony if such a horrendous event had taken place. She would be torn and bloody from the battering of her body. Other than the marks on her legs and a strange sensitivity in her private area, there was no indication that an assault of that nature had occurred.

But *something had* happened. And she wasn't sure she wanted to know. The situation was horrible enough without adding more trauma. Maybe it was a blessing she could not remember.

Tap, tap.

Londyn startled, clutching the towel closer as she whirled to look at the door.

Her captor rapped on the door again. Harder this time. Impatiently.

"Time's up, Londyn. Open the door."

She swallowed at the rough irritation his voice contained. There was no choice but to obey him. Instinct screamed that was the safer option. Defying him, or attempting to, was a dangerous gamble.

Grabbing the bathrobe robe, Londyn thrust her arms through the sleeves and tied the belt tightly around her waist.

"Just-just a minute," she answered in a high, thin voice. Clearing her throat, she tried again in a stronger tone. "I'm coming."

"Unless you want to see me when I'm angry, I suggest you unlock this door immediately." There was a deceptive silkiness to his words now. As if he welcomed the opportunity for a violent display of force.

Londyn hated herself for the fear clawing its way up her throat. She ran to the door, fumbling with the lock and throwing it open.

Oliver leaned against the door jamb, arms crossed. His eyes, so icy blue with a darker, indigo-colored ring encircling the irises, darkened in appreciation at the sight of her in the robe.

"I'm sorry," Londyn stuttered. "There's no clock in here, so I didn't know-"

"Be quiet," he ordered softly.

Londyn's explanation abruptly ended. She nervously shifted her feet as he examined her before his eyes quickly scanned the room behind her. He was checking to see if she'd managed to find a weapon and was just waiting to use it on him.

A smirk played across his lips as his gaze slid back to her. "Don't ever lock a door on me again, Londyn. I've no patience for it. Do you understand?"

Londyn's nod was terse.

His smile grew. "I want to hear you say it. Say you understand, Londyn."

Her eyes closed briefly before she stared steadily ahead. "I understand."

He watched her as if considering his next move while Londyn's heart pounded. Then he reached out, hooking his fingers into the top of the robe and pulling until she had no choice but to go where he wanted.

Pressing her back against the door frame, Oliver braced an arm above her head and leaned in. His gaze flickered over her pale features. His firm lips quirked in amusement at her obvious fear.

"Jesus Christ, you are beautiful. I didn't realize how much until just now," he murmured almost to himself. Placing an index finger beneath her chin, he lifted it until she met his gaze. "And when your eyes flash at me like that, you're fucking stunning. Such a pretty color, too. The same shade as the mourning doves my father had me use for target practice as a kid. I deliberately missed them, of course, which never failed to end with a beating for my ineptness." His jaw tightened, irritation evident in the clench of his teeth as he revealed more than he intended.

Londyn swallowed a whimper. What sort of parent encouraged a boy to shoot harmless birds for practice? It was barbaric and cruel. She flattened herself against the door frame. She didn't want him to think she was beautiful. She didn't want him to be attracted to her in any way, but that was a very foolish thing to hope for. Like other predators in her life, this one was drawn to her face and figure. And because she was smaller and weaker than him, he believed it was his right to take whatever he desired.

Standing like this, trapped by his muscular arms and the rock-hard solidness of his body, Londyn became aware of several things. First, he had to be at least six-four, which meant he towered over her measly five-three height. And his muscles... they rippled beneath the tight black T-shirt he wore. A faint scruff covered his chin, and the horrifying thought that this had caused the mysterious scrapes on her thighs sent panic scurrying along her veins.

"What are you thinking, little killer?" His head inclined until their foreheads were nearly touching. "How you might get away? You *can't*. How to talk me out of taking what is mine? You *won't*."

Londyn tried to remember everything she'd learned so far about dealing with sociopaths and troubled individuals. But it all jumbled in her head, mixing like a deadly cocktail spiked with fear and recklessness.

"How did I get the marks on the inside of my legs?"

Her impulsive demand sent a genuine smile skating across his face.

"Marks?" he teased. "What marks? Let me see. Maybe I can tell you what caused them."

"I don't remember what happened last night. For all I know, the three of you took turns assaulting me." Londyn's mouth tightened in outrage.

"No one touched you in that way other than me, Londyn. And no one will as long as you live."

"The one guard, Carl, he liked hurting me. Maybe he—"

"Carl is dead. I snapped his neck," Oliver stated with nonchalant coolness.

Londyn stared at him. Had she heard him right? "You did what?"

Oliver trailed his finger down from her chin until it landed in the hollow of her throat. "You heard me. He struck you hard enough to knock you out. So, I broke his neck. You are my property. No one hurts you unless it's me."

A wave of nausea swept her. She couldn't believe what she was hearing. Knowing another man had lost his life because of her was more than she could comprehend. Even if the two men were monsters, knowing she was the catalyst for their deaths was disturbing. "Did the three of you... There-there are scrapes and what I think are marks that weren't there before. Like bite marks."

"I told you, dove. No one touched you except me." There was a smugness to his tone that could not be ignored. Londyn's stomach dropped as his words sunk in.

"You touched me..." Her words came out in a breathy exhale of horror, too overwhelmed by his admission to pay much attention to the nickname.

Oliver brushed his nose along hers before softly pressing his mouth to her lips. He kissed her gently between words. "Silly little girl. Of course, I touched you. I kissed. I licked. I tasted. Fuck. I *feasted* until you nearly came on my tongue. Your body enjoyed it. It responds because it understands what your mind hasn't yet grasped. You belong to me. Your body is mine.

Your delicious cunt is mine. Your mouth. The air in your lungs..." He kissed her more forcefully then, curling his hand around her throat, his tongue stroking hers until Londyn moaned in panicked surrender, and he allowed her to take a breath. "That's mine, too. Every piece of you is mine. Mine to play with. Mine to use. Mine to destroy."

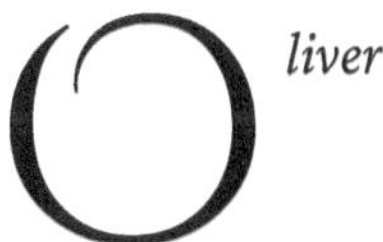 *liver*

LONDYN's bottom lips quivered at his declaration.

Fuck. Why was he admitting his actions from last night? Why admit anything, for that matter? Although he certainly enjoyed the glint of fear in those dove-gray eyes, he relished far more the tiny sounds she made when he kissed her.

Taking pity on her, Oliver stepped back. "I've made coffee if you want some."

He didn't miss her frown of mystified confusion as he quickly moved past the admission of murder on her behalf and the confession that she'd been violated. Yeah, maybe there was an ick factor regarding eating her pussy while she was unconscious, but he'd fucking do it again in a heartbeat.

Lacing his fingers through hers, Oliver led Londyn down the hall to the elegantly rustic kitchen. He pushed her to sit on a barstool at the black granite island, watching with avid interest as she fought to keep the robe from gaping and exposing her long legs.

"How do you take your coffee?" His question snapped her gaze back to him. "And while the kitchen is fully stocked, I'm afraid I'm not much of a cook."

"Cream and sugar, please," she said in a small voice that made his cock twitch with anticipation. He imagined her saying "Yes, Sir," in the same tone when he commanded her to get on her knees.

All in good time.

He slid a cup in front of her and leaned back against the opposite counter. His gaze fixated on the motion of her throat when she took a sip of the steaming beverage. Just watching her swallow, and imagining his cum trickling down her throat, was making him uncomfortably hard.

Her eyes briefly closed in appreciation. "Thank you," she murmured, her eyes meeting his before darting away again. Tangling a lock of hair around her forefinger, she scanned the open space. No doubt, she was searching for any opportunity to escape.

"Would you like some scrambled eggs? I can manage that much and some toast." Oliver's mouth tightened when an unmistakable look of hunger flitted across Londyn's delicate features. "When's the last time you ate something?"

Her brow furrowed in confusion. "Yesterday morning. An apple from one of the guards." A derisive laugh escaped her as she cupped her hands around the coffee mug. "Well, half an apple, anyway. That's all he threw into the cell."

Oliver tamped down his rising temper. How in the hell was this girl still upright and lucid? After everything he knew of her captivity, the drugging, the abuse, and being hunted in the woods, she should be curled up on the floor in a helpless heap. "The Ranch hasn't fed you?"

Londyn shook her head. "Why waste resources on a girl you intend to have murdered?"

The bitterness in Londyn's tone belied her submissive appearance. She was such a contradiction, and Oliver loved solving a puzzle. Unraveling her was going to be a pleasure.

Oliver reached into one of the lower cabinets, pulling out a frying pan. Because the gas stove sat in the middle of the large island, he could easily keep an eye on her as he cooked. Assembling the items he needed, he whisked the eggs, added some cheddar cheese and a bit of cream, and then poured them into the pan. Londyn sipped her coffee, but her silent attention remained mainly focused on him.

When it was ready, he pushed the plate of steaming eggs and toast toward her.

"I-I need a fork." Her voice was soft and non-confrontational.

Oliver let out a sharp laugh. After seeing what a woman could do with an innocuous utensil, he sure as hell wasn't about to place one in his captive's hands.

Londyn's head tilted. "Why is that funny?"

"My brother's fiancée once stabbed someone in the back with a fork. So, out of an abundance of caution, a spoon will do you just fine."

She held the spoon he gave her as if considering how best to turn it into a weapon. But hunger won out over bloodthirsty intentions. With a tiny sigh, she began eating while he did the same.

"Picking up our conversation from earlier, tell me how you came to be involved with the auction?" Oliver questioned as she nibbled on her last piece of buttered toast. He had remained on the opposite side of the island, standing in case there was a need to act quickly.

"For the same reasons as other girls. I needed money. It seemed like the only option to get a large sum fast."

"A *large sum?*" Oliver's brow arched. "I know Vanderbilt is expensive, but surely you have access to student loans. Scholarships. I imagine you are smart enough for such things. What kind of debt have you racked up? Or maybe it's something else." He studied her closely while she squirmed under the scrutiny. "Tell me why this was your only option. Do you like to gamble? Drugs? Something else as illicit as an auction where young women are paid obscene amounts of money for their time and their bodies"

Her eyes flashed with lightning at his crass insinuations. "No," she snarled, raking a hand through her damp hair in frustration. "I did it because I had no other choice. I did it because I am the only one who can take care of my sister. She-she was beaten and abused and then injected with so many drugs she should have died. Paris is in a nursing home after being in a coma for nearly a month. Now, there are so many bills. There's no money, and the insurance only goes so far. And since she lost her job because of all this, that will soon be gone." Londyn's chin trembled, and damn, if Oliver didn't feel a slight twinge of something... foreign.

Maybe shame. Or empathy.

Fuck if he knew.

"I need money to make sure the person who hurt her suffers, too," Londyn said, her eyes now glossy with unshed tears. There was a fierceness in her demeanor completely at odds with the sweetness of her face. "I need money to destroy him. Ruin him."

"Why not just go to the police? If this man is responsible,

you could have reported the crime. Let them handle it. And I'm sure whatever medical bills your sister has acquired could have been resolved with a repayment plan." Oliver's eyes narrowed in shrewd assessment. "Unless you wanted a break from all that. Maybe your motivation wasn't your sister at all. Maybe it was the idea of spending thirty days being catered to. Having gifts lavished on you. Eating in the best restaurants, drinking the finest wine, flying around the world as arm candy to the winning bidder."

Londyn met Oliver's gaze. She did not seem aware of the tears streaming down her pale cheeks, turning her eyelashes into dark spikes of inky black.

"The police? Go to them?" She laughed, a harsh sound full of disdain. "They are the ones who did this to her. The chief of police where we live... he did this to her. He wants her dead. And since I'm now trapped in this nightmare, he'll get his wish."

Oliver's head cocked to the side. "None of that matters now, dove. You realize that, don't you? Your sister. The sheriff. College. Your life before now is done. Everything that happens from here on out is in my control. You no longer have a say in what happens. You no longer have any concerns other than submitting to me and ensuring my happiness and satisfaction."

Londyn choked on a sob, turning her face to stare out the expansive set of windows overlooking the lake. The water glistened in the distance, the nearly bare trees creating a frame for the lake and the mountains around them. Ten miles in all directions from the main ranch house was nothing but streams, steep mountain ledges, and vast wilderness. She did not say anything for a long moment, and when she turned to face him, her chin was set at a stubborn tilt.

"I know this: I know my life is in your hands now. No matter how wrong it is. No matter how depraved and horrendous this situation is. I've been thrust into a world of evil that is incomprehensible to me. And I know you have no reason to consider it, but I wonder if we might come to some kind of agreement."

Oliver smiled, enjoying this back-and-forth exchange. There was something exhilarating about this cat-and-mouse game they'd begun. Londyn was revealing so much about herself in these moments. Showing him the different ways she could be manipulated and molded into the perfect captive. For example, she was undoubtedly submissive, but there were these brattish elements about her that made his blood rush. Taming a brat would be fun. "You've no bargaining power here, Londyn."

"I know that. But still...will you listen to my proposal?"

Shrugging his shoulders, Oliver nodded. "If it makes your situation easier to bear in your mind, then propose away. Nothing will probably come from it, however. I'm not known for extending mercy."

She met his gaze steadfastly, a hard glint within the soft charcoal-hued depths of her eyes that sent a pang of foreboding throughout Oliver's veins. He may have underestimated her ability to twist his intentions to suit her purpose. Whatever she requested was likely to be agreed upon. The inevitability of a compromise battered him like a tidal wave. He would give in with irrational, rare benevolence. He would grant her this one concession while using it as an opportunity to exert further control. Like a wolf playing with a newborn fawn, allowing it to totter on wobbly legs before devouring it whole, Oliver would get what he wanted.

"I will not fight or try to escape or beg for freedom. I will submit to anything you want from me. But I ask for two things in return."

"You have my attention, although realistically, you know I can and will do whatever I want anyway," Oliver coolly replied.

Londyn took a shuddering breath at his calm assertion, then blurted out, "Deposit the money I would have received from the auction into an account in my sister's name. It will be used strictly for her care. And when you are done with me, instead of giving me back to these men just to be sold again... you promise me a quick and painless death."

Oliver schooled his features into his usual mask of indifference. Her demands shocked him, although he would never let her know that. The unexpected acceptance of her fate almost made him angry. She should be fighting tooth and nail to escape him. Like she had in the woods last night. He wondered when she would use the knife she'd stolen from the knife block earlier. Hopefully, soon. He couldn't wait to teach her a lesson. All he had to do now was wait for her to do something foolish.

"Why would I agree to that? I've already spent a fortune on you."

"True." Londyn's gaze drifted to Oliver's hands, then quickly averted. "But will you consider it?"

A grin spread across Oliver's face. "Are you promising to be a good girl for me? You'll let me do anything I want without fighting me?" No doubt the tattoo inked onto his knuckles frightened her. It should. Whatever he held in his hand belonged to him, and this enchanting creature was now one of his most valued treasures.

"If you swear to do as I ask, then yes." She looked paler than before. The dire bleakness of her situation was finally sinking in.

Oliver stalked toward Londyn at the same time as she slid off the barstool. Pain twisted her features when her bare feet touched the coolness of the wooden floor. He would check out whatever injuries she suffered, but for now, that must wait.

"You cannot negotiate something you have no control over, Londyn. You *will* be my good girl regardless of your wishes. You *will* do whatever I want, whenever I want. But just so you understand that I'm not completely unreasonable, I will meet one of your demands. It's your choice as to which I accept."

CHAPTER

TEN

L*ondyn*

His cruelty was stunning.

Londyn's breath hung in her throat. He could not actually mean to make her choose between her sister's fate and the pain she would suffer at this monster's hands.

The glint of desire in Oliver's icy-blue eyes was unmistakable. They darkened the longer he stared at her. His lean, muscular body grew taut in anticipation of her next move. He wanted her. Wanted to *hurt* her. To take what he had paid a small fortune to possess. Londyn was dizzy with fear and anger that her life had come to this.

"Why offer a choice at all? Or is this just a game to you?" Londyn inched away, instinctively creating distance between them. "No matter what I choose, you will not honor it. You are a criminal. A sadistic user of women. You prey on the helpless

73

and the weaker sex. We both know you will do as you please. Spare me the insinuation that you might keep your word."

A muscle ticked in Oliver's jaw. That her words stung him seemed highly improbable. In the robe's deep pocket, Londyn recklessly gripped the handle of a small paring knife. Earlier, she'd snatched it from the butcher block of knives next to the stove while Oliver gathered items for their breakfast from the refrigerator.

"Your soul is so black and so diseased that *imprisoning* a woman is the only way you can have one." She took another small step back. "Decency and innocence are so offensive to a man like you that you must destroy it by any means possible."

A smirk flitted across Oliver's sculpted features at the hurled insults. "I might be the villain in this fucking story, Londyn, but I'm giving you a choice. A death free from pain or the relief of knowing your dear sister will be cared for after you've taken your last breath. But my patience is growing thin. I'll decide for you if you can't."

"My sister. I choose my sister!" Londyn cried out.

Oliver pulled his cell phone from his front jeans pocket and dialed a number.

"Hey, I need you to set up a bank account at Georgia State Bank for Paris Yvette Sky. Immediately, that's when. I'll text the details in a few minutes. Two million. Establish Lex as attorney of record for all approvals and distributions. Line up private nursing care while you're at it. The very best you can find. Yes. Indefinitely." There was a pause as Oliver listened to whatever was being said on the other end of the line, but his gaze did not waver from Londyn's. "I'll explain everything later. Thank you, Bridgette." He ended the call and returned the phone to his front pocket. "Satisfied?"

It was a trick of some sort. A cruel, heartless trick designed to mess with her heart and mind. If her sister was truly provided for… with more money to cover expenditures than Londyn ever would have made auctioning off her virginity, it proved one inescapable fact. Oliver Winter was a monster of epic proportions, blessed with a web of power and money so vast it could swallow an insignificant nobody like her in the blink of an eye. A dark, terrifying monster graced with the face and body of a Greek god and the wicked charm of an archangel banished from heaven.

Londyn's panic swelled until her chest was tight with it, her body damp from cold sweat that drenched any hope of survival. This man. This killer.

He truly owned her now.

She had sold her soul to the Devil himself.

Oliver came closer, anchoring his hands on the top of her shoulders. Hard fingers dug into her flesh through the robe's thick fabric. "So damn noble of you, Londyn. Putting your sister before yourself." His voice was husky and low. "But who knows? If you do as I say, if you please me, maybe I'll give you what you want. Maybe I'll kill you while you are coming on my cock at the fucking height of your pleasure. You'll have to work hard to earn that kind of mercy, though. Fuck, now is as good a time as any to see if you can pull it off. This is your chance to prove you really want it."

Releasing her shoulders, he grabbed her hand, but Londyn abruptly tore away from his grasp. She whipped the knife from the robe's pocket. Although Oliver moved out of reach, he did not appear surprised that his prisoner was armed.

"Stay away from me," Londyn warned, dashing hot tears from her cheeks while keeping the knife pointed at him. "Give me the security code so I can open the door."

"You're that eager to be chased through the woods again, are you? We'll arrange that later on my private property,"

Oliver drawled. "You run; I chase. You hide; I find. You fight; I fuck. I like that game."

"I'm not going anywhere with you." Londyn's voice trembled. Another tear rolled down her cheek. It was suicide to defy this man, but she had no choice. "I'm not..."

"Did you forget the bargain we just made, Londyn? You will do anything and everything I tell you. For your sister's sake, remember?" He advanced until the point of the knife touched his stomach. "So, what's it gonna be, little killer? Stab me or cry for mercy?" His gaze turned harder. More predatory. An endless, fathomless black well of savage depravity that made her tremble. "I can choose for you. And just so you know, I'll enjoy both."

"Get away from me!" Londyn nearly screamed. She teetered on the edge of full-blown hysterics as the knife pierced Oliver's T-shirt, but he merely laughed and leaned closer.

"You've killed one man, but I wonder if you have the guts to carve me up, Londyn." His voice was soothing, his eyes dark with excitement. He was getting off on her fear. The realization left Londyn nauseous and terrified of the repercussions of her actions. He would not let her get away with this. Even if she somehow escaped this cabin, this man would hunt her to the ends of the earth.

"Please... I'm begging that you let me go. I-I'll repay you the money from the auction somehow. Just let me go."

A stain, darker than his black T-shirt, spread from under Oliver's ribcage as the knife sank into his flesh a little more. Londyn chewed her bottom lip in agitated despair. What was he going to do to her now?

"Let you go? Last night, I gave up two and a half million dollars for the pleasure of fucking you. And an additional two just for the thrill of breaking you." Oliver laughed, his hand suddenly latching around hers. Ignoring her gasp of pain, he twisted her wrist until the small blade sliced even deeper into his flesh. Londyn stared in horror as he deliberately exacerbated the injury.

"We're just starting to have some real fun. And the only way I'm letting you go is if you leave in a coffin." Yanking the blade from her hand, Oliver tossed it into the sink. "You're a naughty girl, Londyn. I admire that fire inside you, that drive for survival. I think we have a lot in common. We'll both do whatever is necessary to get what we want—even murder."

Londyn glared at him as he laced his fingers through hers and brought them to his firm lips. He brushed her knuckles with his mouth deceptively soft, pressing warm kisses as he regarded her. His eyes crinkled at the corners, acknowledging her fear and contempt.

"I'm nothing like you," she hissed.

"Keep telling yourself that." He grinned as he spun her around. Within seconds, he had stripped her of the fluffy robe and pinned her naked body over the kitchen island.

It happened so fast, his hands so brutal and determined that Londyn barely registered how effortlessly he manhandled her. She was like a ragdoll he played too rough with.

"I'm disappointed you didn't think it was worth keeping your end of our bargain, Londyn," he tsked while anchoring her hands in the small of her back. She cried out, struggling when he pulled another pair of zip ties from his back pocket. He probably owned stock in the thin plastic strips, which would explain his ready supply. Londyn kicked and squirmed while he effortlessly held her down and secured her. "I've spent far too much money on you not to have earned a certain degree of respect. How can I trust you when you turn on me like a feral cat?"

Londyn bucked, breathless with sheer panic when Oliver

pressed his lower body against her buttocks. His cock was hard. Like a metal pipe bruising her flesh as he deliberately forced her to feel his arousal. The material of his jeans scraped her skin. Leaning down, he murmured in her ear, his breath warm, "You shouldn't have pulled that knife on me, baby. Now, you will be punished, and your sister won't get the care she needs."

"I'm sorry..." Londyn gasped. "I'm so sorry. Please don't punish her because of my actions. I'm to blame. And I-I promise I'll be good if we can keep the bargain."

The heat of his body lifted from her back, leaving behind a warm wetness she realized was probably blood from his wound. Bile rose in her throat.

"Hmmm." Cool air swirled between them as Oliver moved slightly to the side. "So, let me make sure we understand one another. You agree that I will use you *however* I like in exchange for the deal made on your sister's behalf."

"Yes! Yes. I agree. Please." Her words were now a whisper of agonized confusion. With her upper body pinned against the cold granite of the island, her nipples contracted into hard buds until they throbbed and ached with mystifying intensity. When Oliver kicked her feet apart, his large hand easily encircling her bound wrists and keeping her immobile; her stomach quivered with desperate anticipation. Something was horribly wrong with her. She should be rigid with fear. Not sinking into a hazy lassitude where her body insisted his hands somehow felt... right. "Give me another chance, please."

Oliver ran a free hand down the center of her back, pushing the tangled mass of her damp hair aside. Calloused fingers gently stroked and danced down her spine until he reached her bottom. Cupping one buttock then the other, his palm burned her skin as he caressed the firm swells. Londyn's muffled whimper of alarm drew a deep chuckle from him. "Not sure you deserve that, but you definitely deserve this."

CHAPTER
ELEVEN

L *ondyn*

The pain did not register at first.

There was a sharp, cracking sound, and a sensation bloomed across her tender skin.

Oliver struck her again, his hand connecting with the fleshiest part of one cheek. Then came another. And another. All in rapid succession and so shocking in the manner of delivery that Londyn was speechless as she tried to make sense of what was happening.

This man... this monster... was spanking her as though she were a wayward child in desperate need of discipline.

"Stop! Stop, you psychotic bastard!" Londyn screamed. She tried standing, but Oliver merely moved a hand to her neck. Now, she was effectively anchored to the countertop, the side of her face flush with the cool granite. She could only writhe

80

and curse as her tormentor leisurely administered the punishment.

"Be quiet," he gruffly commanded. "Or I'll find something else to use besides my palm. Remember you just agreed to accept anything I do to you."

The threat worked. Londyn swallowed her cries, trying to be silent. It went on forever until she wondered if his hand was as sore as her buttocks. Realistically, he'd held back from using his full strength, but that did not hurt any less.

"Please," Londyn finally begged in desperation when he gave no indication of ever stopping. For some strange reason, the last few swats felt different as the pain eased from a thousand stinging bees to a dull, almost comforting ache. That in itself was enough to cause confused panic. "Please, you're hurting me." Her legs wobbled, unable to support her weight, but Oliver responded by shoving a knee between them to balance her.

The heavy thickness of him there, pressing hard on vulnerable areas, sent searing waves of shock through her. Her entire body was instantly hyperaware of him—his crisp, spicy scent, his large, warm hands, and his calm breathing. But mostly, she was tuned to his leanly muscled form and how everything inside her quivered in response.

Majoring in the field of psychology taught her many things, but never had those lessons been as intensely personal as her current situation. Two things were blatantly obvious.

One... this man was a seriously disturbed individual with a desire to punish women for some unknown wrong.

Two... she was just as fucked up as he was because her body was drowning in acceptance.

"It's a punishment, Londyn. It's supposed to hurt. Now, are you going to be a good girl and stay fucking still so I don't leave you with any lasting damage? "

She could not articulate a response. Her brain was too fuzzy to form words. She sagged against the countertop and onto his thigh with a soft, helpless moan of contentment. Why and *how* did any of this feel good? Where had the pain disappeared to? Experimentally, she rocked back and forth against the muscular thigh wedged between her legs. A breathy sigh of bliss escaped her as the endorphins spiked higher. Why had he stopped spanking her? She wanted more, although it made zero sense to want that.

Oliver groaned, his distant voice raspy with lust. "You're fucking perfect. Do you know that, Londyn?" He pressed harder, applying direct pressure to her clit in the most delightful way. "I shouldn't give you a single moment of pleasure. Not when this was supposed to be a goddamn punishment." He slapped her ass again, and another moan slipped between her lips when the strike jolted her. "But fuck if I can help myself. Do you know why? Do you? It's because your skin is now a beautiful, glowing pink, branded with my handprints. And your sweet cunt is dripping all over my thigh. You enjoy riding my leg like a whore in heat, don't you? You liked that spanking, too. And now you want me to make you come while you're flying in subspace."

He bent over her, his thigh remaining steady in pressure but adding a rotating movement that made Londyn whimper. Is this what it felt like to pass out? This floaty, dreamy state she was now deep inside?

"Are you going to come for me, dove?" His growl reverberated through her as he spanked her again. "Fucking come on my thigh, Londyn. Show me that you understand every inch of you, willing or not, belongs to me. Come for me like this. Beg me. Plead me to make you come."

"Please..." Londyn could not stop the tsunami building inside her. As if from a great distance, she heard him spit, followed by a muttered curse. She didn't understand until something wet and warm, something intrusive but so damned exhilarating, pressed against the puckered ring of her ass. It hurt just enough to clear some of the cobwebs from her dazed mind but not enough to make her fight back. When he dipped his thumb into her, carefully but insistently stretching the small hole until her body allowed the violation, she sobbed harder. "Please."

"Please, what, Londyn?" he mocked, in full control of her at that moment and forcing her to accept it. To revel in it. To push against it, silently demanding more. Londyn surrendered to the darkness of his possession. The pressure, the shocking fullness invading her private region, along with the firm press of his thigh, drove her over the edge. Nothing else mattered except her captor and his hands as they molded her to fit his cruel grip. He was imprisoning her in a web of her own confusing desire. She had no shame. No pride. No sense of herself and her own identity. All that mattered was reaching a climax with his hands and words guiding her.

Her first-ever orgasm—orchestrated by a man she did not know.

"Let me come... let me..." she moaned almost incoherently. "Please let me..."

"Fuck, yes. Come for me, Londyn. With my blood and spit in your tight little ass, my thumb fucking you here, and my thigh drenched from your soaked cunt. Come for me." He groaned as shudders racked Londyn's body in response to his growled command. When the orgasm took her under, the pleasure was so intense that black pinpoints exploded behind her closed eyes.

Oliver's voice seemed to come from a million miles away. She focused on it as she drifted toward unconsciousness.

"If you could see how gorgeous you are right now, Londyn.

Your ass is all pink and marked with the imprint of my fingers. I cannot wait until I have you stretched out and taking my cock in all your sweet holes. I can't wait to hear the sounds you make when I fuck you for the first time. I can't wait to hear you beg me again. And you *will* beg. For more. For me to stop. And then for more again. Because this is just the beginning."

Without warning, Oliver moved so that his entire body was between her legs, keeping them spread wide. His thumb remained lodged inside her, but now, one broad finger of the same hand thrust inside her pussy, sliding into the depths of her body with shameful ease. But it was too much. Too full. Too painful. She was filled with him whether she wished it or not. Reaching beyond the endorphins coursing through her, pain nudged at sensitive nerve endings until the sensation outpaced the pleasure. Her hips rolled in shocking tandem with his every move.

"You're hurting me," she whimpered. Tears rolled down her cheeks, leaving tiny puddles on the granite.

"Fuck, your pussy is so goddamn tight." Oliver ignored her accusation, the sound of his low chuckle chilling Londyn to the bone. He continued plunging and withdrawing his fingers, his other hand keeping her pinned to the counter. "Better get used to it, Londyn. Because my cock is a hell of a lot bigger than what's inside you right now."

Everything inside her screamed in horror. Because Londyn finally understood. Understood why her mother had pursued a lifetime of bad choices with abusive, horrible men who berated her and used her body. She got why her sister allowed Sheriff Adam Franklin to do awful things until she stood up to him. It had taken less than twenty-four hours to discover what three years of psychology studies failed to reveal about Londyn's own psyche. She was as fucked up as the man holding her down. As drawn to the darkness as her mother and sister. She'd buried it for so long. Avoiding men in general. Ignoring guys who asked her out on dates in high school and while attending classes at Vanderbilt. Throwing herself into her studies had worked.

But now, everything she tried so hard to suppress was slamming into her like a runaway freight train hurtling down the tracks. She could kick and scream and despise what was happening, but deep down, inside the darkest and secret parts of her inner soul, she found this exciting. Eventually, she would become addicted to Oliver Winter's brand of dominance. Because some depraved part of her *liked* the way he hurt her. She liked how the bite of pain was tempered with overwhelming pleasure and how her body responded to his commands. How she quivered in anticipation of the violent yet calm way he took control of her.

Despite the burning ache from his thick finger in her pussy and his broad thumb invading her *there*, Londyn's body was tightening again. The fullness morphed into a need that could not be denied. If Oliver did not stop, she would come a second time. And that was a devastating realization.

Oh, God. What is wrong with me? What is happening to me? This can't be who I am inside. It can't be...

"Tell me something, little killer," Oliver murmured. "Why did you kill the man delivering you here? Did you change your mind at the last minute? Try to escape, and he stopped you? Tell me what you did. And why."

Londyn squeezed her eyes tightly. If only she could force her body to stop responding to him. If only she could blink this all away. Go back in time to the day before two guards from Diamond Lake Ranch picked her up at the airport in Denver. She would never have gotten in the car had she known the horrors awaiting her. Chewing her bottom lip, she stubbornly remained silent until Oliver's cruel fingers bit into the back of her neck.

"I asked you a question, Londyn. I expect an answer."

"He-he wanted to have sex with me in the back of the limo. Said it was my last chance for the next thirty days to have a real man," Londyn mumbled, remembering how the man held her down, telling her that girls heading to a Diamond Lake Ranch auction always enthusiastically agreed to his proposition. "When I told him I was a virgin, that this was my chance to make the most money at auction, he laughed. Said whatever old man bought me wouldn't know the difference. I fought back, but it only made him angry. He ripped my jeans off, tearing my shirt. There was a gun strapped into a holster under his arm, and I-I grabbed it. I clicked off the safety, and then there was a big boom. Blood was coming out of his mouth and from a hole in his side. I don't remember anything else until we were at Diamond Lake Ranch. The other guard driving the limo told them I tried to get away." She trembled as Oliver abruptly grew still. Despite reliving that terrifying experience, her body ached for him. It still wanted the strange, painful pleasure from her captor's touch.

The truth of that made her sick to her stomach.

"He tried to rape you?" Oliver's voice was a low growl of angry disbelief. Which was ironic, considering what he was doing to her at that moment. "Is that what you are telling me, Londyn? Don't fucking lie to me."

"It's the truth," she whispered.

Oliver withdrew, and Londyn cried out. The pain from his digits leaving her body was almost worse than when he'd thrust them in.

"Don't fucking move from that position, Londyn." The words sounded like they came from between clenched teeth. Londyn obeyed. She stayed bent over; legs spread wide, her cheek pressed flat against the cold granite. Something warm and wet trickled down the inside of her thigh, but she did not dare squirm.

His blood... and my own arousal.

Oliver bent over her, his breath warm in her ear. "I mean it, dove. Disobey me, and what I just did will seem like a pleasant daydream."

TWELVE

liver

RAGE, both hot and cold, ran through Oliver.

Rationally, he knew acting on his first impulse was impossible. He wanted to hunt down any man, living or dead, who had hurt this girl bent over his kitchen island. This girl with his blood and spit smeared across her flawless, pinkened skin. How hard would it be to exact revenge from those Diamond Lake Ranch employees?

Difficult but certainly possible.

Londyn held her breath as he moved to the sink at the other side of the island and carefully washed his hands. Watching her obey his commands while fighting the urge to stand was incredibly enjoyable. It might become his favorite past-time while she was alive and thinking of the many scenarios where he could force her submission was arousing as hell.

After drying his hands, Oliver cleaned the blood from his stomach. The wound wasn't serious, although it bled copiously. Turning his back on her, he rummaged through the same upper cabinet where he'd found the ibuprofen last night and pulled out a small stash of bandages, medicated ointment, and a tube of super-glue. With quick, efficient movements, he took care of the injury, sealing the wound with the glue and slapping a bandage over it.

Scooping up the knife used in the attack, he sauntered back to London's side. He loved how her eyes widened when he crossed her line of sight. She was frightened of him. Of retaliation. Or maybe she was just scared in general.

He took her wrists and sliced through the zip tie, then stood her upright, turning her to face him. She trembled uncontrollably, staring ahead as he smoothed her hair away from her face. Oliver couldn't help but admire her as she wobbled on weak legs. She really was stunning with her rounded breasts and gently flared hips. Running a thumb over her bottom lip, he contemplated how her mouth would feel on his cock. How he could fuck her throat, and she would let him because she promised to do anything he wanted.

Gray eyes locked with his, flashing with renewed indigna-tion when he pushed his forefinger into her mouth and stroked her tongue until she instinctively closed her plump, pink lips around the digit. For a second, he relished the feeling of the warm depths of her mouth but mentally shook his head at where his lust was heading.

Before he changed his mind and bent her back over the island for his own selfish pleasure, Oliver let her go. Grabbing the robe he'd stripped from her earlier, he wrapped Londyn in it and led her to the living room. There was a plush sofa overlooking the lake, and as he pushed her down to sit, his cell phone buzzed.

Fishing it from his front pocket, he checked the caller's identity, and his jaw tightened. He clicked the call open.

"Ruel."

"Good morning, my friend," Ruel said jovially. "Did you enjoy the evening with your new possession?"

"I did," Oliver calmly replied. He did not say anything else. Giving Ruel ammunition of any kind was far from wise, and it was a serious matter when the owner himself called to check on them. A few seconds of uncomfortable silence stretched between the two until Ruel finally cleared his throat.

"That's good. Good. But we have a small problem, my friend."

"And what is that?"

"You must pay for the most recent loss of a Ranch employee. Not much, but something," Ruel explained. "One hundred thousand."

Oliver laughed softly. "Your employee abused my property. And everyone knows how fiercely a Winter defends and protects what's his. It's not a matter of funds; it's a matter of a man assaulting an asset that *belongs* to me. There was a price to be paid for his audacity, and I exacted full payment."

"I'm short of two guards now because of this girl," Ruel complained. "Someone must pay."

"Speaking of which, you should do a better job vetting those men. They're fucking your girls before they ever arrive here. My property tells me the one she killed attempted to rape her." Oliver paced to the wall of windows, leaning a forearm against the glass as he gazed out over the woods below the cabin. "A regrettable accident, according to her version of events."

"Bah!" Ruel snorted. "Women never tell the truth. Virgin or not, this one is no different."

"She has no reason to lie to me, of all people. You know me well enough to know I didn't give a fuck about circumstances before I took ownership. I'm just alerting you to a problem with those you hire. Consider it a favor."

Ruel was silent on the other end of the line before grumbling, "I will look into it. But still, someone owes me for the man I lost yesterday. Seeing that Number Fifteen is the catalyst for both situations, she can pay the debt on your behalf. We will offer her for use in the main clubhouse. One night for those men who pay for the privilege. We understand her worth is diminished now that she is no longer a virgin, but we can easily get one hundred thousand for her. You can watch, of course."

Instant, possessive rage flooded Oliver; an emotion more potent than anything he'd ever experienced. His hands clenched with such force that his phone was in danger of cracking apart.

Over my dead, fucking body, will I ever let that happen. No one touches her but me. No one fucks her but me. And no one hurts her but me.

"Like I said, Ruel. A Winter defends and protects what's his, and I've paid a fortune to claim this one as mine. Listen very carefully, as I will not repeat myself. I will personally slice off the balls of any man who dares to touch her and make him eat them off a plate. Is that unclear in any way?"

Londyn's faint gasp swung Oliver's attention back to where she huddled on the sofa. Her eyes were wide as she clutched the robe tighter around her body. But was it the blunt statement displaying his obsession that disturbed her? Or was it the sight of the hollow-eyed skull etched in black ink emblazoned across the width of his back? His motto, *Bleed For Me,* was inked below it.

"This puts us at an impasse, my friend. In this case, I cannot extend your invitation at Diamond Lake Ranch. I must regrettably request that you end your stay."

Oliver stalked back to Londyn, lifting her chin with a forefinger while Ruel spoke. Her pulse beat rapidly in the hollow of her throat, and as she stared up at him, he slid his hand around the slender column. Her eyes fluttered shut at his overt display of dominance.

His lips curved into a smirk of approval. He didn't give a fuck that Ruel was evicting him. He hadn't planned on staying anyway. The resort's management could not be trusted. Oliver suspected they would try snatching his prize from his grasp, especially if it was discovered Londyn was still a virgin.

"Understood. I hope my stance on this situation does not hinder future dealings with Winter Enterprises." Oliver's fingers tightened until a whimper escaped Londyn. To her credit, she did not move a muscle. She remained frozen in place, like a rabbit caught in the stare of an apex predator.

"We will revisit this when tempers are not so high," Ruel responded, agitated. If the Russian were smart, he'd let this insult go and remember the obscene amount of money Oliver had spent at the Ranch. Not to mention the influence the Winter name carried. Even halfway across the country, it was understood how unwise it was to cross Kingston and Oliver Winter.

"I look forward to it." Oliver abruptly ended the call, bored with the entitlement in Ruel's tone. Management had gotten sloppy when it came to the treatment of their girls, but that was not an issue Oliver could rectify on his own. He could, however, take the necessary steps to protect his new possession. And serving her up as the unwilling main course in a gang bang by Ranch members was not going to happen. Just the thought made him want to go on a blood-fueled rampage.

Keeping his hand around Londyn's throat, he willed himself to calm down. He thought back to how she looked at him. How her eyes drifted over his body, sizing him up and taking note of his strength. In the eyes of someone so young, someone as innocent as she was, Oliver realized he must appear scary as fuck. And if Londyn was frightened of his tattoo, it stood to reason that the words inked just above his barbell-studded cock would terrify her.

He couldn't wait to introduce her to every surprise he had in store. But that momentous occasion would come soon enough.

"Londyn."

Her eyes popped open at his soft murmur.

"Go clean yourself up. When you are done, I want you to get dressed."

"What-what shall I wear? I have no clothes—" Her gaze slid to the phone he still held. She watched as he set it on the coffee table. He saw her fingers twitch as if she were barely restraining herself from snatching it up and dialing for help. Even if she did something as foolish as that, nothing would come of it. After all, the local sheriff's department ran cover for Diamond Lake Ranch. Hell, the mayor and the sheriff himself were both honorary members and accepted occasional weekend passes to enjoy the Ranch's many pleasurable offerings.

"There will be something on the bed," Oliver cut her off, sliding his grip from her throat. He dragged her up from the sofa, his hands hard and unyielding. Guiding her toward the hallway, he ignored the pained furrowing of her brow at his rough handling. She was hurting after being bound and spanked, but there were also cuts and bruises on her bare feet.

If he weren't careful, if he didn't keep his wits about him, he'd probably wind up swooping her into his arms. Then, like a goddamn romance novel hero, he'd carry her anywhere she wanted to go. "Don't take too long. We'll be leaving within the hour."

"Where are we going?" Londyn asked hesitantly, and Oliver immediately wondered if she might try attempting another escape. Despite her tearful vow to obey him in all things, he suspected she would take advantage of any opportunity to get away.

"To my cabin." His grin stretched wider when uncertain panic flashed across her pale features. "That's where the real fun starts."

THIRTEEN

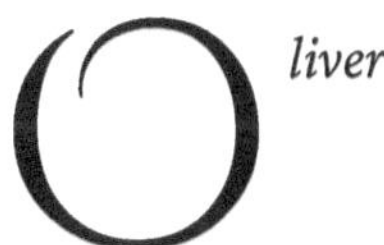 *liver*

WHEN LONDYN EMERGED from the bathroom with a towel wrapped around her body, Oliver was waiting for her in the bedroom.

"That's my stuff," she noticed, wariness filling her tone as she nodded toward the overnight bag on the bed.

Oliver nodded. He could hardly look away from the perfection of this girl. Her dark hair was wet, streaming down her back in a silky waterfall as her dove-gray eyes met his. She clutched the towel closer to her as if that would ensure the cloth would not be wrestled away.

"One of the guards gave it to me when they dragged you inside. I'm guessing you have suitable clothes in there?"

Surprise lifted her eyebrows high. She obviously expected

him to rummage through her private belongings. "Unless they kept my things, there should be something I can wear."

"Get dressed then," Oliver ordered, waving a hand in her direction. He had finished packing his few items into a rolling suitcase and began pulling on a fresh black T-shirt.

Londyn hesitated. Her gaze flickered over his muscular body, briefly landing on the bandage covering his wound. Then her features hardened, and she clutched the towel even tighter.

Oliver found her shyness amusing. After everything he'd done, Londyn was reluctant to reveal her gorgeous body to his lustful stare. Which was smart. Because his cock ached to be inside her. The innocently seductive image she presented was severely testing his willpower. He wanted to fuck her. Fuck her hard. Fuck her senseless. Fuck her until their bodies fused and merged into something created by the Devil himself.

"Londyn..." Oliver's tone was stern. "I've already seen you. *All* of you. Every goddamn inch. I've even tasted you. But I swear to God, I have no intention of fucking you here. Now, get dressed before I change my mind."

Her cheeks flushed pink, her gaze flitting to the bed at the reminder of *that* unforgivable act while she lay helpless and unconscious. With a tilt of her chin, she dug through the travel bag. A virginal set of nude panties and matching bra emerged along with a pair of jeans and a cream-colored, long-sleeved blouse. Turning away from his prying gaze, she let the towel fall to the ground while fumbling with the panties. When she dropped them, she bent at the waist to retrieve them, and Oliver hissed a groan of desire. Palming his erection through his jeans, he fought for control.

"Are you purposefully trying to drive me mad, Londyn? Because I'm *this* close to saying fuck it. I'm this close to taking what I want."

"I'm sorry," Londyn whispered, tugging on the panties

with such haste she nearly toppled over. In record time, she was dressed, panting from exertion, and her face flushed with embarrassment. "You don't have to watch, you know. I'm quite capable of dressing myself without guidance or criticism."

Oliver's jaw ticked. Londyn's quiet yet resentful snarkiness ignited a desire to show her just how cruel he could be. Up to this point, he had handled her with an odd sort of tenderness completely foreign to his brutal nature. And she had no idea the depths of depravity to which he could sink. No clue of the darkness of his soul. Under the tutelage of his deceased father, he had mastered the fine art of torture and would gleefully exhibit those skills if she continued pushing him.

"Someone needs an attitude adjustment," he growled. "Settle that shit before I blister that sweet little ass of yours a second time."

Little brat.

It was becoming clear that his captive did not like being told what to do. Which only made Oliver want to order her around even more.

Her lips tightened into a thin line at the threat as she forcefully plopped onto the bed. A wince of pain creased her brow when her bruised buttocks hit the mattress. Yanking on socks and a pair of doe-brown ankle boots, she kept her silence, although he was sure the cuts and scrapes on her feet and lower legs were probably hurting, too. He would take care of that once they reached his cabin.

"I have a car coming for us soon, but I need to know if you can behave yourself. Can you do that, Londyn? Can you behave? Or must I physically restrain you for the ride?" He watched as she pulled the length of her hair over one shoulder and quickly wound the wet strands into a thick braid that hung to the middle of her back.

"I'm not a child," she shot back, eyes flashing. But when

Oliver took a menacing step toward her, she held out a hand to stop him. "Yes. I will behave myself. I promise. I know any escape attempt will not end well for me."

Ignoring the pathetic attempt to ward him off, Oliver prowled closer until he towered over her. She was still seated on the bed, her eyes level with his mid-chest. The pulse in her neck thumped rapidly. How sick was it that Oliver found her fear as heady as any aphrodisiac?

Wrapping the braid around his fist, he jerked Londyn's head back. His gaze narrowed as he stared down into her wide eyes.

"I'm warning you, little killer. Keep mouthing off like that, and I'll stuff your throat so full of my cock you won't be able to breathe without my permission." His dick swelled more, throbbing with painful intensity, demanding that he follow through on the threat.

This wasn't like him. Keeping his cool, staying calm and collected while doing the most unhinged things, was his signature. And this girl was fucking all that up. He could barely think straight, especially when he remembered how she tasted. And how it felt when her tight cunt and ass squeezed his fingers when he made her come.

Fuck, fuck, fuck.

Oliver abruptly tugged her off the bed using the braided rope of hair like a handle. "Get on your fucking knees."

Londyn yelped in alarm, tumbling to the floor, only to be hauled upright and put into position with a hard hand gripping her elbow. She instinctively braced herself with her palms flat on his thighs, balanced on her knees for what he had planned. Although her eyes filled with tears and her breath escaped in panicked gasps, that delicately mutinous chin tipped high.

It fucking pissed him off that she did not seem particularly scared of what he might do to her.

Time to remedy that.

Still holding her hair in his fist, Oliver ripped at the button of his jeans with his free hand. The material gaped open in a V, revealing a couple of the letters inked above his groin.

"You are about to get a valuable lesson, Londyn. I hope you learn something since that spanking didn't accomplish shit." His grip tightened, and she let out the most delicious whimper. Her fingernails dug into his jeans with such force Oliver felt the pinch through the thick material. "Open your fucking mouth."

Londyn shook her head, a choked whimper bubbling up from her throat.

That sheer defiance she exhibited rattled Oliver. It disturbed him more than he wanted to admit. This fucking girl had more steel in her veins, in her spine, in her tiny goddamn pinky than most of the men he knew. He almost admired her for it, even if she was stupid for believing she could fight him and prevail.

"Remember your promise to obey me, Londyn. Don't make me tell you again," he snarled. "Now, open your fucking mouth." This was wrong, but he couldn't help himself. His need to dominate her was inescapable. A need unlike anything he'd ever experienced before.

BUZZZZZ.

It was the security system monitoring the cabin sending an alert. Someone was on the front porch, pressing the doorbell. Next came a succession of sharp, forceful raps from a hard fist. Most likely, it was Joey, the same Winter Enterprises driver who had dropped him off the day before.

Oliver snatched Londyn to her feet, grinning as relief flashed across her stunning features.

"Don't think this interruption means your instruction is

over. Because I'm far from done with you, Londyn. And since our destination is about two hours away, I've got plenty of time and opportunity to prove my point." Leaning close, he brushed her mouth with his, nibbling on her bottom lip until her eyes squeezed tightly. "During your time left on this earth, I'm going to teach you how to be a good girl... *my* good girl."

DESPITE HER OBVIOUS TREPIDATION, Londyn was asleep within the first half hour, her head propped against the window's panel, arms crossed protectively over her chest as if that would save her. Oliver watched from his corner of the limo as she twitched and mumbled. His piece of property was exhausted. Everything from the past twenty-four hours was finally catching up to her. So, he allowed her to slumber while considering the best way to exert control over her.

And doing nothing about it.

This... *empathy*... was annoying. And confusing. Londyn belonged to him. He paid a fortune for the right to fuck her whenever and however he wanted. And yet, he hesitated to follow through with the threats he had made earlier. For some reason, some goddamn, fucking reason that didn't make fucking sense, he wanted to take care of her.

You almost forced her to suck your cock because you were angry. Is that some fucked-up method of taking care of someone?

Oliver clenched his teeth. Why he felt so strongly about this girl was bewildering as hell. He had never cared for anyone. All he'd ever done was hurt people. Gladly. Willingly. With enthusiasm and pleasure.

In particular, he enjoyed hurting women.

It was fucked up. Every depraved thought, calculated act, and desire revolved around forcing a woman's submission. He accomplished that by following the teachings of his father. Sometimes, the women were complicit and willing to be dominated; and sometimes, they required more than a little *persuasion*. Until now, he'd never come across one who he wanted to protect from himself.

Or from others.

Maybe this confusing state of emotions was what his brother experienced when he fell in love. Maybe he should examine Kingston and Ava's relationship to determine the root cause of why he felt this way now. While it was understandable that Kingston wanted to possess and protect Ava, Oliver found their deep love for one another mystifying. Even more so now when he wondered if the same capacity to place a woman's happiness and well-being above his own needs and desires existed within him.

No. It doesn't. You are a killer, just like your father. You are an abuser, just like your father. You love to see women bleed and cry for mercy. You want them to suffer at your hands. You are a psychotic piece of shit. Just like your father. And you know you will torment, abuse, and torture this girl until the day you end her life.

Just like your father would have. Kingston would have followed the same path had he not fallen insanely in love.

But there had always been a difference between Oliver and his older half-brother. Kingston somehow retained a thread of decency. A sliver of morality. The things he'd done over the course of a lifetime were a result of cruel manipulation by their sick father and the consequences of assuming the responsibilities of their criminal kingdom.

Oliver did awful things because he *wanted* to. He did them because he grew up full of hate and fear of his father and despised his mother for her weakness. The same woman who fucked her stepson behind her husband's back and used Kingston's love to get her hands on a gun. The day Rebecca shot Alan Winter and put a bullet in her own head at the dinner table—while he and Kingston watched in horror—was the day any semblance of decency died in Oliver.

"I'm a fucking monster," he muttered to himself, gulping down the last dregs of bourbon in the crystal tumbler. "A monster."

Wasn't it about fucking time to prove it?

His gaze drifted over his sweet, little prisoner—his prize, his fucking possession. Any weakness he showed toward her would come back to bite him. He couldn't let himself be swayed by her pretty gray eyes and a gorgeously curved body.

Not even if something inside him, something strange and unknown, demanded otherwise.

Stretching his legs so that he could touch the seat opposite of him, he leaned toward her. She was curled up with her feet tucked beneath her body. He ran a hand up her calf until he reached her knee and palmed it.

Londyn's eyes fluttered open, sleepy confusion clouding the clear depths of dove-gray. She stared at him for a moment as though trying to place him. When he squeezed her knee, his fingers gripping her flesh even through the jeans she wore, clarity tightened her lips into a thin line. She was silent as they regarded each other, and Oliver's mouth quirked in a wicked grin.

"Wake up, little killer. Time to play a game."

FOURTEEN

L *ondyn*

LONDYN SWALLOWED HARD, forcing herself to remain still as her captor's cold, blue eyes roamed her body.

"Stop calling me that," she whispered. The reminder that she'd killed a man—no matter how much he deserved it—made her stomach turn.

Oliver laughed, rolling the tumbler in his hands until the ice clinked against the sides of the crystal. "But it fits you so well."

If this man was ugly, had offensive body odor, or if his breath smelled terrible, nurturing an aversion would be easier done. But that was not the case. Her owner had the bone structure, body, and good looks of a male model. She couldn't help the stupid part of her that found him attractive, even if it was completely irrational. How could she consider him good-looking when he was a real-life, brutal monster?

"I guess I can always call you little dove." He squeezed her knee and pulled so that her legs fell open. "Sit. Up."

Londyn ignored his sardonic reminder that he grew up shooting those helpless creatures but followed his command. His warm hand rested on her leg before sliding up to tightly grip her hip. It was a heavy, inescapable reminder that she was under his control.

"Strip." The directive was a low growl. "I want to see you naked."

Londyn's gaze darted to the smoked-glass panel separating them from the driver. In the vehicle's low interior light, she saw Oliver's mouth curve even more.

"Don't worry. Joey can't see you. Now, strip. I want every inch of you bared for me."

Londyn shuddered. "I don't want to..."

Oliver's hand left her hip, shooting out to capture her chin in a hard grip. He squeezed so hard that his fingers dug into her cheeks, leaving indentations. His head cocked, blue eyes darkening as he regarded her. "What makes you think I give a fuck what you want? Remember the rules, Londyn. I command. You obey." Leaning closer, he brushed his mouth over hers. "Refuse me again and I'll rip every stitch from your body. You won't be allowed clothes at all."

Londyn nodded, a tear slipping down her cheek. She wasn't even aware of it until Oliver's grip loosened. After catching the droplet on the tip of his index finger, he rubbed the moisture across his firmly molded lips.

"Fucking delicious. Almost as mouthwatering as your sweet pussy." Letting her go, he reclined against the black leather seat opposite hers, stretched his legs, and motioned with the hand still gripping the crystal tumbler. "Get on with it."

It only took a handful of seconds to shed the jeans, blouse, socks, and shoes. The hard part was removing her bra and panties. When she was finally naked, she hunched her shoulders, folding her arms across her chest in an attempt to hide from his hot stare. He looked at her like she was his next meal. She shivered at the thought, hating how her body liked that idea. Despite the chill in the car, her body burned with embarrassment. Between her legs, a distressing moisture grew, leaving her damp and even more confused.

"Good girl," Oliver drawled in a low voice that made Londyn's stomach clench. "Now, lean back against the seat, facing me. Spread your legs. I want to see you."

Londyn steeled herself, swallowing a sob. *I won't cry this time. No matter how perverted and degrading this is, I won't cry. I won't let him break me or beat me down to his level.*

Staring straight ahead, she willed herself to disassociate from the situation. She could do that... she'd become an expert at it while growing up. Being resourceful sent her scurrying into the woods often as a way of escaping male attention, but sometimes that just wasn't practical. Sometimes, the "uncles" her mom hooked up with got too grabby or decided her mom needed a lesson. When they beat her up in front of her daughters, Londyn could close her eyes and pretend she wasn't there. She could be someplace else. Anyplace else.

"*Tsk, tsk,*" Oliver murmured. "Come back to me, Londyn. You don't get to disappear inside your head. You don't get to go someplace without me. No, I want you right here. Your eyes on me. Now, do as you're told. Spread yourself open so I can see the pretty, pink pussy I purchased."

Londyn met his gaze, helpless rage coursing through her

body in swirling tendrils at the callous order. How dare this man take away the only weapon she had left to endure this nightmare. Her ability to slip away inside her head was the most valuable coping mechanism she'd taught herself. She needed it to survive.

He chuckled, taking a sip of bourbon. "I like it when you get angry and fight back. I like it almost as much as I love your submission. It's a curious thing. I've never realized how arousing the combination of defiance and reluctant surrender could be."

Londyn's eyes involuntarily dropped to his crotch. He was erect, straining against the denim. The size of his cock made something inside her flutter. Horrified by her reaction, she quickly looked away.

"Don't worry, little dove," he laughed beneath his breath. "You'll get that soon enough. But not right now. I want to watch you make yourself come."

"I-I don't understand," Londyn stuttered in a panic. *Oh, God. Please make this stop. Please. Please. Please.*

"I think you do." Amusement laced his tone. "But I'll explain, so there is no question. I want you to rub your clit. Pinch your nipples. Fuck yourself with your own fingers. Make yourself come so I can watch you shatter."

"I can't. I won't," Londyn bit out. "It's depraved. Sick. *You're* sick."

"Sick? Probably. But I'm also dying to fuck you, Londyn. So, either you do what you're told, or I'll take care of my needs as best as I know how. Believe me, I have no aversion to getting blood all over these seats." His demeanor darkened, a muscle ticking in his square jaw. Excitement sparked in his pale blue eyes. This unexpected glimpse into his psyche revealed everything. He hoped she refused his demands so he'd be justified in assaulting her, but he was also giving her a choice of sorts. A devil's bargain where no matter what she chose, she would lose. "Slide your hand down to your pussy. Spread yourself for me." He hesitated as if making a difficult decision, then said in a husky voice, "Make yourself come and I'll leave you alone for a little while."

"Do you promise?" she choked out, moving her hand down the trembling plane of her belly. "You won't... you won't touch me?" Her fingers rested on her smooth pussy. It was strange that the soft, silky flesh beneath her fingertips was her own. She was frozen in place, hoping there was a shred of humanity somewhere behind his savagely handsome features. Some sliver of emotion that would show her the slightest hint of mercy.

"As much as I am capable of, I give you my word."

Londyn nodded. This was as much as she could coax from him. A promise to let her be. And if she refused to do what he commanded, she knew he would take her in the back of this limo with no thought. Slowly, she moved her fingers over the tender flesh, hating how her thighs naturally fell apart so he could see everything.

"Have you touched yourself before, Londyn?" he asked. "Masturbated using your fingers or anything else?"

"No," Londyn whispered, humiliated at the thought of this man knowing all her secrets. He had no right to them, no right to wiggle his way into her head and play his sadistic games.

"Don't fucking lie to me." The words were a whiplash of domination and consequences. His features were even harder than before, his eyes burning into hers. It frightened her.

"Yes... yes, I've touched myself before." Without being told, she circled her clit with her forefinger before sliding it inside her body in a shallow thrusting motion. Every fiber of her body went taut with anticipation.

This is so wrong. Wrong. Wrong. Wrong.

"Good girl. Fuck." Tension stretched Oliver's voice until it was a tight string ready to snap. "You are fucking gorgeous, Londyn. So goddamn beautiful. Show me how you make yourself feel good. How you take yourself right up to the edge. Do that again. Again. You like me watching you like this, don't you, dirty girl? You wish it were my hand rubbing your cunt. You wish my mouth were there between those silky thighs of yours. You know, I can still taste you from last night. Still taste how wet and sweet you were when I thrust my tongue up inside you. You might not have been aware of it at the time, but your body fucking knows who it belongs to. Do you remember what it felt like this morning when I had my fingers inside your pussy and my thumb deep in your tight, little ass? Remember how you exploded for me? Remember how good it felt... how desperately you wanted my cock inside you instead of my fingers fucking you and making you come all over my hand."

Londyn could not help it. Her body responded to every filthy word that poured out of Oliver's mouth. The darkness of what he said, the darkness of what he'd done to her, sucked her into an abyss she might never crawl out of. She closed her eyes, hating how the pressure between her legs built into an overwhelming crescendo. She'd never done anything so depraved before. So dirty. So unhinged. How could she like this? *Why* did she like it?

Now, she was panting, her hips circling mindlessly, focused on chasing the pleasure rippling through her. Her eyes screwed tightly shut, but she was distantly aware that Oliver had moved to the seat beside her. His body was as hot as a furnace. It took everything inside her, every ounce of willpower she possessed, not to curl toward him. To let him take what he wanted. To make her submit to his control.

Her eyes flew open when piercing cold enveloped one of her nipples. Oliver swirled an ice cube across the pebbled button. He did the same for the other, and Londyn whimpered, her hand between her legs slowing in her confusion.

"Look at me." He waited until her eyes refocused on him. "Don't you fucking stop, Londyn. Keep going until you come." His mouth closed over her nipple, the heat of it contrasting sharply with the ice. He sucked and nibbled, alternating between her breasts until she moaned in helpless lust. "God-damn, your tits are so sweet. They'll look so pretty when I pierce them. I think you'll like that. The slightest brush of my hand on them will set you on fire. Maybe I'll pierce your pussy, too." Londyn's hips bucked upward, straining for release, and Oliver laughed softly. "Yeah, you like that idea, don't you? Show me how much you like the idea of being pierced, little killer. Fuck that sweet little cunt harder. Fuck *my* little cunt. Come for me, Londyn. Come for me now and thank me for it like the good girl you are. Come for me using your own fingers because this is the only time I will allow it. Your pussy. Your pleasure. Your body. It's mine now. If you live or die, it's my decision. I decide when and where you come. I decide if you receive pleasure or pain. Or both."

He bit her nipple just hard enough to jolt her forward, her back arching as the pain merged into a soul-rattling orgasm that swept over her. Her pussy clamped down on her fingers, drenching her hand and the leather seat. It was an endless minute of riding out the waves of pleasure as Oliver devoured, sucked, and teased her breasts. The orgasm left her wet and weak and stupidly aching for more.

As the last of the ecstasy ebbed away and sanity returned, Londyn weakly pushed Oliver away. Drawing her knees up to her chest, she curled into herself. Tremors shook her body as she buried her face in disgusted shame.

She refused to look at him as scalding hot tears ran down her cheeks and soaked the skin of her bare knees. Even when she felt him move away and rustling reached her ears, she would not look at him. Only when something soft settled over her shoulders like a drift of snow did she dare raise her head.

Oliver said nothing as he wrapped the lap blanket around her. The unexpected kindness had nausea rising like burning lava in the back of her throat. She forgot about her plan to appease this man. All she could see was red, her fury tinged with the blackness of despair.

"I hate you," she whispered, clutching the material closer. "I hate you so much."

Oliver smirked. "Good thing this is just temporary, then. You know, I can only imagine the kind of psychological damage I'm causing you right now. Because what kind of self-ish, twisted monster would let you have all the pleasure while denying himself? Hmm? It takes a particular sort of villain to deny himself a body like yours, especially when it's been bought and paid for." He tucked a strand of her hair behind her ear. The gesture was almost tender, but then he ruined it. "And what does it say about *you*, little killer, when you so obviously enjoyed it? Maybe I should have you lick the seat clean where you came all over it."

She trembled at the threat, thinking he would make her do something so disgusting for his sick enjoyment, but he slid back into the seat across from her. Pouring himself another finger of bourbon from the built-in bar, his gaze roamed her body while Londyn glared back at him. His dark hair was rumpled, as if he'd repeatedly thrust his hands through the thick waves in frustration. The letters tattooed across his fingers mocked her. Reminding her when he'd curled his hand around her throat and claimed her as his.

MINE.

Seeing where her gaze had landed, Oliver smiled with satisfaction. Londyn wanted to rake his smug, handsome face with broken fingernails until he was bleeding and tattered. Her hatred filled the limo's interior, suffocating enough to make an impression on her captor.

"Take a moment to collect yourself, Londyn, then get dressed. We'll arrive at our destination soon. I don't want the driver to see you in this state."

"Why not?" she snapped back, her nerves frayed and fluttering in the wake of her coerced performance. The one consolation was Oliver had not demanded that she satisfy him. Thank God for small mercies. "Why should your driver be different from those animals back at the Ranch? After all, I'm nothing more than a whore to be passed around. Someone you'll use to pay off debts and favors."

Oliver shook his head at her heated accusations, a frown tugging the corners of his mouth. "I meant what I said back at the cabin, Londyn. I'll fucking gut *any* man who touches you without my permission. When and *if* I share you, it will be at my discretion. Not because someone else demands or expects it. Now, get dressed like I told you. Because I'm this close to flipping you onto your stomach and fucking you so hard you melt into that damned seat."

CHAPTER

FIFTEEN

liver

Maybe he was too rough with her.

Oliver silently watched as Londyn quickly dressed and curled up on the opposite seat as far away from him as she could. She even refused to look in his direction, instead turning her face to the window. But he could see the tears tracking down her cheeks, and they annoyed him.

Or maybe it was more that they bothered him, and *that* was annoying. This girl, this goddamn girl, was too fragile for this world. Too sweet and fucking innocent for the things he had planned. Maybe he should do as she wished and slit her throat when he was done with her. It would be a kindness. A mercy killing from a man who barely knew the meaning of the word. Would extinguishing her light exonerate him? Erase all the bad shit he'd done over the years?

Ending her life was far more merciful than allowing Ruel and Erik to resell her to an even crueler master. Londyn would never survive a second auction, let alone another hunt. Speaking of which, how in the hell had she even discovered the existence of the Russians' underground operation, anyway? One of the largest organizations of its kind, it was a closely guarded secret reserved for some of the most powerful men in the country.

"Who told you about the auction?" Oliver abruptly asked her.

Londyn startled at the sudden question but did not answer. Her lips thinned, and her arms tightened their grip around her knees as she drew them closer to her body.

Oliver ground his teeth. Stubborn little dove, she'd soon learn that his will was much greater than hers. There were so many delicious ways of getting what he wanted from her.

"Londyn," he intoned with deceptive calmness. "Do not make the mistake of believing I will grow tired of playing with you anytime soon. If I am constantly required to force you to do what I want, to make you obey me in all things will only cause *you* misery. Now, before you learn how unpleasant I can be when I'm angry. How did you find out about the auction? Who told you?"

Londyn's gray eyes flashed like lightning. She glared at him and then snapped, "No one told me. I found out what I wanted to know on my own."

"On your own?" Oliver's head tilted, an eyebrow arching high. "That doesn't seem possible."

"It wasn't that difficult. I went on the dark web and found what I needed to know. We discussed it in my criminal-psychology class last semester. My professor said you could find anything you wanted there and told us how to do it. I searched for private auctions where the organization's reputation and reports of the women's safety were stellar. I bypassed those that gave any indication of being involved with human trafficking." Chewing her bottom lip, she shrugged her shoulders. "Obviously, I got that part wrong. I should have delved deeper. Researched others before taking the first offer thrown out there."

Oliver frowned. "It was very foolish of you, Londyn. The people running these auctions, like those at Diamond Lake Ranch, hell, people like me, can never be trusted. They will take and take and leave you with nothing. You'll end up being a pawn. A toy for their amusement while you are destroyed in the process."

Londyn met his gaze, the soft gray depths liquid with tears of frustrated anger. "I learned that lesson a long time ago, Mister Winter. The depravity of men is not new to me. I am very aware of the monsters in this world."

"You have no idea what kind of monster you've been sold to, Londyn, nor have you ever experienced what I have planned for you. But you will see soon enough." His voice roughened as he swallowed the rest of the bourbon in the glass. "I promise you that."

LONDYN SAT CURLED-UP on the seat, facing away from the gates as they slowly swung open to admit the car. She could not see the long driveway ahead of them or the coach house reserved for the use of his security and household staff. She showed no interest that they had reached their destination. Oliver wondered if she was possibly shutting down on him.

He had purchased this house and property nearly a year earlier, specifically for its remoteness and the security measures already in place. While the previous owners had tastes similar to his—both in decor and sexual proclivities—Oliver had never brought a woman to Big Sky Cabin before today. He preferred utilizing the property as a private retreat. Londyn would be the first to experience all the pain and pleasure in the well-appointed playroom built into the mountain's base beneath the main house. Thinking of her entirely at his mercy with no intervention from outside parties or restrictions enforced by private clubs had Oliver's cock hardening with anticipation.

It was another fifteen minutes before the cabin came into view, and as the limo pulled around the circular driveway, Londyn's gaze slid to meet his.

"Is this yours?"

"It is. Before you consider making a run for it, be aware that the woods surrounding the cabin are just as dense and thick as those surrounding Diamond Lake Ranch. My security team is far more diligent."

"Who else lives here?" Londyn asked softly.

"No one. I come here when I want to shut out the world," Oliver replied in a brusque tone.

Londyn's gaze dropped to Oliver's hands. "So, everything here belongs to you?"

He gave her a tight smile. "Yes. Now, that includes you."

She said nothing more as Joey opened the door and extended a hand to help her exit. A possessive twinge assailed Oliver when Londyn accepted the limo driver's assistance. Fuck. Even that innocent gesture was almost more than he could bear to witness.

After climbing out of the limo, Oliver brushed past Londyn and bounded up the stone-terraced steps of the cabin. Keying in the code that unlocked the front door, he motioned for her to follow him. He watched as she glanced at Joey, who was gathering the luggage from the limo's trunk and knew exactly what she was thinking. She thought she could establish some kind of ally. Someone who could help her escape this predicament.

But she would find little sympathy or commiseration in Joey. The man wasn't nearly as sadistic as Malcom, but his loyalty to the Winter family was unwavering. The same could not be said for Oliver's former right-hand man. Malcolm had been like a wild animal and controlling him had been difficult. His death at Kingston's hands was justified. If he was still alive and tried assaulting Londyn in the same manner he had attacked Ava Blue, Oliver knew he would have tortured the man for days and days and in much more creative ways than Kingston had devised.

"Londyn. I'm waiting." Oliver snapped his fingers as if summoning a wayward pet, knowing it would piss her off.

Londyn's eyes narrowed, but she straightened her shoulders and obediently trudged up the steps to enter the house. Joey followed behind her, setting the bags down in the spacious foyer.

"Want me to carry these up to your rooms, boss?" Joey asked respectfully.

"No. I'll manage it from here."

"Need me for anything else?" Joey asked with a small smile.

"Not for a few days, at least. Feel free to go into town if you like or stay at the coach house. I'll let Miss Miller know when I need her services."

"Thanks, boss."

Joey closed the front door behind him, leaving Oliver and Londyn alone. She quickly retrieved her small duffle bag, clutching it to her midsection like a shield.

"Who is Miss Miller?" Her gaze darted around the luxurious foyer.

"My housekeeper. She stays at the coach house when I come here."

"Oh." Londyn blinked as Oliver untangled her bag from her grip. He cupped her elbow in his hard hand.

"Come with me. I'll show you where you will sleep."

He guided her down the hallway, past the enormous great room, with its wall of windows and expansive view overlooking the valley. A stunning staircase constructed of deer antlers led to the cabin's upper floors. Oliver grabbed her hand, pulling her up the wide steps until they reached a landing and a corridor lined by multiple doors. The hallway curved around a bend.

"Down there, at the end of another hallway," he gestured toward the furthest end of the corridor, which curved around the bend and continued out of sight, "are my rooms. This one will be yours." Pushing open one door, he let her enter the spacious bedroom first. He dropped her bag into an overstuffed chair.

"I have my own room?"

Her surprise amused Oliver. He nodded, leaning against the doorjamb as she moved to the center of the airy space. It was tastefully decorated in natural shades of ivory and pale green. Mounded high with decorative pillows, a four-poster king-sized bed made of lodgepole pines provided an obvious focal point. An attached bath with granite countertops in shades of brown and cream and a matching, glassed-in shower was also well appointed with every amenity she might require.

"I won't cage you, Londyn, unless necessary." Oliver's gaze drilled hers. "Will it be necessary?"

Her head moved in a short, jerky shake, her lips tight. Oliver stalked toward her, closing the distance she had placed between them.

"There is a cage in the playroom, and I thought of placing

you in it. But if you are a good girl and cause no trouble, you may sleep in here."

Her lips tightened even more with his words. "Playroom?"

Oliver's mouth twisted with a smile. "You'll see soon enough. In the meantime, you will stay where I put you. Do you understand?"

Londyn nodded slowly, and Oliver could practically see her mind turning with a thousand questions. Sliding his hand around the nape of her neck, he forced her to look up at him. Her breath hitched as he handled her, her body taut with apprehension.

He was so much larger than she was. Taller. Wider. More muscular. At six foot five and two-hundred-and-fifty pounds, he towered over her. She was terrified of him, and while that was usually cause for delight, the unease in her soft gray eyes was also mildly disturbing. Oliver craved that fear, but he wanted it in a sensual setting with Londyn. He wanted her off-balance, wondering what he might do to her body. He wanted her writhing with need and frightened that he wouldn't let her come on his dick.

"Good." Squeezing her neck as a reminder to behave, Oliver stepped back before surrendering to his base urges. Goddamn. He wanted to throw her on that bed, tie her down and fuck her until she was screaming his name. "Freshen up if you need to. I'll be back in fifteen minutes."

A QUICK CHECK of his phone revealed several missed calls from Kingston. Oliver's silence no doubt worried his older brother, but the conversation he knew was imminent was not one he wanted Londyn to overhear. After keying in the code to his suite of rooms, he entered and went to the attached bathroom.

He set the cell phone on the counter and tugged his shirt over his head. The bandaging over the wound remained intact, and Oliver peeled it back slightly to check for further bleeding. There was no fresh seepage, but it was best to keep it covered. At least it didn't require stitches.

A smile tugged at his lips when he remembered Londyn threatening him with the paring knife. She was an intriguing contradiction. A mix of both innocence and fierceness. Even more appealing was her intoxicating response when he played with her. She enjoyed every minute of it, but the shame was obviously something she couldn't reconcile.

If Londyn was conflicted over what he'd done so far, Oliver could only imagine how she would survive their future interactions. He planned on pushing her to the very limits of endurance. Possessing her completely would be the ultimate erotic experience. He damned sure intended on enjoying making her his new little toy.

His phone buzzed, vibrating against the countertop. Fuck. It was Kingston. Oliver placed the call on speaker, answering it as he pulled his shirt back on.

"What's up?"

"What the hell have you done, O?" Kingston's tone was low and intense. He was pissed.

Oliver rolled his eyes. Raking a hand through his hair, he checked his reflection in the vanity mirror. "What are you talking about?"

"You know damn well what I'm talking about," Kingston hissed. "You bought a girl. An unwilling one. Have you lost your fucking mind?"

Oliver laughed. "Which pisses you off more, King? The fact I made a purchase? Or that it was a Diamond Lake auction?"

"Both," Kingston huffed. "And the amount you paid—"

"Who told you?" Oliver interrupted.

"Ruel. After demanding compensation for some guard that you apparently eliminated last night, he mentioned you purchased a girl they offered up for permanent sale. And she hadn't volunteered for that spot on the auction block. Fuck, Oliver. Two million dollars…"

"Two point five, if you want an exact number. Should I remind you that it's my money?"

Kingston was silent, then heaved an exasperated sigh. "After what happened last year, I hoped you would stay away from that shit."

"That's ironic, coming from you. At least I didn't abduct this one off the street and hold her hostage for repayment of a debt."

"Watch yourself, Oliver," Kingston growled. "If I could go back and do things differently, I would. For Ava's sake. This is wrong… and I'm telling you this based on experience."

"It's my mistake, and it's done now." Oliver wasn't in the mood for a lecture from his older brother. The criticism was unwarranted and unwelcome, especially considering what Kingston did to Ava before he fell in love with her.

"You could let her go."

"Or I could keep her. Did Ruel tell you I beat Barlow on the main bidding? And when we were both required to hunt her down, I beat him at that, too." Oliver's tone hardened as he recalled the bruises marking Londyn's body. "As for the man I terminated, he abused my new acquisition in front of me. There was no other option."

"You know they cannot be trusted, Oliver. You cheated them out a great deal of money when you backed out of that agreement."

"And I just gave them a great deal of money in exchange for a woman," Oliver calmly replied. "Between Barlow and me, they collected nearly five million dollars for her. I also gave them enough money before to smooth over everything that happened last year."

"We both know the Russians are unpredictable. What is your plan when you grow tired of her?" Kingston pressed.

Oliver hesitated. He still hadn't decided what to do with Londyn when this was all done. The thought of executing her made him slightly dizzy. And he knew he couldn't physically return her to Diamond Lake Ranch for a secondary sale. He'd won her. She was *his*.

"Do you have feelings for this girl?" Kingston asked when Oliver remained silent. "That's too much money to say you don't."

"I haven't even fucked her yet, so your theories are completely off-base," Oliver softly laughed. "The terms of the sale were pretty clear. She's mine until I no longer want her. Then, it's either eliminate her or return her to the ranch. They will sell her again if I decide that option."

"Bring her to New York. Neil has spots open in the charity... she can stay as long as necessary. I'll arrange a new life for her. A new name. Ruel and Erik will never have to know."

Oliver's jaw clenched. His older brother was the secret creator and largest donor to a charity aiding victims of domestic violence and abuse. At any given time, there were at least a hundred or so women who were part of the organization and received medical care, therapy, and job skills to rebuild their lives. Oliver had never understood Kingston's involvement. Winter Enterprises ruled the underground criminal syndicate that dominated the East Coast; helping women in desperate situations was a contradiction of enormous proportions.

But then again, knowing the pain and torment Kingston's mother and his own mom endured at the hands of their monstrous father, it made perfect sense.

"Oliver, think twice about this. You aren't the same person you were last year. You aren't the same person our shitty father beat and tortured. You don't have to be like *him*. I chose not to be, and you can choose that, too. You can do the right thing. You can save this girl's life," Kingston urged. "Bring her to New York."

"Don't be so fucking dramatic, King. I plan on fucking her, not marrying her."

Being told how to handle Londyn rubbed Oliver the wrong way. Irrational resentment bubbled inside his gut, although at the same time, he knew Kingston was only trying to help. "I'll think about it," he finally muttered, unable to hide the anger in his tone. Being angry was not the best mindset when dealing with his new treasure, but there was only one way to calm his internal demons. His usual method for calming those beasts was a good, hard fuck.

"That's all I can hope for. While you are handling this next job, I want you to consider the possibilities open," Kingston said in a weary voice. He quickly rattled off the details for the job he was sending Oliver on and closed with these parting words. "You've come to a crossroads, Oliver. I hope you take the right direction."

CHAPTER

SIXTEEN

L *ondyn*

AFTER USING the restroom and splashing her face with cool water, Londyn put away the contents of her duffle bag. Her clothes fit into one drawer of the sleek system built into the walk-in closet. The pair of tennis shoes she had packed from her sister's house were placed neatly on the built-in rack where they appeared embarrassingly out of place.

Perching in one of the chairs by the row of windows, she looked out over the stunning view. There were endless swathes of trees and the distant glimmer of a lake in the distance, but no other houses could be seen. If she managed to escape the cabin, there was nowhere to go. She couldn't even be sure where this house was located, although she suspected she was still in Colorado.

She shifted on the chair, the soreness of her bottom a

blazing reminder of the spanking and the humiliation of having a thumb shoved inside her. Her captor had no mercy in his twisted soul. He would kill her the moment he grew tired of her.

"What am I going to do?" Londyn wiped tears from her cheeks, hating how easily they flowed. She had to be stronger than this. Stronger and smarter. She must remember her psychology studies and use everything she knew against Oliver Winter.

It would not be easy, especially since he had so easily tapped into a hidden portion of her psyche and discovered how to manipulate her. He commanded, she folded. Realizing that she was complicit in her destruction made her sick.

She had sworn to obey him. Promised to willingly kneel in exchange for her sister's care and safety. There was no other choice but to do what he demanded and survive long enough to get away.

He had not locked her inside her bedroom. Maybe it was some kind of test. If she could gain his trust and show him that she would not run, he might grow comfortable with her submission and drop his guard. And as much as she feared the reality of being at his mercy, she would do what was necessary. She would obey him. Appease him. Make him trust her.

And strike when he least expected it.

When Oliver returned as promised just a short time later, he had a bottle of water and a ham sandwich for her.

"Best I can whip up in a hurry." Setting the tray on the dresser, he waved a hand toward it. "I took a chance and decided you liked ham."

Londyn nodded. She wasn't really hungry, but she would devour that sandwich if it meant keeping him calm. She must appear appreciative of everything he did for her, regardless of how small. It was how one stroked the ego of a sociopath—

making them feel like the most important and most interesting person in the room. She did not get up from the chair where she'd sat, waiting his return. She didn't want to move and give him the impression that she might be thinking of darting past him.

"I like ham and cheese. Thank you," she said softly, frozen like a rabbit avoiding the predatory gaze of a wolf.

His head tilted as if he knew her game plan. "You're welcome, Londyn. Make yourself comfortable. In fact, I advise that you take this opportunity to get some rest. We'll both need it." His beautiful light-blue eyes darkened as they raked her body. "You, especially, will find the coming days exhausting."

Without another word, he turned, exiting the room as Londyn slumped in relief that he had not tried to touch her.

For days, he left her alone in her room. She was positive it was a test to ensure she followed his commands. Londyn obeyed. Not once did she attempt to leave the bedroom, although she was aware that the door was unlocked. Oliver delivered her meals, silently watched her eat, and took the dishes with him when she was done.

Londyn was glad that their interactions were brief. But she could not ignore the uneasy feeling that something momentous was coming. So, she remained on high alert while she spent the days watching the woods outside the large windows, sleeping, or reading a book from the selection provided in the room's built-in bookcase. Eventually, Oliver would claim what he had purchased, and that reality was so terrifying that it gave her nightmares.

One morning, the soft sound of the door clicking open

made Londyn leap from the chair. Wrapping her arms around her midriff, she stared at her captor as he leaned against the doorjamb. He was tense, an unsettled air emanating from him had grown since they arrived at this house.

His eyes, so piercingly blue, pinned her in place, and Londyn couldn't do anything other than tremble. Something bad was about to happen. She could feel it.

"What a good girl you are. Staying put, like I told you," Oliver said in a low voice. He held a bundle of clothes in his arms and tossed them onto a small bench beside the door. A few of the items appeared to be very expensive and exquisitely designed lingerie. In different circumstances, she would have squealed with delight at seeing the lovely items, but the sight of them caused her heart to thump wildly.

"Where would I go?" Londyn was afraid even to blink as the corners of his firm mouth quirked up.

"Where indeed?" His gaze swept over her body, then narrowed. "You're crying."

Londyn quickly wiped her cheeks clear of any lingering moisture. She did not respond to the accusation. Of course she had been crying. She was at the mercy of a monster and held as a prisoner inside this room for three days.

Oliver studied her for a few more seconds, then crooked his finger. "Come here, Londyn."

As if approaching the execution block, Londyn glided toward the man holding her hostage. The closer she got, the more uneasy she became. The dark frustration rolling off him scared her. When she reached him, she stood silently, dreading what might happen.

His hand came up, and Londyn could not help herself when she flinched. The ice blue of his eyes darkened as he trailed a forefinger down her cheek and across her jawline until he reached her chin. Applying pressure to the underside of it, he forced it upward so there was nowhere else to look other than him.

"My brother believes I can be a hero," Oliver remarked, his tone distant and contemplative. It was as though the possibility was a foreign concept and one impossible to obtain. "But he knows me. Knows how we grew up. Knows the things I've done. There is nothing *good* inside me; he knows that better than anyone. He doesn't want to see it. He's fucking in love, and now, he's blind to everything else. But in our world, it's dangerous not to recognize the wickedness of others."

Londyn said nothing. Oliver had a brother? Did he have any influence over the man imprisoning her? Was it possible that he could help?

Her thoughts ran rampant until Oliver slid his thumb over her bottom lip, demanding entrance. He stroked her tongue and then thrust it further into her mouth in a crude imitation of a blow job.

"You are going to bleed for me, Londyn. You will do it because you want me. You will do it because you know I'll hurt you and then lick the wounds I create. You will discover that I am no fucking hero. So, you can cut me open even more if you want. See for yourself that I have no heart; that any pleas for mercy will be wasted."

His voice was soft and resolute. He meant every word, and Londyn shivered as she recognized the truth of his statement. Her life lay in the hands of the Devil, and that's where it would end eventually.

Oliver removed his thumb and rubbed it over her mouth, painting her lips with salvia before wrapping his hand around her throat. He gripped it so hard that Londyn could hardly draw in a full breath. Then he leaned forward, licking the tears from her cheeks. His lip brushed over hers with brutal tenderness until she tasted the salt. "Are you ready to see just how much of a villain I am?"

Londyn's heart pounded with such ferocity she felt sick. "I'll do whatever you want, just please, don't hurt me."

"I'm afraid that's not an option. So much of what I'm going to do to you will be painful. But I promise I'll make it feel good."

She could not grasp that concept, her brain struggling to understand how pain could be pleasurable. Oliver laughed at her obvious confusion.

"Oh, Londyn. We're going to have so much fun. You had your first lesson when I spanked your sweet little ass. Now, it's time for another— only this will be for *my* pleasure." Letting her go, he grabbed something black and silky from the pile of clothes he had dropped on the bench. It was a slip of a night-dress with spaghetti straps and a plunging neckline. It hardly looked long enough to cover her ass, and Londyn knew that was intentional.

"Put it on," he directed with a smirk. "And don't worry about underwear. I want you bare beneath it."

Almost woodenly, Londyn did as she was told. She carefully folded her yoga pants and T-shirt into neat squares, tugged off her bra and panties, and then slipped the negligee over her head. It settled over her body like it was made for her, the material soft against her skin and hugging her curves. Oliver reached out, quickly ripping off the tag still attached to the garment. She caught sight of the price stamped on the item before he crumpled it and tossed it onto the bench. A thousand dollars. A thousand dollars for this scrap of silk.

"Much better. From now on, I don't want to see you in anything other than the clothes I give you." His voice was husky with desire. With a frown, he picked up the tail end of the braid she'd woven her hair into early that morning and pulled off the elastic band that held it all in place. With tender care, he untangled the plait, combing his fingers through the strands until it lay in dark, wavy curls.

Londyn stood like a statue, not daring to breathe as he pushed the dark mass of her hair until it tumbled down her back. Then he grabbed a handful of it within his fist, tilting her head back. Oliver studied her carefully, holding her gaze for so long she thought he might be reconsidering whatever he had planned for her.

"You are so beautiful, Londyn. And while I'm sure my money was well-spent, now is the time to confirm it."

She did not resist as he took her by the hand and led her from the bedroom toward the downstairs portion of the house. Londyn caught quick glimpses of elegant rooms decorated in an eclectic mix of both sleek modernism and edgy rustic touches. Everything was black and dark wood with chrome accents and luxurious furs that she couldn't be sure were real or not. The fox fur blankets, the bearskin rugs... it all certainly looked real.

Behind a gourmet kitchen outfitted with all the newest and shiniest chef-grade appliances was a steel door that looked like the entrance to a vault. A fingerprint keypad was an additional security fixture to the heavy locking bolt. Oliver halted before it and turned to Londyn, smiling at her wide eyes.

"Before we go any further, I want to make sure you understand what I expect from you." His hand curled under her chin. "You will give me your complete obedience inside this room. Defiance or refusal will result in punishments, which will vary depending on the severity of your transgression. Remember, Londyn, you agreed to this in exchange for your sister's care and the money I have directed to be utilized for that purpose. Do we understand one another on this?"

Londyn clenched her teeth, her stomach roiling with fright

and anger. "Yes. I understand." She could not stop the words that poured from her next. They were like a runaway torrent; she could no longer hold it back than she could dam up a tidal wave. "And I understand that you are a sociopath with an undiagnosed need for control. A need to prove ownership of things you've never earned or deserve. Tattooing the word on your knuckles does not give you the right to take or steal whatever you want. You've no right to demand my submission while dangling my sister's safety over my head like some damn carrot. But I have no choice. I will do what you want. I will do it, and I will hate you with every breath in my body. You need therapy, Oliver Winter. Or maybe a bullet. I believe the latter is the only cure for the depths of your sickness."

Oliver stood motionless, his blue eyes cold and hard as he stared her down, listening silently to her vitriol. A muscle clenched in his stubbled jaw, and his lips tightened. His fingers flexed around her chin before slowly lowering his hand to her throat. His right hand—the tattooed one. That hand encircled her neck, pushing until her back was flush against the wall. That same hand began to squeeze as a smirk flitted across his face.

"Mouthy little dove," Oliver murmured, removing her ability to breathe with frightening calm. "Don't you think I know that? I'm very aware of my shortcomings. And as for therapy... you're going to help with that in more ways than you could possibly dream of."

Keeping her pinned to the wall, he raised his free hand and pressed his thumb to the keypad. The lights blinked red, then green, and the sound of a lock opening reached Londyn through the roaring in her ears. She clutched the hand around her throat to loosen his grip, but Oliver simply chuckled. Only after he had thrown the bolt to the door and let it swing open did he let her go so she could frantically suck in a breath of air.

All Londyn could see were stairs leading into darkness, but as he pushed her ahead of him, sconces on the wall immediately lit up, activated by their movement. She stumbled down the concrete steps, holding a hand to the cold stone wall to keep her balance as Oliver prodded her to keep moving. When they reached the bottom, she sucked in a whimper of alarm as he flipped on a light switch. Illumination filled the entirety of the space, revealing gadgets and devices of all kinds. She had no idea what most of this stuff was, but it all appeared to be instruments of pain.

A cage of thick steel bars took up one corner. It was not nearly as ornamentally pretty as the one at Diamond Lake Ranch. This one seemed designed to contain a dangerous prisoner. A small twin-size bed with iron bars for a footboard and headboard stood in the middle of the enormous room. No linens other than a white fitted sheet covered the mattress. Nearby, a harness-type contraption resembling a diabolical swing hung from a lowered truss system.

Along dark-gray walls, silvery chains with manacles dangled from rings embedded in the thick mountain stone. An illuminated cabinet closer to the steps they had just descended held a dizzying array of whips, paddles, and crops, all contained behind glass and lit up like a rare art display. In one corner stood a large formation in the shape of an X. Cuffs hung from rings drilled into the wood, and Londyn swallowed hard. She knew what that was. She saw one on the dark web while searching for auctions she could enter. A blindfolded girl had been strapped to it, a man standing behind her with a leather whip gripped tight in his gloved hand.

Oh, God.

This is what Oliver had planned for her.

Torture. Degradation. Pain.

She could scream and scream, and no one would ever hear

her. They were far below the main foundation of the house above them. The air was cool, the room windowless with corners as dark as midnight. But despite the obvious, dungeon-like atmosphere, there were undeniable touches of expensive luxuries. Recessed lighting cast warm, golden pools of light over the main components of the room. A beautiful couch upholstered in blood-red velvet occupied one of the many alcoves, and a thick abstract rug of black and gray defined that area. Hidden speakers played a hauntingly seductive tune Londyn had never heard before, and sconces crafted of black iron and diamondlike fractured glass adorned the walls and threw off a low, flickering light.

Oliver watched Londyn as she gazed around the room. She could tell that he liked the fear she could not hide. Liked the horror in her expression as she took in the implements of torture. He liked scaring her. It was part of what made him tick. It excited him.

For some unholy reason, her pulse began racing. Adrenaline scorched her veins, and for reasons she could not yet completely face, Londyn trembled with realization.

She felt more alive in this moment than she ever had. Knowing she had no control over what would happen next, no way of stopping this man from doing anything he wanted with her, was incredibly freeing. And knowing he would encourage her to scream, cry, and curse was almost cathartic. If she let everything out, screamed out all her frustration, all her pain and fears, he would most likely praise her for it. It was both a sobering revelation and a frightening thought.

Maybe... she needed therapy, too. And this was only the first session.

SEVENTEEN

L *ondyn*

"LONDYN, LOOK AT ME," Oliver commanded in a smooth, low voice. He waited until her gaze drifted back to him before continuing. It seemed he was choosing his words with care. "If you please me, if you do exactly as I say and give me your complete submission, I'll do what you asked of me that first morning. I will end your life rather than send you back to Diamond Lake Ranch."

Londyn's eyes watered at the finality of his tone. "You could let me go. I-I won't tell anyone what happened. I'll go back home. Take care of my sister. Find justice for her and punish the man who hurt her. Let me go, and I won't say a word about you. About us. This. I swear it."

Oliver shook his head, eyes darkening. "I can't let you go, nor can I keep you. Because once I fuck that tight little virgin cunt, I won't rest until I'm certain no other man ever experiences the pleasure of you squeezing his cock like you will soon squeeze mine. The only way to ensure you aren't sold to another man is to watch you take your last breath while I'm buried deep inside you." His blue eyes glittered like diamonds. "Be a good girl, and I will make it quick and painless."

The unspoken threat of what would happen should she fail to meet the vague qualifications for being *a good girl* hung in the cool air of the underground playroom. Her chest tightened until she felt faint, but she nodded in agreement.

A smile tugged at his lips, but it was a cold one. It never reached his eyes. Londyn closed hers, swaying with terror while tremors swept her body. She gritted her teeth to control the shaking as her bare toes curled against the stone floor. Her legs were suddenly so weak that she teetered on the verge of collapse.

"How do I know you will keep your promise? How can I be sure you let my sister have the money once I'm dead and gone? How do I know you won't just take the money back?"

Oliver's head tilted at her accusation. For a moment, he looked offended. Then he shrugged. "You don't know, Londyn. I can't even swear that I'll keep my promise because there's not a fucking thing in this world that I hold dear enough to swear against. So, bad luck on that. You'll just have to hope I keep my word. If it makes you feel better, you can haunt me from the afterlife if I fail to keep my end of our deal." He smirked at her, his features darkening as he softly commanded, "Down on your knees, Londyn. Hands behind your back. No more speaking unless I permit it."

The room spun as she quickly obeyed. The black slip was too short to cushion her bare legs, but the discomfort of kneeling on the hard floor was overshadowed by apprehension.

She could not see what he was doing. The clink of something metal ratcheted her breathing to the point of hyperventilation.

"Deep breaths for me, dove. I don't want you passing out yet. Not when we are only just beginning." His breath brushed the hair behind her ear as he bent over. Taking her wrists, he clicked a pair of handcuffs around them.

When she gave her hands an experimental twist, Londyn realized the cuffs were constructed of butter-soft leather. The sound she heard was the chain linking them together.

Oliver spoke again in low, soothing tones. "For the last week or so, I've gathered items essential for our time together. The furniture in this room, the St. Andrew's Cross, the bedframe, the couch, and the swing were installed before I purchased the cabin, but they've never been used, not even by the prior owner. The restraints and the implements I will use are new."

Londyn's fists clenched at the unspoken revelation. "There's never been another... you mean..."

Oliver's fingers laced through her hair, tilting her head back until she could see his face from where he still stood behind her. "You are the first, Londyn. I've never felt strongly enough about another woman to do half the things I plan on doing with you." From this awkward position, he kissed the tip of her nose. "And you've earned yourself a punishment."

Keeping one hand entangled in Londyn's hair, Oliver moved to stand before her. He held the tresses tight for a long moment, then abruptly released her. His mouth curved with the ghost of a smile as he unbuttoned his white shirt, slowly rolling up the cuffs to reveal muscular forearms. When the shirt fluttered around his chiseled body, Londyn could see the white, square bandage from the stab wound. Her pulse accelerated with dread.

"Open your mouth."

Londyn did not move. *Oh, God. What is he going to do?*

Oliver's hand curled around her throat, snapping her back to attention. "Open. Your. Fucking. Mouth."

She complied, a tear running down her cheek that Oliver immediately scooped on the end of his forefinger. He sucked the teardrop before sliding the digit so deep into her mouth she nearly gagged. His smile grew wider at her involuntary response and the way her legs clenched together.

"Sweet as nectar. Oh, Londyn. Everything about you is so fucking delicious. I'm going to devour every part of you. Worship every part of you. And I will *possess* every part of you. Starting with this beautiful mouth and throat."

Withdrawing his finger, Oliver's large hands went to the black leather belt around his trim waist. Deliberately, he slid it free from his jeans, then passed its end through the buckle so that it fashioned a loop.

Londyn closed her eyes as he gently placed the noose around her neck. It hung loose, but the implication was quite clear. He meant to choke her with it. To extinguish her life at that very moment. A sob escaped before she could swallow it back down.

"Shhhh. I've no intention of killing you right now," he laughed softly, pulling the belt until it tightened around her throat. It did not hurt, but the implication of what was coming next made her quiver. "Remember what I said. Please me and I will do what you want. Now, open your eyes."

She did, staring up at him from her knees.

"Normally, I would have you pull my cock out, but with your hands bound, I'm afraid that's not an option. Next time." Oliver undid his jeans before pushing the material down to ride low on his hips. "You see what it says, don't you? Good. Now, take your punishment like a good girl."

Londyn's eyes watered, a cry bubbling up in her throat. *SWALLOW.*

The word was tattooed in an ornate script across the lowest portion of his sculpted abdomen, stretching from one side of the V to the other. His large cock loomed below it, thrusting up from the neatly groomed pubic area studded with things that looked like barbells. She counted six of them; shiny silver bars that captured the light and reflected it. With his free hand, Oliver stroked himself as Londyn watched, his thumb caressing the barbells and the head of his cock until a groan was wrung from his lips. The noose around her neck tightened like a leash used to control a wayward pet.

"Take a deep breath, little dove. You're about to get all nine fucking inches of me. I'm going to fill that sweet throat with cum, and you will swallow every drop. Now, open for me."

Everything seemed to move in slow motion and a very surreal fashion. Londyn automatically parted her lips, and then he was pushing his way inside, gliding past the barrier of her teeth and hitting the back of her throat until she gagged. Oliver *tsked* and withdrew a few inches. Reaching down, he cupped her chin in his hand and forced her to meet his icy-blue eyes. They had noticeably darkened until the irises were indistinct from the dark-blue ring surrounding them.

"Have you never given head before?"

Londyn shook her head the best she could with the belt holding her head immobile. Tears streaked down her cheeks. Not because Oliver was hurting her but because her own response frightened and confused her. Trembling with emotion, her body was betraying her. Between her legs, moisture gathered, and beneath the silky gown, her nipples were diamond-hard points so sensitive that every brush of the fabric had her swallowing back a moan.

Oliver huffed out a laugh. "I'm going to be all your firsts,

Londyn, and all your lasts." He slid back in and quickly withdrew so she could breathe. "Fuck, your mouth is amazing. Open wider for me and flatten your tongue." He thrust deeper, the cold barbells on the underside of his shaft clinking against her lower teeth. The mushroom-shaped head of his cock impaled the back of her throat again until she choked. "Breathe through your nose, dove," he instructed in a rough voice. "Fuck, I'm not going to fucking last long. Not when your mouth is so goddamn hot and tight. Even your fucking teeth feel good."

Dropping the end of the belt, Oliver's hands buried themselves in the thick waves of Londyn's hair. He held her, cradling her head in his palms as he began steadily fucking her mouth. When she tried pulling away, salvia dripping down her chin, he jerked her back into place, his grip tightening as he chased his pleasure. But although it was brutal and degrading and easily the most frighteningly arousing thing she'd ever experienced, Londyn sensed Oliver was restraining himself from losing control. His thrusts were shallow enough that she could breathe but still so deep that he brushed the back of her throat, swelling her cheeks with the thickness of his cock each time his hips flexed.

Was he really trying not to hurt her? The flash of gratitude she felt even as his hands cruelly held her in place was disgusting. How could she be grateful for this tiny drop of kindness after everything she'd suffered at his hands? Why wasn't she biting his dick off? Or ripping out one of the barbells with a quick snap of her teeth? Why, *why* was she allowing this? And why did she want his hands to snake between her legs and make her come?

"Goddamn, you're gonna make me come before I'm ready," Oliver warned, the words coming out in a strangled curse that invaded her disjointed thoughts. "Swallow me, Londyn. Swallow every inch of my cock and every drop of my cum."

Hearing his filthy words, Londyn clenched her thighs tightly, rubbing them together to get some relief. From what, she wasn't sure. Something was wrong with her. Something so terrifying that she couldn't begin to understand it. It was dark and insidious. Overwhelming. A craving that must be fed. Something must be done to ease the ache deep inside her. She needed something to quiet the roaring in her head. To soothe the blood rushing through her veins.

"Fuck…" Oliver hissed, hands clenching her hair with such force that she would have screamed if her mouth hadn't been so full. Then he was exploding, warm salty liquid pouring down her throat in what felt like a gushing river. She was drowning. Coughing. Semen and spit mingled together, spilling from the corners of her mouth. Oliver did not stop rocking his hips as his release filled her. A groan of immense satisfaction rumbled through his body, and Londyn was light-headed as the sound washed over her.

For an eternity, Londyn waited. Accepting. Crying. Swallowing.

Just like the tattoo across his lower stomach predicted she would.

EIGHTEEN

liver

CHRIST.

Oliver's breath escaped in harsh grunts. His head swam with the force of his orgasm. He couldn't remember ever coming so strongly from a simple blow job. In fact, he might not have ever come so hard in his life.

As he came to his senses, he became aware of many things simultaneously. First, his little prisoner was sobbing at his feet with his cock stuffed in her mouth. Tears tracked down her cheeks in salty trails, and his cum glistened at the corners of her mouth and on her chin. She was still trying to swallow his release, which was quite admirable. Second, he held a fistful of her hair in such a tight grip that it was likely excruciating. And third, her body was quivering almost uncontrollably while her thighs shifted together in a restless motion.

Pulling out of her mouth, Oliver tucked himself back inside his jeans but left them unbuttoned. Londyn stayed where she was; lips parted from her shaky breaths; eyes closed. She was silently crying, and Oliver's cock stirred despite the explosive orgasm he'd just experienced. He was ready to go again in an instant.

Swiping a finger across her chin, he gathered the remnants of cum and pushed it back into her mouth. "I told you to swallow every fucking drop, Londyn."

Her eyes flew open at the taunt, the gray depths cloudy with angry tears and frustration. Glaring at him, she swirled her tongue around his forefinger, erasing the evidence of his climax as they stared at one another. For a long moment, Oliver allowed her to do as she wished, remembering just moments ago how her tongue felt against his piercings, how she gagged on his thick length and swallowed reflexively each time he went a little too deep down her amazingly tight throat. He probably shouldn't have used her so roughly—especially when she was so inexperienced. He'd been with women far more experienced at fellatio who couldn't deep-throat a cock of his size. Yet, this innocent girl, all five-foot-four and one-hundred-and-fifteen pounds of her, had taken every inch he shoved in her mouth.

"Good girl," he crooned as she continued licking and sucking his finger. He liked how her eyes glittered with the brilliance of diamonds when he praised her. Her reluctant need for it was something he was already addicted to. She was exquisite. A goddess. A toy he would enjoy fucking over and—

Like an angry little cat, Londyn's teeth clamped down on his finger with such force that Oliver knew she had drawn blood. The pain was barely acknowledged. It was insignificant compared to the things he'd endured. In fact, her attack only hardened his dick and his resolve.

"Oh, that was a mistake, dove. Cute, but a mistake. And you were behaving so well," Oliver *tsked* when she finally let go so she could spit out his blood. Her eyes flashed like thunderstorms rolling across the seas as she glared at him.

He grinned, wrapping a hand around her upper arm and abruptly snatching her onto her feet as if she were nothing but a ragdoll. "I guess my cock down your throat wasn't punishment enough?" he murmured, staring into her eyes. "You want more, don't you? Well, I can certainly accommodate that."

Ignoring her whimper of protest, he dragged her to a vertical pole anchored to the floor and bolted to the ceiling. A chain dangled from its upper portion, a closed-hinged hook at its end. With deftly swift movements, he freed her wrists from the cuffs and just as quickly restrained them again. Her hands rested over her stomach for a brief second before he snatched them over her head, securing the cuffs to the hook. She was barely tall enough to reach the end of the chain, and now, she was practically on her tiptoes.

"You are excited by what I'm doing to you, Londyn. You can't hide that from me." His bloodied finger trailed down her cheek, then her neck, until he reached the top of the silky nightgown. "I watched you rubbing your thighs together, wishing I would touch you there. I think you like the pain. Like me using you." With both hands, he abruptly ripped the gown into two halves. The material separated as easily as crepe paper.

Londyn cried out in shock as the cool air rushed over her naked form. Her nipples pebbled as Oliver drank in the bewitching sight of her restrained and bare for him. Letting out a groan, he cupped her full breasts, smearing his blood over the creamy flesh. "You are fucking exquisite." He took one peak into his mouth, lavishing it with strokes of his tongue before grazing the tight bud with the sharp edge of his teeth.

"Oh, God," Londyn feverishly moaned, shaking her head side-to-side. Her voice accelerated into a squeal, her body arching away when he bit her in response.

"No gods here, little dove. Just the Devil and you." His soft laughter galvanized Londyn. With a ferocity borne of desperation, she kicked her legs, trying to hurt him, but Oliver only chuckled again, taunting her, "Is this your way of asking me to tie your legs as well? Because if you don't want that, you'd best settle. There. That's better. You'll learn that no matter how ferociously you fight, I will do what I want, Londyn. This is the second time you've made me bleed, and while I usually do not allow such incidents to go unanswered, my intention right now is to continue your punishment in a manner that is pleasurable for me. Do you know how I will do that?"

Londyn's head lolled as he continued licking and sucking her nipples until they were painfully hard. "N-no," she gasped when he nipped again.

"I'm certain you've never been edged. It's also called orgasm denial by some. It's a combination of pleasure and torment that can be useful in teaching a lesson. It can be a way of taming a brat or even inspiring obedience. In your case, I plan to accomplish all those objectives by repeatedly bringing you to the edge. But you will never be allowed to come. It's an exquisite torture, really. I'm so fucking excited to initiate you."

Her body began shaking with his words. Oliver could not resist taking the finger she'd chomped and sliding it into the warm folds of her pussy. The blood still welling from his bite wound should have been a lubricant, but Londyn was already dripping wet.

"Oh, little dove. You are drenched for me. What a pair we are, you and me. You see, I enjoy inflicting pain, and your body apparently loves it." Oliver pressed a soft kiss to her open mouth as she panted, using his tongue to outline her lips before dipping in and swirling it around hers. "This pleases me more than you realize. You are a special kind of prize. I'm so fortunate to have acquired you."

He began stroking her clit, moving with her body when she arched away from his touch. With a mix of his blood and her sweet juices, he occasionally thrust his finger inside, making her cry out at the shocking intrusion. "Do you feel that, Londyn? How wet you are for me? How the pain turns you into a needy little whore desperate to be used by a monster like me? You are fucking my fingers right now... and it's fucking hot. Maybe I'll let you come after all. I'll enjoy watching your sweet cunt drip with all that hate and lust you've got bottled up inside you."

Oliver knew the signs of her impending orgasm. They were scorched into his goddamn brain. Every night, he'd replayed them like they were scenes from an X-rated movie. He'd fucked his hand to those images... swearing at himself for being so weak. But allowing her those three days of recovery only meant it would be all the sweeter when he broke her.

Oliver cruelly withdrew his hand when her eyelids drooped heavily, and her toes began to curl. She receded from the edge, her eyes flying wide open with confusion. He roughly shoved his fingers in her mouth, stifling her moan of protest.

"Lick them clean, dove, and we'll start again. That was the first of many orgasms I'll withhold from you today, so take a deep breath. I'm going to ruin you to the point where you are on your knees begging me to fuck you. And hopefully, you will have learned your lesson by the time we are done. Defy me, and I'll punish you. Hurt me, and I will hurt you. Deny me, and I will take what I want anyway. You can't win, you will *never* win. And I'll make you sorry you *ever* thought it was an option."

Many hours later, he carried her up the stairs and laid her unconscious body across the bed.

He had lost count of how many times he denied her completion. After the first five or six times, he simply enjoyed the moments. He carefully watched her responses to his touch. Filed away the knowledge of what made her squirm and jerk against the chain. Noted every nuance of her body as she shivered and sweated and cried from sheer frustration and his cruel denial. But as a testament to her incredible stubbornness, she never begged for anything. Not even to stop the erotic torture. She remained mute until her body finally gave in to exhaustion, her eyes shooting daggers at him until the moment they fluttered shut and she sagged against the restraints. He immediately unchained her from the post before the weight of her body could cause any harm to her shoulders or arms.

She was fucking magnificent in her suffering, and over the hours spent trying to break her today, Oliver's obsession expanded into something more twisted. Before ending her life, he would hear her sweet voice begging for his mercy. Begging for his cock. Begging that he fuck her into oblivion. But while he had not accomplished those goals with this session of punishment, he thought his next plan would do the trick.

Londyn sighed heavily as he tucked the coverlet around her shoulders. She would be sore tomorrow—her muscles taxed to the limit. He was worn out as well, maybe even more so than her. Fighting the urge to let her come, fighting the overwhelming need to bury himself deep inside her was probably the most difficult thing he'd ever done. Even after he used her mouth two more times and jacked off over her round ass once, marking the pinkened globes with his cum and handprints, Oliver wasn't satisfied.

Fuck, far from it. His cock knew what it wanted, and what it wanted was her virgin cunt. He wanted it sucking him in the same way her hot, sweet mouth enveloped him. He wanted it pulsing around him, bleeding for him and soaking his flesh with her pleasure. That's what he wanted, and goddamn if he could hold off from taking every piece of her for much longer.

But... maybe she had earned a small reprieve—one day of rest to regain her strength. One day of contemplating her situation and how completely he held her life in his hands. After her initial resistance, Londyn accepted the punishments he gave her. Maybe she deserved a tiny display of his benevolence.

No. Fuck that. We'll start again tomorrow. Only this time, I'll give her so many goddamn orgasms that she won't remember or even be able to say her own name. The only words I'll allow are "Oliver" and "Please."

"Rest easy, little dove," he whispered, brushing her tangled hair away from her forehead. Unable to help himself, he brushed her lips with his, taking advantage of her soft mouth and kissing her deeply. He had painted her lips with her arousal many times while he played with her, and now, he relished the tangy sweetness on his tongue. She was so delicious. He just wanted to lick and bite and suck every bit of her into his mouth. Inhale her into his lungs and cut his veins open so he could absorb her like an addict injecting a fix. "Very soon, you will bleed for me, and I will relish every drop."

NINETEEN

L *ondyn*

LONDYN JERKED UPRIGHT, clutching the sheets to her bare breasts.

For a brief second, she wasn't sure where she was. Her eyes darted around the darkened room, taking in the quiet hush as she took a deep breath. Slowly, she settled against thick, fluffy pillows.

She was still Oliver Winter's prisoner. His *toy*.

Somehow, she had survived God only knew how many hours of degrading torture in his chamber of horrors. She wasn't sure how she'd ended up in this room. Everything was a complete blur of pleasure, pain, tears, and euphoria.

Shifting her naked legs, Londyn winced. She was so sore, her muscles screaming each time she moved. When she threw back the coverlet and perched on the side of the bed, her actions were wobbly and slow.

Everything hurt. *Everything.* Her breasts. Her arms and shoulders. Her bottom. The tenderness between her legs had her biting back a sob. How many times did he invade her flesh with his long, thick fingers while denying her the orgasm her body craved so desperately? She couldn't answer that question. At some point during her time in the underground room, she'd lost count and blacked out.

But it was her throat that hurt the most. Oliver fucked it three times that she could recall. The piercings... Oh, God... the piercings. She could still feel the cold metal bars clinking against her teeth and sliding across her tongue until the head of his cock touched the back of her throat. Even though she had the strange feeling he had held back from abusing her far more than he could, it did not erase the way he forced her submission. How he made her swallow and accept *everything* he gave her. How would she survive when he decided it was time to claim her virginity? Those piercings would likely tear her to pieces.

Londyn lowered her head, wrapping her arms around her waist. She bent over, rocking slightly. Her hair was a tangled mess. After being drenched with sweat, it had dried into stiff waves. She needed to wash it. God, she must be a mess. Glancing down at herself, she expected to see skin smeared with his cum and blood and her own arousal. But surprisingly, she was relatively clean. He must have wiped her in between those moments of insanity. A faint memory of a warm cloth passing over her lower spine made her shudder. When he had swiped it between her legs, she had moaned at the sensation and bucked her hips in desperation.

"Ah-ah," he chided. "You don't get to come, Londyn. Not now, and certainly not in the near future. Should you think about getting yourself off when I'm not around, I would advise you to think again. I will know if you do something so foolish. You won't be able to hide

it from me, and your punishment will be severe if you disappoint me. Your orgasms are mine, dove. I decide when, how, and where you may have one."

Clenching her teeth, Londyn shoved aside those memories, refusing to dwell on her body's betrayal when Oliver touched her. And his cruel words when he forced her to acknowledge how much she liked him touching her.

She ached all over, but she was also alive. *Alive.* He hadn't killed her, and he finally promised to do it quickly and painlessly when the time came. She must be grateful for that, at least.

Despite the soreness and the aches rippling through her body, Londyn could no longer ignore more pressing needs. She was starving. Thirsty, despite the cool sips of water Oliver had occasionally forced on her. And she needed to pee, although her insides clenched at the thought. That was likely to be painful, considering how swollen and sensitive she was *down there.* She rose from the bed, holding one of the posts for support. The longer she stood there, the steadier she became. Steeling herself, she shuffled to the attached bathroom.

It didn't hurt as much when she urinated, which was a small miracle. A cup of water from the tap alleviated her thirst for the moment; now, she needed to find something to eat.

Londyn made her way into the walk-in closet, pulling her favorite Vanderbilt University sweatshirt and a pair of panties from the small pile of clothes stored in the dresser drawer. She refused to wear anything from the stack of high-end garments Oliver left on the bench by the door. Ignoring those clothes, she went to the door. Was it locked to prevent her from leaving? So far, that had not been the case, and only his admonishment to stay put had kept her from attempting to venture out before now. Now, she wondered if she was brave enough to defy him.

Quietly, she turned the door handle, her heart pounding.

It was unlocked. But only when her stomach growled hungrily did she make a decision.

Peeking into the dark hallway, Londyn saw nothing that would prevent her from leaving the room. She chewed at her bottom lip, wincing when she belatedly remembered that it was also swollen from Oliver's kisses and nibbling bites.

Black iron sconces illuminated the corridor with low light. Holding her breath, Londyn quietly closed the door behind her and approached the stairs. Glancing over her shoulder, her eyes searched the shadowy darkness. Somewhere at the opposite end of that dark hall was Oliver's room.

What would he do if he caught her roaming through the house? What awful punishment would he devise?

Londyn paused. Contemplating that very real possibility was almost enough to send her running back to the safety of her room. But her stomach clenched again with hunger, and her lips tightened. She had not eaten since dinner the night before.

She crept down the massive staircase, anticipating Oliver Winter bearing down on her at any moment. Ready to crush any sign of bravery or rebellion. But the house remained eerily quiet. Stepping into the large great room, she could only hear the tick-tock of an enormous wall clock, its exposed gearwork steadily clicking and whirring away the seconds and minutes toward the midnight hour.

The room was empty, and Londyn hesitated, gathering her bearings as she tried to remember where the kitchen was. Maybe to the left. Yes, the left. And the front door, where Oliver ushered her in just four days ago, would be to the right.

Indecision trickled through her body. Should she even attempt to escape? Would this be the only chance she had to get away? The temptation sent a shiver down her spine, but she closed her eyes against it; her breaths shallow and ragged in the still air. What if he was waiting to pounce on her? Waiting for her to make the fatal error of thinking she could get away? The house must be under surveillance... armed with cameras in every corner. Glancing around the area where she stood, she could see no evidence of a camera system, but those things were so discreet. A criminal like Oliver was bound to have the latest technology when it came to security. There were probably cameras, all right. Several of them, and all the size of a coat button, scattered throughout the house like tiny eyes watching her.

Although her sense of survival screeched in protest, Londyn turned left. After feeling her way down another short corridor, she entered the kitchen. It looked different in the dark, the slabs of white marble gleaming starkly in the dim light cast by subtle undercabinet illumination. Opening the doors of the gigantic refrigerator, she rummaged through its contents, locating a block of expensive cheddar cheese with a few slices already conveniently cut, a bowl full of red grapes, and a bottle of Evian water. Placing the items on the large island in the center of the room, she noticed a fruit bowl and grabbed a banana and an apple.

Pulling up a barstool, she gingerly perched upon it and drank half of the water before quickly eating the cheese. Her stomach grumbled in appreciation, and she polished off the banana and the apple before starting on the grapes. Popping one into her mouth, Londyn chewed it slowly while inspecting the kitchen. A large, sleek knife block sat beside the gas stove, and for a moment, she considered arming herself.

Bad idea. Remember what happened the last time?

She squirmed uncomfortably, remembering how badly it hurt when Oliver had pushed inside with his thumb during that first punishment back in the cabin at Diamond Lake

Ranch. It was stupid to consider taking a weapon when he would undoubtedly discover the reckless theft and punish her again. The man had eyes like a hawk. He missed nothing.

Sighing, she popped another grape into her mouth and swallowed a mouthful of water. Her gaze drifted until it landed on the steel door leading to the underground room. Her pulse fluttered with frightened awareness. The things he'd done to her down in that dark, scary space could not be forgotten, no matter how hard she tried to erase the memories from her brain. Not only had Oliver used his fingers to drive her to the edge of multiple orgasms, but he'd also used his tongue and teeth. And several times, he used the length of his cock, sliding the hard shaft and the barbells up and down her clit without actually entering her pussy.

That had been the worst. Because she desperately wanted him inside her, filling the ache his hands and lips had created. The cold steel of his piercings had been slick with her arousal, easily slipping over her clit again and again until she nearly screamed with pleasure. But every time she was close to falling over into the abyss, Oliver softly chuckled and eased off from tormenting her until the impending climax waned. Then it started again, an endless cycle of arousal and denial, punctuated by interludes where he fucked her throat or masturbated over the curve of her ass.

And each time, she wanted more. More. More. More.

Frightened by her thoughts and the reality of how easily Oliver controlled her body, Londyn frowned. She tugged at the hem of the tattered and threadbare sweatshirt. It was a far cry from the thousand-dollar slip he ripped from her body, but no doubt it would tear just as easily with a tug of his fingers. The cotton was thin from multiple washings, but it was soft and comfortable, and, most importantly, it was *hers*. A memento of her former life. A token of her dreams and aspirations. A reminder of Paris and the fragile, dangerous world where her older sister would soon be alone, helpless, and unprotected.

London sniffled, dashing the tears away from her cheeks with an angry swipe of her hand. She would not cry. It did no good.

"If you are weeping over the current state of your clothing, I can't say I blame you. What the *fuck* are you wearing, dove?"

CHAPTER

TWENTY

AN ALERT SOUNDED the moment Londyn's bedroom door opened. Propping himself against the pillows, Oliver pulled up the camera system on his cell and watched as Londyn stood indecisively in the corridor. When she headed for the stairs, he immediately threw the covers back and pulled on loose pajama pants.

The cameras next picked her up as she stealthily entered the dimly lit great room. Oliver ground his teeth when she suddenly stopped, her gaze drifting to the front door. Surely, she must realize all entry points were armed by the security system, complete with fingerprint-activated locks and deadbolts to prevent anyone from coming in or leaving. If she attempted slipping past those extensive measures before he made it downstairs, he would beat her sweet little ass black and blue once he caught her.

Relief mixed with disappointment when she continued creeping along the dark space. Punishing her for an escape would have been an enjoyable way to pass the hours. It didn't mean he wouldn't take his pound of flesh from her luscious hide for this particular transgression, but she had not compounded the error by making him chase her.

He was moving down the hallway, following her footsteps as she turned toward the kitchen. Clicking on that camera revealed her opening the fridge. She rummaged through the drawers, grabbing various items. Her movements were stilted, as if turning a certain way caused pain. No doubt she suffered some discomfort after being restrained and used for hours earlier. He'd tied her up in a variety of positions, and being forced to *almost* climax over and over would certainly cause a few strained muscles and soreness.

A twinge of guilt assailed Oliver when Londyn plucked an apple and a banana from the crystal bowl on the counter, adding it to the impromptu feast. It wasn't that he had forgotten to feed her; it was that he'd been so caught up in his own desires and the need to punish her that it became an afterthought. After she passed out in the playroom, he decided it was best to let her, ignoring his body's demands that he continue using her regardless of her unconscious state. Fuck. He should have at least made sure she was staying hydrated beyond the few sips of water he allowed her while learning every inch of her body. She was already too thin for his liking. Starving her wasn't his intent.

Standing outside the open archway, Oliver waited in the shadows as Londyn ate. Her gaze roamed around the kitchen, and his hands tightened into fists when her attention landed on the expensive block of gourmet-styled knives.

If she made a move toward those... if she so much as twitched with the intent of filching a fucking butter knife, he would lock her in that cage in his playroom and keep her there for weeks.

But she did not move from her perch on the barstool. She drank the rest of the water and tugged at the hem of a ratty, white sweatshirt with the word "Vanderbilt" emblazoned across her chest in gold. Then, she started to cry, and for reasons he could not quite explain, Oliver couldn't bear it. Leaning against the doorway's thick molding, he crossed his arms.

"If you are weeping over the current state of your clothing, I can't say I blame you. What the *fuck* are you wearing, dove?"

Londyn screamed, jumping off the barstool and holding the empty water bottle over her head as if it were a wooden club before blindly chunking it in his direction. Oliver easily dodged the lightweight missile as he stepped fully into the kitchen.

"Good thing that wasn't sharp," he chuckled while moving around the island until he stood before her.

Londyn glared at him, a mixture of distrust and fear illuminating her gaze. She was breathing heavily. "What are you doing sneaking up on me?"

"Why are you roaming around my house after midnight?" Oliver countered calmly. "It's against the rules."

She swiped at her cheeks again and sniffed. "You never really told me the rules. I know where *not* to go, but everything else is as clear as mud." Her gaze skittered away from his, dropping to study the grape stems on the marble countertop. Picking one up, she twirled it between her fingertips, eyes remaining downcast as though it would prove her rebellion was a simple misunderstanding. He might have been fooled had it not been for the dislike roiling around her like a tsunami.

Oliver's lips twitched. "Maybe you're right about that. I'm still easing into the role of your owner. I should be clearer about my expectations."

Londyn did not reply, but her gaze flitted to the bandage he still wore from where she'd cut him back at the cabin in Diamond Lake Ranch.

"Look at me, Londyn." Once he had her attention, he brushed the hair out of her face to easily see her features. "You may go anywhere within the house apart from the playroom, my personal suite, and my study. This does not, however, mean you may venture outside. I forbid it unless I'm with you."

Her breathing hitched as he trailed a forefinger along her jawline, but she remained silent.

Oliver's smile was cold and hard. "Say 'thank you,' Londyn."

Her eyes flashed, her lips pressing flat into a line of disapproval. "Thank you."

"Thank you, what?" he murmured, wrapping his arms around her waist and pulling her against his body. His bare chest grazed the tips of her breasts, and she flushed with shame when they immediately hardened into tight little buds beneath the thin material of her shirt. "Thank me in a proper manner."

The look she gave him was quizzical. She had no idea what he was talking about, which almost made him laugh. This new rule was bound to piss her off. Did he care? No. Did he want to hear the word falling from her perfect, pouty lips? Abso-fuckinlutley.

"I don't..." She squirmed in the circle of his arms, but he squeezed tighter, a blatant warning that he wasn't ready to let her go.

"Sir," he supplied helpfully. "Thank you, Sir. That's what I want to hear from you. That's my new rule, Londyn. I expect to see your gratitude when I grant you mercy or show you kindness." He could almost hear her teeth grinding with frustration. "Come on, dove. Is it really that unreasonable?" Pulling her closer, he nuzzled the space below her ear, pressing a kiss there and smirking in triumph when he felt her body subtly melt in response.

"You don't really mean I—"

"Yes. I mean precisely that," Oliver interrupted, enjoying this power play between them. The push and pull. The cat and mouse. It was the most entertainment he'd had in months. Playing with her was so much fun, and although he knew it wouldn't last forever, he would relish every moment spent teasing and tormenting her. "You don't want to disappoint me, do you?"

"No," she breathed, slumping in defeat at the unspoken threat in his tone. "Thank you, Sir," she added a few seconds later, her voice small and submissive.

Oliver suspected she simply played along for her own ulterior motives. Maybe it was even a weak attempt at manipulating him, but that was okay. She would not emerge a winner in these little mind games. He was a fucking master at such things and had been taught from an early age how to crush an opponent before they even realized what was happening.

"Good girl." Keeping one arm snug around her waist, he lightly rested his free hand against her throat and stared into her wide eyes. She smelled like fresh apples. If he kissed her right then, he'd taste the tartness of the fruit on her lips. But while losing himself in a kiss with his little prisoner was tempting, he had a different agenda in mind. "Tell me why you were crying."

Londyn blinked, her brow furrowing in confusion over his concern. Her chin trembled as he waited expectantly for an answer until, finally, she gave in with a tiny sob.

"I'm worried about my sister. I'm the only person she has, and when I'm gone, there will be no one left to care for her like I do."

Oliver frowned. "I've arranged the most expert care available, dove."

"It's not the same thing!" Londyn cried bitterly. "Sure, she'll have people taking care of her basic needs, keeping her comfortable, and all that. But they won't love her like I do. Paris will be alone. And if she ever... gets better... she won't be safe. The man responsible for her condition will finish the job. He'll get rid of her to protect his reputation."

Slowly rubbing his thumb up and down her throat in a rhythmic motion, Oliver huffed. "I can't do anything about forcing the nursing staff to fall in love with her, but I can do something about the danger you think she's in. Tell me the man's name, and I will eliminate him."

Londyn froze as his words sunk in. She looked horrified by his blunt suggestion, but fuck if Oliver could understand why. It was a logical solution, and he had no qualms about following through. Killing people was something he excelled in doing. In fact, deep inside whatever was left of his twisted soul, he *wanted* to do it. If it made Londyn happy—if it provided a smidgen of comfort when the time came to face the end of her own life—he would gladly slice a man open from groin to throat.

"I-I don't want that," Londyn stuttered, her voice hoarse.

"No?" Oliver's eyes narrowed. "Why wouldn't you? It's a simple thing, really. Easy. Quick. I'll make it look like suicide if you're worried about it reflecting on your sister. Or I can make him suffer in as many gruesome ways you can imagine."

Londyn swallowed hard, her eyes filling with fresh tears. Oliver watched the motion of her throat, feeling it beneath the pad of his thumb. His dick hardened to painful extremes as he remembered how tight and warm her throat had been. How she struggled to keep swallowing him so fucking deep when he occasionally thrust past her gag reflex.

Focus, Oliver. Focus.

"You want to be there when it happens, little killer? Is that it? Maybe you'd rather be the one wielding the knife or holding the gun?" He would do that for her, too, if she wanted. He was genuinely curious about why something so simple should require second thoughts or even soul searching. Eliminating a threat was a basic rule of self-preservation. She needed to learn that lesson, and he'd help her if necessary. Because if she wanted to shoot the guy herself, he'd give her the bullets. If she planned on slitting his throat, he would hand her the knife while tilting the man's head back. And if she would rather set the man's house on fire, burning him and everything he treasured, Oliver would supply her with the matches and then fuck her in the glow of the flames. Whatever would make her happy in that situation, he would do.

She looked conflicted by the suggestion. "I thought I wanted to kill him... but now, I don't know." Her lower lip trembled, and Oliver kissed it, tugging it between his teeth until she let out a soft whimper. Of course, considering the state he'd driven her to earlier, the sexually suggestive nature of his actions would rev her body right back up until it was begging for release.

"Think about it, Londyn. If that's what you want, I'll make it happen. You can watch from the sidelines." Oliver paused, then said, "I've already killed a man for you. What's one more?"

"That was different. I-I didn't ask you to do that. I didn't know until you told me."

"If you think killing a man bothers me, rest assured that it does not. It's how I was raised. My brother and I both." Oliver spun her so her stomach was pressed against the kitchen island, and he stood behind her. She was shaking as he continued speaking in a low, husky voice, his hands gathering her mass of dark curls tumbling down her back. He held most of it in one fist, exposing the nape of her neck and pushing until she was sprawled over the island's surface. "Place your arms out flat. Do not move." She did as he ordered, her body as tight as a newly strung violin as he continued speaking.

"I grew up on violence and death, Londyn. Indoctrinated in it like it was a fucking religion," he murmured huskily, his lips brushing her skin. He could not explain why he was telling her these things, but something about her made him want to confess his sins. To come clean and sin again. "My father's number one priority, his only concern, was making sure Kingston and I knew how to kill and destroy things. We weren't allowed to get attached to people or things. It's so easy to lose them. It is far too easy for the things you love to be used as weapons against you. So, I learned not to feel. Not to care. To look after myself and my own interests no matter what."

He trailed his finger down her back, tracing her spine through the thin material until he reached the sweatshirt's hem. Sliding a hand beneath the edge of the material, he skimmed her hip with his palm before dipping his fingers into her panties.

"Does your brother feel the same?" Londyn asked in a strangled voice, her body jolting forward at his touch. But there was nowhere to go, pinned as she was against the island's marble edge.

Oliver laughed at the question. "At one time, yes. Now, not so much."

"What changed?"

"Love. Stupid fucking love changed him. But don't worry, little dove. I won't be so foolish. My father made sure of that.

My mother made sure of it, too, when she shot him between the eyes at the dinner table and then blew her own brains out in front of Kingston and me. I thought he learned a lesson from that... watching my mother kill our father... but I was wrong. It only made him more determined to break the vicious cycle." His fingers slid over her bare flesh, dipping into her swollen cunt. She moaned and rocked back against his hard dick. "I'm different from him, though. King's got a streak of decency inside him that our dad never could slice out, no matter how hard he tried. I'm more like our father, and sometimes that even scares the shit out of me."

"Why?" Londyn's choked whisper hung in the cool air.

Oliver hesitated, then, without warning, shoved two fingers inside her pussy, the damp flesh giving way to the onslaught. She cried out, an agonized sound of helpless lust that made his cock throb where it pressed against her ass. He felt her warmth even through his gray silk pajama bottoms. His little prisoner might not realize it, but she wanted him to fuck her, and soon enough, he would oblige her.

"Because I'm the fucking villain, and I will destroy what I treasure most in this world without blinking an eye." His breath stirred the air beside her ear as he took the delicate lobe between his teeth, gently biting it as he slowly and deliberately finger-fucked her. Londyn trembled, her legs nearly giving way as he expertly made her aware of her own needs and how futile it was to deny them. "I'll destroy you, too, Londyn. But I'll make sure you enjoy every second of it. I'll fuck you senseless. Use your body. Your mouth. Your cunt. Your gorgeous ass. I'll do anything I want. Everything I want. And you will beg me for all of it."

Her body tightened with his words, her legs shaking as she whimpered with the truth of his words. Untangling his hand from her hair, he gripped her throat and tilted her head toward him. "Do you want to come, little dove?" His fingers plunged in and out, driving her to the edge again. Only this time, he would allow her to fall over. The first of many climaxes she would have over the next twenty-four hours. And while he had not intended to do this so soon after their last session, circumstances demanded otherwise. "Do you want to fucking come on my fingers, my tongue, or my cock? Or better yet... how about all three?" His words were a silky promise that caused her body to involuntarily rock back against him.

"Y-yes!" Londyn gasped before his hand tightened around her neck, cutting off her air. She fought him, clawing his hands, but he squeezed harder until her motions slowed. He would choke her until she passed out if she kept fighting him, but such brutality wasn't necessary. Her body stiffened suddenly, tremors racking her form as she came so hard and so violently it drenched his fingers. The orgasm rippling through her made her compliant and weak. Oliver was surprised at how quickly it overtook her, but fuck, he loved it. He loved that his little dove liked it rough. Liked being forced. Liked being turned into his little whore.

"That's it, Londyn. That's my good fucking girl. I want that sweet little cunt soaking my fingers. This is just the first of many times you will come for me. You'll be begging for it to stop before we're done. Now, let's ensure we don't lose count, dove." Letting go of her throat, he quickly opened a drawer and pulled out a small paring knife from the selection there. Roughly shoving the sweatshirt up until the material bunched up between her shoulder blades, he slid his hand down the small of her back, where it began to curve into the roundness of her ass. Londyn was so high from the endorphins coursing through her body that she did not react when he carefully sliced a tally mark in her soft skin with the sharp edge of the blade.

Blood welled up from the single line. It wouldn't leave a permanent scar, but he'd have no trouble counting the marks he gave her for at least a few days. His dick hardened even more as Londyn remained slack against the island's surface, her breathing harsh and unsteady.

"This fucking shirt is in my way," he growled, pulling his fingers out of her pussy. "And the panties, too. From now on, I only want you to wear the things I give you. Do you understand?"

Grabbing the edge of the shirt, he was ready to slice through it when she sobbed, "No! Please...don't. My-my sister gave me this. Please... it's all I have of home."

Oliver paused, knife in hand. He itched to follow through. He wanted nothing on her body that he had not provided, but a tiny sliver of his heart responded to her anguish. Sentimentality did not usually affect him. Such emotions were beyond his comprehension, to be honest. How could someone place value on possessions or gifts? It had never made any sense to him. Cocking his head, he recalled how Kingston acted about his mother's china set. How he only used it for very special occasions and special people. The first Mrs. Allan Winter, Kingston's mother, died from a miscarriage after being horribly abused by her husband when Kingston was only three. The china was all Kingston had of hers; he guarded it over the years as though it were a priceless treasure.

Oliver had no such trinkets left to him by his own mother. Rebecca's marriage to Allan Winter was a nightmare of abuse and screaming matches, topped off with the secret seduction of her sixteen-year-old stepson. Kingston had been both a distraction and a way to obtain what she wanted. After all, it was Kingston who gave her the gun to kill their father before taking her own life. And Kingston was to blame for the twisted path Oliver careened onto in the aftermath. Only recently had he reached a level of understanding matters from his half-brother's perspective. Such retrospection was slowly opening his eyes to irrefutable facts; Kingston had suffered, too.

"Please... don't cut it," Londyn hiccupped. "I'm begging you."

"Calm down," Oliver murmured, pushing the shirt higher between her shoulder blades so it was out of his way. "I won't cut it, but these panties? Well, that's another story. I don't want you wearing any unless I give you permission." He quickly sliced through the cotton underwear, ignoring her intake of breath when he wadded up the pieces and tossed them aside. "There... that's better." He admired the thin line just above the dimples of her ass before swiping the blood away with the edge of his thumb. "I just marked you, Londyn, and you *will* keep count. Let me hear you say it. What number is this?"

"O-one," she whispered in a shaky voice. Tears fell from her thick, dark lashes. "One."

"That's right," he crooned, smoothing her hair back from her wet face. The high from the climax was waning, leaving her skin sensitive and reactive to the slightest stimulation. She was quivering all over. "And what do you say when I give you something?"

"T-thank you, Sir."

"Good girl. Now, let's get you ready for the next one. And since I'm in a generous mood, I'll let you choose if you come on my cock or my tongue."

CHAPTER

TWENTY-ONE

L *ondyn*

LONDYN'S HEAD lolled against Oliver's chest as he carried her up the stairs. To her surprise, he did not turn down the hallway toward the room he'd given her but continued striding down the corridor and around the corner until he reached a set of double doors, one of which was slightly ajar.

After pushing it open with a nudge of his foot, Oliver entered the dimly lit room. Londyn barely had the strength to lift her head to peek at the room's interior as he strode through it. She caught a quick glimpse of an enormous bed crafted of what looked to be twisted, blackened branches and sleek chrome and glass furniture. Several pieces of framed artwork decorated the walls, echoing the modernistic style she'd glimpsed in the great room before. Abstract landscapes in

166

tones of white, black, and gray. Metal etchings of wolves and horses. It was all cold, scary, yet visually striking.

She screwed her eyes shut as Oliver shouldered through another door. He flicked a switch. The room instantly flooded with light that stabbed Londyn behind her closed eyelids.

"Stand up."

Londyn obeyed as Oliver set her on her feet. Slowly opening her eyes, she gazed around the room. It was so bright that it was nearly blinding. It was decorated with glass and mountain stone, a mix of rugged surfaces, gray-veined marble, and fixtures so high-end they probably cost more than the shitty trailer she'd grown up in. A freestanding, curved tub, big enough for three or four people, sat in front of a floor-to-ceiling window. A huge, ornate crystal chandelier hung over it. Londyn swallowed hard, fighting a wave of dizziness that threatened to buckle her knees.

"Let's get you out of this."

Before she grasped his meaning, Oliver tugged the sweatshirt over her head, tossing it onto the vanity counter along with the knife he used to cut off her panties. Londyn caught a quick glimpse of herself reflected in the mirrors above the double sinks. She might have been a waif he'd found in the forest. Naked and trembling, her hair wild, and her skin pebbling with goosebumps. Crossing her arms over her chest, she quickly averted her gaze from the mirror.

Bad idea. Because Oliver had stripped off the pajama bottoms and was now as naked as her.

She couldn't look away from him. She wanted to. God, how she wanted to. But there was a silken string of fascinated horror tethering her eyes to the broadness of his chest. And his trim hips. His well-formed, muscled legs and bulging arms were encircled with barbwire. He had the physique of a Greek god. A perfectly sculpted man inked with tattoos bound to haunt her for the remainder of her short life. When her eyes drifted toward his midsection, she swayed.

Tattooed above his groin, the word SWALLOW stretched from one side of the V to the other. His cock was so hard it was nearly upright against his lower stomach, its thick length blocking out the A and both L's.

All.

He'd made her swallow all of him.

She'd blocked out the reality of what he'd done to her just a few hours ago.

The piercings...those barbells. Sliding against my pussy. Cold steel hitting my teeth. Oh, God. Down... down my throat.

Why did I let him do that? Why didn't I fight harder in the playroom? Or down in the kitchen just now?

"Stop thinking, Londyn." Oliver stepped closer, sliding his hands alongside her cheeks. He cradled her face, peering down into her wide eyes. "Stop thinking and take a deep breath for me."

Why she followed his calm instructions made no sense, but Londyn did as he commanded. The moment she exhaled, Oliver kissed her, his mouth gentle and searching on hers. When she whimpered in pain, stiffening in his arms, he kissed her with increasing pressure until she sagged against him, her hands fisting against the corded muscles of his broad chest. She was no match for his strength, much less his size and insistence. He wouldn't release her. Her body agreed with that scenario, even if she was screaming inside.

One of his hands sank into her hair, holding her still for the onslaught while his free arm slid around her waist. He kept her anchored against his tall, hard body while Londyn sank into the kiss despite the fact her mouth hurt from being used earlier in the day. Oliver groaned at her surrender, kissing her with such ferocity she wondered if he was trying to steal her soul through the crush of his lips on hers.

When he finally let her go, Londyn gasped in relief. Her eyes watered with his grip on her hair, and her skin tingled with awareness. She wanted him to kiss her harder. It scared her... this need to have his hands and mouth on her, taking whatever he wanted. She did not know why she craved it, but she did. Her hands fisted tighter with the desire to strike him. To make him pay for showing her what it meant to want with madness ruling you.

"That's enough, dove," he breathed against her mouth as she panted. "If I don't stop, I'll end up fucking you here on my bathroom floor. While I would enjoy that, I doubt you would."

He stepped away from her and approached another open door cut into a wall of mountain stone. The skull tattoo emblazoned across his back watched her with fathomless, soulless eyes as he punched the buttons of the rectangle-shaped panel set in the rock. After adjusting a few things with a stab of his finger, Londyn heard water running. It sounded like rain pouring through a hole in the ceiling.

"Come on." Oliver reached for her. He tugged her through the wall's open doorway into a vast shower designed to look like a rock grotto. There was one large rain-shower head and multiple wall jets, but the true focal point was the waterfall. The water tumbled from a wall expertly constructed to mimic the side of a mountain. It fell in a rushing curtain, splashing on the rocky outcroppings and the stone floor. It was breathtaking.

Oliver immediately pulled her into the waterfall, using his hands to slick her hair and the warm water away from her face. When he turned her to face the wall, she instinctively braced herself with hands flat against the stone. She hissed as the water washed away the blood from the tally mark, but the pounding of the waterfall was already easing much of the tension in her overused muscles. She was relaxing into the sensations, lulled by how good it felt, when he suddenly tugged her away from the feature, moving her to stand beneath the gentler rainfall of the overhead shower.

Then, for reasons Londyn could not understand, he poured shampoo into his hand and began lathering her hair, his fingers massaging her scalp and the aching tendons in her neck. A moan of pleasured distress slipped from her. She shouldn't be enjoying this so much.

"Shhhh," Oliver murmured, rinsing the suds away with capable hands. "I did a very poor job of seeing to your needs after our time in the playroom. It's important to do these things. So, let me take care of you right now, Londyn. Okay?"

Londyn nodded as he followed the shampoo with conditioner before washing her body. The body wash smelled like him, a blend of spice and oak that was intoxicating and erotic. It surrounded her, infiltrating her senses. His large hands were everywhere as he rubbed liquid into her skin, his palms slicking over her breasts and stomach, kneading her shoulders, and sliding to her hips and butt cheeks. She fought to contain the sighs of pleasure. She'd never been touched with such care and attention before. It was amazing. Wrong and confusing— but amazing, nonetheless. Had this occurred in a different life, in a different place and time, she would have melted into this man and done anything he asked.

"Fuck, you are gorgeous, Londyn. Addictive. I can't keep my goddamn hands off you."

Londyn opened her eyes. Oliver was brutally beautiful, the water sluicing down his hard body, finding and traveling along the crevices and ridges of his abdomen. His pale-blue eyes gleamed like rare topazes as he touched and explored her curves. Why was he being gentle with her now after using her without a thought for her comfort? And why had he revealed so much about himself when speaking of his childhood and the relationship with his older brother? It sounded like he'd had a traumatizing childhood, much like her own. Maybe touching her like this satisfied his unvoiced need to comfort and be comforted. Maybe he was starved for human connection, and this was the only way to fulfill it. It was very puzzling. Londyn didn't know what to think.

When he pinched her nipples between his forefinger and thumb, it proved impossible to think at all.

"Sit on the bench."

Londyn frowned, shaking off her lassitude, as Oliver pushed her toward a wide ledge carved into the stone. It was slick with water but not in the direct path of the waterfall and the rain-shower nozzle. She sank onto it, his hands gripping her shoulders while guiding her.

Gazing at him, Londyn remained motionless as he thrust a hand into her hair. He held her still, his large palm cradling her scalp as he studied her features. His cock bobbed in front of her. The piercings caught the water, beaded up on the metal, and then dripped off to land at her feet. Much like her saliva had done before.

She licked her lips, her throat tightening painfully. The memory of how he fucked her mouth with absolute ruthlessness made her thighs clench.

What was wrong with her? Why? Why did she wish he would do it all over again?

"You're sore, aren't you?" he asked softly. "But that's not what's bothering you, is it? You liked what I did to you before, and I suspect you will love what I've planned next. I think when I fuck you for the first time, you're going to come all over my cock like a good fucking girl. Isn't that right, little dove?"

Londyn bit her lip, shaking her head in denial, but she

couldn't ignore the truth his words contained. Blood roared through her veins in response to his filthy accusation, her nipples tightening into hard buds that almost hurt. Her eyes fluttered shut.

"Spread your legs for me, Londyn. Spread them wide."

She did as she was told. Oliver sank to his knees between her outstretched thighs. Hooking his muscled forearms beneath her legs, he jerked her forward until her ass was nearly hanging off the bench seat.

Londyn braced herself on her elbows, meeting his gaze over the flat plane of her stomach. The position in which he had anchored her meant *everything* was bared to him, ready to be devoured. His mouth twisted into a small grin, a lock of wet, dark hair falling over his brow as he took in the sight of her.

"You're going to come for me like this. On my tongue. As many times as I demand. Do you understand? Your cum is a goddamn aphrodisiac, dove. And I don't plan on stopping until it coats the inside of my mouth and drips down my fucking throat." Leaning forward, he ran his tongue over her bare pussy and groaned. "Jesus Christ, you taste so damned good. You are so pretty. So soft and pink. I'm going to feast until I'm fucking full of you."

"Oh, God," Londyn breathed, and Oliver's teeth flashed white as he bit the inside of her thigh, leaving another mark on the pale skin.

"Not God's name, Londyn. *My* name. And I want you to scream it."

He lowered his head, and with the slightest brush of his lips against her sensitive clit, Londyn came undone. The rapid orgasm was as shocking as it was quick. It rolled over her, leaving her mangled and gasping for air. Her channel pulsed, aching for something to fill it as her clit throbbed from the feather-light pressure of Oliver's tongue.

"Oh, Londyn. You didn't follow my instruction," he chuckled, raising his head and studying her. Although his chin was shaded by dark stubble, she could see it glistened with her juices. Her stomach clenched in embarrassment as he said in a husky voice, "I want another climax from you, and this time, I want your screams as well."

When he forced her to reach the pinnacle again, she did scream. How could she not when his mouth ravaged sensitive flesh, and two large fingers were embedded in her vagina up to his knuckles? He rubbed a spot deep inside her, and she combusted with disgusting ease, her cry a long, wobbling wail of satisfaction and a craving for more.

"Fucking hell. That's it, dove. Scream for me just like that. You are so fucking gorgeous like this. At my mercy. Coming for me. Clenching my fingers so goddamn tightly. Your pussy looks so pretty with my fingers deep inside it. *Mine*. All mine. Come for me again."

"I-I can't," she moaned, her body sinking against the rocky ledge. "Please..."

"You can, and you will," Oliver promised. He thrust his fingers in harder, his mouth latching onto her clit. When his teeth bit down on the sensitive nub, her weak scream filled the cave-like enclosure as she came so hard she blacked out.

When her eyes fluttered back open, she focused on Oliver as he pulled his tattooed fingers out of her and rose to his feet. Towering over her, he sucked those same fingers clean of her wetness, his eyes burning with lust and possessiveness as he made a show of licking the letters emblazoned on his skin. Glancing to his left, he contemplated the detachable shower nozzle while Londyn quivered at the obvious pathway of his thoughts. "Stand up and turn around. I want you on your knees. Ass in the air."

When she did not move quickly enough, he grabbed her by

the arms and yanked her upright. Spinning her, he arranged her in the position he desired, slapping her bare ass almost playfully once her chest was flat on the bench.

"Put your hands behind your back."

Londyn hesitated but quickly did what he ordered when he slapped the other side of her bottom. That one stung, but she choked back a squeal of pain and adjusted herself with the side of her face on the bench, her knees bent beneath her, and her ass high in the air. She looked like a deranged cat in heat, but Oliver's low rumble of approval told her he liked it.

"Should I tie you up like this, dove?"

She heard him detach the showerhead from its holder, and her heart pounded so hard that she thought it might explode. Oliver did not expect an answer, so she did not bother forming a response. Oliver would do whatever he pleased. If he wanted to tie her up, he would. If he wanted her hands free, he'd do that, too.

When the warm water spray hit her butt cheeks, she jolted, but Oliver gripped her hands on the small part of her back, holding her in place. "Maybe I should grab some restraints."

"I'm sorry. I-I didn't mean to move. I'll be still. I promise."

Oliver's response was to slide the shower wand between her legs from behind. The steady stream of water aimed directly at her clit. The intensity sent a moan from her chest bubbling up into her throat. It felt so good, but it was too much. Within seconds, her body tensed with another looming orgasm.

"Hold this against your cunt. Don't you dare fucking drop it or move until I say." Releasing her hands, he waited until she shoved them down the front of her body and between her legs. With her arms now trapped between the weight of her upper body and the bench, he thrust the shower nozzle head into her palms, then reached over to twist a lever on the wall-mounted holder.

The stream of water slowed to an intermittent pulse, but Londyn had no time to appreciate the slight reprieve. Oliver began slapping her ass cheeks with leisurely purpose, first one and then the other. The combination of sharp pain and pulsating heaven quickly drove her back to the edge, and she sobbed. How many more of these intense orgasms could her body take?

"You're going to come again for me, but before you do, tell me—how many does this make so far?"

Londyn's body shook. She could not think, not with the water beating against her clit and his large hand cracking against her ass.

"Th-three," she stuttered, her legs trembling uncontrollably.

"Wrong." One hand slapped her ass harder, while two long, hard fingers on his other hand slammed into her pussy, stretching her as he spanked her. "It's four, counting the one in the kitchen. And you're about to give me number five," he chuckled as she gasped, her body bowing up tight. "Look at you, little dove. Fucking my fingers like a good little whore. I don't know which is prettier: My hand wrapped around your throat or your pussy sucking my fingers in deeper. I should fuck you right now since you won't fight back. Maybe I will. Would you like that? My cock ripping you into pieces while you're coming all over it?"

She exploded before he finished talking, her pussy clenched on his fingers as the pulsing of the shower nozzle pushed her into a world of darkness. The climax seemed to come from everywhere, sending her flying into a hazy subspace where she simply floated. The roaring in her ears faded, leaving everything quiet and still. All that remained was the pleasurable waves undulating through her and pinpoint lights drifting across the darkness in a waterfall of sparks.

She was no longer in the shower with her tormentor. She was soaring somewhere in the clouds and hurtling into blackness, far above heartache, pain, and pleasure. She might have screamed, or maybe she was sobbing. She didn't know. She didn't care.

She was slipping away, and it didn't matter.

TWENTY-TWO

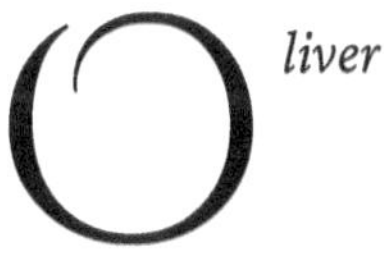 *liver*

OLIVER TURNED the water off and scooped Londyn up from the shower bench.

He carried her out of the shower enclosure, grabbing a couple of towels off the nearby rack as he entered the bedroom. When he'd placed her on the bed, he dried her off, then snatched up a blanket from the bench at the foot of the bed.

As he wrapped it around her shaking body, Londyn stared ahead as if in a daze, her eyes unfocused. Her entire body quivered from an overload of sensations, the tremors rippling through her like invisible shock waves.

Oliver swore under his breath, tucking the extra towel around his waist. He'd pushed her too far. It was too much—the orgasms too quick in succession and too intense. *Fuck.* He loved seeing her this way, but he should have considered her lack of experience. Should have weighed it against the intensity of everything he'd previously done to her in the playroom. She wasn't ready for this, and he was a selfish bastard for forcing it upon her. His next step should be providing true aftercare for her.

The housekeeper had fully stocked the kitchen before his arrival, which meant his favorite chocolate was in the fridge. A few pieces would ensure Londyn did not crash after she emerged from the subspace he'd driven her to. She needed to be kept warm as well. Oliver tucked the blanket tighter around her shoulders, then passed a hand over her tousled, wet hair.

He was still aroused, having focused all his attention on Londyn while they were in the shower. His plan had been to make her come several times while he jacked himself off, but when she slumped forward in a boneless heap, something inside him snapped.

But why?

Why did he care? This was what he wanted, right? Londyn at his mercy. A toy to play with. An object existing solely for his amusement and to endure anything he wanted. Her feelings, her pain, or even pleasure... none of it mattered. She was there because he paid good money for her. Any inclination to show sympathy or administer care other than the absolute minimum must be squashed.

Oliver ducked into the bathroom, retrieving the knife from the countertop. When he stalked back to the bedroom, he saw Londyn had not moved from where he placed her. She was still in a fog. Good. She probably wouldn't feel a thing.

Oliver carefully pulled the blanket away from her body before pushing her back against the bedcovers. From there, he rolled her onto her stomach.

Londyn did not resist his arranging her like an inanimate

doll. Even when he sliced her skin with a series of superficial tally marks, she didn't flinch.

Wiping the blood away with the towel used to dry her, Oliver stared at the smooth, creamy skin of Londyn's lower back. The five straight lines did something unexpected to his insides. Something that felt suspiciously like shame even while his cock thumped so hard it was painful.

God, how he wanted to fuck her. It was a raging need inside him, vying with the urge to take care of her, too. A strange contradiction. One that left him desperate to grant her the sharp bite of pain while also soothing it with overwhelming pleasure.

The warring principles pissed Oliver off. He contemplated fulfilling his base urges when she mumbled something and tried rolling onto her back.

"Don't."

The single-word command stopped her. She froze, still on her stomach, damp, thick hair tumbling down her back. It was so pretty, like a mass of dark ink spilling across a cream canvas. Oliver wanted to grab handfuls of it. Let it sift through his fingers like reams of silk and bury his face in the fragrant waves. Instead, he raked his fingers through it, separating it into three sections. He braided her hair into a single, thick plait with quick, efficient motions. Then he ripped a string from one of the blanket's tassels, tying off the braid to secure it.

"Stay where you are, Londyn. Don't fucking move a muscle unless I say so."

A tiny whimper indicated she understood the growled order. Before leaving her, Oliver again swiped fresh droplets of blood from her back with the ruined towel. He traced the wounds with the pad of his thumb. Fucking hell, seeing her marked like this made his cock rock hard.

He planned on giving her more of those lines; only these

orgasms would happen while his dick was buried deep in her virgin cunt. A muscle ticked in his jaw as he covered her with the blanket. She would bleed for him, and he would enjoy every second of it.

And if she expected mercy from the Devil, she would be very disappointed.

WHEN OLIVER RETURNED from the kitchen, he discovered Londyn had obeyed him. She lay on her belly, face turned toward the headboard, and her cheek pressed to the coverlet. She was so still, so silent, that for a second, he worried he might have pushed her past the point of no return.

But then her legs shifted slightly, and he huffed a sigh of relief. Sitting on the bed, he spread out the items he'd gathered, then pulled the blanket off her. He slid an arm beneath her stomach and tugged her upright so that she leaned against him for support.

"Londyn," he said softly, watching her gray eyes grow less hazy with every passing second. "I want you to eat this for me. Open your mouth."

Her brow creased with a frown as she obediently closed her lips around the small bar of mint chocolate. It wasn't fancy or gourmet. Hell, it wasn't even very good chocolate. Hotels routinely used candy for turn-down service, but it had been his favorite since childhood. On the rare occasions he had traveled with his parents, his mother always ensured he got the little treats on his pillow. It was one of a few positive memories he'd retained.

After she swallowed the chocolate, Oliver held an open bottle of water to her lips, waiting patiently until she drank her fill. Pinching her chin between his thumb and forefinger, he tilted her head and stared into her eyes. The gray depths were less unfocused now, but her eyelids drooped heavily. Her small body was succumbing to exhaustion, instinctively curling into him and seeking warmth.

Oliver hesitated before chucking the towel still tucked around his waist. Pulling the covers back with one hand while keeping his free arm wrapped around Londyn, he maneuvered her beneath the cool silk sheets. Settling beside her, he propped himself up against the mound of pillows and dragged her closer. She resisted at first, but his hold was unyielding until she gave up, sagging weakly against him.

"I can't sleep here," Londyn murmured, her long, thick eyelashes fluttering closed.

"I want you to. For a little while, it's okay."

"But only for a little while?" she questioned as his arm tightened around her.

"It isn't safe," he admitted begrudgingly. "I might hurt you in my sleep, and that's a problem."

Londyn made a little sound in the back of her throat. "Why?"

Oliver's mouth tipped upward in a smile. "Because I want to be awake and in full control of my faculties when I hurt you."

"That's not what I meant," Londyn grumbled, tilting her head so she could study him. "Why would you hurt me in your sleep?"

He was silent for a moment, then bit out, "I have nightmares."

She lowered her head once more before whispering, "What kind of nightmares?"

Oliver picked up the braid he'd woven her hair into, winding it around his wrist. The idea of anchoring her to him was appealing. *Or you to her...* something inside him slyly suggested. "The kind that doesn't end well for women who spend the night in my bed."

Londyn huffed out a breath of exasperation. "I have them, too. Everyone does at some point. Tell me about yours. It might help if you talk about them."

His laughter was cruel. "Trying to psychoanalyze me, little killer? Won't work. Besides, I guarantee the things haunting me are far more violent and depraved than anything you can imagine or have experienced."

She shrugged. "What would it hurt? It's not like I'll tell your secrets to anyone. Once you're done with me, anything you say goes with me to my grave."

Oliver did not respond. Being reminded of the day he would end her life did not sit well with him, especially when her soft body was warm and pliant beside him.

"I woke up once with my hands around a woman's throat," he said slowly after several minutes of silence.

Londyn snuggled closer, her voice sleepy. "That doesn't seem out of character for you, to be honest."

"Her face was already turning blue. My hands were scratched from her nails. I don't even know why I woke up when I did. It wasn't the first time something like that happened, but a few seconds more, and she would have been dead." His voice turned husky. "I was dreaming... reliving an incident with my father. A flashback to the first time I hurt a woman. He told me what to do, but first, I had to watch him and my half-brother so I wouldn't fuck it up. Kingston hated it as much as I did but telling my dad 'no' wasn't an option. I wanted to kill him for making me make her scream. "

"Your dad was not a nice man."

Oliver chuckled at her naivety. "He was a fucking monster. Evil incarnate. An abuser. A cold-blooded murderer. And he passed all those wonderful attributes onto his children. He killed Kingston's mother. Well, kill is too mild a word for what he did. He fucked her to death and left her to bleed out from a miscarriage when he was done with her. A few years later, he married my mom. After she had me, it only got worse. And when he found out that his firstborn was fucking his stepmother, that's when the crazy really got out of hand."

"How old were you when that happened?" Londyn prodded gently.

"Old enough," Oliver replied cryptically. He wasn't sure why he was spewing this out to her, but what she said was true. Whatever bullshit he got off his chest in this moment would go no further than this room. Londyn was right about one thing. She would carry this pathetic confession straight to her grave. "I was ten when Kingston started sleeping with her and twelve when she killed our father and herself at the dinner table."

"You saw that?" A sound of distress escaped her. "That must have been so traumatic to see at such a young age."

Oliver stared at the vaulted wood-beamed ceiling overhead. No matter how long he lived, he'd never be able to unsee the gaping hole in his father's head, nor the pieces of tissue that discolored the dining-room wall behind his mother's chair. "That's an understatement. And overshadowed by the fact my brother was the one who gave her the gun. I hated Kingston so much for that. Hated him because he promised to protect me, and he failed. Hated him because he loved my mother. Hated him because his adoration wasn't enough for her. She used us both in different ways to escape our father. I was the one left behind with the pieces." He sighed heavily. "But I think I hated my father more because he made me just like him. Hard. Cruel. Sadistic."

"Would you say your nightmares," Londyn swallowed

hard, "are a result of your mother murdering your father and committing suicide in front of you?"

"I'd say they are a direct result of being tutored on torturing and raping women, murdering and disposing of his enemies while my father directed me on the most efficient methods to serve him." Oliver's jaw tightened at how easy it was to share these painful memories with Londyn. Somehow, he felt lighter. Less burdened. Which was almost comical, considering how fucked-up he truly was. Telling her his secrets shouldn't leave him feeling cleansed. He was his father's son in all ways, and confessing these sins to an innocent and naive girl would not bring absolution.

"Did you... did you love your mother?" Londyn asked softly.

Oliver was silent for a moment, then gruffly replied, "I'm sure at some point I did, but I'd say the answer to that is no. Did you love yours?"

"Sometimes, I did. I felt sorry for her more than anything. She had an abusive childhood and never learned to trust anyone. She didn't know how to love. How to be caring. It would have been better if she'd never had children, although sometimes, it seemed like she was truly trying to do what she thought was best. I think our mothers were likely very much the same. Scared. Overwhelmed. And betrayed by others. I dream about her sometimes." Londyn's voice was growing faint, exhaustion catching up to her. "She kisses my forehead like I'm a little girl and tells me she's sorry. And I hug her back... then the dream goes black and I'm alone again. Do you ever dream about your mom?"

"I don't want to talk about this anymore." He knew his tone was cruel. He meant it to be because she was bringing feelings and memories to the surface that he had suffocated a long time ago. "Go to sleep, Londyn. Get some rest before we start again. I plan on fucking you until I don't remember my nightmares. For one night, at least. Maybe you'll find a reprieve from yours."

Londyn stiffened, but her body was succumbing to everything he had already done. Slumping against him, her voice was drowsy and full of regret as she said, "Some may be scarier than others, but everyone has nightmares, Oliver. Now, you are one of mine and will be for a long time after this."

CHAPTER

TWENTY-THREE

L*ondyn*

LONDYN CAME AWAKE IN STAGES.

LONDYN CAME AWAKE IN STAGES.

When her eyes fluttered open, the room was dimly lit, the early-morning sunlight filtered by automatic blinds tilted just enough to provide illumination. Stretching her legs, she moaned softly as the muscles protested.

Turning her head on the pillow, she rolled to her side, her breath catching as she came face to face with the sleeping visage of her captor.

Thick, dark eyelashes cast shadows on his upper cheeks; his lips parted slightly as he murmured something in his sleep. With his brow unfurrowed and mouth not twisted into his customary cynical grin, Londyn could appreciate his masculine beauty. He might have been a male model in another life with his diamond-sharp jawline and high cheekbones. She was breathless just staring at his face, and when her gaze drifted down, skimming over the broad shoulders and chest, she wondered how something so outwardly gorgeous could conceal such wickedness.

The sheets twisted about his waist so low on his trim hips that the letters tattooed above his groin were almost completely visible. Londyn swallowed against the lump in her throat, remembering how she'd stared at those letters as he thrust repeatedly into her mouth.

It wasn't fair that he should look like this and still possess the soul of a heartless monster. It wasn't fair that after everything he'd done, her pussy was wet for him even now.

In his own way, he took care of me last night. Why? And why did he open up to me like he did? Why tell me about his parents and his brother? Why tell me about his nightmares unless there is something inside him searching for forgiveness?

Oliver had purchased her nearly two weeks ago and had yet to fully possess what he paid millions for. Why was he waiting? What did he hope to accomplish by drawing it out? They both knew he could force her to do whatever he wanted, and he would, eventually. There seemed to be no logic for dragging out the torture. Did he think she would be more easily controlled once he proved how much her body craved being used and dominated?

A whimper escaped her. The truth left her stomach in knots. If this man was a monster, what did that make her?

"You're thinking too hard, dove. I can hear your thoughts without you saying them."

Londyn gasped, her gaze flying back up to scan his face. With his eyes closed, the corners of his mouth were tilted in a smirk. Before she could scurry away, Oliver settled deeper into the pillows, one arm tucked beneath his head while the other curved around her waist. He hauled her closer, snuggling his face into the hollow between her neck and shoulder. She suddenly realized she was as naked as he was. Every inch of his body was branding hers, burning her skin and leaving every nerve ending she had raw and tingling with hyper-awareness.

Breathing deep, Oliver rumbled his contentment while lightly nipping her tender skin.

"Fuck, you taste good." Tilting his head back just enough to gaze at her, his eyes gleamed like rare, blue topazes in the morning's golden light. "And congratulations are in order, I suppose."

"For what?" Londyn choked out. Oliver held her so close, so tight, there was no mistaking his erection prodding her belly. The way her insides melted was infuriating and terrifying. If her mouth and throat were sore from the size of his cock and all those piercings, she could only imagine what he would do to more vulnerable areas.

"You survived the night in my bed," he laughed softly. "Guess that's a sign we're meant to be." Taunting further, he pressed a tender kiss to her open mouth, his lips brushing over hers, teasing.

Londyn said nothing as he kissed her gently but with increasing pressure and intensity. When his tongue delved into her mouth, stroking hers, a helpless moan fluttered in her chest. She could not stop her thighs from clenching, her pussy aching with immediate lust for him. She was becoming a creature she did not recognize. A woman desperate for physical contact. Hungry for affection and attention. And even if it came with strings attached, such as her eventual demise, she could not deny how alive she felt with his hands on her.

"So, what were you thinking about just now? You looked... distressed... is the best way to describe it," Oliver murmured between long, deep kisses Londyn was sure were designed to scramble her mind.

"Nothing. I-I wasn't thinking about anything."

He laughed at the blatant lie. "Someone is looking for a punishment this morning. I don't like when you lie to me."

The way her insides clenched, her channel getting wetter with his threat, was the stuff of nightmares. She couldn't even cry out in protest. Not with his mouth moving over hers, his tongue diving and searching out all her secrets.

"Tell me, little dove. What nightmares keep you awake at night? Hmm? Tell me. I really want to know. Is it because your body responds to me?" His hand slid from her waist to her butt cheek. Squeezing one rounded globe, he chuckled when she gasped into his mouth. "Is it how your cunt is so wet, I can feel it soaking into my skin? Or is it the way your nipples are hard and begging for my mouth? Are those the nightmares you suffer from?"

Dipping his head, he took the tip of one breast into the burning heat of his mouth, his teeth gripping her nipple so that his tongue could flick it. When her hands clutched his hair, trying to dislodge him, Oliver moved his arm from beneath the pillows and anchored both her wrists in his hand. Jerking them above her head, he held her in place as he continued tasting her.

"Be still, dove. Or I'll have to tie you down." Sharp teeth nipped tender flesh, and Londyn whimpered. It felt so good that her head was spinning.

"I'm waiting for your answer. I told you my secrets last night. Now, I want to hear yours." His mouth moved to her other breast, rolling the nipple between his teeth. Then he laved it with his tongue, soothing the sting. "Nightmares, Londyn. Tell me what scares you. Tell me what you've suffered. Tell me *everything*."

Londyn shook her head, lips tight with stubborn denial.

"Aww, don't be like that," he chuckled. "Don't you want to share like I did last night?"

"So you can use it against me?" she bristled.

Oliver's head lifted, his eyes boring into hers, his jaw set with determination. "Isn't that what you plan to do? Use my words against me? Exploit any weakness I might have?"

Londyn looked away from the accusation in his eyes. "I wanted to help you."

His hands tightened around her wrists. "And you did. After all, you're still alive, aren't you? I didn't kill you in your sleep, and now"—his hips shifted so that she could feel his cock against the side of her thigh— "tell me about your nightmares so I can fuck you."

Londyn trembled as Oliver pushed her onto her back. Rolling on top of her, he easily spread her legs using the width of his body. She tried bucking him off, but it was impossible. He was so much bigger. So much stronger. Tears pricked her eyes as her worst fears became reality. Whatever this man wanted to do, he would succeed. Her brain, her looks, not even her education in understanding the sociopathic mind would stop this. A helpless sob escaped her as he hovered over her, his gaze searching hers.

"You told me you entered that auction because you needed to take care of your sister the way she took care of you. You said she protected you," Oliver murmured. He still held her hands above her head, the way he regarded her almost tender.

"Paris shielded me many times from danger when we were growing up." Londyn's throat closed with the admission of Paris's sacrifices. Whenever one of their mother's numerous boyfriends began showing too much attention toward her, Paris always found a way to gain their interest. How often had Londyn been awakened by Paris slipping out of the room, her hand held tightly by whatever man was living with them?

Hours would pass before her sister would crawl from under the smothering weight of the covers. Cheeks wet with tears, Paris's hand would find Londyn's. Squeezing it, she conveyed without words that they were safe for the time being. And when some men proved more persistent than others, the two sisters would hide in the woods surrounding the trailer park.

"Go on. Tell me more. I want to know just what frightens you. I want to know what chases you when you close your eyes," Oliver said. "I know my demons, Londyn. I fight them every night. Do you know yours? Are you brave enough to say them out loud?"

Londyn's chin rose at the challenge.

"I have nightmares of being buried alive. It's awful. Terrifying. I can't breathe. Can't move. It's pitch black, and things move around me. But I must be still. I can't make a sound because if I do, the monster will find me."

Londyn closed her eyes, suffocated by memories. Those moments waiting for her sister to return were dark and heavy. In her mind, burrowing beneath the covers to escape the boogie man was the same as being buried alive. It wasn't that she was afraid of enclosed spaces. And she certainly wasn't scared of the dark. But thoughts of being smothered, of not being able to see the danger, had imparted claustrophobic fear she could never fully overcome.

"My mom... our mom was an alcoholic. Drank every day. Couldn't hold down a job for long. She would disappear for days and then show up with a new boyfriend. Sometimes, they were nice. Most of them were not. Paris would... She made sure I was never abused in the same way she was. I would take a beating here and there, but I never went through what she did. She took the brunt of it all, and later, when Mom was dying, Paris worked two jobs to pay the bills and keep a roof over our heads. I was a senior in high school. She gave up her own hopes and dreams so I could go to college. She stayed behind and took care of our mom. I owe her my life. Whatever is left of it, anyway."

"These men you mentioned... What are their names?"

Oliver's tone was darker than any other time he'd ever spoken to her. It was the voice of a killer. A reaper of souls. Londyn shivered, wondering how many men had heard him speak before taking their last breath.

"I was young. There were so many over the years that I can hardly recall first names. My mom collected men as a hobby. None of them ever lasted long enough to become a permanent part of our lives. Why would you want their names, anyway? It's not as if they'll ever be held accountable for what they did to us."

"I want names so I can track each one down and put a bullet between their eyes. Consider it another aspect of your sister's care. I'll do the same for that fucking sheriff if you tell me he abused or threatened you, too. And I don't care if it happened before I bought you or after. Any man who dares touch what is mine... who dares to touch you... I will slit his fucking throat and make him drink his own blood."

Oliver kissed her with such savagery that it took her breath away. Londyn was shaking from her confession and the intensity of his kiss when he stripped the covers away, baring their bodies to the cool air. Releasing her hands, he slid down her body, his mouth worshipping the fullness of her breasts, the smooth flesh of her stomach, and the soft curves of her hips. Reaching her pussy, his fingers spread her wide so he could see just how wet she was. Londyn flushed with shame.

How could she find any of this exciting or pleasurable? She had no say in what would happen. No voice. No rights. The fact she was sinking into his possessiveness was horrifying.

"Please..." She did not even know what she was begging

for. Did she want him to stop? Or was it a plea that he continue doing whatever he wanted with her?

Oliver grinned as her hands clutched his shoulders. "I like the sound of you begging, dove. As long as it's for me to keep going. Anything else, and I'm afraid I'll have to gag that pretty mouth." Rising to his knees, he gripped her hands again, holding them against the ridged muscles of his abdomen. "I don't like being touched when I'm fucking a woman, but for you, I might make an exception. But leaving your hands free will bother you a hell of a lot more than if I tie you up. Do you know why? Because being restrained makes you the victim. You can fight and scream. Tell yourself you did everything to get away. But it won't hide the truth that you are dripping for me, will it? When I shove my cock into you, your body will welcome me. When I fuck you without mercy, *you'll* welcome the pain and the humiliation of knowing you want this as much as me."

He released her wrists, watching as they slowly fell to her sides. They stared at each other as Londyn's chest rose with panicked breaths. She refused to look at the part of him straining toward her center. She could not admit that everything he said was true. She ached for him. Even after the multiple orgasms he'd forced on her, she wanted more. It was like she was addicted to him.

Oliver's smile was sly when she remained silent. "I'm giving you a choice, Londyn. I can gag you, strap you down with that sweet little ass sticking up so you can't fight back, or you can accept the fact that this is happening and submit to me. Either way, I am going to fuck you." He trailed his knuckles down the valley between her breasts, his eyes darkening when Londyn's nipples hardened into aching peaks. "Now that I've discovered you like a bit of pain, I know you will enjoy it. No matter which scenario you choose." His head tilted, his eyes roaming over her body. The heat from his body increased by the second, and the tension rose until the air snapped with electricity.

Londyn was shaking. The logical choice was to demand that her hands remain free, but that's not what her body wanted. Her body was screaming for restraints and a gag. It wanted to be dominated and used. It wanted to be at this evil man's mercy. It wanted her mind to shut down and just... accept it. And if she did, if she surrendered completely, there would be no decision to make. No right or wrong choice. There would only be submission and acceptance. Nothing else would matter. Her life would be held in this man's iron-tight grip. She would have no say as to her fate.

"Time's up, dove. What's it gonna be?"

CHAPTER

TWENTY-FOUR

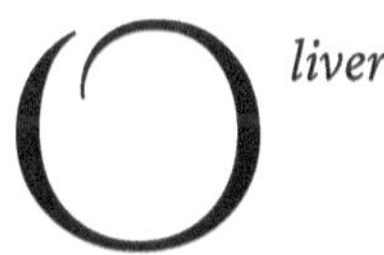*liver*

"Please don't restrain me."

Her voice trembled, but she glared at him without submission or fear. The look in her eyes was almost challenging. Oliver sat back on his haunches, pulling her knees until they were bent and framing his body. He gripped one of them, his fingers digging into her skin while he palmed his cock. "You don't want to be tied up? Don't you think I'll do it anyway if that's what I want?"

"Then why even ask me?" Londyn shot back.

Oliver smiled. "I like giving you choices. You see, it's how I learn what makes you tick, Londyn. You give me little tidbits of information every time." He stroked his massive length, passing his thumb over the barbells and smearing precum across the mushroom-shaped head. When Londyn's gaze

195

dropped to his hand, he nearly groaned. He knew how large he was, and he knew she was panicking over how he would fit inside her. God, he couldn't wait to show her.

Her eyes lifted, the gray depths now the color of steel as they locked with his. "Maybe I'm using reverse psychology on you. Have you considered that? That I might be playing *you*?"

A huff of a laugh escaped Oliver. "Are you so sure I haven't already accounted for that? I grew up surrounded by criminals. Rubbed shoulders with the worst this world has to offer. Safe to say, I've learned a thing or two about human nature and how to manipulate and control a person. You might have the schooling and all the smarts, but I have real-world experience."

"Tie me up then," Londyn snarled. "Force me to submit like the animal you are."

"But that would give you exactly what you want, dove."

Tears filled her eyes with his quiet assertion, her gaze moving to his midsection and the wound that was now hardly a scratch.

"Don't worry, little killer. It's healed."

"Don't call me that." Her face flushed, full of shame. "I-I didn't mean to kill him. I told you that. It-it was an accident."

"Oh, baby," he murmured. "Do you think it bothers me that you killed a man? It doesn't. In fact, I would have loved to have seen it. Mostly, I'm glad you did it. Because your actions saved this sweet, virginal cunt for me." He accelerated the stroking of his cock, knowing that even against her will, her gaze zeroed in on the movement of his hand, fascinated. "And when you cut me? You have no idea how goddamn hard it made me. I wanted to fuck you right then and there while my blood dripped over your body. But I knew I couldn't. I couldn't because I realized that I couldn't control myself. I knew if I did what I wanted, it would destroy you, and that's the last thing I want. Even someone like me knows when to exercise some restraint. But understand this. I would have fucked you until you took your last breath with my cock buried inside you. And I would have enjoyed every second of it."

"I wish you would have," she whispered. "Then this would all be over."

Oliver released his cock, sliding his fingers over her wet center and smearing his precum there until the moisture was a combination of the two of them. He loved how wet she was, how she fought it. How she hated and feared him, and yet her body responded to his touch. It was a heady sense of power, knowing he held this much control over her. "This won't end soon, Londyn. You can count on that."

Londyn whimpered. Whether the involuntary sound was a result of his resolute statement or the fact his fingers caressed her so thoroughly, Oliver wasn't sure. His thumb found her clitoris, and he began circling mercilessly. Her eyes fluttered shut.

"You promised… you promised you would kill me quickly." Londyn's hips arched upward, seeking more while Oliver allowed himself a triumphant smile.

"And I will. When the time comes. But, sweet little dove, I plan on keeping you for a long time."

He thrust his index finger inside her, crooking it until he could press it against her G-spot while maintaining the pressure on her clit. When she came in a glorious rush, and her cries echoed throughout the bedroom, he swiftly replaced his finger with the head of his cock and pushed his way inside.

Her pussy latched onto his dick, instinctively fighting his invasion. Letting out a panicked gasp, Londyn tried dislodging him by desperately pushing his midriff. Her fingers scrabbled against the muscled planks of his stomach, unable to find anything to grab in the smooth tautness of his body.

Oliver responded by clamping his hand around her throat,

holding her in place as his other hand remained on her knee, pushing it so her legs were spread wide.

"Fuck, you feel amazing. Let me all the way in, like a good girl," Oliver groaned, pushing even further until the first barbell was inside her snug channel.

The scream that fell from her lips was a breathless, strangled sound. Her hands grabbed his forearms, her nails digging into his skin. It only heightened Oliver's sensations. He laughed helplessly as the fire inside him burned higher and more intensely. He thrust a little more, feeling her flesh give way as she trembled and clutched at his cock. When he looked down at the junction of their bodies, he saw that he was embedded almost to the second barbell. The sheer fucking pleasure of it was making him lightheaded.

"You're doing so well for me, dove. Such a good fucking girl," he panted. Somehow, he restrained himself from plunging in to the hilt, but it was hell. "Just a bit more... breathe for me, Londyn. That's it. Just like that. Only eight or so inches and five barbells more to go."

She began thrashing, her movements so frantic that Oliver could only do one thing to keep her from getting hurt. Tightening his hand around her throat, he restricted her breath just enough until every molecule of her attention focused on him. She stared at him, wild-eyed and shaking, tears tracking down her flawless cheeks. Her lips parted, trying to draw a proper breath beneath the shackle of his fingers.

"Fighting me only makes it worse, Londyn. Relax for me, and I promise I'll make it feel good," he murmured, surging forward with every word. "You're so fucking wet for me; your cunt is strangling my cock. And I know it's painful, but your body has already accepted this." His gaze softened as he watched her trembling, and something that might have been tenderness fluttered in his stomach. "Do you want me to make you feel good, Londyn? Do you want me to make you come again?"

Her soaked pussy reacted by squeezing his dick tighter. She whimpered, her eyes closing in shame as she nodded.

"Eyes on me, dove. I want your words."

Her wet eyelashes were dark spikes as her eyes fluttered open. For a long moment, they stared at each other before she choked out in a whisper, "Yes, Sir."

Oliver groaned. "Yes, what?" She would be the death of him, eventually. That sultry mix of innocence and sex was natural to her. God help him if she ever learned to use it to her advantage. He wouldn't stand a chance.

"Yes, please make me come," she mumbled as his fingers loosened enough to allow her to speak. "It hurts so bad... It feels like you are tearing my insides apart. You're too big... It hurts too much."

"Oh, baby," Oliver crooned. "It will only hurt like this once. After this, there will be only pleasure when I fuck you. So, dig your nails into me. Scratch me all you want. Hell, you can bite me, too, if that's what you feel like. I'm going to make you come, and you will scream like I promised."

She stared mutely up at him, her nails impaling his fore-arms until little blood-filled divots appeared. Oliver leaned forward, taking her mouth with his, kissing her deeply as he rubbed her clit. Each time she moaned, his cock slid inside her, inch by inch, until he reached the unmistakable tight barrier of her virginity. He hesitated in moving any deeper, concentrating on driving her to a toe-curling orgasm even while his cock breached her defenses. When he felt her muscles tighten, when her pussy clamped tighter, and the walls began pulsing around him, Oliver abruptly canted his hips, shoving the rest of the way inside. Tearing through the thin membrane, he swallowed her scream and began moving in a rocking motion until she arched against him.

"That's it, baby. There you are, my sweet, sweet girl." Moving his hand back to her throat, he squeezed lightly as she moaned again, the vibration tickling his fingers. His hips snapped in a rhythmic fashion, grinding her clit until her hands gripped his arms tighter.

But she no longer pushed him away.

She pulled him closer.

CHAPTER

TWENTY-FIVE

L *ondyn*

"GODDAMN, Londyn. You are so fucking beautiful like this. Twitching around my cock, struggling to breathe with my hand around your throat," Oliver said in his cruel, casual way. With each slow, deliberate thrust, he made sure she felt his piercings, the cold bars quickly heating until they matched her warmth.

His words set her on fire. Everything about this... her captivity... his dominance... her surrender to her own dark desires was wrong and confusing. She shouldn't want any of this. But she did. And while she burned under his possession, Oliver continued stoking the flames, fucking her until the pain and intensity of her stretching to accept him became secondary to what her body demanded.

"I can feel you coming on my cock, dove. Your pussy is contracting around me, little flutters that vibrate my piercings. It's fucking amazing." Bracing himself on one arm, Oliver kept his hand around her throat. It was a simple act of dominance and not intended to make her lose consciousness, although Londyn knew that could change without warning. Her body responded in the most humiliating way, soaking his cock and pulsing desperately.

"Will you come again for me?" His sly inquiry was accompanied by his hips pumping in a series of shallow movements that seemed designed to drive her crazy. Oliver huffed out a laugh, burying himself until he could go no further before withdrawing enough to glance down between their bodies. "My dick is coated with your blood and your cum. I want more of it."

Londyn's weak, strangled whimper of greedy acceptance amused him. A dark angelic grin curved his lips.

"You looked gorgeous choking on my dick in the basement. Every time I shoved myself down your throat, it made you wet. Maybe wetter than you are now with my cock buried in this tight pussy. Should we try that again and see if I'm right? Or should I keep fucking you like this until you pass out?"

Oh, God. Remembering what he had done to her in the basement made Londyn convulse in a mixture of desire and absolute terror.

"It scares you, doesn't it? Thinking about all the ways I'll use you. It frightens you, but you're getting off on it, too. I can tell because you squeeze my cock so tightly when you are scared." Oliver released her throat.

She drew a quick breath before he slid his hand into her hair and gripped the nape of her neck. Tilting her head back, he stared into her wide eyes as he glided in and out of her. "I think I should chase you through the woods again." His voice was raspy with lust. "I should let you believe there's hope of escape. I'll wear a mask again. Only this time when I catch you, I'll fuck you in the dirt while you scream and try to get away. Ahhh," he laughed suddenly, "your pussy likes that idea. It's fucking strangling me. I can't hold it off any longer. Let me feel you coming on my cock, Londyn, while I come inside you."

His movements became more erratic, more forceful, and uncontrolled. Letting out a low growl, his body tensed as he thrust harder, deeper inside her, and Londyn responded as he commanded.

The room dimmed, stars exploding behind her eyes as an overwhelming climax swept through her. She screamed in pleasure, crying out as Oliver slammed into her one last time. The barbells that studded his cock dragged over every sensitive nerve ending inside her, hitting spots she never knew existed until it all exploded in a dizzying avalanche of sensations; a final climax riding the tails of the last one with no break in between.

"You'll be the death of me, Londyn. Take every inch and every drop. Take it all." Oliver's mouth slammed onto hers.

Londyn could not breathe. She could only shake and submit to the darkness as he shuddered with the force of his orgasm. Her body melted around him as the hot heat of his cum filled her. And she could do nothing to stop it. She wasn't even sure she wanted to. It was a strange sense of belonging that overcame her as he pumped into her. She reveled in the security of his embrace even though she knew it wasn't real. Because nothing with this man at its center could ever be the truth. Everything was a lie. A smokescreen. A mirage.

That feeling of being safe with Oliver Winter? It was a dangerous illusion and trusting it would be her downfall.

SHE MUST HAVE BLACKED OUT.

When she came to, groggy and disoriented, she discovered Oliver still looming over her, his body shaking as he came down from his climax. Their heavy breaths filled the room while beyond the sleek glass doors leading to an expansive balcony, birds twittered and sang in the early-morning sunshine. It was such an odd thing. Outside this room, the world continued revolving as if nothing had happened. The fact she'd just surrendered her soul and virginity to the Devil was inconsequential to everyone but her.

"Fuck me," he muttered. "That was worth every penny." He eased out of her, smiling when he saw the evidence of their mutual orgasms mingled with her blood. Rearing back on his haunches, he grabbed a section of the sheets and leisurely wiped himself off before doing the same to her swollen sex. He noted the way she flinched, and surprisingly, when he passed the silk over her a second time, his touch was gentle but sure. "Next time, I'll push all my cum back inside you, Londyn. You'll keep everything I give you until I say otherwise."

He tossed the soiled silk aside as Londyn lay frozen, her heart racing and her blood turning to ice. She could feel something welling up inside her. A roiling ocean of emotions and feelings. It was barreling through her; she couldn't stop it. Her eyes filled with tears, and before she knew what was happening, she was sobbing hysterically, overwhelmed and out of control until she couldn't breathe. Her chest swelled like it was stuffed full of dynamite and a second away from exploding.

"Shit." Oliver moved quickly until his back was against the headboard. "Stop crying."

Londyn scrambled into his lap, frantically holding on to him like a lifeline. Why she clung to the one person who was the catalyst for her pain was a mystery. But something inside her soul was drawn to his darkness. She could not fight how it wrapped tendrils around her mind and refused to let her go. And it was pathetic how she craved his touch, his attention. She'd not experienced affection or even something so simple as a hug in such a long time. Was it any wonder she gravitated toward this man? He made her feel things she had never experienced before.

The realization that she wanted more of him was frightening. Humbling. Humiliating.

For a moment, Oliver did nothing. Even amid her hysteria, Londyn recognized his reluctance to embrace her, although he did not try dislodging her. It was as if he were overcome with indecision at the sight of her tears. When she pressed her face into his chest, clinging to him and hating herself for it, he stiffened, his body rigid and unyielding. She whimpered, squirming until she was nestled firmly in his lap.

Letting out a sigh, Oliver finally gathered her close, his arms encircling her waist as she huddled against him, soaking his skin with hot tears.

"Sshhh," he crooned, stroking her hair. "It's okay. You're okay. I've got you. Don't cry now."

His assurances only made Londyn sob more.

Okay? How is any of this okay?

He shifted her until he could frame her face in the cradle of his large hands. Peering into her eyes, he watched as she tried to bring herself under control. Beneath his impassive gaze, Londyn could see an unexpected softening in the icy-blue depths as he studied her. A smile twisted his lips as she stared back, unblinking.

"Tell me, little dove. Why are you crying?"

Fresh tears welled in Londyn's eyes. She bit her bottom lip, a little hiccup escaping when she took a deep breath.

"I-I don't know," she lied.

The corner of Oliver's eyes crinkled, but he was oddly sympathetic. "Oh, that's not true. You may not understand why you started, but you know the reason for your tears now. Let me help you figure this out because I suspect I understand you better than you probably do. You're feeling violated, but you are also content. You've experienced an overload of plea-sure, but your mind cannot accept that. It is actually rebelling, so as your body and your mind fight, all that confusion and turmoil needs an outlet. You cry so bitterly, and yet, you seek comfort from me. The man keeping you prisoner. It's over-whelming, I know." He pressed a soft kiss to her lips, brushing them gently as he spoke. "I do understand. More than you can realize. I know what it's like to want to scream at the top of your lungs. To flail and rage and feel like there's not a goddamn soul on this earth listening to you. I understand. So, you cry on my shoulder for as long as you want. I won't think any less of you."

A muscle ticked in the firm line of his jaw with his confes-sion. Londyn could almost hear him grinding his teeth as he cursed softly under his breath as he seemed to realize what he had inadvertently revealed.

She could not withstand the vulnerability she saw in him. Could not fight the silky thread of commiseration she suddenly experienced. To think he truly understood her based on his own experiences was unfathomable, but the connection between them shimmered like water in bright sunlight. This man was a killer. An abuser. A monster. And yet, his admission did something unexplainable. It made him almost... *human.*

What Londyn did next shocked them both.

Winding her arms around his neck, she hesitantly kissed him; her lips barely pressing his, her breath coming in helpless gasps. She could not rationalize *why* she initiated the kiss. She only knew, in that moment, she could do nothing else to express the emotions raging inside her.

Oliver shuddered; his eyes fluttering shut as Londyn shyly explored the firmness of his mouth. The pillow-like softness of the center of his lower lip and the rough scrape of the morning stubble were contradictory but addictive just the same. His breath remained slow and even, but where her breasts pressed into his broad chest, his heart was thumping as rapidly as her own. His hands dropped from her face, instead, resting lightly on her hips. When she finally leaned back, her eyes wide with shock at her actions, Oliver's mouth pulled into a tight line. His brow furrowed, and Londyn's stomach dropped with irrational fear.

"Don't make the fucking mistake of thinking you might soften me. I may understand you and, surprisingly, even feel a bit of sympathy for your situation. But this doesn't change anything. I'm the fucking villain in this story, Londyn. You should remember that and never forget it."

He removed her from his lap and rolled to sit on the edge of the bed with his back to her. The skull tattoo grinned at her as if confirming his words. Londyn shivered, wrapping her arms around herself while drawing her knees to her chest. She watched him, breathless and confused, as he continued speaking without looking back at her.

"I've have business to attend over the next couple of days. While I'm gone, I expect you to be a good girl. If you are, if you cause no trouble, I'll take you to the lake for some fresh air when I return. Would you like that?"

Londyn desperately wanted that. She needed the sun's warmth on her face. A fresh breeze ruffled her hair. But she couldn't help but think this might be a trick. A test of some sort. Maybe he wanted to see if she would run. Maybe he wanted her to try so he could punish her again and feel vindicated for whatever torture he dreamed up. Or maybe this was all a setup for the day he ended her life. After all, he'd taken what he wanted. Her innocence. Her blood. Her soul. "If that's what you want."

Oliver glanced over his shoulder at her, his mouth a hard line. "Miss Miller will be coming to clean the house and restock things over the next couple of days. I don't want you interacting with her. Not because she doesn't know why you are here, but because I don't like making her uncomfortable. And if I know you, you will try enlisting her help in escaping. Which would be a useless endeavor on your part."

Londyn nearly choked on her outrage. He didn't want to make his housekeeper uncomfortable, but he sure as hell didn't mind taking what didn't belong to him. He hadn't felt such remorse about making her cry. His lack of regard was so hurtful it left her breathless. Her hands clenched into fists.

But still... if she indicated in any way that his statement bothered her, if she let her mask of acceptance slip, he might take back the offer of eventually taking her outside.

"Okay," she said tersely while swallowing past the lump of resentment in her throat. "I will stay in my room."

He studied her from over his shoulder; his gaze narrowed as if he expected her anger to manifest. When she calmly wiped the tears from her cheeks in silence, he let out a heavy sigh and turned back.

"Go there now." Oliver's voice was gruff. "And Londyn? I owe you five more lines in addition to the ones already carved into your back. Don't think I've forgotten."

Londyn gasped. When had he added the additional lines? After the shower? When she was high on endorphins and crashing? The entire experience was a hazy blur in her mind, but she almost remembered him rolling her onto her stomach when he placed her on the bed. Was that when he did it? She felt sick that she could not remember.

His cruel smile told her he knew exactly what she was thinking, and he enjoyed her horror. "They will be a reminder of what you have given me—your submission and your innocence."

TWENTY-SIX

O*liver*

FUCKING HELL.

Oliver rubbed his hands through his hair once he was alone. His weakness was not something he planned on letting Londyn see.

But how could he not melt just a little when her pretty gray eyes searched his, hoping to find a sliver of humanity? How could he resist the tenderness wiggling into his heart when her tight, little body gave in to his demands? His obsession was growing by the second, and damned if he could see any way of escaping its clutches.

You're supposed to end her life, remember? You even promised to do it quickly. Mercifully.

Fuck that.

After tasting her, using her, drinking in her sweetness and

her fear until he was giddy, Oliver wasn't so sure he could follow through on his promise. He didn't want to kill her. He didn't think he could endure a moment without her. She was unique in a way that didn't make sense. His feelings for Londyn were not rational. Or smart.

Becoming attached to a woman wasn't normal for him. He used them. Fucked them. Discarded them. That was his way. That was his life. Never get too close. Never let anyone or anything become so vital that it could be used as a weapon.

This world he and his brother inherited from their bastard of a father was cruel and unforgiving. It twisted love into hate. Acceptance into cruelty. And dependence into a curse. Loving someone could get you and that person executed.

Kingston didn't believe that, of course. No, Oliver's older brother had fucking rainbows and stars in his eyes, despite the lessons of their lifestyle. Because of Ava's love, Kingston thought himself invincible. Although things had calmed down over the last year, Oliver was under no such illusions. If Kingston were honest with himself, he'd realize Oliver was right. The people you loved were never safe if you were stupid enough to claim them publicly. There was always someone waiting in the shadows. Waiting to destroy what you cared about. Waiting and watching for the moment weakness presented itself, allowing for total destruction.

Oliver wouldn't allow that to happen to Londyn. He wouldn't let another man ruin and tear this girl to pieces. Her fate was in his hands, and there it would stay until the day she took her last breath. He would hide his obsession from the world—keeping her for himself for as long as it took for the situation to play out. And he would harden his heart against the softening he was beginning to experience. It wasn't safe for either of them.

Rising from the bed, Oliver grabbed the towels he'd used

last night to wipe the blood from her back. He considered stripping the bed of the sheet. He shouldn't care what his housekeeper thought of the soiled fabric, but something niggled at his insides. Shame, maybe, that he had so brutally used his prisoner, and now he wanted to conceal any evidence of it.

Crumpling the towels, he shoved them into the bathroom hamper along with the bed sheets. Miss Miller could just fucking deal with it and do the damn job he paid her to do.

Turning on the shower, he waited for the water to heat before stepping into the grotto. Some of Londyn's blood was smeared across his groin, and faint traces of it still stained his cock even after he'd wiped himself. Placing a hand against the stone wall, he leaned forward, watching the water rinse it away until it flowed down the drain in little pink rivulets. His body hardened as he remembered placing Londyn on her hands and knees on the shower bench. His entire body throbbed with savage hunger at the memory of her sleek body shaking while his fingers thrust into her. He couldn't wait to fuck her in that same position—on her knees and with her ass in the air.

Fuck. He needed to come again.

While it would be ideal if Londyn were there handling his current condition with her sweet mouth or tight cunt, Oliver realized he should curb his appetite. Taking her again so soon would likely hurt her. That left him with the option of jacking off alone. It might temper his hunger for a while. With a low groan, Oliver took himself in hand, gliding a palm over his rigid length until he finally came in a rush.

The release felt strangely empty. Unsatisfying, although his cum splattered across the stone walls. It wasn't good enough. Hell, jacking off would probably never be good enough again.

He doubted he'd be able to fuck another woman for a while after his prisoner was gone.

Rinsing the shower wall clean, Oliver cursed his own goddamn weakness. And his stupidity. He was doing exactly what he promised himself he would never do. He wasn't the type to get attached. He wasn't a man who cared. But everything was changing. Dangerously and recklessly, things were becoming different.

He was addicted to Londyn. She was all he wanted.

OLIVER UNDID THE TIE, tossing it into the passenger seat of the black Mercedes S580 with a grunt of annoyance. He always wore a dark suit and matching tie when undertaking business on behalf of the family, and he hated the constrictive nature of the clothing. It was fortunate that recently, the jobs Kingston tasked him with were usually very easy to complete. Securing and arranging transportation of women that Winter Enterprises selected for rescue and dispatching the men who abused them while the law looked the other way was one of the relatively simple aspects of what he did.

Pulling away from the tarmac at the small regional airport, he considered the fastest route available to get back to the cabin when his cell phone chirped.

The caller was listed as unknown. Very few people had this number, and Oliver knew every single one of them. He clicked the call with a frown, waiting for it to connect to the car's Bluetooth. Whoever it was, he didn't have time for their bullshit. He wanted to get back to Londyn and resume where they'd left off.

"Yeah."

"Winter? Lee Barlow here."

Oliver's jaw clenched with annoyance. "How did you get this number?"

"Doesn't matter-"

Oliver cut the man off with a growl. "The fuck it does. Who gave it to you? Because I sure as fuck didn't."

Barlow paused and then said smugly, "You and I know that anything can be bought for the right price. Tell me, are you tired of her yet?"

"What the fuck are you talking about?" Oliver's hand curled into a fist. One of the Russian owners of Diamond Lake Ranch was the likely culprit in passing along his private cell number.

"It's been three weeks. Maybe you've already disposed of her? If not, I will pay your price to transfer ownership."

"Fuck off. She's not for sale," Oliver replied calmly, his blood simmering with rage, although he maintained his composure. How dare this fucker *think* he stood a chance in hell of taking Londyn. "Not now. Not ever."

"Thought I'd do you a favor by throwing the offer out there. Ruel says a third party is interested in taking her. Said if the funds come through, they'll hold another auction and hunt. Of course, since she's no longer a virgin, the bidding will be greatly reduced. But I hope we can avoid that." Barlow hesitated. "I'd like to work out a deal before they take her back..."

"Take her back? Not fucking happening."

"That goddamn sale should have been voided that night, Winter," Barlow said, his tone rising in anger. "You cheated—"

"Cheated? I cheated?" Oliver snarled softly. "You were fucking about to rape the girl."

"So what? I caught her first. She was mine to fuck right then and there."

"You may have caught her, Barlow, but I'm the one who tracked her through the woods. I'm the one smart enough to take out my opponent by any means necessary. And I'm the one who carried her back and was recognized as the obvious winner."

"You almost gave me a goddamn concussion."

Oliver laughed. "You were compensated for your loss. Ruel gave you your choice of women and the freedom to do whatever you wanted."

"I was not given free rein. And I certainly did not have permission to do what I would have done to Item Number Fifteen. She was why I bid in the first place. It was the perfect opportunity to hunt human prey and decide the manner of her death. You stole that remarkable experience away from me," Barlow grumbled. "The Andrey brothers have promised a second hunt, open to other bidders. If we handle this ourselves, we won't get screwed over by those fucking Russians."

"I don't give a fuck what they've promised. I hunted her. I caught her. I'm keeping her. She's fucking *mine*."

Barlow's laugh was dry. "Don't be so sure of that, Winter. They have their own sick methods of getting what they want. With certain law-enforcement factions behind them, I don't doubt they will succeed. But maybe I will beat them to it."

"Barlow, I want you to understand something. I'm like my brother. Only I'm worse. I've tortured more men than I can count and eliminated far more. I am not secretly tormented by this necessity in my life. The Andrey brothers are aware of this, but you don't know me as well as them. I'm saying this because I want you to remember this. It's the only time I'll give you a warning. Don't fuck with me. And if I ever see you near *her*, regardless of how innocent the circumstances may be, I will rip you limb from limb and use your head as a paperweight on my desk. Now, lose my fucking number."

Oliver ended the call.

Over his dead fucking body would he ever give his prize up. Yeah, he'd cheated during the hunt, but that was to be expected. He did what was necessary. That's what a Winter did. They cheated. Lied. Stole. Killed. And all in the name of getting what they wanted.

"Fuck!" Oliver shouted into the emptiness of the car's luxury interior.

Barlow's call was a warning. It was likely already in the works if the Russians had publicly stated their intention to hold another hunt. And what law-enforcement entity was driving the reversal of the permanent sale?

The biggest question was why the apparent fixation on Londyn? Oliver knew some men relished the opportunity to hunt and dispose of a woman. It was a depraved excitement available to the wealthiest, most powerful men in the world. That Londyn was a quiet nobody was a bonus. Being a beautiful, innocent girl made her invaluable. With her background, she would never be missed. No family would be looking for her. No close friends organizing search parties or candlelight vigils. With the overwhelming obligations of school and caring for a seriously ill sister, would anyone raise an eyebrow at the suggestion that Londyn ditched her problems to start over somewhere?

But then again, maybe this didn't have anything to do with Londyn herself. Maybe this had everything to do with his botched deal with the Russians the year before. They'd been furious when he backed out of selling Ava to them. He hadn't cared then, and he didn't now. Especially since he'd reluctantly paid a fortune to smooth things over. Oliver never gave the organization a reason for his decision to back out, but murdering his own partners and reconciling with Kingston made it obvious to the casual observer. It was possible that Ruel and Erik still held grudges even while they smiled, took his money, and kept his membership active at Diamond Lake Ranch. Maybe he'd been too arrogant, too assured of his own ruthless reputation to recognize they hadn't let *any* of it go.

Oliver's teeth clenched with frustration. None of these conjectures or theories mattered. He didn't give a fuck what the Andrey brothers wanted and/or expected. Londyn wasn't going back to them, nor would Lee Barlow *ever* get his hands on her.

She was his. No other man would have an opportunity to take her from him.

He drove the winding mountain roads as if he were a professional racecar driver. It was dangerous, but he could not dispel the sense of urgency hounded him. He'd left her alone for too long. Of course, he'd checked the camera system often during his absence, ensuring that Londyn remained in the house. But his fingers itched to touch her silky skin. His lungs couldn't expand to full capacity without her nearby. And his heart thumped sluggishly when he couldn't hear her soft breathing. He wondered if he might be going a bit insane. Never had he felt such an overwhelming need for physical contact with someone to feel whole.

It was a four-hour trip to reach the cabin. Oliver made it in three.

While waiting for the gate to swing open, he pulled up the cameras. He didn't want to search the entire house for her. This was a more efficient method of quickly locating her so he could go straight to her. But her bedroom was empty. As was the library.

For a second, Oliver's heart stuttered. Had his little dove foolishly attempted an escape?

His footsteps were hard, heavy, and impatient as he ascended the terraced porch steps in a rush. Entering the open living room and attached foyer, Oliver considered checking the cameras again but stopped when he heard voices, feminine voices coming from the kitchen. Londyn's sweet voice was instantly recognized, but the giggle that followed was not.

A pang of regret slammed the inside of Oliver's chest, bouncing off his ribs almost painfully.

He'd never heard Londyn laugh. Hell, he'd never even seen her really smile. The fact he suddenly wanted to bask in the sunshine of her happiness was alarming.

Even worse?

He wanted to be the reason for her joy, which was both terrifying and infuriating.

TWENTY-SEVEN

L *ondyn*

LONDYN SENSED Oliver standing behind her long before he made his presence known.

This connection she felt with her captor was awful. She hated how her skin prickled when his spicy cologne drifted to her nostrils. She despised the tightening of her sensitive nipples and the lightening sharp tingle between her thighs as the atmosphere in the kitchen grew heavy. Maintaining her composure while smiling at his housekeeper as if nothing was wrong was an exercise in hiding her emotions. How she stood there, exchanging pleasantries as if she were a temporary guest here by choice, she could not explain. Pretending she was not affected by the memory of this man rutting over her was impossible.

Although she'd yet to look in his direction, the weight of

his stare could not be ignored. Tiny tremors of apprehension rippled through her when the housekeeper finally noticed her employer.

"Good morning, Mister Winter. It's good to see you back from your business so soon. I was just introducing myself to Miss Skye. It's so nice having guests here at the house. How about I make you both some breakfast before I get started cleaning?" Miss Miller asked, her voice cheerful and bright. She was a middle-aged woman; if Londyn hazarded a guess, she would say the housekeeper was somewhere around fifty.

Inwardly, Londyn cringed, but her chin tilted higher in a pathetic show of defiance. She regretted not returning to her bedroom the instant she realized the housekeeper was in the kitchen. She'd only come down to grab something for breakfast, then she would have isolated herself as Oliver had commanded. But the woman's open, friendly smile had her ignoring those draconian orders. Her captor had hidden her away from the world for three long weeks. Londyn did not realize how much she missed speaking to someone other than Oliver until the housekeeper introduced herself. Did he really expect her to never have contact with another living soul other than him?

I've allowed him to control me. And that is my downfall.

Her gaze clashed with Oliver's when she turned to face him.

Dear Lord. He looked like a god in that suit. All crisp and businesslike, other than a tie that seemed to be missing and the top few buttons of his black shirt undone. The dark-gray material clung to his hard body in smooth perfection, and his blue eyes were hard as steel and as cold as the deepest ocean as he regarded her.

Londyn's nerves fluttered like a million butterflies in her gut, despite the flash of bravery. She couldn't gauge his reaction to the interaction between herself and the friendly house-keeper. Was he angry? Indifferent? Or did it go beyond that to murderous?

She averted her gaze from his and flashed a smile at the housekeeper. "That's not necessary, Miss Miller. I'm fine with a piece of toast and some fruit."

Miss Miller laughed, her blue eyes crinkling at the corners. "It's no trouble at all. Mister Winter likes my omelets, so if you are okay with that, I'll whip up a couple for you. And I've already made coffee. Is that okay with you, Mister Winter?" Without waiting for an answer, the housekeeper began pulling out the necessary items and cookware to make breakfast.

"That's fine. Thank you, Miss Miller," Oliver murmured, stepping closer to Londyn where she stood at the kitchen island. Leaning into her space, his lips hovered around her ear as he pulled out one of the barstools for her. "Should I bend you over this counter like I did last time we were here, dove?"

He did not touch her, but he might as well have. His husky words slid over her like warm honey, and Londyn immediately blushed at the imagery of his statement. She couldn't get a read on him. There was an edge about him, but oddly enough, she didn't think it was related directly to her. Maybe he wouldn't punish her for defying his orders to avoid his house-keeper. Her lips thinned at the insidious thought that perhaps it was what she secretly wanted. His large hand crashing on her bottom. Snaking between her legs. His mouth, so hard and brutal, plundering her own as he took what he wanted.

Londyn wasn't sure she could form words with her breath hanging in her throat and her heart pounding from the path of her thoughts.

It was a blessing when Miss Miller saved her from respond-ing. "Sit, sit! It will only take a few minutes to get everything ready. While you wait, here's some coffee."

Londyn carefully slid onto the barstool, gratefully accepting the steaming cup of coffee from the housekeeper. Removing his coat, Oliver did the same, his lips twitching as if he recognized the reason for her careful movements. While she blushed even more, he watched as she prepped the drink the way she liked it—more cream than sugar until it was the color of cashmere. She noticed he drank his coffee black, and her nose scrunched at the thought.

"What's the matter?" Oliver asked, sipping from his cup. "Is it not to your liking? Or was it not enough?"

The innuendo in his tone was unmistakable. He was referring to her obvious soreness and the reasons behind it. Londyn's attention focused on the cup she held in her hands. She didn't want him to know her pussy still ached from the thorough fucking he'd given her just a couple of days before. She didn't want him to know she had slept restlessly for the last two nights, strangely ill at ease with his absence. She certainly did not want him to know she spent the long hours alone, alternately dreading and hoping for his return. "Nothing's the matter."

"Tell me."

She set her cup down, cut her gaze at him, and shyly remarked, "You drink your coffee with nothing in it. It's so bitter without sugar and cream, don't you think?"

"Mister Winter always drinks his coffee black," Miss Miller said cheerfully while whisking eggs and cheese in a small mixing bowl. "I was surprised he requested creamer be included with the grocery order before realizing he wanted it for you, Miss Skye."

Oliver's lips tightened with the housekeeper's revelation. "The butter is burning in the pan, Miss Miller."

Miss Miller waved her hand at Oliver. "I've got it, I've got it! Don't worry. I'll not burn your breakfast."

Londyn fell silent, drinking her coffee while contemplating Miss Miller's statement. She couldn't imagine Oliver doing anything so... thoughtful. And especially not on her behalf. But there was so much about him that was a mystery. Just when she thought she had him figured out, he shattered her perception.

As they ate breakfast, the housekeeper busied herself cleaning the kitchen. Londyn was starving, and she quickly downed half her omelet while Oliver made small talk with the older woman.

Oliver smiled his thanks when the housekeeper refilled their coffee cups. "I have some items being delivered to the front gate today. I would appreciate it if you would place them in my bedroom once they arrive."

"Of course, Mister Winter. Is there anything else you would like from the store? I'm placing another order today."

"That won't be necessary, the house will be empty in a couple of days."

Londyn paused—her fork midair and loaded with a bite of steaming omelet.

Oh, God. Does he mean what I think he means? He's going to finally do it. He's getting rid of me.

Her hand was shaky as she laid the fork across the plate. Although it took every bit of willpower she possessed not to jump from the barstool, she remained calm. If she could get outside and away from the cabin, if she acted like nothing was wrong, there was a better chance of escaping the fate he had planned.

"Oh, that's too bad," Miss Miller *tsked*. "Your time here is always too short." Her friendly smile was directed at Londyn. "I hope you come back and visit us, Miss Skye."

Oliver pushed his plate away and stood to move behind Londyn's chair. "She would love to, wouldn't you, Londyn?"

His fingers rested on either side of her neck, lightly skimming the skin over her collarbone. To the casual observer, it would appear to be a sweet, caring gesture of affection. Or a display of ownership from Londyn's point of view. She could not help the way her body trembled in response, and when he squeezed her in warning, Londyn swallowed a whimper.

"Of course," she quickly answered and was rewarded when Oliver's mouth brushed her ear, his breath warm and spine-tingling.

"Good girl," he murmured before raising his voice for Miss Miller's benefit. "I wonder if you could prepare a basket that we can take to the lake this afternoon. Just simple things... fruit and cheese. And a bottle of wine from the cellar. Red, I think, would be nice. Maybe the Hundred Acre Dark Ark Cabernet Sauvignon?"

Oliver waited for Londyn to stand up, then entwined his fingers with hers, pulling her closer as Miss Miller beamed in approval. "If you will excuse us, Miss Miller, I have some matters to discuss with Londyn in private. If you will leave the basket on the dining room table, and we'll grab them on our way out later today."

He dragged Londyn from the kitchen, taking her down a hallway she'd not dared to venture down during her exploration of the house. It was dark, dimly lit by the window at the far end, and paneled in rich wood with matching recessed molding. A moment later, Oliver turned the handle on a heavy oak door and pulled her inside a room paneled in the same manner. It was an office. A huge desk crafted of black-stained wood occupied a space in front of tall windows. With the drapes pulled open enough to admit a swath of morning sunlight, Londyn could see the trees beyond and a glimpse of blue sky above them.

Kicking the door shut and turning the lock, Oliver swiftly

pressed Londyn flat against the paneled wall. He leaned into her space with a wicked smile. "Did you miss me, little dove?"

He smelled like rich coffee and his signature, spicy-sharp cologne. Londyn's hands fisted in his black shirt, pulling him closer without meaning to, which was an answer itself.

Untangling her fingers from the fabric, Oliver gripped her wrists in one large hand and pinned them to the wall above her head. His gaze raked over her body, his mouth quirking upward at the Vandy sweatshirt, khaki shorts, and tennis shoes she wore. "These are not the clothes I purchased for you." Those icy-blue eyes smoldered as his free hand snaked around her waist. Slipping his fingers beneath the sweatshirt's hem, he ran a gentle finger over the cuts he'd given her.

Londyn's eyes fluttered shut as she swallowed a cry. She had examined those marks several times, craning her head and looking over her shoulder to see them in the reflection of the bathroom mirror. They tingled as he traced them, one by one, until she finally opened her eyes. His gaze bore into hers, a spark of possessive triumph deep in the blue depths.

"No," she admitted softly. The things she wore were familiar. Comfortable. She didn't feel bought and owned when she slipped them on.

"Are you still bleeding?" he asked softly, his fingers still exploring her back.

"No," Londyn choked out. She would have arched away from his touch, but that would only press her body closer to his. "They don't hurt..."

"I'm not talking about the cuts I gave you." His gravelly voice cut her off. His hand left the small of her back, sliding to the front of her body and between her legs until he cupped her sex. His palm was firm, hot, and inescapable. Londyn gasped in shock as he ground it against her, leaving no doubt as to the nature of the bleeding he referred to.

"Are you bleeding, dove?" he questioned again. "Because that will determine your punishment."

She quickly shook her head. An alarming spark ignited with the movement of his hand, and although her flesh was sore, Londyn closed her eyes in disbelief at how good it felt. "Punishment?"

"You deliberately disobeyed me."

"You-you said I could go to different areas of the house. The kitchen—"

Oliver laughed. "Don't twist my words, Londyn. I instructed you to avoid interacting with my employees. Instead, I return to find you and Miss Miller chitchatting like best friends."

"It was an accident." Londyn's voice was shaky. "I did not know she was in the house this early. And I couldn't help but talk to her. It would have been rude not to. Besides, I've not spoken to anyone other than you for three weeks. I'm going crazy in this house by myself."

"I understand that, dove. I really do. But it doesn't change the fact you disobeyed me. Now, you will either wrap those pretty lips around my cock in the next five seconds or face the consequences for your defiance. What's it going to be?"

"Fuck you," Londyn whispered, knowing Oliver would take that as a challenge.

His smirk grew. "That's the spirit. And while I really do admire your feistiness, right now, I'll settle for fucking your mouth and enjoying the sounds you make while you choke on my dick." Releasing her hands, Oliver wrapped his fingers around her throat and brushed his nose against her cheek, breathing deep as his grip tightened. "You smell so goddamn good when you're scared, Londyn. I can't get enough of you."

Londyn held her breath as he nuzzled the space below her ear. When he took the earlobe between his teeth and bit down,

Londyn's throat closed around a moan. She hated how quickly her resistance faded, but Oliver cast a seductive spell that was difficult to resist.

"Down on your knees for me, dove."

Londyn shook her head, her lips pressing into a thin line. "No."

"Oh, this is non-negotiable," he replied with a chuckle, flexing his fingers until her breath came out in little pants.

"You told Miss Miller the house would be empty. Where are you going?" Londyn countered abruptly.

Oliver tilted his head, curiosity edging out the lust in his gaze. "You mean, where are *we* going? But that's not important right now, Londyn. You've earned a punishment, and I'm going to fuck your mouth."

"You'll take my corpse with you?" Londyn's voice was shaky, ignoring the last part of his statement. "Thats-that's sick."

"What the fuck are you talking about?" Oliver murmured. "You're going with me when I leave here. I've told you it will be a while before I'm tired of you."

"Where are you taking me?" Her persistence was likely annoying him, and ideally, she would not be asking these questions with her thighs wet from arousal.

His jaw hardened as one hand buried in her hair, wrapping it around his fist like a rope. "To my family's estate. There is an army of men whose only job it is to provide absolute, unwavering protection. It will be safer there."

"Safer? What does that mean? Why would you worry about keeping me safe if you are just going to kill me at some point? It doesn't make sense."

"There have been recent developments." Oliver swore under his breath. "It's the only way I can be sure you aren't stolen from me."

"Who would take me? No one knows I'm with you except..." Londyn's voice was hardly more than a frightened whisper. As bad as Oliver Winter was, Diamond Lake Ranch and the men running it were the stuff of nightmares. "They want to take me back, don't they? Th-those monsters at the ranch. They want me back. They won't let you keep me, will they?"

"Understand this, Londyn. I don't answer to anyone, especially bastards who think they can fuck me over. They will *not* take you from me, but it is an unfortunate reality that this house is not as secure as my brother's stronghold. The Den is a fucking fortress, so that's where we will go."

"You paid for me. Played their sick game when they offered me up to the wolves as a sacrifice. What will they do? Resell me to someone worse? Someone who would slice my throat the moment he fucked me?" Londyn's voice was laced with panic. She wasn't sure if she should be grateful Oliver had no intention of murdering her just yet, worried that he would imprison her in a place that probably rivaled Alcatraz or terrified that she would end up back at Diamond Lake Ranch.

"No one is taking you from me, Londyn. No one. Not now. Not ever. Now, the subject is closed. So, let's return to the issue of your punishment, shall we?" Oliver said firmly. "I won't tell you again to get down on your knees." His hand tightened in her hair, his other resting on her shoulder, exerting pressure until Londyn had no choice but to sink to the floor. The wooden planks were cold and hard beneath her bare knees, and she shivered at the absolute power this man held over her. Why she obeyed was unexplainable. The only explanation was that she was just as sick and twisted as he was.

"That's my good fucking girl," Oliver murmured, rubbing his thumb over her lips as she stared at him. He must have noticed the softening in her gaze when he praised her because the depths of his icy-blue eyes sparked with flames. She was becoming as addicted to hearing the words as he was to saying them. Pushing the digit into her mouth, he smiled when she automatically pressed her lips together. "Suck," he commanded softly, and when she did, a guttural groan escaped him before he pulled his thumb free. "Your mouth is fucking amazing. Unfasten my belt, unzip my trousers, and take my cock out, Londyn."

Removing his cell phone from the pocket of his suit coat, Oliver tossed it toward the desk, where it landed and slid across the smooth surface. Londyn's gaze followed its path until it came to rest on the desk blotter. She wished for the bravery required to jump from the floor and grab it. Was Oliver quick enough to grab her before she scrambled to his desk? Would his hands be around her throat before she could dial 911?

"Londyn." Shrugging off his suit jacket, he tossed it aside and then made a show of rolling up his shirtsleeves to expose his forearms. "Do as you're told."

The stern way he spoke jerked Londyn's attention back to him. He kept one hand entangled in her hair as she obeyed his command, pulling his trousers and silk boxer briefs down past his trim hips. His cock was erect, the crown glistening with moisture as it strained toward her mouth. The six barbells glinted in the light filtering through the half-drawn drapes. Londyn's throat tightened, remembering how those piercings felt when he was thrusting in and out of her mouth during their time in the basement. And her pussy clenched, aching for the painful pleasure she experienced the morning he ripped through her virginity and claimed her as his own.

There was nowhere she could go. Not with the wall at her back and his large, muscular body standing before her. Her gaze rose to meet his, her hands bracing on top of his hard thighs, her fingers digging in until she was sure Oliver could feel the bite of pain. Lust illuminated his eyes as they stared at one another for an eternity. His mouth was tight with tension, the cords in his neck visible, and the veins in his forearms prominent. He was a man on the edge. A heartbeat away from taking and taking and taking. A kiss away from falling into the abyss.

Her body ached for him. Longed for his domination. For his hard hands and even harder possession. When his mouth curved that cruel and familiar smirk, Londyn realized he knew exactly what she wanted.

"Open your mouth, Londyn. And keep your eyes on me."

TWENTY-EIGHT

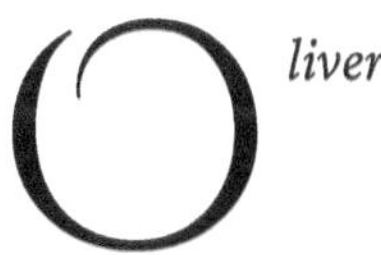

liver

Oliver tugged her to her feet, his large hand cupping her elbow. She was shaking, her cheeks wet with tears. She wiped her mouth with a trembling hand and swiped the moisture from her face. A deep, shuddering breath escaped her lungs when Oliver reached out, pushing her hair back until it flowed over her shoulders.

A twinge of shame threatened the glow of satisfaction that suffused his body. He had used her without mercy, holding her hair in an iron grip as he thrust over and over into the warm softness of her mouth. But she had not fought him, not even when he plunged so deep that she gagged on his thick length, and those pretty tears streamed down her flushed cheeks in tiny, salty rivulets as she swallowed him as deep as she could.

She did not fight him because she got off on it, too.

Oliver's hand encircled her throat. He didn't squeeze, but Londyn grabbed his wrist to keep him from holding her tighter, her breath coming in soft gasps. With his free hand, he flicked away the lingering tears while she stared wordlessly at him, her legs shifting.

"You want to come, don't you? Sucking my cock made you wet," Oliver murmured. "Answer me, Londyn."

Her lips tightened, but she nodded, eyes squeezing tight in defeat.

"I won't allow it, dove. That's part of the punishment." Releasing her until she sagged against the wall for support, Oliver yanked his trousers and boxers back up and retreated a few steps. He raked a hand through his hair, watching as she kept her eyes shut and bit her bottom lip. "Do you understand?"

"Yes," Londyn replied softly, but there was a thread of rebellion in her tone that she could not conceal.

"Be a good girl today, and maybe you'll be rewarded."

Her eyes flew open at his taunt.

"You realize that I can make myself come, Oliver." She glared at him, eyes narrowed and flashing sparks. "I don't need you to accomplish that."

Oliver laughed. "You'll need me for the most basic functions if I tie your hands behind your back like I want to. Let this be a warning. Do anything on your own that results in an orgasm, and I'll spank that little ass of yours until it's ten shades of red."

Londyn clamped her mouth tightly, fists clenching until Oliver decided this approach was getting him nowhere. Changing his methods, he moved until she was flattened against the wall. Her breathing spiked, her pulse hammering in the hollow of her throat so hard he could see every erratic beat. It was difficult, but he restrained himself from exploring the shallow space with the point of his tongue. But fuck, how he wanted to taste her. To lick and savor every inch of her skin until she was crying his name and pulling him closer.

"Let's call a truce, dove." Sliding his hand along her jaw, he cupped her face. Tilting it back, he stared into her eyes. He didn't like the tears he saw in the silvery depths, which was entirely out of character. He usually loved watching a woman cry, and in particular, he loved Londyn's tears. "Even if it's only for a single afternoon. Agreed?"

"Do I have any other choice?" she asked bitterly.

"You do." His tone was husky with desire. Fuck. He was ready to go again. Something about Londyn Juliette Skye made him absolutely feral. "You could spend the day down in my basement. Tied up. Gagged. Completely at my mercy. Is that what you want, Londyn?"

She slowly shook her head as Oliver leaned in, brushing his mouth over hers. She accepted it with a sigh, frowning when he did not deepen the kiss. Her body was trembling with need. He could do whatever he wanted, and she would love it. However, with a self-deprecating nod to his fragile self-control, he let her go.

Striding over to a tall cabinet on the opposite side of his office, Oliver pressed his thumb to the biometric reader and punched the corresponding code. The door popped open, revealing an array of weapons and ammunition illuminated by interior lights. He quickly selected a semiautomatic, the bullets to go with it, and a shoulder holster. Once the weapon was loaded and secured, he glanced at Londyn.

Her anger had dissipated, leaving behind a frightened girl with pale skin and wide eyes. She stared at the gun as though she believed he would shoot her between the eyes on the spot.

Oliver shook his head, giving her an amused smirk. "This is not for you, dove."

"Why should I believe that?" she replied, her voice as shaky as her hands as she tugged at the neck of her sweatshirt. "Why should I believe anything you say after what you've done?"

Oliver shrugged. "You've enjoyed most of what I've done to that tight little body of yours, so maybe you should trust me?"

A shadow of uncertainty crossed her features before her chin tilted upward in that adorable gesture of defiance. "I can't afford to trust you, Oliver. That would be suicidal."

A pang of something foreign and sharp pierced Oliver in the vicinity of where his heart once resided. It was infuriating that he suddenly wanted what she would not give him. Disappointment and regret made his voice rougher than it should have been.

"You can't afford not to trust me, little dove."

LATER THAT AFTERNOON, Oliver collected Londyn from the library and picked up the basket Miss Miller had prepared for them. Leading her onto the stone deck stretching across the back of the house, he tugged her toward the series of wide stairs and landings that descended to ground level. She dug in her heels, refusing to move forward.

"Wait," she asked softly, eyes pleading as she resisted this pull on her hand. "Can I— Is it okay if I stand here for a minute? The sun feels so good. And the air is so fresh. Clean." She let out a pained smile. "I'd almost forgotten how it feels to have the breeze on my face."

Oliver cocked his head. Fuck. Her simple request twisted his guilt-filled insides. He had locked her inside his prison of a house, never considering how cruel it might be to deny her something so simple as fresh air and sunshine.

Letting go of her hand, he retreated until his backside was

against the railing. He set the basket down, crossed his arms over his chest, and watched as she closed her eyes and tilted her face back to feel the sun's warmth. Her smile did not fade as she stood in the middle of the expansive deck, dust motes floating around her, caught in the sunbeams and illuminating her. She looked like a bright woodland fairy who had landed in the middle of his dark, ugly world accidentally.

And Oliver watched, entranced by the sight of her.

Finally, she opened her eyes and met his gaze. There was such a sadness about her as she stared at him that Oliver's breath caught in his throat.

"Okay. I'm ready now," she said, her tone more resolute than he'd ever heard it.

Reaching out, Oliver took her hand again before retrieving the basket. He took the stairs to the forest floor, giving Londyn no choice but to follow. Blue jays and sparrows trilled and cried from the trees as the wind shifted the leaves. The sun's rays were warm, but in the shadow of the trees, the air was cool and crisp. Once they were on the lower level of terrace steps, he released his grip, trusting she would follow him.

Londyn was silent as they moved further from the house. The trail leading to the lake was well-marked and broad enough that they could walk side by side, but she hung back, her footsteps soft on the fallen leaves that blanketed the dirt trail. He deliberately kept his pace easy and slow, knowing that she was likely still hurting from being fucked two days ago. He'd left bruises from gripping her hips so hard. Bite marks along the inside of her thighs. And he'd battered his way inside her tight virginal cunt. Yeah, she was sore, but Oliver could not find it in him to feel sorry for what he'd done, just regret for the way he'd gone about it. He should have exercised some restraint. Some gentleness.

Those thoughts irritated him as he stomped along the trail

leading to the lake. Along the way were several spots where large rock slabs served as terraced stepping-stones. They made the steeper areas of the terrain easier to navigate. And for miles all around them, nothing existed but woods and mountains. It was as though the house and lake had been plopped in the middle of a wilderness.

When the trees finally thinned out, the path ended and revealed a small, pristine lake surrounded by foliage and a small range of mountains in the distance. The water was clear, so clear that it reflected the sky above. It shimmered in the sunlight, bright blue in the deeper parts and a dark turquoise nearer the rocky shoreline.

Londyn let out a soft gasp when she saw the beauty before her.

"How lovely it is," she breathed, walking past Oliver until she stood at the water's edge. "So beautiful and perfect. It doesn't look real."

"You can see this lake from the living room and my bedroom suite, especially during the winter when the trees have lost their leaves. It's one of the reasons I purchased the house." Oliver watched as she shielded her eyes from the sun with one hand and took in the scenery. He barely noticed the beauty of the landscape. All he could see was *her*. And fuck, she was gorgeous like this—the breeze ruffling her hair, the sun warming her cheeks until they were a pinkish glow. She looked like the college student she was before becoming a victim of Diamond Lake Ranch and his own selfishness.

Fresh-faced. Innocent. Sweet.

"Only one of the reasons?" Londyn murmured under her breath, turning to kick one of the several pebbles and rocks littering the shore. Bending, she picked up a few of the smaller stones and threw one into the lake. The ripples from the pebble's impact spread quickly through the still water. "I thought it might be the torture chamber that swayed your purchase decision."

Oliver laughed, setting the basket on a patch of grass. "I won't lie and say the basement wasn't the driving factor for my initial interest. I've not had any use for it, though, until recently."

Londyn swung around to face him, her shoulders squared and hands pressed tightly at her sides. "It's strange to be grateful in a moment like this but thank you for bringing me here. At least when I take my last breath, I will be surrounded by beauty. Not chained up in that basement, begging for mercy."

"What the fuck are you talking about?" Oliver scowled, perplexed by her statement.

The light in her gray eyes hardened to flinty steel. "Please stop with this farce now. It's pointless. If this is where my life ends, you can, at the very least, give me whatever honesty that cold heart of yours can muster." Her gaze dropped to the gun holstered across his chest, one eyebrow lifting to accentuate the path of her thoughts.

Oliver sighed, raking a hand through his thick hair. "Londyn, I told you. *This* is not for you."

Londyn waved an arm, her words sarcastic and cutting. "Oh? Who else would it be for? Are you expecting assassins by your perfect, beautiful lake?"

Oliver crossed his arms over his chest, pinning her with a dark glare. "No, although I never rule any possibility out. It will soon be fall. And winter is right behind that. Bears in this area will be more active. Snakes—rattlers, to be precise—are still out. And let's not even mention the mountain lions. I'm not carrying this gun to use on you. It's for protection from the wildlife around here. *Your* protection, for fucks sake."

Her features were stone-like, the twist of her lips

accusatory. "The only animal I need protection from is the one standing before me."

Tilting his head, Oliver regarded her for a long moment. "You are racking up yet another punishment, dove. Are you sure you want to continue down this road? Are you that hungry for my hands to be on you? My dick inside your mouth again? Or even better, buried deep inside your tight cunt?"

Londyn stomped her foot. "Stop this! Stop equating everything with sex!"

"Why should I?' Oliver stepped closer while she took an unsteady step back, tripping over the stones beneath her feet. "You *love* the things I do to you, Londyn. You just don't want to admit it. You don't want to admit that you've been dripping wet for me since you sucked me off this morning. You don't want to admit that when I made you bleed, you came all over my dick like a bitch in heat. And you don't want to admit, especially to yourself, that you want me to fuck you again and make you cry at the same time."

"You're sick," Londyn whispered in anguish. Her features paled with the truth of his words, and she looked as though she might throw up. "Sick. Twisted in the head..."

"So are you, dove. But don't you think we make a pretty pair?"

Before he could grab her by the arms and shake some sense into her, Londyn reared back and threw a handful of rocks at him. She'd cleverly concealed them in her hand, and now they became stinging missiles. Most bounced harmlessly off his chest, but one larger stone, the size of half-dollars, struck his cheek with enough force to make him stumble.

Londyn dashed toward the woods surrounding the lake. She was smart enough to avoid the trail, recognizing that Oliver could easily overtake her there. She was extraordinarily quick, disappearing into the thick foliage before he could stop her. Maybe she thought she could elude him; her smaller size letting her squeeze through the dense trees and narrow spaces hewn into the rocks by the force of nature. But Oliver was fast on her tail, just heartbeats behind her as she nimbly ducked and scrambled over the obstacles.

But her feet quickly tangled in the thick vines snaking across the forest floor. Like leafy, green chains, they wrapped around her ankles as she cursed and tried kicking free. Within minutes, Oliver had her within his grasp, her flowing hair captured tightly in his grip as he yanked her to a halt. She fought like a wildcat, biting, scratching, kicking until he sank onto the trunk of a fallen tree and hauled her over his lap. Before she could wiggle free, one of his legs had both of hers anchored in place. Her wrists were captured and pinned to the small of her back as he shrugged out of the gun holster and placed it behind him.

"I'm shocked you have it in you to run from me, Londyn. I was thinking to myself that I should have been gentler with you these last few weeks. More patient and careful because I know I hurt you. Now, I can see that I was wrong. I'm beginning to think you only respond to punishments. Punishments are the only way you will ever learn, and any mercy I show you is completely unappreciated. So, I will oblige you on this point. I will punish you until you beg my forgiveness and accept the fact that there is no getting away from me. Until I'm done with you, you will not know a moment of freedom."

"Go to Hell, you fucking monster," Londyn cried, wrenching her body back and forth, trying to free herself of his grasp. "What do you expect me to do? Calmly let you kill me? Sit still while you slice my throat? You are a psychopath, and I'm just one of your many victims."

"Little dove, I have no intention of taking your life today." He ripped her shorts off her body while also wrangling her legs back under control as she struggled in real panic. Her sweat-shirt was jerked toward her shoulders, exposing her back and the tally marks he'd given her. The sight of those thin, scarlet lines made his dick immediately rock hard. The tiny pair of cream-colored panties she wore were ripped away next, the thin fabric shredding in his hands. Londyn shrieked as the cool air touched her bare buttocks, but Oliver was unmoved. "But by the time I'm done with this punishment, you will probably be wishing you were dead."

CHAPTER

TWENTY-NINE

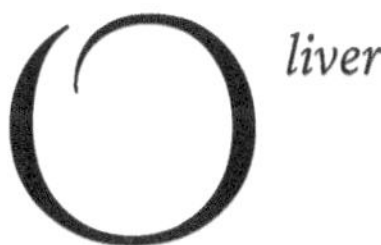

liver

WITH METHODICAL INTENT, he began spanking her. He ignored the screams, the curses, and eventually her pitiful cries as he smacked both smooth, pale globes of flesh with hard, stinging swats. He did not ease up, even when the skin turned pink and then bright red. It certainly hurt like the very devil; spankings always did, but Oliver was careful not to damage her fragile flesh, careful not to bruise her, and mindful of the tiny slashes on her lower back. He wanted this to be a painful reminder of what happened when he was directly challenged or disobeyed, but he did not want to destroy her. In fact, he deliberately tempered his anger before starting this punishment, afraid his emotions would cloud his judgment and he would end up causing irreparable harm.

"Stop, please stop," she sobbed weakly. "Please..."

Oliver paused, resting his hand on the curve of her buttocks and lightly massaging the area he had just spanked. "Ready to beg for forgiveness so soon, little killer? I've only just started."

Londyn did not respond, her tears soaking through the leg of his joggers as she gasped. The only other sounds were the birds singing high up in the trees, the occasional chatter of squirrels, and Oliver's own harsh breathing. He caressed the flesh of her ass, loving how the heat of it burned his palm. His dick was so hard it was fucking painful. It didn't help his state of arousal when Londyn kept squirming in his lap. His grip tightened around her wrists to stop her, and she moaned at the discomfort.

"Answer me, Londyn. Should I continue? Or will you beg?"

"Please, I'm sorry..."

"Sorry for what?" he prodded in a raspy voice full of lust. "Sorry that I caught you? Or sorry for throwing rocks in my face?"

She didn't answer, so Oliver slapped her ass again, enjoying the crisp sound it made when his hand connected with her bare skin.

"I'm sorry for throwing rocks!" she cried out, trying to lift her head to look back at him. Her tangled hair hung in her sweaty face, the strands sticking to her wet cheeks. "I'm sorry, Oliver. Please stop... it's too much."

The same devils that drove Oliver to ruthless savagery were the same ones that prompted him to slip his hand between Londyn's thighs.

A groan of lust rumbled in his chest when soft, warm wetness coated his fingers. He moved them inside her in a shallow motion, gathering her arousal and spreading it gently over her clit.

Londyn cried out, violently bucking upward to dislodge his

hand. Oliver groaned again, forcibly pushing her hands still in his grip into the hollow of her back while the fingers of his other hand explored the folds of her pussy.

"Fuck, your cunt is drenched for me, Londyn. "

She sobbed, desperately thrashing about to escape his touch.

Oliver couldn't help himself. Although this was supposed to be a punishment, he could not stop from circling her clit until she was crying out incoherently and riding his hand. In a matter of seconds, she stiffened with a climax, her clit pulsing rhythmically against his forefinger as she sagged limp and boneless across his lap.

"Now, tell me thank you, Londyn," he growled, bending low until his lips brushed her ear. "Thank me for allowing you to come in the middle of a punishment. Thank me for my restraint when I didn't wring your pretty little neck for that stunt. Thank me, because right now, I want to fuck you more than I need to breathe."

She was still crying softly and sweetly, but she obeyed in a barely audible voice. "Th-thank you, Sir."

Oliver pulled her sweatshirt down so it covered her buttocks, then tugged her upright so that she was sitting sideways and cradled in his lap. Pushing her hair back from her tear-stained face, he cupped her chin, forcing her to look at him.

"I'm holding myself back because I know I'll hurt you, Londyn. Do you realize what that means coming from a monster like me? I don't do gentle, little dove. I'm not considerate. And I sure as fuck don't usually care if a woman comes when I'm doling out punishment. In fact, not coming *is* the punishment. Do you understand what I'm saying to you?"

"Yes," she hiccuped softly. "I'm sorry. I don't know why I did that. It just... it just happened."

Oliver's lips clamped shut, afraid he would reveal too much of his thoughts if he spoke. So, he simply held her close while she cried. When she finally quieted, Oliver set her on her feet and handed over her pair of shorts. The mangled scrap of her panties was stuffed into his pocket.

She avoided his stare while pulling the shorts on, then stood with her arms wrapped around herself. Picking up the gun holster, Oliver shrugged into it, noticing how her gaze latched onto the weapon before she bit her lip and looked away.

"Do you want me to take you back to the lake? Or would you rather return to the house?" Oliver asked, holding his hand out to her once the weapon was secured. He had a feeling she would make a grab for it the first time an opportunity presented itself.

She hesitated before slipping her small hand into his. "I'd rather not go back to the house if that's okay."

"Come on, then." Oliver's lips curved. His little dove feared her punishments would continue in his basement. "I think we could both use a glass of wine or two after this."

It was while they made their way back to the house a couple of hours later that Londyn finally asked the question Oliver was waiting for.

"You said we will be leaving soon." Her voice was meek, and her entire demeanor was one of submission. She'd been like that since the spanking earlier, and honestly, Oliver didn't like it as much as he should. It was confusing as hell. After demanding she accept her situation, he enjoyed it far more when she fought back.

"Yes."

A few moments of silence passed before she cleared her throat. "Will we be flying or driving?"

"Flying for the most part." Oliver's reply was deliberately cryptic. He didn't want her to know too much about his plans and was already considering how he would transport her with minimal effort. As a safeguard, he had already instructed Joey to obtain a small supply of GHB.

Two glasses of wine made Londyn brave. "May I ask you something, Sir?"

Oliver stopped walking and turned toward her. Her subservient manner irked him. He wanted her spitting and snarling at him. But was that because he could use it as an excuse to punish her? Or because there was no pretending for his benefit? "What?"

Londyn chewed her bottom lip, tears welling in her wide eyes. Whatever she was about to ask was heartfelt. This girl would not use tears to sway him; that level of deception didn't exist in her.

"It's been more than a month since I've had contact with my sister. Would you—would you allow me to talk to the nurses you've hired to care for her? Or maybe let me FaceTime with her? I know she can't respond to me; she's incapable. And I know I don't deserve that privilege." Her gaze drifted to the welt under his eye where one of the rocks had grazed him. She continued, her cheeks flushing, "I just want to see her face and let her hear my voice."

Oliver's heart tightened at the pain in her voice, but he slowly shook his head. "I told you before, Londyn. Your old life is no longer yours. You must forget all aspects of it. There's no going back."

"It won't matter if you allow me this. It won't change what happens to me or sway you from your plans," Londyn argued, tears rolling down her cheeks. "I just want to see her before I die. I love her. She's all I have. Can't you understand that?"

You have me! Oliver swallowed the words, shocked at how much he wanted to shout them at her. He was off balance with their weight as they jumbled his thoughts, swelling until he was sure the true depths of his feelings were engraved on his skin from the inside out.

"I cannot allow it. Be content with the concessions I've made so far. Your sister has expert care in place for the rest of her life. I've sworn to give you a quick, painless death. That's all I can give you, Londyn." Stepping closer, he gripped her chin in his hand, tilting her face so he could search her eyes. "Don't ask me for more."

Londyn's eyes flashed silver, her tone bitter. "I expected you to say that."

"Then you should have known better than to ask me."

"I keep hoping a heart will grow inside that empty chest of yours," Londyn retorted; all hints of deference disappearing. "That you will realize how wrong and depraved this is and set me free."

"It's a foolish thing to wish for, dove. Foolish and pointless."

Releasing her, Oliver turned to the trail as Londyn followed, her footsteps much slower than his.

CHAPTER

THIRTY

L *ondyn*

LONDYN GINGERLY SANK onto the dining room chair Oliver held out for her.

Her bottom was on fire. Although she had carefully examined herself in the bathroom mirror, there were no visible bruises from that awful spanking. Only the five tally marks on her back spoke to her captor's obsession with her body, along with the bruises on her hips where he'd gripped her so tightly while fucking her that first time. But no evidence of abuse existed on her backside—just the lingering heat caused by his palm.

He said he owes me five more cuts for the orgasms he gave me. Will I feel them this time? Will I even notice the sting of the knife if I'm coming at the same time? Will I feel it when he slices my throat? Or will it, too, be painless and wrapped in pleasure?

Londyn shook those thoughts out of her mind. She was angry—at him, at herself, and at the world for allowing this to happen. And she was angry that she wasn't fighting harder to escape. It was stupid to feel this way, but Londyn could not help the unsettled turmoil rolling through her. How could she get away when being near Oliver only made her feel safer? It did not make sense, but it was the truth. Even his punishments made her feel as though this was where she belonged. And when he calmly tended her afterward, carefully setting her to rights, straightening her clothes, and feeding her; she could not deny the attachment and dependency that was slowly but surely developing.

Stockholm Syndrome... I got an A on a paper regarding that same subject in Psychology 101 during my first semester at Vandy. How could I know I'd have firsthand experience in a debunked theory. And prove that it truly existed?

Oliver recognized her agitation. After ensuring she was seated, he took the chair at the head of the table, watching closely as she downed the glass of wine in a couple of gulps.

"You're upset," he murmured, leaning across the table to refill her glass.

"You're very perceptive," Londyn mocked. She sipped the wine much slower this time, studying him over the crystal. "Maybe it's because I cannot sit comfortably on my own ass, thanks to you. Or maybe it's because a monstrous tyrant is holding me prisoner."

Oliver smiled at her display of temper, which only infuriated Londyn more. Her palm itched to slap his handsomely sculpted cheek. To see what kind of punishment that sort of behavior would earn her.

Stop dreaming up reasons for Oliver to punish me!

"Stop laughing at me," she demanded, irritated with her train of thoughts.

"But you're so damn adorable when you are mad."

Londyn's mouth thinned into a hard line. There was no talking sense to this man. He was cruel. Stubborn. And powerful. Sparring with him was exhausting, and if she could bring herself to face the truth, pointless. He'd been very clear from the beginning that he wouldn't let her go. He might take excellent care of her after using her body, but he truly didn't care about her. It was a fact she must accept.

She glanced down at the elegant gown she wore. It was one of many packages that had arrived while he was gone. She wasn't sure how he managed to get so many things for her, things that all seemed crafted specifically for her.

Oliver dished up the pasta Miss Miller had prepared for their dinner, his lips still curving upward with a grin. "Miss Miller's an excellent cook. Not gourmet, of course, but still, her dishes are among my favorites."

"I've never had gourmet food, so I wouldn't know what I'm missing." Londyn picked up her fork, testing the tines with her forefinger. "I'm glad I met her. She's very kind."

"She is. She takes excellent care of the house during my extended absences and spoils me when I'm here."

His casual statement was a reminder of their impending departure. Oliver had not given her any details about the trip. She had no idea when they would leave or the exact location of where they were going other than to his brother's estate. She didn't even know if she was expected to pack the items he'd given her or leave them behind for future disposal. And the question lingered—why would he buy these things for her, wasting that money, if he was going to dispose of her soon?

"Does your brother know we are coming?" she asked in an attempt to glean even a small bit of information from him.

"Oh, he knows. It's bad timing, but he knows," Oliver said,

swirling his glass and watching the Pinot Grigio catch the light from the iron chandelier overhead.

"Bad timing?"

For a split second, he looked as though he would not respond. A muscle ticked along the steel cut line of his jaw before he shrugged. "He's getting married in a month."

Londyn's eyes widened. "Married?"

"Yeah. Married. Oh, I've told him it's a crazy idea, but he won't be swayed. But I guess if he's going to marry anyone, it should be Ava. She's turned his world upside down."

"You don't like her?"

"On the contrary," Oliver said before taking a long swallow of wine. "She's an amazing girl. They are meant for one another; love each other to the point of madness. She's got the backbone and strength it takes to be in our world. It's just... this is the type of thing that leaves you fucking vulnerable. Gives your enemies a way to hurt you. Kingston is giving them ammunition by marrying her."

"Isn't that your brother's concern?" Londyn asked. "I mean, it shouldn't matter what he does or who he marries."

Oliver's head tilted. "But it does. Because he loves her, I will do my part in protecting her. And him, if it ever comes to that again. Although I doubt it would ever come to that. Kingston would slaughter anyone who hurt her."

"What do you mean, again?"

He hesitated, his brow furrowing. "Last year, I betrayed Kingston. Tried to sell the woman he loves to the same men who sold you to me. I wanted to take over his empire. Steal his throne. But taking her would have destroyed him and me, too, eventually. So, I eliminated the men I had taken as partners and backed out of the deal. Seems I couldn't stab my brother in the back, after all. Although I desperately wanted his crown, I realized it would never fit me like I wanted it to." Oliver's voice dropped to a low murmur of remembrance. "He forgave me, of course. And so did Ava. But the fact remains, I planned a coup, even if I never went through with it." His fingers closed tight around the wineglass stem. "Kingston trusts me now, but I keep warning him it's my fucking nature to do what is in *my* best interests."

Londyn let out a shaky breath. "Why are you telling me this?"

"Why? I don't know. Maybe I like telling you my deepest, darkest thoughts. Seeing your reaction when you learn my secrets." His icy-blue eyes held her hostage, a hand raking through his thick, dark hair in obvious agitation. His gaze dropped to her breasts, where they swelled against the black silk evening gown she wore. He had commanded her to dress formally for dinner, and she had obeyed, of course. Donning the elegant gown and matching Dior heels, arranging her hair in an elegant updo that Paris had shown her how to do long ago, and applying a bit of mascara and lipstick from the toiletries he had provided. When she entered the dining room earlier, Oliver's gaze lit up in appreciation.

Londyn could not deny the preening satisfaction that sent butterflies flitting around her heart before she shoved the feeling down deep into her gut. She wanted him to like what he saw. Wanted him to want her, which was crazy, considering her current situation.

"Maybe... maybe I'm considering the possibility of keeping you alive. You can be my live-in therapist." Oliver mused, twirling the wineglass between his long, blunt fingers. "How could I be sure you wouldn't try to escape me if I spared your life?" Rattled by his shocking confession, Londyn was silent. She could not promise that if an opportunity to get away presented itself, she wouldn't take it. But what did it matter, anyway? His murmured suggestion wasn't genuine or even a truthful consideration. It was just another way to torment her. Dangling the hope of freedom and waiting for her to snatch at it.

"Would you try?" he asked, pinning her with those perceptive eyes.

For a moment, Londyn caught a glimpse of something else deep in the depths of his steady gaze. A flash of... longing. A vulnerability that made him very human. It was apparent in that split second that this hard, brutal man wasn't as immune to fear and uncertainty as he wanted the world to believe. Suddenly, Londyn understood the reason for the word tattooed across his knuckles. She understood the possessiveness. The way he wanted to completely own and rule her. Everything in his life had been won in bloody fights for dominance and ownership. He held tightly to his possessions and savagely protected them by whatever cruel means were necessary. What he feared most was losing what he treasured most.

And in dawning awareness, she knew that *she* was that treasure. He may have meant it when he swore to end her life, but things had changed. He did not want to lose her now.

The revelation made her breathless. And sick. Because she did not want to leave him any more than he wanted to let her go. Her eyes filled with tears, both for herself and for Oliver. What was between them was hopeless. It would not end well. It was a grim reality Londyn could not ignore.

"I have a gift for you, Londyn," Oliver said suddenly, rising from his chair and standing behind hers.

Londyn did not dare crane her neck to look at him, wondering if he had guessed the track of her thoughts. She sat silent and still as his large hand rested on the curve of her shoulder, his fingers lightly tracing her collarbone while his thumb rubbed the nape of her neck. Every nerve inside her both tightened with anticipation and softened with desire.

Oliver had the terrifying ability to scramble her brain with fear while stoking every illicit craving her body harbored. She subtly leaned into his touch, soaking it in and savoring the tingles of hopeless excitement.

Her eyes fluttered shut as she sensed him reaching into the inner pocket of his jacket. There was a shuffling of something being opened, followed by a muffled pop as it closed. She couldn't be sure, but it sounded like it might have been a jeweler's box.

Cold and heavy, a chain was placed around her neck. No... not an actual chain, but a necklace. It nestled into the hollow of her throat like a lump of ice.

Her hand automatically moved to touch it as Oliver secured it around her neck. There was a quiet click, and his fingers brushed the hair on the nape of her neck, twirling the small curls around his finger as he caressed her.

"I had this made just for you, dove. A symbol of my owner-ship. And my devotion."

Londyn could hear the smile in his words, and her heart pounded. *Devotion? What does that mean? Does he realize that the word carries the weight of forever?*

"I am the only one who can remove it, so don't even try," he continued in a soft murmur. His free hand came up to encircle her throat from the front, tilting her head back until her eyes opened to see him standing above her. "It's a diamond collar, set in platinum with a two-carat stone pendant in the shape of a heart. A ring at the top of the pendant allows a leash to be clipped to the collar. Useful if you decide to crawl away from me instead of to me."

Londyn whimpered at the image his words conjured. A leash? A diamond-encrusted collar? What was next? Caging her as though she were a mischievous kitten?

Please, keep me in a cage if it means I will be yours.

Oliver kissed the tip of her nose and pulled her up from the chair. "Come see so that you can thank me properly."

A large mirror framed in sleek black metal hung over a sideboard, and Oliver guided Londyn there until she could see her reflection.

Her breath caught in her throat. The diamond choker fit around her neck perfectly, the heart pendant sparkling like a chunk of ice in her throat's hollow. She traced it, stunned by its terrible beauty and horrified that its embrace somehow felt… right. As if it had always belonged around her neck, shackling her to the man behind her.

"I'm going to fuck you while you are wearing this, Londyn. Just this and nothing else." Oliver's gaze caught and held hers in the reflection. His eyes were as cold and hard as the diamonds around her neck. Breathless under the weight of his stare, Londyn stood frozen as he continued in a low, husky voice, "I will watch you crawl for me, and I want you to wonder if I will choke you with the leash until you pass out or give you enough slack to hang yourself when you try running. And you will try it, Londyn. I know you won't be able to help yourself."

"I won't…" she argued, but his laugh cut her off.

"Don't lie to me, dove. You would have kept running today if I had not caught you. This makes it a hell of a lot easier to keep you close."

Oliver turned her until she faced him. His fingers hooked the necklace, although there was barely enough room to fit between it and her skin. Leaning forward, he brushed her mouth with his, kissing her softly and licking the tears she did not realize were trickling down her cheeks—tears that spoke eloquently to how lost she was to this man. He had managed to break her. She wondered if he even realized it.

"Don't cry," he murmured. "At least, not yet."

He stripped the dress from her body, tossing the designer

gown to the floor as if it were no more than a used dishrag. She was bare beneath the garment, just as he liked her, and Londyn immediately wondered if her obedience pleased him.

Allowing her to keep the high heels on, Oliver clipped a black leather and jewel-encrusted leash to the small ring at the top of the pendant. Londyn's heart pounded like a war drum as he commanded her.

"Hands and knees, Londyn. I want you to crawl for me like a good girl."

Humiliation stung Londyn with the force of a thousand bees, but, God help her, she obeyed. Willingly. Obediently. Sinking to her knees, she placed her palms flat on the floor, choking back tears and hating the flood of arousal that dampened her thighs. She was his now. Completely and utterly his. And she would have crawled a thousand miles for this man to simply pat her on the head and give her a smile of approval.

Oliver led her to the table, pulling out a chair at the opposite end so that he could sit. With legs spread wide, he might have been a dissolute king sitting on a throne. A tyrant to be pleased. A god to be worshipped.

He tugged the leash, dragging Londyn forward until his muscular thighs bracketed her slender form. When she tried rising on her knees, bracing her hands on the top of his legs to steady herself, Oliver shook his head.

"No. Stay as you are," he breathed, passing a hand over the top of her head and shoving her back into her previous position. Before she could think to protest what he was doing, Oliver pulled her hair free of the updo, spreading it with his fingers until the dark waves cascaded over her shoulders and across her bare breasts. "Lay your head on my knee, Londyn." He spoke softly, his hand slipping down to tweak her hard nipples until a moan escaped her, and she did as she was told.

"I do understand you, dove," he continued in a soothing

manner. "I know the darkest corners of your heart, and you know mine. You *want* this. You want the praise. The degradation. The domination and the punishments. You need the security of my hand around your throat as I command you. You are hardwired to obey me. You might not understand it all yet; this is all so new to you, but you crave the peace that submission gives you. The way it quiets your mind. I've given you the freedom to let go of everything and worry about nothing. You can let go, Londyn. Let go and let me take care of you."

Londyn struggled, her independence fighting the truth in Oliver's words. She wanted to scream. To kick and bite and shake her head because that was not her.

I'm not like that! So easily led and manipulated.

She was strong and smart. Proud and stubborn.

But she was also a woman with a horrible weakness. For Oliver. For those insidious words of praise. For his brutal, unyielding strength. For the way he handled her so carefully. So tenderly. Even when he fucked her mouth like he hated her, he took care of her afterward. He treated her like a prize possession. Like the woman he adored and cherished. And she craved that. Not from just any man. But from this man. This tortured, dark, twisted, soulless man had ripped her heart from her chest and wrapped glittery chains around it. She belonged to him. She was his.

The realization toppled her resistance. Oliver had given her more over the past few weeks than any other man. And if it ended up being the death of her, she could not deny her feelings toward him. When she sank into the promise of his words, she let them drown and pull her under the current.

She was tired of fighting. Tired of the struggle to survive. To breathe. To live.

She did not resist when he rose from the chair and dragged her to stand. She did not fight when he handed her a glass of wine and made her drink until it was empty. And she did not fight when he bent her over his expensive dining-room table, unfastened his trousers, kicked her feet apart, and plunged his pierced cock deep into her pussy.

"You're fucking drenched for me, dove. Is it the weight of the collar that makes you so wet? Or was it crawling for me that got you so hot?"

Londyn let out a muffled scream at the burning, stretching sensation, but how could she fight him when her body sang out in ecstasy with his savagery? Even when he looped the leash around her neck, gripping it with a handful of her hair and pulling so tightly that stars flashed before her eyes, she did not fight. It felt too good. Too overwhelming and too right. It was everything she never knew she wanted or needed. It felt like she finally belonged somewhere in a cruel world, and she was safe in the arms of the monster.

She surrendered with a cry, melting, loving every minute of his brutal, half-crazed possession. Craving his every thrust into her fragile flesh. Wanting more even after she came so hard that she must have stopped breathing. Everything faded to a soft black until the only sounds were her quiet sobs of bliss and Oliver's harsh groans as he fucked her without mercy.

When he jerked her head up until her body bowed, she was already flying into oblivion, soaring among the stars and clouds and adrift on the wind. She rocked in tandem with his thrusts, the edge of the table digging into her hips and bruising her. Her legs shook as he used his thighs to spread hers more, and she bit back a depraved plea to fuck her harder.

"You're mine, Londyn," he growled, plunging so hard and deep that Londyn dazedly wondered if he was trying to rip her apart. "Now and forever. Life or death. Pain and pleasure. Good or bad. You are *mine*."

THIRTY-ONE

liver

AFTER LONDYN PASSED OUT, Oliver carried her through the house and to his room. There, while his cum leaked from her swollen, pink pussy, he laid her on his bed and gathered the items he needed to place the tracker in the nape of her neck. When that was done, he unhooked the leash, coiling it and putting it next to his cell phone so he wouldn't forget to pack it with his things.

The GHB had worked faster than he anticipated. That could be attributed to the fact Londyn had not been eating very much lately. He'd also allowed her to drink wine at lunch and dinner, which certainly left her more susceptible to the drug's effect.

Before he changed his mind, he rolled her onto her stomach, wincing when he caught sight of the bruises on her hips.

Some were the shape of his fingers, while a few were caused by the edge of his dining-room table.

After setting up the tattoo gun and necessary inks, he yanked on a pair of surgical gloves and went through the procedures of prepping her skin. Rather than leaving her with something so transient as superficial cuts, he intended to give her something permanent. Something he would see every time he fucked her. A branding that declared to anyone who saw it that Londyn Juliette Skye was his until she took her last breath.

He worked quickly and efficiently, paying attention to the letters so they were precise and perfect. When it was done, he swiped the blood from the soft skin of her back and leaned back to admire his handiwork.

He and Kingston both learned how to tattoo as a lark when they began getting their own flesh inked. But until this moment, the only person Oliver had ever tattooed was Kingston himself. He was responsible for the motto, *"Crush, Conquer, Protect,"* emblazoned on his brother's flank. And while he wasn't a professional by any stretch of the imagination, he was proficient enough to undertake something this simple.

Covering the fresh tattoo with protective film, he rolled Londyn onto her side, smoothing the tangled hair away from her tear-streaked face. There was no explanation or even understanding of the level of his obsession with this girl.

It defied reasoning or explanation. Watching as she surrendered, knowing she craved him with the same bewildering intensity, was changing him in ways he never anticipated let alone thought possible. She had infected him with something magical and bewitching. He needed her to feel whole. To remind him he was human and not just the monster everyone believed him to be. The more he was around her, the more Londyn sank into his bloodstream, and the more he realized that a life without her was impossible.

It terrified him. His stomach twisted into knots because the first and most important lesson he'd learned long ago was never to get attached. Never give the enemy a target that could be used against you. And never, ever fall in love. It was too dangerous and far too painful.

Dark eyelashes shadowed Londyn's upper cheekbones, brushing her skin like tiny raven feathers. Using his forefinger, Oliver traced the straight line of her nose and the faint freckles dancing across it. Moving to the pout of her lips, he rubbed their pillowy softness and marveled over their tempting fullness. She tasted so good every time he kissed her. It was a flavor akin to cotton candy or the sweetness of overripened apples. Whatever it was, it was undeniably addictive. He couldn't stop kissing her. It was impossible.

Londyn barely stirred, unfazed by the pressure of his mouth moving over hers. She slept so deeply that he worried he might have overdone it on the dose. But when a hum of contentment fluttered in her throat and her mouth curved upward on one side in an unconscious smile, Oliver breathed a sigh of relief. The drug made it easy to insert the tracker chip while ensuring she would still be under its effects in the morning for transportation to the airfield. It probably would not last long enough to reach The Den, but he could always administer another dose if needed during the journey.

Giving her the drug also allowed him to mark ownership of her body. He would have tattooed her at some point, but the idea of this being a surprise was appealing. He could not help but wonder how horrified she would be once she discovered his motto inked along the delicate line of her spine.

Bleed For Me.

It's appropriate. After all, she's the only one I will bleed for in this lifetime. The only one worth spilling blood for. And I will do whatever is necessary to protect her from my enemies. If I must slaughter every motherfucker in my orbit to ensure that, I will do it with a fucking smile on my face and bathe in their blood.

When his phone beeped with an incoming call, he hesitated in picking it up. He was still reeling after the encounter in the dining room and high from the pleasure he'd gained from simply marking her with his motto. Dealing with business at this moment wasn't something he was interested in, but he picked up the call when he saw who it was.

"Lost sight of the target, but the asset remains secure," Bradford dryly reported.

"Lost sight?" Fuck. That wasn't good. Bradford was ex-military, one of a team of four Oliver had hired to keep tabs on Sheriff Adam Franklin in Georgia. They also kept watch over Paris in the new facility where he'd moved her to. If Bradford could not locate the sheriff, that was a bad sign.

"It was determined the target arranged for a leave of absence from his employment using a family emergency as the reason. Examination of online activities revealed dark web searches, with one of those sites being Diamond Lake Ranch."

Oliver breathed deeply. Fear—an emotion he'd not truly felt since his days as a child—permeated his body. It left him physically nauseated.

"Any indication where he might be?"

Bradford replied, "Target appears to have never left the house; although the wife and child were tracked and confirmed to be at the wife's parental home in the same city. A deputy sheriff arrived at the target's home, after which our own search confirmed the residence was empty." Bradford sighed heavily in frustration, the only chink in his otherwise robotic report. "The subject's cell phone records indicate contact with several unknown numbers last night and into the afternoon hours, with the last ping coming from a tower in Dallas approximately one hour ago. Cell transmission has been cut off since. We believe the deputy sheriff has provided cover and assisted the target in eluding our surveillance."

"I'd say that's a strong likelihood," Oliver agreed. The team were experts in surveillance, extermination, and disposal of specific problems in this line of work. He trusted them implicitly. "I want you and another man immediately on a plane to Colorado. I want to know if Franklin is within fifty miles of the ranch or my cabin. Find him, Bradford, and stick to his ass like glue once you locate him."

"That's an affirmative. Tyler and I will handle it."

Oliver tossed the phone onto the bedside table, swearing under his breath. Losing track of the sheriff could be nothing, or it could be something. The surveillance, while useful in uncovering Adam Franklin's illegal activities when it came to his job, had not revealed any interest the man might still have for Londyn's sister. He had not made any attempt to see his former lover nor checked on her after she was moved to the private facility, although random deputies made the occasional drive-by.

But Oliver could not shake the feeling that the sheriff was linked with Diamond Lake Ranch in some manner he had yet to uncover. Maybe the man had close associates in that area of Colorado. And maybe that's what Barlow was talking about when he mentioned law-enforcement entities being interested in a second sale and hunt with Londyn serving as the offering. Maybe Ruel Andrey reached out through his covert connections with state and local police agencies and his deep involvement in state politics in finding ways to get Londyn back within the ranch's grip.

If that was true, Londyn was not safe. While not as powerful as the grip Winter Enterprises had on the criminal underworld, the Andrey brothers, with their Russian ties and corrupt relationships in this part of the country, were a force

Oliver could not ignore. Which left him with few options when it came to ensuring Londyn was never under their control again. Taking her to The Den was still the first option, but eventually, he would take her away from that stronghold. He wouldn't be able to go too long without her, and neither of them could stay there indefinitely. His second option was to cave in and fulfill his promise to end her life before the Russians stole her back. That option made Oliver want to throw up. And his third option... his third option was the most extreme thought ever to cross his mind.

He could make Londyn his wife.

My wife. Mine.

For eternity. Mine.

As his legal wife, no one would dare take Londyn from him. It would be absolute suicide for a man even to consider it. Such drastic measures would ensure her safety no matter where they were. Stealing something so precious from the Devil meant instant annihilation.

Or you could circulate the news that she's already dead. Once she's in Kingston's program and a new identity has been created for her, she can fade away and live a new life. A better life. A life without you in it.

His heart clenched painfully. That would be best for Londyn—a new life, free from danger and men who would use her until she was broken. Men like himself. He could do the right thing for her. Salvage a bit of his own soul by selflessly giving her up. The price for such a sacrifice would mean never seeing her again. She would be dead, as far as the rest of the world was concerned. Including being dead to him.

Fuck that.

Grabbing his phone, Oliver clicked through the contacts. "Change of plan. We're flying to Vegas before heading to New York. Yeah, I have her replacement driver's license and passport. They arrived at the cabin while I was on my last job. Yeah. I'll need a limo, a marriage license, and Judge Cramer to sign off on it. There will be no questions about whether this marriage is legal or not." His eyes narrowed at the surprise evident in the tone of the other man at the end of the line. "Don't worry, there will be no need to forge her signature. She'll sign it. In blood, if necessary. And I know I don't have to say it but keep this confidential. On a need-to-know basis."

Ending the call, Oliver quickly sent a series of text messages to several members of his crew, filling them in on the latest developments and giving instructions as to what he would need from each of them. But one person he did not tell was his brother. For now, he wanted the news confined to those within his close circle. Kingston would find out soon enough, he acknowledged with a faint smile.

Behind him, Londyn made an unintelligible sound as she moved in a restless search for warmth. Now that he'd finished with her tattoo, he itched with the need to commemorate his decision in a more personal manner, but hearing her sweet sounds of slumber made him as hard as a rock. Fuck, he really was obsessed with this girl. The urge to claim her, again and again, permeated his thoughts and dictated his actions even while some small part of his conscience cringed.

Stripping out of the rest of his clothing, Oliver climbed back onto the bed and settled his nude body between her creamy thighs. Hovering above her, he stared down at her beautiful face while tracing a finger over the soaring dark eyebrows and the smattering of freckles that cartwheeled across her nose. She was so goddamn gorgeous. So sweet. So kind. And now, she would truly be his. *Forever.*

Before he could stop himself, he was pushing into her, the way eased by the cum he'd left behind before. His cock glided, a bit rough at first, but arousal gathered inside her pussy the longer he moved his body over her unconscious one. Gentle kisses were pressed to her mouth, his lips worshipping her breasts and the sweet nipples that pebbled so enticingly when his teeth nibbled on them. It was wrong to make love to her when she could neither consent nor struggle, but Oliver was beyond that now. He would do everything for Londyn. He'd take care of her. Ensure her safety. Give her so many orgasms that she would be weak for days.

Oliver's groans were uncontainable as Londyn unknowingly accepted his adoration. His obsession. His madness. He was crazy for her, and he would make her crazy for him in return. When he finally climaxed with a grunt of satisfaction, he withdrew from her and pushed a finger deep inside her to keep his cum from leaking out. And with a sigh of acknowledgment for how insane this all was, he wished his little captive was not on birth control. He wanted to watch her belly swell with his child. Wanted to see her eyes soften with affection when he caressed her. He wanted... no, he *needed* something which would permanently tie them together. Something other than his unhinged obsession and her burgeoning desire for his dominance and her own submission.

He rolled off her after a few moments, covering her body with the silk duvet so she wouldn't become chilled. She snuggled into the covers, blissfully unaware he'd fucked her as he got out of the bed to fire up the tattoo gun a second time. Then, he dragged the freestanding mirror out of the walk-in closet and positioned it at the foot of the bed. Sitting on the leather bench that spanned the width of the bed, Oliver considered his bare chest, rubbing a hand over its expanse until he traced the tattoo emblazoned across his pelvis.

There was only one logical spot for the tattoo he planned, and he smiled as the idea of what he wanted came to life. With careful, methodical movements, he began etching over his heart. He worked for a long time, paying close attention to the delicate shading of the feathers and the gentle curve of the bird's breast. With infinite patience, he was able to match the soft gray of Londyn's eyes.

When it was done, Oliver sat back, wiped the blood and excess ink away from his skin, and smiled at his reflection.

Now, no matter what happened, he would always have a reminder of her. A dove captured in midflight, a diamond-studded collar encircling its delicate neck, and a chain that dangled free but entwined around Oliver's own heart. That was his Londyn. His captured dove. An innocent to his villain.

And in the very near future... his wife.

CHAPTER

THIRTY-TWO

L*ondyn*

A LOW HUM WOKE HER. It was a persistent rumble that infiltrated her consciousness. For a moment, Londyn thought it was simply a noise embedded in her head. However, it permeated the environment. The sound was consistent, steady, and did not deviate.

Cracking one eye open, she peered at her surroundings. She was in a reclining seat of buttery soft leather. It was so cushioned that it felt as though she were lying on a pillow made of clouds. There was hardly any illumination in the space, just a blue glow that shimmered in the darkness as her eyesight slowly adjusted. Her mouth was as dry as sandpaper, her throat parched. And her head ached a little. Was she dreaming? Or awake? Confusion furrowed her brow, and she lifted a hand, intent on massaging her pounding temples.

"Wake up now, Londyn."

She turned toward Oliver, a relieved smile tilting her lips at his calm voice. A sense of safety washed over her as she reached for his hand, seeking the comfort of having him close. Oliver was always so warm despite the frozen heart he sheltered from the world. She drowsily wondered if he would ever let her or anyone else inside.

Oliver took her hand, kissing it and holding it against the hard line of his jaw. The stubble that shadowed his skin sent slow, unwelcome pinpricks of alarm shivering through her body. She frowned, a buried sense of self-preservation reminding her of the danger this man presented. She tried sitting up only to discover she couldn't. Seated beside her, Oliver's smile was oddly reassuring despite confirming that she was restrained.

"Shhhh, you're okay, dove." Oliver's hand covered hers, holding it and pinning it to the armrest. "I've strapped you into your seat as a precaution. The pilot says we'll be hitting a bit of turbulence in a few moments."

Resisting the urge to pull away, Londyn stared at his sinfully handsome face before croaking, "We-we're in the air?"

When had they boarded this plane?

Straining to remember the last moments she was conscious and aware made her head pound even harder. She couldn't remember anything. She didn't recognize the clothes she wore. The cream-colored Chanel sheath dress ended above her knees and dipped so low in the back that she felt the coolness of the seat's leather against her skin. Her feet and legs were bare, a pair of delicate high-heeled pumps sitting in a heap on the floor in front of her. Her pulse beat rapidly, realizing it was likely that Oliver had been the one to dress her.

"Yes. Winter Enterprises's private jet. Well, one of them. Would you like a sip of water?" Raising an eyebrow, Oliver tipped a water bottle toward her, silently asking if she wanted it or not.

Without thinking twice, Londyn grabbed it and twisted the cap. She drank half of it before something caught her attention. A huge diamond ring glittered on the third finger of her left hand.

She froze, staring at the piece of jewelry, confused.

"No. No, no, *no*." The words trailed off in a moan of despair, her gaze snapping to his. "What-what does this mean?"

"It means we are on our honeymoon, dove," was his sardonic reply. "I hope you like the ring. Harry Winston's was kind enough to open their Las Vegas showroom after hours for me. When the manager pulled this from their private collection, I knew it was perfect for you. You were a bit... incapacitated... at the time, so I gambled and selected this for you. It's one of a kind. Quite spectacular and very rare. A blue diamond, cut from one of the most famous diamonds before it was donated to the Smithsonian." He smirked at her. "No one is supposed to know about that, so keep it confidential, will you? It is a closely guarded secret, after all."

"We're not married," Londyn breathed, barely listening to his explanation for why she was wearing this ring. She felt faint. She thought she might throw up. This could *not* be happening. *How did this happen?* He would never marry her. He had made his thoughts on marriage painfully clear. "We cannot be married."

"We most certainly are," Oliver countered almost cheerfully, waving his left hand at her so she could see the beautifully simple platinum band on his own finger.

"You're lying. This isn't real."

"Oh, Londyn," he tsked in mock disappointment. "I may withhold information and sometimes even keep the truth from you, but I will *never* lie to you."

The cushion cut, blue stone nestled in a halo of sparkling white diamonds was enormous on her finger. A thin band of matching flawless diamonds completed the set. The stone itself had to be at least five carats. She couldn't stop staring at it, and her stomach swooped in horror when Oliver laid a heavy hand on her knee, steadying her while taking the forgotten water bottle from her nerveless fingers. Had she been standing, she would have fallen to her knees. Her entire world was tilting and spinning.

"There's that turbulence..." Oliver murmured, and Londyn abruptly realized her dizziness was the jet reacting to the unstable atmosphere, not her surprise marriage.

"I would never agree to this. I would not have said yes..."

Oliver leaned closer, his eyes gleaming as cold and bright blue as the diamond on her finger. "You *said* yes, Londyn. Driving down the Las Vegas strip, you were so excited to say yes that I couldn't keep you off my dick." His voice lowered in heated remembrance. "You were so insistent that I happily let you do whatever you wanted. Take whatever you wanted. I leaned back against the leather seat of that limo while you climbed onto my lap. Then you straddled me with those beautiful long legs of yours, and I watched while you fucked me. With the limo sitting in the driveway of the judge's home, while he waited to hear us exchange vows. My driver was snickering because he knew exactly what was going on in the backseat; you came all over my cock and screamed my name. So, yeah, you said yes. Several times, as a matter of fact."

"There-there were other people there?" Londyn bit back a sob, covering her mouth as nausea rose in her throat. To know there were possible witnesses to her behavior, even if she could not remember it, filled her with shame.

His eyes hardened, his features growing tight. "One of my Las Vegas crew driving the limo and the judge who performed the ceremony. Don't worry about them. The judge would never betray us, and as for the driver... I cut his tongue out."

Londyn stared at Oliver, not sure if she heard him correctly. "You-you cut out his tongue."

"Stupid bastard asked if I intended to pass you around. Now, in all fairness, he can't be blamed for thinking I'd share a woman I had just fucked with my men. I've done it many times, tossing them my scraps to use however they wanted. But to think...to *insinuate* that I would share my *wife*? That I would ever consider such a thing?" Oliver shook his head, reaching out to tuck a tendril of Londyn's hair behind her ear, his touch tender despite the brutality of his words. "I made sure he understood the gravity of his error. Word will quickly spread just how seriously I take such transgressions."

"This is crazy... You took me to Nevada, married me in a ceremony I don't recall, and afterward, you cut out of the tongue of one of your men. Do you not see how insane this sounds? It's something you've created to make me think I'm crazy. Because I don't remember any of that. I don't remember anything since... since we had dinner at your cabin. When you put a collar around my neck... made me crawl to you..." Londyn's eyes widened in horror as she shakily touched her throat. Feeling the choker still locked around the slim column of her neck, she could no longer hold back her tears, realizing what he had done. "You monster... you drugged me? That's why I cannot remember what happened." Her voice climbed higher and higher until it was almost a shrill shriek. "You drugged me!"

"I couldn't take the chance that you would try escaping or fight me when we exchanged vows." Taking her hand with the wedding ring on it, Oliver pressed a soft kiss to it. He ignored her hysterical reaction. "I used the lowest dose possible to mitigate any effects. The GHB made you compliant, but you were still functional. Mostly. You could walk. Talk. Sign your name on our marriage license and recite your vows."

Londyn snatched her hand from his grasp, frantically tearing at the ring to remove it before he took her elbow in a painfully tight grip.

"Take that ring off, and I'll have it permanently attached, Londyn," Oliver warned ominously. "Believe me, you don't want to know how I will accomplish that,"

Londyn did not think. She slapped him with all her strength. Fumbling with the belt cinched tightly around her waist, she got the latch undone and scrambled out of her seat.

Oliver sighed heavily as she fell in a heap, her legs numb from a combination of the GHB and from sitting in one spot for so long. "Where do you think you are going, Londyn? There's nowhere to go." Releasing his own seatbelt, he rose from his seat, following her as she got to her feet and darted toward the rear of the jet. "If you just calm down, you'll see that this is not the end of the world you think it is."

"Calm down? Are you crazy?" Londyn flattened herself against the wall as he stalked toward her. The sky was pitch black outside the small window across from her. It was night-time. How long had she been drugged? How long had it been since the dinner they shared in his dining room? Hours or days? How long had she been his wife?

He drew closer, and Londyn whimpered at the sight of the reddened imprint of her hand on his lightly tanned cheek.

"Why are you doing this to me? Is it not enough that you've tormented me for weeks? Stolen my life? You've taken *every-thing* from me."

"That's true." A strange look crossed Oliver's features as he caged her in, his hand coming up to caress the collar around her throat. He traced the outline of the diamond pendant nestled in the hollow of her throat. "But now, I'm giving you a new life, little dove. This is the only way I know how to accomplish that while also keeping you safe. Being my wife is your only option if you want to stay alive."

"A life spent in captivity, in servitude, is not a life," Londyn whispered. "A lifetime as your plaything does not mean safety, Oliver. You're killing me. Slowly. Surely. I'm dying every minute that you keep me as your prisoner."

Oliver's hand slid into her loose hair, tilting her tear-streaked face until there was no choice but to look up at him. He was so gentle it was almost disarming; so tender that Londyn questioned herself and what she knew of him. The tattooed hands holding her so carefully had inflicted unimaginable cruelty on God only knew how many people. Those hands had murdered. Tortured. Maimed. How could she feel even a flicker of safety while in his embrace?

"I know that, Londyn. Believe me, I know. But you must realize that every minute I am without you, I am dying as well. I-I want things with you that I cannot explain. I want to feel things I've never felt before. Things that scare the fuck out of me. Things I never wanted before you. And I want to feel it all with *you*, Londyn. I want to feel *everything* because of you. Most of all, I want to keep you safe."

Oliver sighed, pressing closer until Londyn's hands braced themselves against his chest. Just touching him, feeling his muscles flexing beneath the black button-down shirt he wore, made her melt inside. She fought against that irrational feeling, determined not to give in. Giving in to him would be her ultimate demise. She was sure of that.

"Is it to keep me safe or is this just your fucked-up way of keeping me for yourself, Oliver?" she spat bitterly, wishing she had the bravery to slap him again. It was deadly foolish to believe he would allow such a direct attack a second time.

"Both," Oliver replied, leaning so close that their foreheads touched. He huffed out a rueful chuckle. "I'm a selfish bastard when it comes to you, but you already know that, too. You've been my wife for almost three hours, and word will spread quickly. No one, certainly not my enemies, will dare try taking you from me." He dropped tiny kisses down the side of her throat. They burned like lit matches on her skin, lighting little fires and igniting her from the inside out.

"What will you do with me now?" She was holding in her screams, fear of the unknown stretching her nerves until they trembled like fragile strings on the verge of snapping. She wondered what the future held for her. Was it easier to get rid of one's legal wife when you tired of her? Would she be tossed aside one day, left to live her own life once he had used her? Or would he simply arrange for her disappearance?

A sad smile tilted the corners of his firm mouth as he pushed his hand against the door to the jet's private bedroom. "I won't hide you from the world. I want everyone to know that you are truly *mine*. This marriage guarantees your safety. I'm taking you to see your sister."

LONDYN FELL BACK into the room with a gasp, Oliver following with a heavy hand on her hip. She could not appreciate the luxurious beauty of the room, not with him prowling after her. She did not stop retreating until the back of her knees hit the king-sized bed.

"My sister?" She latched onto his cryptic statement, wondering if she'd heard him correctly.

Oliver took her hand, entwining his fingers with hers. "Yes. You do want to see her, don't you?"

Londyn nodded, gratitude welling inside her. Was he really

taking her to Paris? Or was it a cruel trick designed to build her trust in him?

"We'll be landing soon." Oliver stroked a thumb over her slender fingers. He hesitated, then said softly, "I need to check the bandage on your back. Then you can pick out some more comfortable clothes to wear."

Her head tilted in confusion. "Bandage?"

A muscle ticked in his jaw. "Let me help you. Put your arms up."

Londyn woodenly obeyed, feeling something tugging at the skin on her spine as she did so. She'd not noticed it before. Had she been injured somehow? Whatever was there did not hurt, not really. It was more of a twinge of awareness, a dull ache localized in one spot.

Oliver dragged the dress over her head, laying it gently across a chair before turning her to face the bed.

"Bend over, wife. I want your hands flat on the bed."

"What did you do to me, Oliver?" Her voice was a shaky whisper while he exerted pressure between her shoulder blades, forcing compliance. Why the word "wife" sent pleasurable shockwaves throughout her body was surely one of the Devil's cruelest tricks.

"I marked what is mine so there will be no doubt who you belong to."

"The ring wasn't enough? Forcing me to marry you wasn't enough?"

Oliver laughed softly. "Sadly, no. I need a more visceral sign to satisfy me. Something I can trace with my tongue before I fuck you."

A shameful shudder of lust melted Londyn upon hearing his blunt words. She nearly collapsed on the bed from the force of it, but gritting her teeth, she remained in the position he wanted, shaking as he examined her back while lightly prodding what must have been a bandage of some sort.

"Did you carve your name into my skin, Oliver? Or did you mark your property with a branding iron?"

His fingers gently touched her, stroking her skin. "Just a simple tattoo, dove. My personal motto along your beautiful spine. And you can be sure I will follow it when it comes to you."

"I don't understand," she confessed softly.

"Bleed for me, dove. You will bleed for me. And I will give my last drop of blood for you." His tongue swirled around the edges of the bandage, reminding her of his words moments before. "Now, I'm going to fuck my wife for the first time, and you will let me, won't you, sweet girl?"

Londyn thought of resisting. She thought of fighting back. But it was impossible when her pussy clenched with need, her flesh wet and aching. She heard the muted jingle of his belt, the unmistakable sound of a zipper lowering, and then he was surging inside her, driving deep until she hissed from the sting. When she fell forward onto her elbows, her body softening for him, he laughed softly and pulled her hips up higher to accommodate his thrusting.

She wanted to both scream with exultation and sob with surrender as her body welcomed him. She was coming within seconds from the angle and the way his pierced cock hit that special spot deep inside her. Gripping the duvet, she trembled, knowing this was *exactly* where she wanted to be. Pinned beneath him, at his mercy and helpless to resist.

"My sweet, innocent wife likes it rough, doesn't she?" Oliver lightly slapped one butt cheek, erasing the sting with a soothing massage of his palm while pumping into her willing body. "Now, come again for me, *wife*. I want to hear you screaming my name. I want you screaming, 'yes, husband,' before this jet lands."

"Oliver," Londyn moaned, her body swaying back and forth with his thrusts. She wasn't sure why she said his name. He would continue taking what he wanted, and she would welcome it despite the war between her mind and her traitorous body. "God, don't stop..."

All motion ceased. Only the sounds of their breathing filled the cabin. With agonizing slowness, Oliver withdrew from her body. Londyn did not move, unsure and admittedly a little frightened by the unexpected action. Her ears picked up the rustling of his clothing, the thump of a shoe hitting the soft carpet, a muffled curse, and the sound of something ripping.

What would he do next? Bind her? Gag her? Fuck her harder and without mercy? Her body flared up in flames. She wanted all those things and more.

"Oliver?" His name was a shaky whisper on her lips.

"I'm right here, dove. I'm not going anywhere."

CHAPTER

THIRTY-THREE

Oliver

HE FLIPPED her onto her back, moving her up on the bed at the same time until the pillows were beneath her head. With the movement, her arms automatically wrapped around his neck, holding onto him as he settled back between her thighs. His body was now as bare as hers and while her brow furrowed with puzzlement, she did not resist him. Then her gaze drifted to the fresh tattoo inked over his heart, and her beautiful gray eyes widened. Her arms dropped from his neck, crossing instead over her bare breasts.

"Oliver... what have you done?"

"I placed you where you belong."

Her chin trembled, her plump pink lips moistened by the tip of her tongue nervously swiping them. "That doesn't make sense."

"It makes *perfect* sense. You've been there since the moment I laid eyes on you. Somehow, you wiggled your way inside this darkness; I don't want to lose that light." His jaw clenched with the confession. He hadn't meant to reveal that; it gave away too much of his power and exposed him to her hatred. To disdain. After all, who could truly love the villain in the fairy tale? When Londyn's eyes softened and glistened with unshed tears, Oliver shuddered with the enormity of what he'd said aloud. "I want you... I want you to look at me like you did in the limo when you climbed into my lap and took what you wanted. I want you to look at me as if you love me."

Londyn let out a little sob. "I don't know anything about you, Oliver, and you know nothing about me. I don't know what your favorite food is. What your favorite color is. Your favorite song or book. We don't—"

"Gray," Oliver interrupted, tracing her cheekbone with his thumb and staring into her eyes. "That's my favorite color. Dove gray, to be precise. Those other things will come in time. Londyn, my darling little dove, don't you understand what has happened? I am fucking *consumed* by you. You occupy my every thought, my dreams. Even my fucking nightmares. Since the night I first met you, you've possessed me."

"Oliver..."

"I won't apologize for buying you in that auction. I won't apologize for the things I've done. I can only swear that even when I hurt you, pleasure will always accompany the pain. If you ask me for something, I will burn down this damn world to get it for you. If you ask me to bleed, I will give you every drop of blood that flows through my veins. And if you want it, I'll carve out this black heart of mine, place it on a silver platter, and bow down before you. But I will never let you go, Londyn. Do you understand? Never. What I feel for you is complete madness, but it's *our* madness, Londyn. Mine and yours. That will never change, and I hope that one day you will feel the same."

Tears tracked down Londyn's cheeks. She said nothing, processing his abrupt confession as the silence hung between them in a heavy curtain of mistrust and shame. Then, hesitantly, as if approaching a wild animal, Londyn's arms lifted again until they looped around his neck.

"I-I feel that way now," she softly admitted. "I don't understand why, but I do. And it's horrible and exciting all at the same time." Then she pulled on his neck, drawing him down until their mouths were mere inches from touching. "I hate this power you have over me, the way you make me want these wicked, dark things, but I want *you*." She lifted her head until the distance was erased, and her lips pressed his with a sweetness that made Oliver's head reel. "Make me yours. Take whatever you want from me. I won't stop you because I can't stop myself."

"I don't want to hurt you, Londyn. I've been so fucking rough with you..."

"I want you. I want the pain and the bliss that always comes with it," she breathed against his mouth, wrapping her legs around his waist and lifting her hips to meet his. "Please, Oliver."

"You don't have to beg me, dove." He moved until his cock nudged the entrance of her body. A moan slipped from her when she kissed him again, and slowly, with excruciating care, Oliver eased into her. The fullness of his possession, the way her insides accepted and clamped down on him, made him tremble. "Fuck, you feel amazing."

With shallow thrusts, he quickly coaxed her body back into a fevered state, one hand coming up so he could hook a finger into the ring of her diamond collar. He held her hostage in that manner, kissing her with growing intensity as his hips moved with increasing force. Londyn whimpered at his actions, her fingers plunging into his thick, dark hair as their tongues tangled and fused together.

Oliver plunged in and out of her as she tightened her legs around his waist and sobbed with pleasure.

"Come for me, wife. But don't you dare look away or close your eyes when you do. I want to see your soul when I give you my own."

WITH THE JET on standby at Walsh Grove's only private airfield, Oliver led Londyn to the car he had arranged. He decided against using a limo, rationalizing it would draw too much attention in the small town. Only the security crew knew they would arrive at the nursing care facility soon, and he intended on keeping their visit as low-key as possible.

Once Londyn was settled into the passenger seat of the Bentley GT Coupe, Oliver revved the engine, and they turned onto the main highway. They drove several miles in silence before Londyn spoke.

"I hope she recognizes my voice," she said softly, smoothing her hands down the front of the jeans he had packed for her. Every now and then, the streetlights would illuminate the car's interior and reflect off the diamond on her finger. It flashed like blue fire, and Oliver couldn't stop staring at it. It was definitely caveman of him, but seeing the small visual reminder of his commitment made his blood thump harder and faster in his veins. Fucking Londyn while she wore nothing but his ring, his collar, and his motto was more addictive than any drug. He couldn't wait until they were back on the jet, and he could do it all over again.

"I'm sure she will, dove."

She smiled sadly when Oliver took her hand in his. "Thank you for this, Oliver. It means everything. I've been so worried."

"I'd like to move her to New York, closer to our estate. You can see her more often if she's closer. With the right kind of therapy and the care of a doctor specializing in this sort of thing, she has a better chance of recovering."

"Move her?" Londyn looked alarmed by that. "Do you think it's possible?"

"Londyn, I can do *anything* you want." He squeezed her hand, convincing her that he spoke the truth. "She'll be safer in New York. Safer than here anyway, even with my men watching over her."

"Sheriff Franklin will still try to hurt her, although he hasn't done so yet. I know the second she's better, he won't let her live long enough to say what he did to her." Her knees bounced with nerves when she mentioned the corrupt sheriff.

"I can solve that *problem* with relative ease."

"I know," Londyn whispered. "And while I know that would be best, I don't know if I can actually...."

"You don't have to do anything, wife. Your husband will handle it." And he would, too. Knowing what he knew about the sheriff of the small town Londyn had grown up in, there was no way the man would be breathing for long. As soon as Franklin was tracked down, Oliver planned on putting a bullet between his eyes.

Londyn shook her head. "It's so strange hearing you call me that. I don't know if I'll get used to it."

Oliver turned the car into the nursing facility's parking lot, pulling into a space near the front door. "You'll be hearing it for a long time." Throwing the car into park, he turned toward Londyn, cupping her face with his large hand. "Once we're done here, we'll return to the jet and continue to New York. But before we go inside, I need to tell you something, and I don't want you to be frightened."

Londyn regarded him, her eyes wide and solemn. "What is it?"

"The sheriff is currently missing," Oliver hesitated and then explained further. "My men have investigated, and we think he is possibly headed for Colorado. There has been some type of communication with Diamond Lake Ranch. My concern is that he is partly to blame for the ranch wanting you back. There must be some connection there, but it's one I haven't uncovered yet."

A deep shuddering breath escaped Londyn. "My sister... she's in more danger than you led me to believe. If you have no idea where Adam Franklin is, he could still hurt her. You don't know what he's capable of."

"My men are watching her carefully, Londyn. No one can get to her. Or you."

"You can't be sure, though. I mean, if he was able to disappear, he could easily slip past your men. I want to take her with us when we leave."

"That's not possible." He stroked her jaw with his thumb, attempting to calm her. Seeing how frightened she was only reinforced his plan to eliminate the sheriff. "Your sister's condition is too delicate, and the jet is not equipped for the type of care she needs. I can arrange it so she is flown out tomorrow once I have a suitable facility lined up. It only takes a couple of phone calls to make that happen."

Londyn's chin tilted in that stubborn gesture Oliver recognized. "Then I want to stay with her until that is arranged."

"That's not going to happen. There is no scenario where I let you stray far from my side."

She pulled away from him, frustration evident in the narrowing of her eyes. "You might as well clip your leash to this collar around my neck. Am I your wife? Or your prized pet?"

Oliver's lip twitched with a smile. "Both. And I'm not fucking around when I say you aren't leaving my side until this business with the sheriff and Diamond Lake Ranch is over. They may not be connected at all, but my gut tells me they are. The Andrey brothers want you back to resell you. To conduct another hunt. And there's someone or something driving that; otherwise, they would have already moved past the auction and onto the next. You came here with me, and you will leave here with me. Now," he tilted her chin with the end of his forefinger, "put a smile on your pretty face and go see your sister. You have an hour before we must get back to the airfield."

Londyn's mouth opened, an argument against his statement clearly formed, but a second later, her lips thinned into a line of irritation. She nodded, remaining silent as Oliver exited the car and rounded it to open her door and help her out. Catching her elbow before she could move past him, he peered into her face.

"You think I'm simply being cruel, but I am doing this for your safety, dove. Can you understand that?"

"Yes," she replied, her body rigid against his. Oliver wished they were back on the jet, back in that magical moment when she had softened for him, her eyes wide and her body bending in willing submission. With an inaudible sigh, he released her arm and let her brush past him. Following her as she entered the facility, Oliver bent his head in subtle acknowledgment to one of the men hired to secure Paris's safety. He leaned against the wall where a locked door led back to the residents of the facility. Only admittance by someone at the front desk would allow a person to move past the facility's built-in security.

Oliver spoke softly to the receptionist, signing the log on Londyn's behalf with her first initial and his last name. A wild excitement zinged along his veins seeing just that tiny example of their connection in black ink. *Londyn Juliette Skye Winter*. It had a certain poetic sound to it.

A buzzer alerted them to the door unlocking, and Oliver ushered Londyn through it, giving Cooper, the stoic ex-military guard on his payroll, a nod as they passed.

The second man working for Oliver sat in a chair outside of Paris's room. Londyn continued into the room while Oliver shook the man's hand when he stood.

"Good to see you, Lawson."

"Winter," Lawson acknowledged. "How goes it?"

"As well as can be expected. Has her doctor been in yet?" Oliver asked as Londyn pushed the door until it was almost shut. He heard her begin crying as she rushed to her sister's bedside, the soft murmur of her voice soothing as she spoke to Paris.

"Due to arrive in about ten minutes. I understand congratulations are in order."

Word was certainly traveling quickly. Oliver realized his next phone call should be to his own brother. He needed Kingston to know what had taken place and why.

"Thank you. Just to give you a heads-up, I'm having her flown to a facility in New York. Ideally, it will happen tomorrow or the day after if necessary. Are you and Cooper available to travel with her? Or should I make other arrangements for security?"

"We're yours until you say otherwise," Lawson assured him. "Still no word from Bradford and Tyler regarding the sheriff's whereabouts?"

Oliver shook his head. "None. But I expect an update shortly. They should be in Colorado by now."

Lawson nodded, then jerked his chin toward the half-shut door. "Let me know if you or Mrs. Winter need anything."

After he entered the room, Oliver quietly pushed the door shut behind him. He watched from a distance as Londyn bent over the girl in the bed, stroking her hair and tucking the covers around her shoulders. She spoke quietly to her sister, and seeing them together, Oliver realized how similar they were in appearance. Both girls possessed dark hair, although Paris's was cut much shorter and barely brushed the tops of her shoulders. She lay motionless, her face blank and eyes dull, without even a spark of life in their pretty hazel depths.

Oliver's jaw clenched. He'd seen death too many times not to notice it in this girl's features. Her skin was pale, her body thin. Fuck, the girl was slowly wasting away, and there was probably nothing that could be done for her.

Londyn glanced up as he approached the bed, tears tracking down her cheeks in the soft glow of a bedside lamp. The room was prettily decorated, its appearance more like a bedroom than a hospital room, although all the necessary equipment for someone in Paris's condition was in place.

"They put a feeding tube in her," Londyn cried, her brow creased in confusion. "A feeding tube. Why would they do that? She was eating on her own the last time I saw her. Slowly, but still, she was doing it. I don't understand why she looks worse than before. I don't understand..."

Oliver reached for her hand, pulling her into his hard body. "I'm sorry, dove. I should have warned you. She stopped eating at the other facility, and the doctors here decided to keep the tube in place. They tell me she's stable for the moment, but the tube is not something that can be removed. I approved their recommendation to keep her on it."

Londyn clung to him, sobbing against his shirt. "You didn't tell me. How could you not tell me?"

Oliver's heart throbbed like it was being cut from his chest as her pain leached into him. "I didn't want to worry you." He almost lifted a hand to rub the pain away before stopping himself.

Her breath came in a shuddering gasp. "I had a right to know, Oliver."

"That's true." He embraced her tighter. "I'm sorry. Sorry, I didn't tell you."

They were words he never thought he'd utter aloud, much less to another person. Londyn's slender body stiffened as he murmured them against the crown of her head.

"Is she... is she dying?"

Oliver couldn't bring himself to tell her the truth, not when it felt like her despair was ripping his insides to bloody, painful shreds. "The doctors here are experts in this field and doing everything possible, dove. When she is transferred to New York, I will make sure the same occurs there as well. She will have the finest care, with every specialist I can find in charge of her." Squeezing her harder, Oliver hoped she would not ask any more questions. He didn't want to lie to her, not when he'd sworn he never would. "Go sit with her, Londyn. Hold her hand. Tell her everything and anything you want to. She'll know you are here with her; I'm sure of it."

He knew that from personal experience. Over the years, the number of men close to death at his hands always knew when someone was close by. And it didn't matter if it was a loved one or someone they feared and hated. They *always* knew.

Londyn sniffled, nodding in agreement and sinking into the chair beside Paris's bed. She took her sister's hand and began talking in a low voice that Oliver would have had to strain to hear. Whatever she was saying was something he had no business listening to.

He retreated from the room, leaving Londyn there. Pacing down the hallway, he pulled his cell phone from his pocket and made two phone calls: one to a private hospital transport company and one to Neil, a physician hired by his father long ago to attend to the family's maladies and a trusted friend of both his and Kingston's. Neil would know exactly what to do and who to hire for Paris's extended care in New York.

Once that was done, he dialed Kingston's number, unable to contain his own rueful chuckle when his brother answered. Kingston's tone was hesitant, expecting bad news because, after all, Oliver never called him up voluntarily or just to chat.

"O? What is it? What's wrong?"

"Everything is fine at the moment, King—no need to call on the troops just yet. I just wanted you to know I took your advice, brother. I married her, and we're coming home. I'll explain more when I see you."

THIRTY-FOUR

L *ondyn*

LONDYN SAT QUIETLY in the car. After wringing herself dry with tears, she had nothing left. She felt numb. Tired. Sad.

The exhausting emotions had her on a roller coaster, but what she felt most strongly was fury. What happened to her sister should *never* have occurred. It was made worse by the fact that the man responsible, the man Londyn swore would pay for his actions, would never know justice at her hands.

And her sister would die. Seeing Paris's condition and hearing the grim prognosis from the doctor on his late-night rounds, Londyn realized the inevitable. Even if transferred to a better facility, with better doctors and better treatment, Paris would likely never recover. Despite the expert care, she was slowly wasting away. The stroke, the overdose's aftermath, and the beating she endured were all too much for her battered body.

Londyn swallowed a choked sob. It wasn't fair. None of this was fair. Her sister, her defender, her protector, and cheerleader deserved so much better—so much more than a wasted life at the hand of a monster like Adam Franklin.

Oliver was deathly silent. Londyn figured he was giving her space as she struggled to accept the reality of her sister's fate. A few times, she glanced his way, noticing how the muscle ticked in his jaw whenever the car was illuminated by streetlights. He had denied Londyn's second plea to remain with Paris while assuring her that arrangements were in place to fly her sister to New York the following day.

It's not enough. Paris needs me.

Oliver reached for her hand. Londyn considered pulling away, but with a small sigh of resignation, she let him entwine their fingers together.

"Are you okay?"

She jumped, his voice startling her. With her free hand, she absently tugged at the choker around her neck before replying, "I'm not sure. I don't think I am. It's just... it's a shock. Seeing her like that."

"I know." He rubbed the top of her hand with his thumb. Tiny, soothing circles that were surprisingly effective in relaxing her a little. Occasionally, he passed over her wedding ring. A jarring reminder that they were actually married.

"I wanted to stay with her."

"I know you did. But I couldn't let you do that," he said, almost apologetically. "I can't take the chance that something will happen to you. You are in danger, Londyn. Far more than your sister is."

Londyn turned her head, looking out the window into the blackness of the passing landscape. When Oliver said things like that, like she really was important to him, it made her stomach swoop. It made her feel like he truly would do whatever necessary to keep her safe, even if he went about it in the most infuriating way. "You promise she's being moved to a facility where I can visit her whenever I want?"

"Yes, dove. I promise."

The road they traveled was a winding, sparsely lit, two-lane stretch. It was the same highway they'd traveled to the care facility. Londyn knew from growing up here that the road was treacherous, with hidden driveways and intersections that only required stopping for approaching side traffic. But Oliver maneuvered the car through the curves as if he'd been driving the area and this particular road his whole life.

"Where will I live?" Londyn asked softly.

"You'll live with me." A smile was evident in his tone as if her question were almost too silly to warrant an answer. "Do you really think I'd allow anything else?"

"But where?"

"The Den," Oliver explained firmly. "It might seem strange at first; believe me, I once felt the same, but the mansion is enormous. We can go days without seeing anyone else if we want to. One section of the house is set aside for my use, although I've rarely used it. I've kept on the move as much as possible over the last few years. It will be different now, though. Kingston and I... we've been working through issues that go back a long way, but I understand him more than ever before." He squeezed her hand and lifted it to his mouth, brushing her knuckles with a soft kiss. "And his fiancé, Ava, she's a very special girl. The two of you will become friends in no time. Both of you are easy to love."

Londyn froze at his unintentional use of the word, but Oliver continued as if he'd not just insinuated he might actually love her. "And there's always the cabin in Colorado if we want a change of scenery. Or some privacy so we can spend time alone with one another."

"You'll be with me, then?" She could not help or hide the trembling hope in her tone.

"Of course." The look he gave her then was dark. Intense. "You are my wife, Londyn. Your place is with me. It doesn't matter where I am, where I go, or what I'm doing."

His gruff voice soothed something untethered inside Londyn. It made her feel wanted. *Safe.* She craved that sensation, melting into its warmth. Did he love her? Was he capable of such an emotion? The man was brutal. Cruel. Hard. But he made her feel like she was the most valuable treasure he'd ever held and that was intoxicating. Her heartbeat accelerated until it raced madly. She may never be able to say aloud what her soul felt, but she could not deny it to herself.

She was in love with Oliver Benedict Winter. Her husband. Her tormentor. Her villain turned unlikely rescuer and savior.

"What will happen if you find Sheriff Franklin?" It was difficult to moderate her tone when she was shaking all over. How could she act normally when her life had suddenly been turned upside down by the realization that she loved him?

"Not *if*. When." Oliver's cell phone rang through the car speakers as he spoke. "Once he's found, I will erase him from existence. I won't tolerate threats to my wife's safety or her happiness." Before Londyn could respond to that surprising declaration, he clicked through to the call. "Yeah?"

"Lawson here. Just confirmed the deputy we've been watching did another drive-by surveillance of the facility. He's headed down Route One toward the airfield. I suspect he'll be coming up on you shortly. I'm in pursuit but currently held up at 5th and Main by a goddamn train that's stopped on the tracks."

"What about Paris? She's still secure?"

Londyn gripped Oliver's hand tightly, terror ricocheting throughout her body until she was dizzy. There was only one reason a deputy would be pursuing them, although what he hoped to accomplish was a mystery. Oliver would never let them be separated, and she knew for a certainty that her husband would kill anyone who even tried it.

"Affirmative. I'm no more than ten minutes behind you. Wanted you to be aware of the development."

"Got it." Oliver released Londyn's hand so he could grip the steering wheel with both hands. The car accelerated, the powerful engine roaring in response to the increase in pressure on the gas pedal. "We're almost at the airfield. I'll call you once we've taken off." He ended the call, scowling as he took a curve so fast the tires squealed. The high-performance luxury car purred as Oliver pressed the gas pedal even more.

"Oliver... I'm scared," Londyn whispered.

"Don't be frightened, dove." He flashed her a sardonic half-smile that was meant to calm her nerves. "Whatever you are thinking, I want you to stop right now. You are safe, Londyn. Safe, do you understand? Nothing is going to happen that I can't contr—"

The abrupt screeching of tires and crashing metal shook the car, sending it into a tailspin off the side of the road and flying into a shallow ditch. Londyn screamed as the car rolled as if in slow motion. She blacked out; the world was dark and cold as the car turned over one more time.

Coming to, she realized they'd finally landed with the wheels facing the sky, the hood sinking into the soft, red dirt. Sobbing, she tried freeing herself from her seatbelt but could not unbuckle the latch. Beside her, Oliver hung upside down from his own, his shoulder grotesquely twisted in the strap. He groaned in pain. A gash on his temple slowly dripped blood as the car shuddered and the engine made strange, clunking sounds. The airbags had gone off in the collision, and now, the interior of the vehicle was cushioned by white clouds of fabric.

"Oliver?" Londyn coughed weakly, her head lolling. Her hair hung in her face, creating a curtain she could not see through. "Oliver, can you hear me?" Her voice sounded muffled. Reaching a hand toward him, her fingers brushed through the thickness of his hair, coming away sticky and wet. "Oh, my God. Oliver!"

He let out a weak grunt but did not respond beyond that. Londyn twisted her body within the tangled seatbelt, desperate to free herself but failing miserably. Shattered glass littered the inside of the car, and the faint odor of gasoline permeated the night air. Because her hands were now wet with blood, her wedding ring easily slipped off her finger, landing somehow in the open center console next to Oliver's cell phone. It glittered like a beacon in the dashboard's slow-blinking lights.

"Come on, hurry the fuck up. We've gotta get her out of there before his crew rolls up and finds us." A man's voice came from the other side of Londyn's busted window and the airbag. She whimpered, realizing the accident was intentional. Someone had crashed into them on purpose, T-boning Oliver's side of the vehicle with the hope it would incapacitate both of them. And possibly kill them.

"Man, this is some fucked-up shit. Why did we let Adam talk us into this?" a second voice breathlessly asked, accompanied by the ear-melting scrape of metal grinding against metal. Someone forcibly yanked on the passenger car door, cursing when it did not budge.

"Why? Because if we don't do it, the bastard will turn us in for every racket we've been running." The first man grunted with the effort of prying open the door until suddenly, something broke free. More glass sprinkled onto Londyn. She shrunk back as a pair of hands appeared in the opening. "I know I don't want to lose all the money we've been making, do you?"

She glanced at her husband, who had not moved since the crash. He looked dead. Panic swelled inside her until she thought she might be sick.

Oh god. Oliver, wake up. Please wake up...

"We've got nothing on our dirtbag of a sheriff and you know it," the second groused. "He's the fucking worst of the worst. Fucking that girl up like he did, and now this. He's more crooked than we are, and he won't keep his word. You know it and I know it."

"Let's just do this and get out of here." Those hands finally reached her, a switchblade knife sliced through the seatbelt harness, and Londyn would have tumbled to the bottom of the upside-down car if not for the grip on her sweater.

A scream escaped her, loud and shrill, as the man dragged her out of the car door opening.

"Fuck, she's still fucking gorgeous, isn't she?" one of the two men said, hauling her upright and turning her around so she couldn't see their faces. "Barely a scratch on her." Together, they army-marched her to a waiting squad car, where she caught a glimpse of the vehicle that had rammed them. It was a beat-up, nondescript model. Older. Cream colored. The front end was smashed in a bit, obviously from crashing into Oliver's sports car. The driver's side of the Bentley was crumpled so badly that Londyn doubted anyone could open that car door without mechanical help.

"Yeah. Get her little ass into the car. We've only got an hour before that plane takes off. We've got to get her to the next county if we're gonna make it. I hope Franklin fucking appreciates this."

They're taking me... kidnapping me... where are they taking me?

Londyn began struggling, and the more upright she remained, the more clearheaded she became. Her screams rang into the night, drowning out the cacophony of crickets and night creatures. She kicked, bit their hands, and swung her arms so wildly that she connected a couple of times with their chests, striking what felt like hard body armor.

"Oliver!" Her voice cracked as she screamed over and over. "Oliver!"

"Shut the fuck up." A balled-up fist connected with the side of her head so forcefully that the world went black for a moment. Stunned, she wobbled on her feet before she was flung over the hood of a police cruiser parked behind the Bentley. Her hands were yanked behind her back. Cold, metal handcuffs clicked into place, and Londyn sobbed in terror. "Be quiet now so we don't have to hurt you," the first man said in a grumbling, mean voice. He tied a piece of cloth over her eyes, cutting off her vision.

She could barely breathe from the panic that overtook her. It suddenly felt like she was being buried alive. Her worst nightmare roaring to frightening life. Two strips of duct tape that crisscrossed each other were quickly slapped over her mouth. The patrol car's back door was opened, and one of the men unceremoniously shoved Londyn into the backseat. She landed on her stomach, unable to right herself. Tears drenched the handkerchief around her eyes until they soaked into the leather seat. She gasped for breath around the makeshift gag as the car door was slammed shut.

"Whadda we do about him?" The owner of that voice was the man who did not sound quite as mean as the one who had struck her.

"Not a goddamn thing. Franklin isn't forcing us to do anything other than get the girl. And *I'm* not going to be the one to put a bullet in his skull, are you?" More doors slammed as the two men got into the front seat of the cruiser. "I don't want or need the trouble that would come with that. He's fucking connected, dude, and if you think he's a bad mother-fucker, you don't want to meet his older brother. The two of them are fucking savages. We got what Franklin wanted, and now, we leave the guy where he is. Do you think he's gonna care that much that we stole this chick from him? Guys like that get pussy anytime they want of all varieties, all shapes and sizes. This one is a nobody, so why create trouble with the Winters if we don't have to? The way I see it, we do this, and Franklin has no reason to turn us into GBI."

Londyn cried silently. These men were operating on Sheriff Franklin's orders. They were abducting her with the sole intention of taking her to Colorado. Her mind frantically worked at putting it all together. She knew that whatever connection existed between the sheriff and Diamond Lake Ranch would soon come to light.

Oliver, please wake up. Please don't be badly hurt. Please don't let them sell me again. Please come for me and rescue me from this nightmare.

THIRTY-FIVE

 liver

"OLIVER!"

The terrible screams woke him.

Shrill and frightened, the high-pitched cries rang in his ears as he hung immobilized, caught in the car's seatbelt. Everything was dark, the only light coming from the dashboard's instrument panel. Various indicators flashed silently, and the stench of gasoline stung his nostrils. A sharp pang stabbed his shoulder, and he closed his eyes against it.

"Londyn..." he groaned.

"Hang on... I'm working on unlatching your seatbelt." The voice seemed to come from a million miles away.

Oliver's eyes flew open, focusing on the broad shoulders of the man working to release him from the car. It was Lawson. Why was the man working on him instead of Londyn? Did this mean she had escaped serious injury? Or did her absence indicate something far worse? The excruciating pain of that thought sent daggers stabbing through his entire body.

"Where is my wife?" The question came out in a weak groan. "Where is she?"

Lawson did not answer but continued working. When Oliver slumped into the car's cabin seconds later, the ex-Marine pulled him free of the wreckage, helping him squeeze through the narrow opening of the mangled door.

"Easy now. You've got a laceration on your temple, a possible concussion, and I suspect your shoulder is dislocated," Lawson rattled off, forcing Oliver to sit on the back bumper of the upended sportscar. With battlefield medical training, he quickly assessed Oliver's injuries and began cleaning the head wound, sanitizing it, and applying surgical strips to the gash.

"Where is my fucking wife, Lawson?" Fighting the dizziness swamping him, Oliver used his uninjured arm to shove the man. The attention to his wounds irritated him when he had no idea of Londyn's condition. "And if you value your life, you'd better say you took care of her first, and she's in your SUV waiting for me." He tried standing but the agonizing pain in his shoulder made him sway on his feet.

"Fuck, Oliver," Lawson swore, guiding Oliver so that he was once again half-leaning and half-sitting on the bumper. "They took her. I pulled up less than two minutes ago, and they were already gone. Looks like there were two of them. My guess is one was driving the car there that T-boned you, the other in the patrol car I saw at the nursing facility." Lawson cursed again under his breath, obviously frustrated by the situation. "No way to know which direction they were headed if they took a side road. I passed no one while driving here, so I doubt they would have returned to town. There's an intersection a few miles ahead between this point and the airfield. It's possible they took one of the two roads headed either east or west, or they could have continued northward toward Atlanta."

Terror welled inside Oliver. It roiled and built into a crushing crescendo that was drowning him. "I can hear her screaming," he grimaced, "like, right now."

Lawson's head tilted. "That's probably the concussion. Or maybe the trauma of the crash? Regardless, stand up so I can do something about that shoulder right now."

Grabbing Oliver's arm firmly, Lawson placed the palm of his other hand against Oliver's shoulder and gave the arm a quick jerk.

There was an audible pop, and the pain instantly melted away. Oliver could think more clearly, and although he was still dizzy, he knew he must move quickly. His focus, his only thought, was rescuing Londyn. When he walked through the front door of Diamond Lake Ranch, he planned on slaughtering anyone in his way *and* the men responsible for abducting his wife.

"My guess is they've headed north to any one of the smaller airfields surrounding Atlanta. They've got to get her in the air as quickly as possible."

"You think they'll show up in Colorado?" Lawson asked, already pulling his cell out. He dialed the other half of the security team on standby near Diamondhead Lake Ranch.

"Yeah, that's exactly what I think." Oliver fought off another wave of dizziness as he turned back to the mangled Bentley. "This must have been planned out in advance. I think they were just waiting for the opportunity to grab her, hoping she would come back here on her own or that I would be goddamn stupid enough to bring her myself, which I was." He reached down into the car, grabbed his phone, and sent up a silent prayer that it still worked. His first call would be to Kingston. He needed an army of bloodthirsty men, and his brother would not hesitate to assemble them. He would also notify his crew from other locations around the country. Poised to dial his brother's number, he hesitated when a blue sparkle caught his attention. Digging into the open console, he plucked two rings from the wreckage.

Holding the priceless gem to the light streaming from Lawson's headlights, Oliver's heart faltered, the air evaporating from his lungs as though it'd been sucked out by a huge vacuum. It was the blue diamond and matching band of diamonds. He'd slid that set of rings onto Londyn's hand just twenty-four hours earlier. He remembered how she stared up at him in dazed adoration in the judge's living room, repeating her vows in the softest, sweetest voice.

A wave of shame washed over Oliver at the memory. He had no right to marry her like that nor to use her in such a heartless, brutal manner over the last month. Londyn deserved the best of everything he could give her. He should have been offering her the moon, the stars, his entire fucking fortune on a silver platter. His knees buckled before he braced himself with a hand against the wreckage of the car.

I should have given her laughter. Embraces. Sweet kisses and whispers for our future. Instead, I gave her nothing but pain. Sorrow. Heartache.

Something was building inside him. A wave of regret and contrition overwhelmed everything he'd once thought important. Money. Power. His brutal reputation. His cruelty. None of it meant anything anymore the longer he stared at the ring in the palm of his hand. The platinum was caked with blood, the sparkling diamonds dulled by it.

Blood.

Londyn's blood.

An anguished howl erupted from Oliver's chest, torn from the very depths of his tarnished, tattered soul. It rang out through the trees and the chilled night air; an otherworldly sound so haunting and disturbing that even Lawson, hardened by combat and the loss of fellow Marines and brothers in arms, made the sign of the cross across his chest.

Oliver stared into the dark, hushed forest around them. Rage, unlike anything he'd ever experienced before, seeped through his body in a tide of scarlet red. It erased the pain he felt. The dizziness. The fog. All of it disintegrated into a single purpose. A deadly focus. A bloodthirsty hunger to cause unimaginable suffering to the men who had done this. Death would be the only reward for those who had stolen his wife.

His very heart and soul.

His love.

Oliver slipped the ring onto his pinkie. It was a tight fit, but it would stay there until he placed it on Londyn's finger once again. On that day, she would smile at him with love and happiness as he swore his life to her.

"Let's go," Oliver said to Lawson, looking back at the man over his shoulder. His jaw clenched tight with the need to destroy and exact his revenge, his hands curling into fists as he envisioned all the many ways he would torture those standing in his way. "I have a wife to rescue and a lot of motherfuckers to kill."

"Tell me what you need, O. Everything we have is available, and I'm headed to the airport now so I can meet you in Colorado."

Oliver rubbed a towel over his head, wincing when the

roughness of his actions caught the sutures of his wound. It would be a new scar to go with the few he already had.

"I need you to stay there with Ava, King. I've got it under control."

Kingston sighed heavily. "You aren't thinking clearly. Believe me, I know just what you are going through. When Ava was taken, I nearly lost my goddamn mind. You don't have to do this alone, Oliver. I don't want you to do this alone."

"I get what you are saying, but if something happens to me, I'll rely on you to finish it, King. Besides, I cannot take you away from Ava. She'd never forgive me if you didn't return. And I sure as hell don't want her to come looking for me in the afterlife. Stay there, Kingston."

"Oliver, you can't expect me to stand by while you blaze your way into the ranch," Kingston argued. "You had my back with Ava. Now let me have your back with Londyn."

Oliver twirled his wedding ring around. "You've been a good brother, King. You always were. Even when you had no reason to be. Even when I wanted you dead because of what went on with my mom. You watched me like a fucking hawk, expecting to be stabbed in the back, but you were always a good brother. I never deserved you or your faithfulness. I hope you will forgive me for every shitty thing I said or did to you over the years. I hope you can forgive me for trying to steal Ava from you. You would have been justified in slitting my throat that day when you came for her at her parents' home. I get it now... your need to protect the one you love more than anything or anyone in this world. I understand that now. Because I feel that, God, how I feel that, for Londyn. I will walk through Hell and fight the Devil himself to get her back. And if I don't make it, I want you to look after her. Will you do that?"

Kingston was silent for a long time, and then his gruff voice came through the line. "Goddamn it, Oliver. You don't have to ask that; there's no need for it. You are going to get her back. And you are going to love her for the rest of your days, just as I do Ava. Someday, our kids will be running around this mansion together as we, the parents, watch and swear to each other that they will have a better childhood than we ever dreamed of. And if you insist on keeping me away, I'm still sending Jack in my place."

"You're sending him?" Oliver asked in surprise. Jack was his brother's right-hand man, and he was as brutal as they came. Along with Paulie, who rose through the ranks under their father, the man had devoted himself to Oliver and Kingston. There was no other man Oliver would have wanted beside him. He breathed easier. Between Jack and his crew sitting on go, there was no question of victory.

"Yes, I'm sending Jack. Now, go fucking slaughter every last one of them and get your ass back home so you and your wife can be in our wedding."

Oliver laughed softly. "That's the plan. I'll see you soon, oh, and King?"

"Yeah?"

"It sounds fucking strange to say it out loud, especially since I've never said it before, but I-I love you, brother."

Kingston's chuckle contained amused exasperation. "Tell me that to my face the next time I see you. Now, go get your wife."

THIRTY-SIX

L *ondyn*

"Wake up, bitch."

Cold water splashed onto Londyn's face. She gasped, coughing as it ran in rivulets down her cheeks. She opened her eyes to see Adam Franklin standing a foot away.

Behind him, leaning against the stone wall, was a man she did not recognize, although he bore a faint resemblance to Adam. She quickly did an inventory of her body, the aches and pains, the scrapes, bruises, and injuries sustained from the car wreck and the journey to this awful place. She was still dressed in the clothes she'd changed into before seeing Paris, but she was now barefoot, her boots were missing. The fact they had not undressed her was a blessing. Once they saw the tattoo on her back declaring her as property of Oliver Winter, Londyn had no doubt they would either slice the ink from her flesh or burn it off while she screamed in agony. In the hours that had passed since the abduction, no one had touched her other than the one deputy who struck her and some rough pawing from the guards outside her cell. They all seemed skittish about abusing her beyond that.

"Even looking like shit right now, you're still quite the stunner." Adam grinned, squatting so that he could peer into her face. "Hell of a lot prettier than your sister ever was. Smarter, too, or so I hear."

"Fuck you," Londyn whispered, her chin tilting. She glared at Adam, contempt oozing from every pore of her body. "That's from me and Paris, you cretin."

Adam's mouth hardened into a thin line, and when he reared back a hand, Londyn kicked out as she scrambled away. The heel of her foot caught him square in the jaw.

The man against the wall laughed out loud as Adam cursed. Then his hard hands were reaching for Londyn's legs, his fingers latching around one of her ankles in a bone-crushing grip. He jerked her to him as she clawed at the concrete floor, trying to escape.

"She's a fucking little wildcat, ain't she? Shit, the men lining up for the chance to hunt her don't know what they're in for. Well, maybe Barlow does," the other man said "You'd think he would have learned his lesson from the first time. Winter bashed his damn head in, and he's still determined to get his hands on her. Gotta admire the man's persistence."

"The Andrey brothers said there won't be a hunt if we had enough money to buy her outright," Adam grunted, flipping Londyn onto her back so that she landed with a thud. The air was knocked from her, but she still fought weakly, using her bound hands to pummel his chest until he gripped a handful of her hair and pulled it so hard that she screamed.

"Don't think that's going to happen." The other man

shrugged. "I heard it's every man for himself when it comes to her."

"They fucking promised they would give us sole consideration Kevin." Adam stood, dragging Londyn with him and using her hair as a handle. Walking her backward until she hit the opposite wall, he glanced over his shoulder at the other man. "Otherwise, I would have kept her for myself rather than have those two dipshit deputies go through all the fucking trouble to get her here. Your job was to have the deal in place, cousin. You vetted the officers who are going to be hunting her tonight. And as an honorary member of this fucking club and sheriff of this jurisdiction, we trusted you to make sure we were the only ones."

Londyn took a deep breath, her eyes closing in despair. There was the connection. Adam was related to the county sheriff the ranch operated out of. The sheriff here was a member. Paid and bribed with sex, and God only knew what else, to look the other way from all the illegal activities happening right beneath his nose. Now, things were going a step further. Now, the ones upholding the law would be the monsters breaking it.

"You don't get it, Adam. The Andreys do whatever the fuck they want, and we go along with it. If they take every penny from every man in this hunt and then decide to keep her for themselves, there's not a damn thing we can do about it."

"It's all bullshit, Kevin." Adam gripped Londyn's hair tighter, tugging her head back until she stared at the stark, fluorescent lighting that illuminated the cell. "That looks like an expensive necklace you're wearing," he leered, fingering the diamond heart pendant. "Is it real? It fucking looks real. Why would Winter give you something like this when he bought you for the pleasure of killing you once he was done?"

Londyn choked back a cry and pressed her mouth shut,

refusing to answer. Maybe it started that way, but things had changed between her and Oliver over the last few weeks. He wanted to keep her safe. He married her to accomplish that. He felt something for her. She knew he did. And if there were a God in heaven, Oliver would come for her. He wouldn't abandon her to this hell on earth. To these monsters.

Oliver Winter was a true killer but deep in her heart, in her soul, Londyn knew one thing for certain when it came to her husband. He was a villain, but he was *her* villain.

Kevin chimed in, "It's fucking real. Only problem is there's no way to remove it. Some kind of locking mechanism. Someone said the only way to get it off is with a special key."

"Oh, that's not the only way," Adam smirked, hooking two fingers into the choker and jerking so close that her face was only inches from his. Londyn stared into his dark eyes, horrified by the unspoken insinuation. "Is it, Londyn? I've got an idea of how we can get it off.

Kevin stepped forward, his boots ringing hollow on the stone floor. "Come on, Adam. You can't be serious right now. Cutting her fucking head off isn't an option. Not if you want to make it off this ranch alive. I suggest you get what you came here for, and let's go. The guards will only look the other way for so long. I'm not giving them more money just so you can get your dick wet before the hunt starts tonight."

"But I'm fucking owed something. I deserve everything I can get from this little bitch and more." Adam rubbed his nose alongside Londyn's, laughing when she strained her head away. "You know. Londyn, your sister was a great fuck. And we had fun until she pissed me off. Threatening to tell my wife about me and her. Saying she was going to report me for all the illegal shit I've done. She had to be silenced. I had to do it. You get that, don't you, Londyn? Sometimes, surviving means keeping your mouth shut. The way you two grew up, I'm surprised that lesson didn't sink in. Keep the secrets; live another day, right?"

"You are pathetic," Londyn breathed. "After everything you did to her, my sister is still stronger than you will ever be. And I will do what she couldn't. I'm going to kill you. I don't know how, but I will. And when Paris takes her last breath, she'll know you are finally where you belong. In Hell."

Adam laughed, pushing Londyn to her knees, where she landed with a sob. "That's a lot of big talk for a girl stuck in a cell and wearing handcuffs. Let's see if you can do something else with that mouth of yours besides making empty threats."

"You know you can't fuck her, Adam. There's no time for that, and the Andreys will have your head on a spike if you even try it," Kevin commented dryly, but he came closer, his eyes darkening with lust as his cousin held Londyn by the hair. "But a little blow job wouldn't hurt anyone; I'd like to get on that action."

"Fuck yeah," Adam breathed, pulling Londyn away from the wall so that Kevin could stand behind her. "Grab her arms and hold them over her head. Get them out of the way so she can't scratch me." Unbuckling his pants, he waited for Kevin to follow his instructions. Londyn screamed as the other man yanked her arms high, pulling them behind her head at the same time until it stretched her body while she was still kneeling.

Adam kicked her thighs apart, stepping between them until she was trapped. "Shhhh, no screaming unless you want the guards to join in. We're doing you a favor right now, Londyn. You only have to suck two cocks… not five or six." Jerking her head back, he stared into her wide, frightened eyes. "If you even think about biting me, I'll yank out every goddamn tooth in your head and fuck the bloody mess left behind."

A second later, he jammed his hard dick into Londyn's mouth, forcing it down her throat while she choked and spat in terrified revulsion. Grabbing the back of her head, Adam grunted in satisfaction, thrusting harder, deeper, holding his position for several seconds until she couldn't breathe. Her face was pressed tightly against his pelvis, the curly hair of his groin smashed into her skin, suffocating her. If there were anything in her stomach to bring up, Londyn would have vomited right then and there. All she could do was gag, swallow, and survive.

"Fuck, fuck, fuck. That's so fucking good. Fucking little whore. You like sucking cock, don't you? I think you might be better at it than your sister was. Did Winter teach you how to give head like that? Did you like it when he shoved his dick down your throat like this?" Leaning back, Adam withdrew from her mouth, using his dick to slap her cheeks and rub the head of it around her parted lips as she drew in deep, gasping breaths.

"I loved it when Oliver did it. I swallowed his cock the best I could, but he's huge, and I could only fit so much of him in," she choked out, glaring up at the sheriff with hate-filled eyes as she let out a little sympathetic laugh. "Can't say the same for you, Adam. Because your dick is so damn tiny, I hardly even know it's there. Paris told me once how small it was. How she always had to get herself off after sex with you because your tiny dick couldn't do the job. We laughed about it for hours."

There was a moment of stunned silence in the cell, and then Kevin burst out laughing. "Oh, shit! What the fuck... oh man, the fucking balls on this girl. Darling," he spoke from behind Londyn, unable to control his hilarity at his cousin's expense while gripping her wrists so tight that the handcuffs bit into her flesh. "That's some funny shit. Not the smartest thing to say right now, but funny as hell."

Londyn's eyes watered helplessly as Adam's face reddened. His eyes molted in pitch-black caverns as he stared down at her. Bracing herself, she knew what was coming, but the blow made her ears ring. Ebony waves crashed over her, threatening to drag her down. She heard him speaking as if from a great distance as he shoved his cock back into her mouth, thrusting so hard and fast that he bruised the inside of her cheeks and the back of her throat.

"Fucking little bitch. Do you think this is funny? Or let me guess. This is some of that reverse psychology bullshit you learned in college," he muttered. "Well, maybe you can analyze this for me. You just talked yourself into a session, not just me and Kevin, but every fucking guard. They're all going to get a piece of you now. Give you a damn fine reason to go to therapy. Kinda a shame you won't live long enough to benefit from it, though."

When he pulled out again, he grabbed her hair even tighter, laughing as Londyn retched. "I like hearing a woman choke on my dick. But I like hearing her scream even more. And I'm going to make you scream. I promise you that."

A commotion going on beyond the cell door snagged his attention as he taunted Londyn. She could barely hear anything over the ringing in her ears, but it sounded like fireworks, accompanied by shouting and clanging metal doors.

"What the fuck is going on out there?" he snapped at his cousin while making sure that Londyn didn't throw up on his shoes.

"Shit, who knows?" Kevin replied, using the handcuffs like a handle to keep Londyn's arms hoisted even higher. The awkward position made it difficult to dry heave, and she choked and wheezed, frantic to spit out the taste of him. "Sounds like some kind of argument between the guards, which isn't surprising. They're as fucking crazy as the damn Russians running this place."

"Maybe they're watching us through the little window there. Maybe they're getting all riled up, fighting over who's gonna be next to fuck this hot mouth of yours. But I'm using you first. Then Kevin. The rest of them will get their turn once we're done with you." Adam's hand was so tight in Londyn's hair that she thought it was coming out at the roots. He leaned down to whisper in her ear, "I'm going to fuck you so hard when I catch you in the hunt. And I'll enjoy watching my fellow officers fuck you to the point of death. That's what I should have done with your sister. I should have taken her out in the woods and arranged my own little hunt. I could have buried her out in the pines; no one would have ever known what happened to her. She would have been just another white-trash whore who moved on to find new guys to fuck."

"Paris trusted you. You used her. Beat her," Londyn choked out. "And-and you raped her, then shot her up with drugs once she realized what an animal you were."

Adam grabbed his dick at the base, ready to thrust between her lips as his jaw tightened. His erection was hard, angry red veins popping up along its ugly length. "She loved every minute of it. Why do you think she stayed with me as long as she did? Guess you don't know your sister as well as you think."

Londyn whimpered in revulsion but gathered her strength for what might be her last moments alive.

"Adam, you put that disgusting *thing* in my mouth again, and I'm biting it off. I don't care what you or anyone else does to me after. Watching you bleed out will be worth it," Londyn taunted weakly, spitting the taste of him out of her mouth until it dribbled down her chin. "So, go ahead. Do it. Put that pathetic little dick in my mouth one more time. I fucking dare you."

THIRTY-SEVEN

liver

IT DID NOT MATTER who Oliver encountered once he burst through the ornate double doors of the main house at Diamond Lake Ranch. Man or woman, if they were in his way, if they tried stopping him in any way, he retaliated with a bullet between their eyes.

With Jack protecting his back, his Las Vegas crew handling matters at the gate and the surrounding grounds, the ex-military team of Bradford, Lawson, and Tyler working to clear a path forward, and Kingston's army eliminating threats from the staff and a few foolhardy club members, opposition to their invasion was sparse.

Not that it mattered to Oliver. Bodies were mowed down in a hail of bullets as he stalked through the sprawling complex. A crazed, avenging angel of death, clad head to toe in black, with a singular mission, while groups of screaming women provided a symphony of sorts in the background.

Two minutes after entering the main building, Oliver executed both Ruel and Erik Andrey, riddling the brothers with a spray of bullets when they rushed him with their guns drawn. Continuing through the hallways and rooms, down long, twisting corridors, Oliver strode in an almost casual manner, methodically taking out men as he moved along. His only thought, his only purpose, was finding Londyn. So, he did what needed to be done and delighted in the carnage left in his wake.

There was no time for discussion. No room for negotiations. No sympathy for anyone who might foolishly expect mercy. When he burst through the set of doors leading to the underground dungeons, he caught Barlow sprinting down one of the corridors, desperate to escape Oliver's terrifying wrath.

Raising a hand in a defensive move, the older man fell to his knees. "Please," he managed to cry out before Oliver shot him point-blank in the chest.

He kicked Barlow's body out of the way as he continued, reloading his weapon.

Rounding a corner in the dungeon's labyrinth of corridors, he saw three guards standing outside one of the cells. Immediately, he knew that his wife was being held behind that door. The guards stared at him in complete shock, not used to facing the real threat of an armed intruder. And although the men were heavily armed, Oliver never slowed in his stride. Advancing on them, he shot two in rapid succession while Jack took care of the third.

Stepping over the bodies, he kicked open the cell door. The first thing Oliver saw was the backside of a man with his slacks around his knees. There was another, standing with his back to the stone wall, holding a woman's cuffed hands high in the air.

Oliver recognized him immediately as Sheriff Kevin Clifton, a member of Diamond Lake Ranch. It was a perk he enjoyed as the local sheriff.

Kevin's eyes widened in surprise. "What the fu—"

Oliver put a bullet through the man's eye before he finished the word. Kevin fell to the floor, and Oliver watched as, in slow motion, Londyn tumbled sideways. The man standing in front of her still held a fistful of her long, dark hair but upon seeing Oliver, her tear-stained face illuminated with joy.

Adam Franklin's face blanched white when he spun around and came face to face with the Devil. Oliver might have laughed had it not been for the rage suffusing every molecule of his body. It was hot. *Burning.* A fire that demanded action. A blood lust that had to be quenched. A veil of red blinding him to anything but what was right in front of his eyes.

Adam's erect penis jutted toward Londyn's mouth. Her bruised, swollen lips and the dull pink handprint marring the side of her face, silently revealed the truth of the assault.

Oliver lost all semblance of civility. In that moment, he became the monster of nightmares. The beast that rampaged and murdered. The Devil who had come to collect the souls of evil.

"Get your fucking hands off my wife."

Adam's mouth rounded in shock, gaping open as he tried making sense of what had just happened. He stared at Kevin, now unrecognizable with half of his face blown off and then back at Oliver.

"Wait-wait a goddamn minute, Winter," Adam cried, releasing Londyn as he threw his hands up in futile surrender. "What the fuck are you talking about? Your *wife?*"

Londyn frantically scooted away while Oliver strode forward simultaneously. He jammed the gun into the man's groin.

"Wait... let's talk this out. We-we can work out a deal that benefits us both," Adam said, frantic in his panic. "There are people who will pay you for her. More money than you can dream of."

Oliver's plans for slowly torturing the man before ending his miserable life shattered into pieces. He wanted blood. Nothing else would satisfy him.

He relished the sheriff's high-pitched scream as he pulled the trigger, blowing a hole in his groin before quickly placing the blood-spattered barrel flush against Adam's forehead. Without a word, he blew the man's brains out, splattering them across the stone wall.

Adam crumpled to the ground, a faceless, bloody heap that Oliver shoved out of his way so he could reach Londyn. She was screaming into her hands, hiding her face so she didn't have to see the bodies surrounding her.

Oliver swooped her up from the floor, squeezing his arms around her so tightly that he worried he was hurting her. She sobbed in his embrace, lifting her handcuffed hands over his head and holding on to him as if she would never let go.

Oliver pressed his lips to her forehead while she trembled uncontrollably. He could not speak for a few moments, realizing how close he'd come to losing her slamming into him like a freight train. *Thank you, God. Thank you for letting me reach her in time. Thank you for not taking her from me.*

"You came for me..." Londyn breathed against the side of Oliver's neck. "You came."

"Of course, I came for you, dove," Oliver muttered hoarsely. "You're my wife. Jack? Get these goddamned cuffs off her."

Jack gently gripped Londyn's hands while her arms were still looped around Oliver's neck. Using a master handcuff key, he clicked open the metal restraints and tossed them aside. "She needs medical attention for those cuts. They're bad, but there doesn't seem to be any other injuries besides the lacerations and the bruises to her face."

What about her psychological wounds? What about those mental bruises she now has from this and from what I've done to her?

"It'll have to wait. We gotta go. Now." Oliver bit out. He would figure all that out later. Once Londyn was safely away from this cesspool.

Jack nodded in agreement. "Everything is secure. Teams are doing cleanup, and once we are gone, no one will ever know we were here."

"Londyn, look at me." Oliver slid his hands into her dark hair, cradling her face so he could stare into her eyes. "I don't want you to look anywhere other than at me, do you understand? Focus on me. Only me."

Londyn wiped her mouth with the back of a trembling hand, her face screwed in disgust. "He-he had his... I tried to stop him, but he..." A low cry escaped her, and Oliver's heart nearly burst with sorrow.

"Shhh, dove, shhh. You're safe now. I've got you. I'm not going to let anything happen to you," he soothed, softly kissing her pink, bruised lips. "Just concentrate on me. God, I don't want you to see what I had to do to reach you. Do you understand? I don't want you to see the monster I became. The massacre I left in my wake. So, will you do this for me? Look at nothing but me as I carry you out of here."

"I can walk..." she protested in a weak voice that made his lips curve up in a rueful smile.

"So stubborn and willful. My headstrong little dove. I'm carrying you, and that's the end of it." Oliver gathered her closer until Londyn was crushed against his chest. With her face buried in his shoulder, he carried her out of Hell.

THIRTY-EIGHT

L*ondyn*

OLIVER CRADLED Londyn against him as the blacked-out SUV raced along the narrow mountain roads to the private airfield. Only when they were safely in the air did he finally loosen his grip.

Londyn was silent as he laid her on the bed in the back of the jet. He gently removed her jeans and sweater before settling her against the covers. She would never admit it, but she had peeked while he carried her away from Diamond Lake Ranch. Blood was everywhere. Dead bodies lay in grotesque heaps, sprawled over furniture and littering the once gleaming wooden floors. There were so many that she lost count, and she squeezed her eyes shut when she witnessed his men dragging some of the bodies by the arms to form piles.

Oliver plumped the pillows behind her head, smoothing

her hair from her face. It was hard to believe, but just thirty-six hours before, she had lain across this same bed while her husband fucked her to prove that she was his.

"Once you've rested a bit, I'll help you take a shower," he said in a low voice. His subdued behavior and careful movements only added to Londyn's anxiety. He was treating her like a fragile porcelain doll, and she hated it.

"I'm not made of glass, Oliver," she whispered, grabbing his wrist so she could mesh their fingers together.

"I know." He laughed softly, raising her hand and kissing her knuckles. "But maybe, right now, I am."

She dragged him closer, burying her head in the curve of his neck. "I knew you would come for me. Even when it seemed hopeless, I knew you would come." She felt him trembling, and her heart reacted, swelling with love.

"I slaughtered everyone who stood in my way, Londyn. Innocent or guilty, if they were in my path, I cut them down to reach you." Oliver's voice was muffled, the words coming out hard and pained as if he hated himself for what he'd done. "I didn't care, either. All that mattered was *you*."

Londyn half laughed, half sobbed. "If it weren't for you, I'd still be trapped there. Or dead."

"I wanted to keep them alive... those men who hurt you, especially Franklin. I wanted them alive so I could hang them from the hooks down in The Den's cellars. I wanted to slowly gut them, watch them bleed out, and hear their cries for mercy while I made them pay for every bruise, every tear, every cut, and every scrape they gave you. But my rage took over. I didn't even think as I ended them. I didn't stop to think that my impatience gave each one of them the easy way out... a quick and painless death that did not equal their crimes." Oliver leaned back so he could stare into her face. "If I had lost you, I would have slaughtered every living soul in that complex. And then I would have turned the gun on myself. Because I wouldn't be able to face a world without you."

"You didn't lose me. I'm still here. I'm *yours* for as long as you want me."

"That will be forever, dove. You are mine. My calm and my storm, Londyn. Sunshine and rainbows. Sin and salvation. You are everything, and I won't give you up. Never ask me to let you go because I won't. My entire fucking world revolves around you. I may go to Hell for my selfishness, but I'll drag you down there just to keep you by my side. I love you, Londyn. I love you so much that it hurts. Nothing you do or say will ever change what I feel for you. But I'll always be the villain in our fairy tale. Because the day I purchased you on that auction block— the worst day and night of your life—that day was the beginning of *my* life."

He hesitated, and Londyn saw the vulnerability he tried concealing from the world. He never wanted anyone to see his weakness. A small part of him still saw love as a liability, but he couldn't help himself when it came to her. She recognized that, and melted even more for him.

"Oliver..."

"I should let you go." He laughed softly at himself. "If I had a drop of decency, I would. But I can't. I *won't*. I'm a heartless bastard. I'm cruel. Selfish. I do awful things to people. I'm a murderer. A thief. A depraved degenerate. And I have no right to think you will ever love me, but I'm not sorry for taking what I want when it comes to you. I'll never be sorry."

Londyn kissed him with such fierceness it felt like her heart would shatter. "I'm not sorry either, Oliver. I can't be because I do love you. *All* of you. Even the darkest, scariest parts of you. You say I belong to you... well, you belong to me, too. And if anyone thinks they can ever come between us, I'll kill them before you have a chance to do it and wear their teeth as a necklace." Her gaze fell to their hands, and her lips quirked with a smile. "Now. May I have my ring back? I don't feel like I'm truly your wife without it on my finger."

Oliver slipped the blue diamond off his pinkie, sliding it and the wedding band onto her ring finger. "When I saw the blood on it, I vowed to hunt every man involved in your abduction. The two deputies responsible for the car accident have already paid with their lives, but still, I went through Hell thinking the blood staining that diamond came from you."

Londyn quickly explained what happened on that dark, quiet Georgia road, filling in the missing pieces so Oliver had a clear picture of the crash and what followed. His arms wrapped around her as she revealed the plans Adam had for her and the fact fellow law-enforcement officers had joined the second sale.

"I'll never put you in that kind of danger again, Londyn. It was reckless and arrogant to think my name alone would give you enough protection." Oliver's jaw tightened with determination, and Londyn wondered if he was already planning to eliminate even more people on her behalf. It was useless to argue the point that his decision to take her to see Paris made it worth any risk.

"Let's not look back anymore, Oliver. We have the rest of our lives together. And I want to spend it with you."

His blue eyes sparkled like the rare diamond on her finger. "I want that, too, dove."

～

Two weeks later

 The Den, Upstate New York

 It was the day of Paris's funeral.

 Londyn slipped her hand into Oliver's as he pulled her

closer. For the past two nights, she'd cried herself to sleep, and her husband had comforted her the best he could. He'd held her as she sobbed, murmured soothing words into her hair, and stroked her back with his large, capable hands. The huge, scary man she was married to even drew her a warm bath, washed her hair, and brought her so many cups of hot tea that she was practically sick of the beverage.

Her sister's death was not unexpected, of course. The specialists Oliver hired all expressed the same opinion when Paris was transported to a facility thirty minutes away from The Den. Her injuries were so complicated that there was no hope for recovery.

Londyn was glad she was there at the end, holding Paris's hand as she slipped away following a second massive stroke. She watched as Oliver grieved alongside her for a woman he did not know. He felt her sorrow as if it were his own, the depths of his devotion bringing Londyn joy even in the midst of terrible sadness.

"I'm so sorry, Londyn," Ava Blue said, leaning in to kiss Londyn on the cheek. A soft autumn breeze ruffled Londyn's dark hair as they stood beneath a towering oak tree in the private cemetery. The Winter brothers had recently purchased a family plot here, and Kingston insisted Paris be buried there so Londyn could visit whenever she wanted.

Over the past two weeks, Londyn and Ava had grown extremely close. The fact they would soon be true sisters in the eyes of the law only cemented their relationship. Watching the tiny, blonde Ava boss Kingston Winter around was quite entertaining, but Londyn knew her own relationship with Oliver was a mystery to his older brother and Ava.

The attentiveness he showed toward her, his obvious love and adoration had many of those living at The Den mesmerized. One night, Ava confessed how utterly astounding she found Oliver's transformation to be, especially regarding his relationship with Kingston. It was as if the strained hatred and mistrust over the years had never occurred. The two men spent a lot of time together, working on business deals, watching football, and playing friendly yet competitive pool games where expensive bottles of scotch were the prize.

Londyn had overheard a conversation between the two men just the day before. And her heart nearly burst with emotion at the conviction in Oliver's tone. Kingston, with a broad smile on his face, had asked him, "Now do you believe me when I told you how different life can be when the right woman loves you, O? Everything is brighter. Shinier. Nothing else matters except the way she smiles at you."

For a long moment, Oliver was quiet, then in a surprising gesture, he embraced the older man. His voice was gruff when he finally replied, "It is more than I ever hoped for a sinner like me, King. She's banished my nightmares and shown me how to love. How to live. I don't deserve her, but I can't be sorry that Londyn loves me. Because I love her more than life itself."

Kingston smiled in understanding. "We all deserve happiness, Oliver. And to share this as brothers... it is a gift I never thought we would have together. Having been so cursed in this life, we somehow ended up blessed with unimaginable riches. We found the love of our lives, O. True love. And there's no price you can place on that."

Oliver's response was to simply embrace his brother. No words were necessary.

Ava's sweet voice brought Londyn back to the present. "I want to tell you how much I admire you for what you did for your sister, Londyn. It was very brave of you to go through that. I'm sure she was very proud of you, too."

"Thank you, Ava. I wish you could have met her. Paris would have adored you as much as I do," Londyn replied, returning the young woman's embrace with a tearful smile. Kingston, waiting his turn, bent down and gave his new sister-in-law a quick, brotherly kiss on the cheek before slipping an arm around his fiancée's waist.

"We all wish we could have met her," Kingston said, nodding at the minister to begin the service.

Ava dipped her head toward Londyn, her beautiful features somber. "I know I cannot take Paris's place, but I already consider you a sister, Londyn, if that's okay. I feel so very close to you, even in the short time we've known one another. And I would love to have you stand with me at the wedding, as a true sister would."

Londyn grabbed Ava's hand and gave it a squeeze that said volumes. The other girl's kindness was a balm to her wounded soul. "I would like that very much, Ava," she whispered as Oliver pulled her closer alongside his body. Turning to him, she released Ava's hand and took his so she could mesh their fingers together.

He brushed his lips across the top of Londyn's head. "You are so brave, little wife. And while they say the pain will ease one day, I will always be here to hold you on those days when the sadness overwhelms you. You know that, right?"

Londyn squeezed his hand tightly, tears springing to her eyes at the sweetness of his words. "Having you beside me makes this easier to bear, Oliver. Your brother... and Ava... everyone has been so kind to me. Paris wanted me to grab everything life has to offer, and I will. The best part of it is having you beside me to face whatever comes next. I love you."

Oliver's smile was tender, his full lips curving upward with devotion for her.

"And I love you, little dove. In this life and the next, I will always love you."

CHAPTER

THIRTY-NINE

O *liver*

"WHAT A BEAUTIFUL WEDDING," Londyn sighed, twirling dreamily. The elegant, formal gown of silvery blue clung to her delicious body when she came to a stop and leaned against the low stone wall. This part of the terrace overlooked the gardens where Kingston and Ava had exchanged vows earlier that evening.

Oliver found it hard to look away. The moonlight reflected off his wife as if jealous of her inner glow. It dipped over her skin, caressing the hollows and highlighting the curves.

Oliver smiled, appreciating that Londyn had already downed two glasses of champagne and was a little tipsy. After giving the toasts as best man and matron of honor, he'd led her to this corner of the expansive terrace. The strains of the band playing in the great hall were barely audible here.

326

Sweeping her into his arms, he spun her about as she laughed in delight.

"I want to give you the same experience, Londyn. I want to see you in a beautiful wedding dress. I want the world to watch me take you as my wife. To hear me say the words that bind me to you forever. Will you let me do that?" Oliver asked with deadly seriousness. His little wife was so damned gorgeous that sometimes it hurt to look at her. It made him feel unhinged and crazy, knowing this girl was his. "I want to give you that moment of walking down the aisle and hearing the whispers of everyone admiring how stunning you look in white. I stole that from you. I wish I could go back and do it differently so you would have a memory you can always cherish. But I can't. So, I'll give you a new memory. If you let me."

Londyn's features lit up. "I don't need those things, Oliver. I already have you; that's enough," she said softly, standing on her tiptoes to kiss him. "But it is very sweet of you to offer."

"It's a selfish demand, really. I want photos of your face and reaction as I promise to love and cherish you. I want something I can look back on and remember the day I made you mine."

"But I've *always* been yours," Londyn whispered, swaying with the movement of his body as they slowly began to dance. "A photo won't change that. My heart knew it was yours the first time you kissed me."

"A wedding is the least of what I will give you, Londyn. I want you to finish school and get your degree. Not because I think you should, but because you want to do it for yourself. I want to marry you with everyone watching. And someday, I want to watch you grow big with our baby in your belly." Oliver was adamant. These were things he could do for her. He could make her every wish come true, even those she didn't know she wanted.

"I would love to get my degree. But how would that work? I'd have to attend classes, and I never want to be separated from you."

"I'll buy us a house down in Nashville. We'll live there while you finish school. I'll cook dinner for you every day, do all shopping, hire someone to do the cleaning..."

Londyn laughed, "You'll do the cooking, huh?"

Oliver's smile was sheepish. "Well, I can manage grilled cheese sandwiches, at least. And scrambled eggs. Maybe we should just plan on eating out a lot."

"A baby would be nice. One day." She trailed her finger over a lock of dark hair as it fell into his eyes. The scar on his temple from the accident was not visible to anyone else, but Londyn knew it was there. When she touched it so carefully, so full of tenderness and love, Oliver could not help but lean into her touch, his eyes closing in contentment.

"I'll give you anything in this world, dove. Anything you want," he swore. "You only need to ask."

"Anything?" she breathed, kissing him again, her lips teasing his until he groaned with desperate lust. "Will you attach the leash you've hidden away to my collar? Will you spank me if I disobey you? Will you fuck me until nothing matters but how good you make me feel? Will you make love to me until the sun comes up? I've missed you so terribly, Oliver. You've kept me at arm's length for a month. Ever since you rescued me... and I'm tired of waiting for you to take what is yours."

Oliver's arms tightened around her at the reminder of what Londyn endured. She had suffered a few nightmares since that day, and he was there to hold her through the aftermath of those dark nights.

As far as the world knew, Diamond Lake Ranch suffered a gas leak and subsequent explosion. It destroyed the complex and killed many of the people staying there, including several members of law enforcement attending a retreat. It was a cover story. One that kept many wealthy and corrupt people from having to answer too many probing questions. It quickly faded from the headlines and was now just a manufactured tragedy where only a few knew the truth.

"I wanted to give you space. Wait until you are ready. Don't think for an instant that I haven't been going crazy, Londyn. Waiting for you to want me as desperately as I want you is probably the hardest thing I've ever had to do. Restraint is not in my nature, but for you, I can wait as long as you want me to."

"I *always* want you, Oliver. Even when you are cruel and heartless, I crave the things you do to me," she confessed shyly, peeking up at him to see his reaction. "I love the way you make me feel. I love the darkness that overwhelms me and how you carefully hold me when it's over. I love how you tremble on the edge of control and how it scares me and thrills me. It's addictive, and because of you, I *always* want more."

Hooking her diamond choker with his index finger, Oliver smiled at her. "If I bent you over this stone wall and fucked you right here, anyone might see us. Would you try and stop me, little wife?"

Londyn's cheeks flushed pink, but a calculating gleam darkened her gray eyes. Her chin tilted, and Oliver's dick hardened when he recognized she was deliberately taunting him. "Maybe. I don't know. Do you think it will be that easy bending me to your will?"

Oliver took her words as a direct challenge to his authority. "I think with the proper punishment, I can accomplish anything I want to with you, Mrs. Winter. Shall we test it and see?"

"It might help with my insubordination, Sir." She glanced

around the terrace, assuring herself they were alone, before flashing him a cheeky grin. "Should I get down on my knees first or—?"

He cut her off with a hand wrapped around the slim column of her throat, squeezing until she moaned in greedy acceptance and sank helplessly against his body. Her hands braced themselves against his broad chest. Every muscle he possessed tightened with desire when she shivered and licked her full, pink lips.

Brushing his mouth against her ear, he murmured, "While you do look pretty sucking my cock, I prefer you spreadeagled and tied to my bed." He bit her earlobe until she squealed. "I want to taste my wife's sweet, tight pussy for as long as I like before I fuck her senseless."

Londyn nodded the best she could with his hand encircling her throat. When he finally released her, his brow arching in question to her next move, she readily took his hand and followed him inside the mansion.

Oliver skillfully avoided the wedding guests as he led her up a back staircase to their private wing. Once inside their bedroom, a huge room decorated in shades of gray and black, he quickly pulled the items he needed from a dresser drawer, then stripped Londyn's clothes from her. She stood nude before him, beautiful and unashamed, clad only in silver Dior heels and her jewelry. Her lips twitched with a nearly invisible smile when she saw what he held in his hand.

Clipping the diamond-encrusted leash to her choker, Oliver gave it a sharp tug, guiding her to the bed.

"That kind of brattish behavior will always earn you a punishment."

"Really?" she replied, her voice husky with longing. "I'll remember that in the future."

Oliver let out a sharp laugh. "Manipulating me to get what you want is a terrible idea, little wife."

"Is it? Maybe you should teach me a lesson," she crooned in response.

Oliver bit his bottom lip. He was going to fucking combust on the spot if she persisted in misbehaving. There was only one way to deal with this sort of behavior, and the end result would be pleasurable for both of them.

"Lean over the bed, dove, and spread your legs for me. Let me see what is mine."

Londyn quickly obeyed, her arms stretching toward either side of the bed, her thighs separating so he could see her cunt glistening for him.

"Good girl," he murmured, running a hand over her smooth buttocks.

She wiggled back and forth in anticipation. "Oliver, please. I need you. Don't tease me. It's been too long since I've felt you inside me."

"You don't dictate what happens here, wife. I'm in control. Do you understand? Or should I retrieve my belt and help to clarify it?"

When she did not respond quickly enough, he slapped one rounded ass cheek. She groaned, spreading her legs wider for him. "Yes, Sir. Whatever you think will teach me a lesson, Sir."

"Jesus, I think I've created a monster," he breathed, trying to conceal a grin of satisfaction before continuing sternly, "Using those reverse psychology methods won't work on me, Londyn. Best that you remember that." Peeling away the various pieces of his dark-gray suit, Oliver leaned over Londyn once he was naked. He traced the tattoo down her spine with the tip of his finger until she shuddered. Then, with the tip of his tongue, he outlined every letter of each word until she squirmed beneath him and panted into the comforter.

Sinking to the floor behind her, Oliver held the end of the leash while spreading her pussy with his fingers. He slapped the end of the leather against the tender flesh once, laughing at her surprised yelp before covering her pussy with his mouth and leisurely teasing her clit with his tongue. She flooded his mouth with her arousal, a moan escaping her as she rocked against him, frustrated she could do no more in her position, sprawled across the bed as she was.

"Oliver, for fuck's sake. Please fuck me," she breathlessly demanded, which earned her two quick strikes of the leash to her ass cheeks. She groaned in response, dropping her head into the covers to muffle the sound. Her pussy was drenched, and Oliver couldn't resist shoving two fingers inside her, roughly fucking her until she was breathing hard and on the edge of coming.

"Hmm. I'm not sure if I should spank you with this leash or fuck you with it wrapped around your pretty neck."

"Both?" Londyn offered, raising her head to glance back at him over her shoulder. Her eyes flashed with impertinence. "I think both are warranted, don't you? Insubordination will not be tolerated. Do you remember telling me that once?"

"Oh, I remember but you need to learn patience, sweet wife. Patience." He chuckled at the impatient nature of her tone. "I've got all night and the rest of our lives to satisfy your every need." Withdrawing his fingers from her tight pussy, he made sure she watched as he licked them clean. "And tomorrow, well, tomorrow, I'll introduce you to the dungeons here at The Den. I'll tie you up, maybe place a vibrating plug up this sweet little ass and fill your pussy with my cock. I'll enjoy making you come so many times that you'll feel me for days after."

Londyn groaned in almost comical frustration at the filthy

suggestion and suddenly rolled onto her back, reaching for Oliver and pulling him up from where he knelt.

He allowed it, flipping her around until she was draped over the top of him as he laid back on the bed.

Her gray eyes glittered with helpless arousal as her delicate fingers traced the dove tattoo emblazoned across his heart. "Boss me around later. I'll let you do whatever you want. Right now, I want my husband to make love to me. Make me see stars, Oliver. Remind me that I'm yours and you are mine. Remind me that you love me because I love you with all my heart and soul."

Oliver tugged the leash until her head lowered. He kissed her wildly, fiercely until she melted over him, her eyes shiny with tears and adoration. What swirled around inside him was almost too big to endure. It illuminated him from the inside out. It made him stupid. Foolish. Incredibly happy. Content with who he was and where he was. And all because this dazzling girl holding him so tightly had decided a villain's soul could be redeemed and loved.

"You've earned yourself a real spanking later, but for now, I will give my wife exactly what she wants." Oliver kissed Londyn again, slowly and more deliberately until they were both breathless and needy. Her thighs spread over the tops of his, straddling him so he could surge up inside her. His piercings rubbed all the right places, and it sent him soaring when her body clenched around his cock.

Pushing her upright so her legs bracketed his hips, he pinched her nipples until she gasped with pleasure, her hand splayed across his chest as he encouraged her to ride him. He thrust upward every time she ground her pelvis over his, moving inside her, stoking their desire until it flamed as brightly and as hot as the sun.

With her fingers, Londyn traced the word tattooed above

his groin where their bodies merged, silently promising to be his forever. When their climaxes hit simultaneously, leaving them both crying out in satisfaction, Oliver used the leash to tug her back down until she sprawled across him. He pressed kisses to her mouth, breathing in her little pants and her whimpers of delight.

"I love you, Oliver," Londyn breathed, cradling his face in her hands and staring deep into his soul. A sweet smile curved her lips when she saw tears glistening in the corners of his eyes.

"And I love you, Londyn Juliette Winter," Oliver whispered, crushing her close. He'd never grow tired of hearing those words from her, nor of repeating them back. He'd done so many terrible things in his lifetime, but it felt as though his sins were washed away every time he kissed this girl. She made him feel wanted. Loved. Needed. And it was more than he could have ever hoped for. "I will love you until there is nothing left of me but dust."

THE END

I HOPE you enjoyed SOUL OF A VILLAIN and thank you for reading! It's been so much fun writing these morally grey heroes and feisty heroines. If you enjoyed this not-so-pitch-black world I've created, I'd love to hear from you! You can follow me everywhere on social media and through my newsletter.

• • •

A HUGE HUG of gratitude goes out to my readers, ARC team, followers, and Honeybees from the Facebook group, especially Linda Kehn. Your support means everything. Thank you to the wonderful author community who have embraced and cheered me on over the years. Hugs and kisses for Cheryl Maddox, the best PA that ever PA'd. Thank you to Dakota Willink for designing such stunning graphics and covers for my books. My gratitude to Katie at Spice Me Up Editing for taking this book on and editing my words until they make sense.

The Savage World
A King So Savage Book 1 of The Savage Duet
https://geni.us/AKingSoSavage
A Heart So Savage Book 2 of The Savage Duet
https://geni.us/AHeartSoSavage
<u>Soul Of A Villain</u>
https://geni.us/SoulOfAVillain

The Taming Series
Taming Ivy
https://geni.us/TamingIvy
The Untamed Duke
https://geni.us/TheUntamedDuke
Untaming Lady Violet
https://geni.us/UntamingLadyViolet

Wicked Rogues Romance

APRIL MORAN

My Darling Rogue
https://geni.us/MyDarlingRogue

The Seven Seconds Series
The Bloodfeather Promise
https://geni.us/BloodfeatherPromise
Seven Promises
https://geni.us/SevenPromises

Standalone Christmas Historical Romance Novella
A Scandal Before Christmas
https://geni.us/AScandalBeforeChristmas

Standalone Office Romance Novella
Whiskey Darling
https://geni.us/WhiskeyDarling

VISIT APRIL'S WEBSITE
www.aprilmoranbooks.com

SIGN UP FOR NEWSLETTER AND UPDATES
http://bit.ly/AprilMoran_BookUpdates
April Moran Book Updates

. . .

STALK APRIL EVERYWHERE
https://www.facebook.com/AuthorAprilMoran
https://www.facebook.com/groups/aprilshoneybees/
https://www.bookbub.com/profile/april-moran
https://www.instagram.com/aprilmoranbooks
https://www.goodreads.com/Author-AprilMoran
https://www.pinterest.com/aprilmoranbooks
https://www.tiktok.com/authoraprilmoran

www.ingramcontent.com/pod-product-compliance
Lightning Source LLC
Chambersburg PA
CBHW030132310726
48970CB00005B/1399